Oscar Fingal O'Flahertie Wills Wilde (16 October 1854 – 30 November 1900) was an Irish poet and playwright. After writing in different forms throughout the 1880s, he became one of London's most popular playwrights in the early 1890s. He is best remembered for his epigrams and plays, his novel The Picture of Dorian Gray, and the circumstances of his criminal conviction for homosexuality, imprisonment, and early death at age 46. Wilde's parents were successful Anglo-Irish intellectuals in Dublin. Their son became fluent in French and German early in life. At university, Wilde read Greats; he proved himself to be an outstanding classicist, first at Trinity College Dublin, then at Oxford. He became known for his involvement in the rising philosophy of aestheticism, led by two of his tutors, Walter Pater and John Ruskin. After university, Wilde moved to London into fashionable cultural and social circles. (Source: Wikipedia)

Literary works:
Ravenna (1878)
Poems (1881)
The Happy Prince and Other Stories (1888)
Lord Arthur Savile's Crime and Other Stories (1891)
A House of Pomegranates (1891)
Intentions (1891)
The Picture of Dorian Gray (1890)
The Soul of Man under Socialism (1891)
Lady Windermere's Fan (1892)
A Woman of No Importance (1893)
An Ideal Husband (1898)
The Importance of Being Earnest (1898)
De Profundis (1905)
The Ballad of Reading Gaol (1898)
The Portrait of Mr. W. H. (1889)

THE SOUL OF MAN UNDER SOCIALISM
&
A CRITIC IN PALL MALL

Oscar Wilde

PRINCE CLASSICS

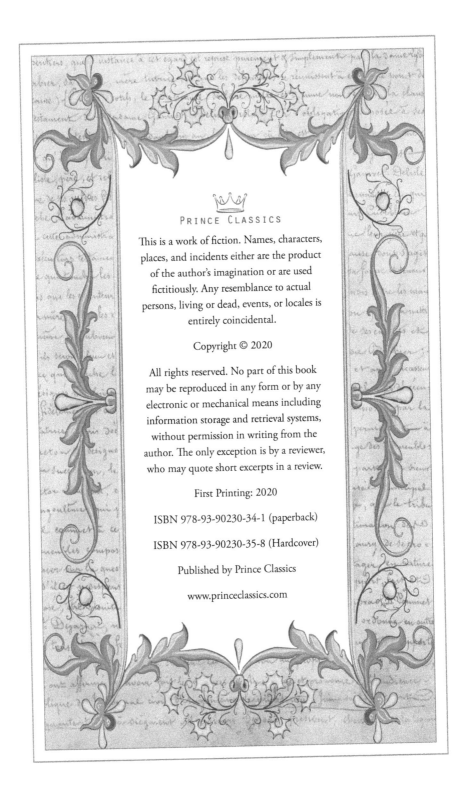

PRINCE CLASSICS

First Printing: 2020

ISBN 978-93-90230-34-1 (paperback)

ISBN 978-93-90230-35-8 (Hardcover)

Published by Prince Classics

www.princeclassics.com

Contents

THE SOUL OF MAN
UNDER SOCIALISM
&
A CRITIC IN PALL MALL

THE SOUL OF MAN UNDER SOCIALISM

THE SOUL OF MAN

The chief advantage that would result from the establishment of Socialism is, undoubtedly, the fact that Socialism would relieve us from that sordid necessity of living for others which, in the present condition of things, presses so hardly upon almost everybody. In fact, scarcely anyone at all escapes.

Now and then, in the course of the century, a great man of science, like Darwin; a great poet, like Keats; a fine critical spirit, like M. Renan; a supreme artist, like Flaubert, has been able to isolate himself, to keep himself out of reach of the clamorous claims of others, to stand 'under the shelter of the wall,' as Plato puts it, and so to realise the perfection of what was in him, to his own incomparable gain, and to the incomparable and lasting gain of the whole world. These, however, are exceptions. The majority of people spoil their lives by an unhealthy and exaggerated altruism—are forced, indeed, so to spoil them. They find themselves surrounded by hideous poverty, by hideous ugliness, by hideous starvation. It is inevitable that they should be strongly moved by all this. The emotions of man are stirred more quickly than man's intelligence; and, as I pointed out some time ago in an article on the function of criticism, it is much more easy to have sympathy with suffering than it is to have sympathy with thought. Accordingly, with admirable, though misdirected intentions, they very seriously and very sentimentally set themselves to the task of remedying the evils that they see. But their remedies do not cure the disease: they merely prolong it. Indeed, their remedies are part of the disease.

They try to solve the problem of poverty, for instance, by keeping the poor alive; or, in the case of a very advanced school, by amusing the poor.

But this is not a solution: it is an aggravation of the difficulty. The proper aim is to try and reconstruct society on such a basis that poverty will be impossible. And the altruistic virtues have really prevented the carrying out of this aim. Just as the worst slave-owners were those who were kind to their slaves, and so prevented the horror of the system being realised by those who suffered from it, and understood by those who contemplated it, so, in the present state of things in England, the people who do most harm are the people who try to do most good; and at last we have had the spectacle of men who have really studied the problem and know the life—educated men who live in the East End—coming forward and imploring the community to restrain its altruistic impulses of charity, benevolence, and the like. They do so on the ground that such charity degrades and demoralises. They are perfectly right. Charity creates a multitude of sins.

There is also this to be said. It is immoral to use private property in order to alleviate the horrible evils that result from the institution of private property. It is both immoral and unfair.

Under Socialism all this will, of course, be altered. There will be no people living in fetid dens and fetid rags, and bringing up unhealthy, hunger-pinched children in the midst of impossible and absolutely repulsive surroundings. The security of society will not depend, as it does now, on the state of the weather. If a frost comes we shall not have a hundred thousand men out of work, tramping about the streets in a state of disgusting misery, or whining to their neighbours for alms, or crowding round the doors of loathsome shelters to try and secure a hunch of bread and a night's unclean lodging. Each member of the society will share in the general prosperity and happiness of the society, and if a frost comes no one will practically be anything the worse.

Upon the other hand, Socialism itself will be of value simply because it will lead to Individualism.

Socialism, Communism, or whatever one chooses to call it, by converting private property into public wealth, and substituting co-operation for competition, will restore society to its proper condition of a thoroughly healthy organism, and insure the material well-being

14

of each member of the community. It will, in fact, give Life its proper basis and its proper environment. But for the full development of Life to its highest mode of perfection, something more is needed. What is needed is Individualism. If the Socialism is Authoritarian; if there are Governments armed with economic power as they are now with political power; if, in a word, we are to have Industrial Tyrannies, then the last state of man will be worse than the first. At present, in consequence of the existence of private property, a great many people are enabled to develop a certain very limited amount of Individualism. They are either under no necessity to work for their living, or are enabled to choose the sphere of activity that is really congenial to them, and gives them pleasure. These are the poets, the philosophers, the men of science, the men of culture—in a word, the real men, the men who have realised themselves, and in whom all Humanity gains a partial realisation. Upon the other hand, there are a great many people who, having no private property of their own, and being always on the brink of sheer starvation, are compelled to do the work of beasts of burden, to do work that is quite uncongenial to them, and to which they are forced by the peremptory, unreasonable, degrading Tyranny of want. These are the poor, and amongst them there is no grace of manner, or charm of speech, or civilisation, or culture, or refinement in pleasures, or joy of life. From their collective force Humanity gains much in material prosperity. But it is only the material result that it gains, and the man who is poor is in himself absolutely of no importance. He is merely the infinitesimal atom of a force that, so far from regarding him, crushes him: indeed, prefers him crushed, as in that case, he is far more obedient.

Of course, it might be said that the Individualism generated under conditions of private property is not always, or even as a rule, of a fine or wonderful type, and that the poor, if they have not culture and charm, have still many virtues. Both these statements would be quite true. The possession of private property is very often extremely demoralising, and that is, of course, one of the reasons why Socialism wants to get rid of the institution. In fact, property is really a nuisance.

Some years ago people went about the country saying that property has duties. They said it so often and so tediously that, at last, the Church has begun to say it. One hears it now from every pulpit. It is perfectly true. Property not merely has duties, but has so many duties that its possession to any large extent is a bore. It involves endless claims upon one, endless attention to business, endless bother. If property had simply pleasures, we could stand it; but its duties make it unbearable. In the interest of the rich we must get rid of it. The virtues of the poor may be readily admitted, and are much to be regretted. We are often told that the poor are grateful for charity. Some of them are, no doubt, but the best amongst the poor are never grateful. They are ungrateful, discontented, disobedient, and rebellious. They are quite right to be so. Charity they feel to be a ridiculously inadequate mode of partial restitution, or a sentimental dole, usually accompanied by some impertinent attempt on the part of the sentimentalist to tyrannise over their private lives. Why should they be grateful for the crumbs that fall from the rich man's table? They should be seated at the board, and are beginning to know it. As for being discontented, a man who would not be discontented with such surroundings and such a low mode of life would be a perfect brute. Disobedience, in the eyes of anyone who has read history, is man's original virtue. It is through disobedience that progress has been made, through disobedience and through rebellion. Sometimes the poor are praised for being thrifty. But to recommend thrift to the poor is both grotesque and insulting. It is like advising a man who is starving to eat less. For a town or country labourer to practise thrift would be absolutely immoral. Man should not be ready to show that he can live like a badly-fed animal. He should decline to live like that, and should either steal or go on the rates, which is considered by many to be a form of stealing. As for begging, it is safer to beg than to take, but it is finer to take than to beg. No: a poor man who is ungrateful, unthrifty, discontented, and rebellious, is probably a real personality, and has much in him. He is at any rate a healthy protest. As for the virtuous poor, one can pity them, of course, but one cannot possibly admire them. They have made private terms with the enemy, and sold their birthright for very bad pottage. They must also be extraordinarily stupid. I can quite understand a man accepting laws that protect private property, and admit of its accumulation, as long as he himself is able under those conditions to realise some form of beautiful and intellectual life. But it is almost incredible to me how a man whose life is marred and made hideous by such laws can possibly acquiesce in their continuance.

However, the explanation is not really difficult to find. It is simply this. Misery and poverty are so absolutely degrading, and exercise such a paralysing effect over the nature of men, that no class is ever really conscious of its own suffering. They have to be told of it by other people, and they often entirely disbelieve them. What is said by great employers of labour against agitators is unquestionably true. Agitators are a set of interfering, meddling people, who come down to some perfectly contented class of the community, and sow the seeds of discontent amongst them. That is the reason why agitators are so absolutely necessary. Without them, in our incomplete state, there would be no advance towards civilisation. Slavery was put down in America, not in consequence of any action on the part of the slaves, or even any express desire on their part that they should be free. It was put down entirely through the grossly illegal conduct of certain agitators in Boston and elsewhere, who were not slaves themselves, nor owners of slaves, nor had anything to do with the question really. It was, undoubtedly, the Abolitionists who set the torch alight, who began the whole thing. And it is curious to note that from the slaves themselves they received, not merely very little assistance, but hardly any sympathy even; and when at the close of the war the slaves found themselves free, found themselves indeed so absolutely free that they were free to starve, many of them bitterly regretted the new state of things. To the thinker, the most tragic fact in the whole of the French Revolution is not that Marie Antoinette was killed for being a queen, but that the starved peasant of the Vendée voluntarily went out to die for the hideous cause of feudalism.

It is clear, then, that no Authoritarian Socialism will do. For while under the present system a very large number of people can lead lives of a certain amount of freedom and expression and happiness, under an industrial-barrack system, or a system of economic tyranny, nobody would be able to have any such freedom at all. It is to be regretted that a portion of our community should be practically in slavery, but to propose to solve the problem by enslaving the entire community is childish. Every man must be left quite free to choose his own work. No form of compulsion must be exercised over him. If there is, his work will not be good for him, will not be good in itself, and will not be good for others. And by work, I simply mean activity of any kind.

I hardly think that any Socialist, nowadays, would seriously propose that an inspector should call every morning at each house to see that each citizen rose up and did manual labour for eight hours. Humanity has got beyond that stage, and reserves such a form of life for the people whom, in a very arbitrary manner, it chooses to call criminals. But I confess that many of the socialistic views that I have come across seem to me to be tainted with ideas of authority, if not of actual compulsion. Of course, authority and compulsion are out of the question. All association must be quite voluntary. It is only in voluntary associations that man is fine.

But it may be asked how Individualism, which is now more or less dependent on the existence of private property for its development, will benefit by the abolition of such private property. The answer is very simple. It is true that, under existing conditions, a few men who have had private means of their own, such as Byron, Shelley, Browning, Victor Hugo, Baudelaire, and others, have been able to realise their personality more or less completely. Not one of these men ever did a single day's work for hire. They were relieved from poverty. They had an immense advantage. The question is whether it would be for the good of Individualism that such an advantage should be taken away. Let us suppose that it is taken away. What happens then to Individualism? How will it benefit?

It will benefit in this way. Under the new conditions Individualism will be far freer, far finer, and far more intensified than it is now. I am not talking of the great imaginatively-realised Individualism of such poets as I have mentioned, but of the great actual Individualism latent and potential in mankind generally. For the recognition of private property has really harmed Individualism, and obscured it, by confusing a man with what he possesses. It has led Individualism entirely astray. It has made gain not growth its aim. So that man thought that the important thing was to have, and did not know that the important thing is to be. The true perfection of man lies, not in what man has, but in what man is. Private property has crushed true Individualism, and set up an Individualism that is false. It has debarred one part of the community from being individual by starving them. It has debarred the other part of the community from being individual by putting them on the wrong road, and encumbering them. Indeed, so completely has man's personality been absorbed by his possessions that the English law has always treated offences against a man's property with far more severity than offences against his person, and property is still the test of complete citizenship. The industry necessary for the making money is also very demoralising. In a community like ours, where property confers immense distinction, social position, honour, respect, titles, and other pleasant things of the kind, man, being naturally ambitious, makes it his aim to accumulate this property, and goes on wearily and tediously accumulating it long after he has got far more than he wants, or can use, or enjoy, or perhaps even know of. Man will kill himself by overwork in order to secure property, and really, considering the enormous advantages that property brings, one is hardly surprised. One's regret is that society should be constructed on such a basis that man has been forced into a groove in which he cannot freely develop what is wonderful, and fascinating, and delightful in him—in which, in fact, he misses the true pleasure and joy of living. He is also, under existing conditions, very insecure. An enormously wealthy merchant may be—often is—at every moment of his life at the mercy of things that are not under his control. If the wind blows an extra point or so, or the weather suddenly changes, or some trivial thing happens, his ship may go down, his speculations may go wrong, and he finds himself a poor man, with his social position quite gone. Now, nothing should be able to harm a man except himself. Nothing should be able to rob a man at all. What a man really has, is what is in him. What is outside of him should be a matter of no importance.

With the abolition of private property, then, we shall have true, beautiful, healthy Individualism. Nobody will waste his life in accumulating things, and the symbols for things. One will live. To live is the rarest thing in the world. Most people exist, that is all.

It is a question whether we have ever seen the full expression of a personality, except on the imaginative plane of art. In action, we never have. Cæsar, says Mommsen, was the complete and perfect man. But how tragically insecure was Cæsar! Wherever there is a man who exercises authority, there is a man who resists authority. Cæsar was very perfect, but his perfection travelled by too dangerous a road. Marcus Aurelius was the perfect man, says Renan. Yes; the great emperor was a perfect man. But how intolerable were the endless claims upon him! He staggered under the burden of the empire. He was conscious how inadequate one man was to bear the weight of that Titan and too vast orb. What I mean by a perfect man is one who develops under perfect conditions; one who is not wounded, or worried or maimed, or in danger. Most personalities have been obliged to be rebels. Half their strength has been wasted in friction. Byron's personality, for instance, was terribly wasted in its battle with the stupidity, and hypocrisy, and Philistinism of the English. Such battles do not always intensify strength: they often exaggerate weakness. Byron was never able to give us what he might have given us. Shelley escaped better. Like Byron, he got out of England as soon as possible. But he was not so well known. If the English had had any idea of what a great poet he really was, they would have fallen on him with tooth and nail, and made his life as unbearable to him as they possibly could. But he was not a remarkable figure in society, and consequently he escaped, to a certain degree. Still, even in Shelley the note of rebellion is sometimes too strong. The note of the perfect personality is not rebellion, but peace.

It will be a marvellous thing—the true personality of man—when we see it. It will grow naturally and simply, flowerlike, or as a tree grows. It will not be at discord. It will never argue or dispute. It will not prove things. It will know everything. And yet it will not busy itself about knowledge. It will have wisdom. Its value will not be measured by material things. It will have nothing. And yet it will have everything, and whatever one takes from it, it will still have, so rich will it be. It will not be always meddling with others, or asking them to be like itself. It will love them because they will be different. And yet while it will not meddle with others, it will help all, as a beautiful thing helps us, by being what it is. The personality of man will be very wonderful. It will be as wonderful as the personality of a child.

In its development it will be assisted by Christianity, if men desire that; but if men do not desire that, it will develop none the less surely. For it will not worry itself about the past, nor care whether things happened or did not happen. Nor will it admit any laws but its own laws; nor any authority but its own authority. Yet it will love those who sought to intensify it, and speak often of them. And of these Christ was one.

'Know thyself' was written over the portal of the antique world. Over the portal of the new world, 'Be thyself' shall be written. And the message of Christ to man was simply 'Be thyself.' That is the secret of Christ.

When Jesus talks about the poor he simply means personalities, just as when he talks about the rich he simply means people who have not developed their personalities. Jesus moved in a community that allowed the accumulation of private property just as ours does, and the gospel that he preached was not that in such a community it is an advantage for a man to live on scanty, unwholesome food, to wear ragged, unwholesome clothes, to sleep in horrid, unwholesome dwellings, and a disadvantage for a man to live under healthy, pleasant, and decent conditions. Such a view would have been wrong there and then, and would, of course, be still more wrong now and in England; for as man moves northward the material necessities of life become of more vital importance, and our society is infinitely more complex, and displays far greater extremes of luxury and pauperism than any society of the antique world. What Jesus meant, was this. He said to man, 'You have a wonderful personality. Develop it. Be yourself. Don't imagine that your perfection lies in accumulating or possessing external things. Your affection is inside of you. If only you could realise that, you would not want to be rich. Ordinary riches can be stolen from a man. Real riches cannot. In the treasury-house of your soul, there are infinitely precious things, that may not be taken from you. And so, try to so shape your life that external things will not harm you. And try also to get rid of personal property. It involves sordid preoccupation, endless industry, continual wrong. Personal property hinders Individualism at every step.' It is to be noted that Jesus never says that impoverished people are necessarily good, or wealthy people necessarily bad. That would not have been true. Wealthy people are, as a class, better than impoverished people, more moral, more intellectual, more well-behaved. There is only one class in the community that thinks more about money than the rich, and that is the poor. The poor can think of nothing else. That is the misery of being poor. What Jesus does say is that man reaches his perfection, not through what he has, not even through what he does, but entirely through what he is. And so the wealthy young man who comes to Jesus is represented as a thoroughly good citizen, who has broken none of the laws of his state, none of the commandments of his religion. He is quite respectable, in the ordinary sense of that extraordinary word. Jesus says to him, 'You should give up private property. It hinders you from realising your perfection. It is a drag upon you. It is a burden. Your personality does not need it. It is within you, and not outside of you, that you will find what you really are, and what you really want.' To his own friends he says the same thing. He tells them to be themselves, and not to be always worrying about other things. What do other things matter? Man is complete in himself. When they go into the world, the world will disagree with them. That is inevitable. The world hates Individualism. But that is not to trouble them. They are to be calm and self-centred. If a man takes their cloak, they are to give him their coat, just to show that material things are of no importance. If people abuse them, they are not to answer back. What does it signify? The things people say of a man do not alter a man. He is what he is. Public opinion is of no value whatsoever. Even if people employ actual violence, they are not to be violent in turn. That would be to fall to the same low level. After all, even in prison, a man can be quite free. His soul can be free. His personality can be untroubled. He can be at peace. And, above all things, they are not to interfere with other people or judge them in any way. Personality is a very mysterious thing. A man cannot always be estimated by what he does. He may keep the law, and yet be worthless. He may break the law, and yet be fine. He may be bad, without ever doing anything bad. He may commit a sin against society, and yet realise through that sin his true perfection.

There was a woman who was taken in adultery. We are not told the history of her love, but that love must have been very great; for Jesus said that her sins were forgiven her, not because she repented, but because her love was so intense and wonderful. Later on, a short time before his death, as he sat at a feast, the woman came in and poured costly perfumes on his hair. His friends tried to interfere with her, and said that it was an extravagance, and that the money that the perfume cost should have been expended on charitable relief of people in want, or something of that kind. Jesus did not accept that view. He pointed out that the material needs of Man were great and very permanent, but that the spiritual needs of Man were greater still, and that in one divine moment, and by selecting its own mode of expression, a personality might make itself perfect. The world worships the woman, even now, as a saint.

Yes; there are suggestive things in Individualism. Socialism annihilates family life, for instance. With the abolition of private property, marriage in its present form must disappear. This is part of the programme. Individualism accepts this and makes it fine. It converts the abolition of legal restraint into a form of freedom that will help the full development of personality, and make the love of man and woman more wonderful, more beautiful, and more ennobling. Jesus knew this. He rejected the claims of family life, although they existed in his day and community in a very marked form. 'Who is my mother? Who are my brothers?' he said, when he was told that they wished to speak to him. When one of his followers asked leave to go and bury his father, 'Let the dead bury the dead,' was his terrible answer. He would allow no claim whatsoever to be made on personality.

And so he who would lead a Christlike life is he who is perfectly and absolutely himself. He may be a great poet, or a great man of science; or a young student at a University, or one who watches sheep upon a moor; or a maker of dramas, like Shakespeare, or a thinker about God, like Spinoza; or a child who plays in a garden, or a fisherman who throws his net into the sea. It does not matter what he is, as long as he realises the perfection of the soul that is within him. All imitation in morals and in life is wrong. Through the streets of Jerusalem at the present day crawls one who is mad and carries a wooden cross on his shoulders. He is a symbol of the lives that are marred by imitation. Father Damien was Christlike when he went out to live with the lepers, because in such service he realised fully what was best in him. But he was not more Christlike than Wagner when he realised his soul in music; or than Shelley, when he realised his soul in song. There is no one type for man. There are as many perfections as there are imperfect men. And while to the claims of charity a man may yield and yet be free, to the claims of conformity no man may yield and remain free at all.

Individualism, then, is what through Socialism we are to attain to. As a natural result the State must give up all idea of government. It must give it up because, as a wise man once said many centuries before Christ, there is such a thing as leaving mankind alone; there is no such thing as governing mankind. All modes of government are failures. Despotism is unjust to everybody, including the despot, who was probably made for better things. Oligarchies are unjust to the many, and ochlocracies are unjust to the few. High hopes were once formed of democracy; but democracy means simply the bludgeoning of the people by the people for the people. It has been found out. I must say that it was high time, for all authority is quite degrading. It degrades those who exercise it, and degrades those over whom it is exercised. When it is violently, grossly, and cruelly used, it produces a good effect, by creating, or at any rate bringing out, the spirit of revolt and Individualism that is to kill it. When it is used with a certain amount of kindness, and accompanied by prizes and rewards, it is dreadfully demoralising. People, in that case, are less conscious of the horrible pressure that is being put on them, and so go through their lives in a sort of coarse comfort, like petted animals, without ever realising that they are probably thinking other people's thoughts, living by other people's standards, wearing practically what one may call other people's second-hand clothes, and never being themselves for a single moment. 'He who would be free,' says a fine thinker, 'must not conform.' And authority, by bribing people to conform, produces a very gross kind of over-fed barbarism amongst us.

With authority, punishment will pass away. This will be a great gain—a gain, in fact, of incalculable value. As one reads history, not in the expurgated editions written for school-boys and passmen, but in the original authorities of each time, one is absolutely sickened, not by the crimes that the wicked have committed, but by the punishments that the good have inflicted; and a community is infinitely more brutalised by the habitual employment of punishment, than it is by the occurrence of crime. It obviously follows that the more punishment is inflicted the more crime is produced, and most modern legislation has clearly recognised this, and has made it its task to diminish punishment as far as it thinks it can. Wherever it has really diminished it, the results have always been extremely good. The less punishment, the less crime. When there is no punishment at all, crime will either cease to exist, or, if it occurs, will be treated by physicians as a very distressing form of dementia, to be cured by care and kindness. For what are called criminals nowadays are not criminals at all. Starvation, and not sin, is the parent of modern crime. That indeed is the reason why our criminals are, as a class, so absolutely uninteresting from any psychological point of view. They are not marvellous Macbeths and terrible Vautrins. They are merely what ordinary, respectable, commonplace people would be if they had not got enough to eat. When private property is abolished there will be no necessity for crime, no demand for it; it will cease to exist. Of course, all crimes are not crimes against property, though such are the crimes that the English law, valuing what a man has more than what a man is, punishes with the harshest and most horrible severity, if we except the crime of murder, and regard death as worse than penal servitude, a point on which our criminals, I believe, disagree. But though a crime may not be against property, it may spring from the misery and rage and depression produced by our wrong system of property-holding, and so, when that system is abolished, will disappear. When each member of the community has sufficient for his wants, and is not interfered with by his neighbour, it will not be an object of any interest to him to interfere with anyone else. Jealousy, which is an extraordinary source of crime in modern life, is an emotion closely bound up with our conceptions of property, and under Socialism and Individualism will die out. It is remarkable that in communistic tribes jealousy is entirely unknown.

Now as the State is not to govern, it may be asked what the State is to do. The State is to be a voluntary association that will organise labour, and be the manufacturer and distributor of necessary commodities. The State is to make what is useful. The individual is to make what is beautiful. And as I have mentioned the word labour, I cannot help saying that a great deal of nonsense is being written and talked nowadays about the dignity of manual labour. There is nothing necessarily dignified about manual labour at all, and most of it is absolutely degrading. It is mentally and morally injurious to man to do anything in which he does not find pleasure, and many forms of labour are quite pleasureless activities, and should be regarded as such. To sweep a slushy crossing for eight hours, on a day when the east wind is blowing is a disgusting occupation. To sweep it with mental, moral, or physical dignity seems to me to be impossible. To sweep it with joy would be appalling. Man is made for something better than disturbing dirt. All work of that kind should be done by a machine.

And I have no doubt that it will be so. Up to the present, man has been, to a certain extent, the slave of machinery, and there is something tragic in the fact that as soon as man had invented a machine to do his work he began to starve. This, however, is, of course, the result of our property system and our system of competition. One man owns a machine which does the work of five hundred men. Five hundred men are, in consequence, thrown out of employment, and, having no work to do, become hungry and take to thieving. The one man secures the produce of the machine and keeps it, and has five hundred times as much as he should have, and probably, which is of much more importance, a great deal more than he really wants. Were that machine the property of all, every one would benefit by it. It would be an immense advantage to the community. All unintellectual labour, all monotonous, dull labour, all labour that deals with dreadful things, and involves unpleasant conditions, must be done by machinery. Machinery must work for us in coal mines, and do all sanitary services, and be the stoker of steamers, and clean the streets, and run messages on wet days, and do anything that is tedious or distressing. At present machinery competes against man. Under proper conditions machinery will serve man. There is no doubt at all that this is the future of machinery, and just as trees grow while the country gentleman is asleep, so while Humanity will be amusing itself, or enjoying cultivated leisure— which, and not labour, is the aim of man—or making beautiful things, or reading beautiful things, or simply contemplating the world with admiration and delight, machinery will be doing all the necessary and unpleasant work. The fact is, that civilisation requires slaves. The Greeks were quite right there. Unless there are slaves to do the ugly, horrible, uninteresting work, culture and contemplation become almost impossible. Human slavery is wrong, insecure, and demoralising. On mechanical slavery, on the slavery of the machine, the future of the world depends. And when scientific men are no longer called upon to go down to a depressing East End and distribute bad cocoa and worse blankets to starving people, they will have delightful leisure in which to devise wonderful and marvellous things for their own joy and the joy of everyone else. There will be great storages of force for every city, and for every house if required, and this force man will convert into heat, light, or motion, according to his needs. Is this Utopian? A map of the world that does not include Utopia is not worth even glancing at, for it leaves out the one country at which Humanity is always landing. And when Humanity lands there, it looks out, and, seeing a better country, sets sail. Progress is the realisation of Utopias.

Now, I have said that the community by means of organisation of machinery will supply the useful things, and that the beautiful things will be made by the individual. This is not merely necessary, but it is the only possible way by which we can get either the one or the other. An individual who has to make things for the use of others, and with reference to their wants and their wishes, does not work with interest, and consequently cannot put into his work what is best in him. Upon the other hand, whenever a community or a powerful section of a community, or a government of any kind, attempts to dictate to the artist what he is to do, Art either entirely vanishes, or becomes stereotyped, or degenerates into a low and ignoble form of craft. A work of art is the unique result of a unique temperament. Its beauty comes from the fact that the author is what he is. It has nothing to do with the fact that other people want what they want. Indeed, the moment that an artist takes notice of what other people want, and tries to supply the demand, he ceases to be an artist, and becomes a dull or an amusing craftsman, an honest or a dishonest tradesman. He has no further claim to be considered as an artist. Art is the most intense mode of Individualism that the world has known. I am inclined to say that it is the only real mode of Individualism that the world has known. Crime, which, under certain conditions, may seem to have created Individualism, must take cognisance of other people and interfere with them. It belongs to the sphere of action. But alone, without any reference to his neighbours, without any interference, the artist can fashion a beautiful thing; and if he does not do it solely for his own pleasure, he is not an artist at all.

And it is to be noted that it is the fact that Art is this intense form of Individualism that makes the public try to exercise over it in an authority that is as immoral as it is ridiculous, and as corrupting as it is contemptible. It is not quite their fault. The public has always, and in every age, been badly brought up. They are continually asking Art to be popular, to please their want of taste, to flatter their absurd vanity, to tell them what they have been told before, to show them what they ought to be tired of seeing, to amuse them when they feel heavy after eating too much, and to distract their thoughts when they are wearied of their own stupidity. Now Art should never try to be popular. The public should try to make itself artistic. There is a very wide difference. If a man of science were told that the results of his experiments, and the conclusions that he arrived at, should be of such a character that they would not upset the received popular notions on the subject, or disturb popular prejudice, or hurt the sensibilities of people who knew nothing about science; if a philosopher were told that he had a perfect right to speculate in the highest spheres of thought, provided that he arrived at the same conclusions as were held by those who had never thought in any sphere at all—well, nowadays the man of science and the philosopher would be considerably amused. Yet it is really a very few years since both philosophy and science were subjected to brutal popular control, to authority in fact—the authority of either the general ignorance of the community, or the terror and greed for power of an ecclesiastical or governmental class. Of course, we have to a very great extent got rid of any attempt on the part of the community, or the Church, or the Government, to interfere with the individualism of speculative thought, but the attempt to interfere with the individualism of imaginative art still lingers. In fact, it does more than linger; it is aggressive, offensive, and brutalising.

In England, the arts that have escaped best are the arts in which the public take no interest. Poetry is an instance of what I mean. We have been able to have fine poetry in England because the public do not read it, and consequently do not influence it. The public like to insult poets because they are individual, but once they have insulted them, they leave them alone. In the case of the novel and the drama, arts in which the public do take an interest, the result of the exercise of popular authority has been absolutely ridiculous. No country produces such badly-written fiction, such tedious, common work in the novel form, such silly, vulgar plays as England. It must necessarily be so. The popular standard is of such a character that no artist can get to it. It is at once too easy and too difficult to be a popular novelist. It is too easy, because the requirements of the public as far as plot, style, psychology, treatment of life, and treatment of literature are concerned are within the reach of the very meanest capacity and the most uncultivated mind. It is too difficult, because to meet such requirements the artist would have to do violence to his temperament, would have to write not for the artistic joy of writing, but for the amusement of half-educated people, and so would have to suppress his individualism, forget his culture, annihilate his style, and surrender everything that is valuable in him. In the case of the drama, things are a little better: the theatre-going public like the obvious, it is true, but they do not like the tedious; and burlesque and farcical comedy, the two most popular forms, are distinct forms of art. Delightful work may be produced under burlesque and farcical conditions, and in work of this kind the artist in England is allowed very great freedom. It is when one comes to the higher forms of the drama that the result of popular control is seen. The one thing that the public dislike is novelty. Any attempt to extend the subject-matter of art is extremely distasteful to the public; and yet the vitality and progress of art depend in a large measure on the continual extension of subject-matter. The public dislike novelty because they are afraid of it. It represents to them a mode of Individualism, an assertion on the part of the artist that he selects his own subject, and treats it as he chooses. The public are quite right in their attitude. Art is Individualism, and Individualism is a disturbing and disintegrating force. Therein lies its immense value. For what it seeks to disturb is monotony of type, slavery of custom, tyranny of habit, and the reduction of man to the level of a machine. In Art, the public accept what has been, because they cannot alter it, not because they appreciate it. They swallow their classics whole, and never taste them. They endure them as the inevitable, and as they cannot mar them, they mouth about them. Strangely enough, or not strangely, according to one's own views, this acceptance of the classics does a great deal of harm. The uncritical admiration of the Bible and Shakespeare in England is an instance of what I mean. With regard to the Bible, considerations of ecclesiastical authority enter into the matter, so that I need not dwell upon the point.

But in the case of Shakespeare, it is quite obvious that the public really see neither the beauties nor the defects of his plays. If they saw the beauties, they would not object to the development of the drama; and if they saw the defects, they would not object to the development of the drama either. The fact is, the public make use of the classics of a country as a means of checking the progress of Art. They degrade the classics into authorities. They use them as bludgeons for preventing the free expression of Beauty in new forms. They are always asking a writer why he does not write like somebody else, or a painter why he does not paint like somebody else, quite oblivious of the fact that if either of them did anything of the kind he would cease to be an artist. A fresh mode of Beauty is absolutely distasteful to them, and whenever it appears they get so angry, and bewildered that they always use two stupid expressions—one is that the work of art is grossly unintelligible; the other, that the work of art is grossly immoral. What they mean by these words seems to me to be this. When they say a work is grossly unintelligible, they mean that the artist has said or made a beautiful thing that is new; when they describe a work as grossly immoral, they mean that the artist has said or made a beautiful thing that is true. The former expression has reference to style; the latter to subject-matter. But they probably use the words very vaguely, as an ordinary mob will use ready-made paving-stones. There is not a single real poet or prose-writer of this century, for instance, on whom the British public have not solemnly conferred diplomas of immorality, and these diplomas practically take the place, with us, of what in France, is the formal recognition of an Academy of Letters, and fortunately make the establishment of such an institution quite unnecessary in England. Of course, the public are very reckless in their use of the word. That they should have called Wordsworth an immoral poet, was only to be expected. Wordsworth was a poet. But that they should have called Charles Kingsley an immoral novelist is extraordinary. Kingsley's prose was not of a very fine quality. Still, there is the word, and they use it as best they can. An artist is, of course, not disturbed by it. The true artist is a man who believes absolutely in himself, because he is absolutely himself. But I can fancy that if an artist produced a work of art in England that immediately on its appearance was recognised by the public, through their medium, which is the public press, as a work that was quite intelligible and highly moral, he would begin to seriously question whether in its creation he had really been himself at all, and consequently whether the work was not quite unworthy of him, and either of a thoroughly second-rate order, or of no artistic value whatsoever.

Perhaps, however, I have wronged the public in limiting them to such words as 'immoral,' 'unintelligible,' 'exotic,' and 'unhealthy.' There is one other word that they use. That word is 'morbid.' They do not use it often. The meaning of the word is so simple that they are afraid of using it. Still, they use it sometimes, and, now and then, one comes across it in popular newspapers. It is, of course, a ridiculous word to apply to a work of art. For what is morbidity but a mood of emotion or a mode of thought that one cannot express? The public are all morbid, because the public can never find expression for anything. The artist is never morbid. He expresses everything. He stands outside his subject, and through its medium produces incomparable and artistic effects. To call an artist morbid because he deals with morbidity as his subject-matter is as silly as if one called Shakespeare mad because he wrote 'King Lear.'

On the whole, an artist in England gains something by being attacked. His individuality is intensified. He becomes more completely himself. Of course, the attacks are very gross, very impertinent, and very contemptible. But then no artist expects grace from the vulgar mind, or style from the suburban intellect. Vulgarity and stupidity are two very vivid facts in modern life. One regrets them, naturally. But there they are. They are subjects for study, like everything else. And it is only fair to state, with regard to modern journalists, that they always apologise to one in private for what they have written against one in public.

Within the last few years two other adjectives, it may be mentioned, have been added to the very limited vocabulary of art-abuse that is at the disposal of the public. One is the word 'unhealthy,' the other is the word 'exotic.' The latter merely expresses the rage of the momentary mushroom against the immortal, entrancing, and exquisitely lovely orchid. It is a tribute, but a tribute of no importance. The word 'unhealthy,' however, admits of analysis. It is a rather interesting word. In fact, it is so interesting that the people who use it do not know what it means.

What does it mean? What is a healthy, or an unhealthy work of art? All terms that one applies to a work of art, provided that one applies them rationally, have reference to either its style or its subject, or to both together. From the point of view of style, a healthy work of art is one whose style recognises the beauty of the material it employs, be that material one of words or of bronze, of colour or of ivory, and uses that beauty as a factor in producing the æsthetic effect. From the point of view of subject, a healthy work of art is one the choice of whose subject is conditioned by the temperament of the artist, and comes directly out of it. In fine, a healthy work of art is one that has both perfection and personality. Of course, form and substance cannot be separated in a work of art; they are always one. But for purposes of analysis, and setting the wholeness of æsthetic impression aside for a moment, we can intellectually so separate them. An unhealthy work of art, on the other hand, is a work whose style is obvious, old-fashioned, and common, and whose subject is deliberately chosen, not because the artist has any pleasure in it, but because he thinks that the public will pay him for it. In fact, the popular novel that the public calls healthy is always a thoroughly unhealthy production; and what the public call an unhealthy novel is always a beautiful and healthy work of art.

I need hardly say that I am not, for a single moment, complaining that the public and the public press misuse these words. I do not see how, with their lack of comprehension of what Art is, they could possibly use them in the proper sense. I am merely pointing out the misuse; and as for the origin of the misuse and the meaning that lies behind it all, the explanation is very simple. It comes from the barbarous conception of authority. It comes from the natural inability of a community corrupted by authority to understand or appreciate Individualism. In a word, it comes from that monstrous and ignorant thing that is called Public Opinion, which, bad and well-meaning as it is when it tries to control action, is infamous and of evil meaning when it tries to control Thought or Art.

Indeed, there is much more to be said in favour of the physical force of the public than there is in favour of the public's opinion. The former may be fine. The latter must be foolish. It is often said that force is no argument. That, however, entirely depends on what one wants to prove. Many of the most important problems of the last few centuries, such as the continuance of personal government in England, or of feudalism in France, have been solved entirely by means of physical force. The very violence of a revolution may make the public grand and splendid for a moment. It was a fatal day when the public discovered that the pen is mightier than the paving-stone, and can be made as offensive as the brickbat. They at once sought for the journalist, found him, developed him, and made him their industrious and well-paid servant. It is greatly to be regretted, for both their sakes. Behind the barricade there may be much that is noble and heroic. But what is there behind the leading-article but prejudice, stupidity, cant, and twaddle? And when these four are joined together they make a terrible force, and constitute the new authority.

In old days men had the rack. Now they have the press. That is an improvement certainly. But still it is very bad, and wrong, and demoralising. Somebody—was it Burke?—called journalism the fourth estate. That was true at the time, no doubt. But at the present moment, it really is the only estate. It has eaten up the other three. The Lords Temporal say nothing, the Lords Spiritual have nothing to say, and the House of Commons has nothing to say and says it. We are dominated by Journalism. In America the President reigns for four years, and Journalism governs for ever and ever. Fortunately in America Journalism has carried its authority to the grossest and most brutal extreme. As a natural consequence it has begun to create a spirit of revolt. People are amused by it, or disgusted by it, according to their temperaments. But it is no longer the real force it was. It is not seriously treated. In England, Journalism, not, except in a few well-known instances, having been carried to such excesses of brutality, is still a great factor, a really remarkable power. The tyranny that it proposes to exercise over people's private lives seems to me to be quite extraordinary. The fact is, that the public have an insatiable curiosity to know everything, except what is worth knowing. Journalism, conscious of this, and having tradesman-like habits, supplies their demands. In centuries before ours the public nailed the ears of journalists to the pump. That was quite hideous. In this century journalists have nailed their own ears to the keyhole. That is much worse. And what aggravates the mischief is that the journalists who are most to blame are not the amusing journalists who write for what are called Society papers. The harm is done by the serious, thoughtful, earnest journalists, who solemnly, as they are doing at present, will drag before the eyes of the public some incident in the private life of a great statesman, of a man who is a leader of political thought as he is a creator of political force, and invite the public to discuss the incident, to exercise authority in the matter, to give their views, and not merely to give their views, but to carry them into action, to dictate to the man upon all other points, to dictate to his party, to dictate to his country; in fact, to make themselves ridiculous, offensive, and harmful. The private lives of men and women should not be told to the public. The public have nothing to do with them at all. In France they manage these things better. There they do not allow the details of the trials that take place in the divorce courts to be published for the amusement or criticism of the public. All that the public are allowed to know is that the divorce has taken place and was granted on petition of one or other or both of the married parties concerned. In France, in fact, they limit the journalist, and allow the artist almost perfect freedom. Here we allow absolute freedom to the journalist, and entirely limit the artist. English public opinion, that is to say, tries to constrain and impede and warp the man who makes things that are beautiful in effect, and compels the journalist to retail things that are ugly, or disgusting, or revolting in fact, so that we have the most serious journalists in the world, and the most indecent newspapers. It is no exaggeration to talk of compulsion. There are possibly some journalists who take a real pleasure in publishing horrible things, or who, being poor, look to scandals as forming a sort of permanent basis for an income. But there are other journalists, I feel certain, men of education and cultivation, who really dislike publishing these things, who know that it is wrong to do so, and only do it because the unhealthy conditions under which their occupation is carried on oblige them to supply the public with what the public wants, and to compete with other journalists in making that supply as full and satisfying to the gross popular appetite as possible. It is a very degrading position for any body of educated men to be placed in, and I have no doubt that most of them feel it acutely.

However, let us leave what is really a very sordid side of the subject, and return to the question of popular control in the matter of Art, by which I mean Public Opinion dictating to the artist the form which he is to use, the mode in which he is to use it, and the materials with which he is to work. I have pointed out that the arts which have escaped best in England are the arts in which the public have not been interested. They are, however, interested in the drama, and as a certain advance has been made in the drama within the last ten or fifteen years, it is important to point out that this advance is entirely due to a few individual artists refusing to accept the popular want of taste as their standard, and refusing to regard Art as a mere matter of demand and supply. With his marvellous and vivid personality, with a style that has really a true colour-element in it, with his extraordinary power, not over mere mimicry but over imaginative and intellectual creation, Mr Irving, had his sole object been to give the public what they wanted, could have produced the commonest plays in the commonest manner, and made as much success and money as a man could possibly desire. But his object was not that. His object was to realise his own perfection as an artist, under certain conditions, and in certain forms of Art. At first he appealed to the few: now he has educated the many. He has created in the public both taste and temperament. The public appreciate his artistic success immensely. I often wonder, however, whether the public understand that that success is entirely due to the fact that he did not accept their standard, but realised his own. With their standard, the Lyceum would have been a sort of second-rate booth, as some of the popular theatres in London are at present. Whether they understand it or not the fact however remains, that taste and temperament have, to a certain extent been created in the public, and that the public is capable of developing these qualities. The problem then is, why do not the public become more civilised? They have the capacity. What stops them?

The thing that stops them, it must be said again, is their desire to exercise authority over the artist and over works of art. To certain theatres, such as the Lyceum and the Haymarket, the public seem to come in a proper mood. In both of these theatres there have been individual artists, who have succeeded in creating in their audiences— and every theatre in London has its own audience—the temperament to which Art appeals. And what is that temperament? It is the temperament of receptivity. That is all.

If a man approaches a work of art with any desire to exercise authority over it and the artist, he approaches it in such a spirit that he cannot receive any artistic impression from it at all. The work of art is to dominate the spectator: the spectator is not to dominate the work of art. The spectator is to be receptive. He is to be the violin on which the master is to play. And the more completely he can suppress his own silly views, his own foolish prejudices, his own absurd ideas of what Art should be, or should not be, the more likely he is to understand and appreciate the work of art in question. This is, of course, quite obvious in the case of the vulgar theatre-going public of English men and women. But it is equally true of what are called educated people. For an educated person's ideas of Art are drawn naturally from what Art has been, whereas the new work of art is beautiful by being what Art has never been; and to measure it by the standard of the past is to measure it by a standard on the rejection of which its real perfection depends. A temperament capable of receiving, through an imaginative medium, and under imaginative conditions, new and beautiful impressions, is the only temperament that can appreciate a work of art. And true as this is in the case of the appreciation of sculpture and painting, it is still more true of the appreciation of such arts as the drama. For a picture and a statue are not at war with Time. They take no count of its succession. In one moment their unity may be apprehended. In the case of literature it is different. Time must be traversed before the unity of effect is realised. And so, in the drama, there may occur in the first act of the play something whose real artistic value may not be evident to the spectator till the third or fourth act is reached. Is the silly fellow to get angry and call out, and disturb the play, and annoy the artists? No. The honest man is to sit quietly, and know the delightful emotions of wonder, curiosity, and suspense. He is not to go to the play to lose a vulgar temper. He is to go to the play to realise an artistic temperament. He is to go to the play to gain an artistic temperament. He is not the arbiter of the work of art. He is one who is admitted to contemplate the work of art, and, if the work be fine, to forget in its contemplation and the egotism that mars him—the egotism of his ignorance, or the egotism of his information. This point about the drama is hardly, I think, sufficiently recognised. I can quite understand that were 'Macbeth' produced for the first time before a modern London audience, many of the people present would strongly and vigorously object to the introduction of the witches in the first act, with their grotesque phrases and their ridiculous words. But when the play is over one realises that the laughter of the witches in 'Macbeth' is as terrible as the laughter of madness in 'Lear,' more terrible than the laughter of Iago in the tragedy of the Moor. No spectator of art needs a more perfect mood of receptivity than the spectator of a play. The moment he seeks to exercise authority he becomes the avowed enemy of Art and of himself. Art does not mind. It is he who suffers.

With the novel it is the same thing. Popular authority and the recognition of popular authority are fatal. Thackeray's 'Esmond' is a beautiful work of art because he wrote it to please himself. In his other novels, in 'Pendennis,' in 'Philip,' in 'Vanity Fair' even, at times, he is too conscious of the public, and spoils his work by appealing directly to the sympathies of the public, or by directly mocking at them. A true artist takes no notice whatever of the public. The public are to him non-existent. He has no poppied or honeyed cakes through which to give the monster sleep or sustenance. He leaves that to the popular novelist. One incomparable novelist we have now in England, Mr George Meredith. There are better artists in France, but France has no one whose view of life is so large, so varied, so imaginatively true. There are tellers of stories in Russia who have a more vivid sense of what pain in fiction may be. But to him belongs philosophy in fiction. His people not merely live, but they live in thought. One can see them from myriad points of view. They are suggestive. There is soul in them and around them. They are interpretative and symbolic. And he who made them, those wonderful quickly-moving figures, made them for his own pleasure, and has never asked the public what they wanted, has never cared to know what they wanted, has never allowed the public to dictate to him or influence him in any way but has gone on intensifying his own personality, and producing his own individual work. At first none came to him. That did not matter. Then the few came to him. That did not change him. The many have come now. He is still the same. He is an incomparable novelist.

With the decorative arts it is not different. The public clung with really pathetic tenacity to what I believe were the direct traditions of the Great Exhibition of international vulgarity, traditions that were so appalling that the houses in which people lived were only fit for blind people to live in. Beautiful things began to be made, beautiful colours came from the dyer's hand, beautiful patterns from the artist's brain, and the use of beautiful things and their value and importance were set forth. The public were really very indignant. They lost their temper. They said silly things. No one minded. No one was a whit the worse. No one accepted the authority of public opinion. And now it is almost impossible to enter any modern house without seeing some recognition of good taste, some recognition of the value of lovely surroundings, some sign of appreciation of beauty. In fact, people's houses are, as a rule, quite charming nowadays. People have been to a very great extent civilised. It is only fair to state, however, that the extraordinary success of the revolution in house-decoration and furniture and the like has not really been due to the majority of the public developing a very fine taste in such matters. It has been chiefly due to the fact that the craftsmen of things so appreciated the pleasure of making what was beautiful, and woke to such a vivid consciousness of the hideousness and vulgarity of what the public had previously wanted, that they simply starved the public out. It would be quite impossible at the present moment to furnish a room as rooms were furnished a few years ago, without going for everything to an auction of second-hand furniture from some third-rate lodging-house. The things are no longer made. However they may object to it, people must nowadays have something charming in their surroundings. Fortunately for them, their assumption of authority in these art-matters came to entire grief.

It is evident, then, that all authority in such things is bad. People sometimes inquire what form of government is most suitable for an artist to live under. To this question there is only one answer. The form of government that is most suitable to the artist is no government at all. Authority over him and his art is ridiculous. It has been stated that under despotisms artists have produced lovely work. This is not quite so. Artists have visited despots, not as subjects to be tyrannised over, but as wandering wonder-makers, as fascinating vagrant personalities, to be entertained and charmed and suffered to be at peace, and allowed to create. There is this to be said in favour of the despot, that he, being an individual, may have culture, while the mob, being a monster, has none. One who is an Emperor and King may stoop down to pick up a brush for a painter, but when the democracy stoops down it is merely to throw mud. And yet the democracy have not so far to stoop as the emperor. In fact, when they want to throw mud they have not to stoop at all. But there is no necessity to separate the monarch from the mob; all authority is equally bad.

There are three kinds of despots. There is the despot who tyrannises over the body. There is the despot who tyrannises over the soul. There is the despot who tyrannises over the soul and body alike. The first is called the Prince. The second is called the Pope. The third is called the People. The Prince may be cultivated. Many Princes have been. Yet in the Prince there is danger. One thinks of Dante at the bitter feast in Verona, of Tasso in Ferrara's madman's cell. It is better for the artist not to live with Princes. The Pope may be cultivated. Many Popes have been; the bad Popes have been. The bad Popes loved Beauty, almost as passionately, nay, with as much passion as the good Popes hated Thought. To the wickedness of the Papacy humanity owes much. The goodness of the Papacy owes a terrible debt to humanity. Yet, though the Vatican has kept the rhetoric of its thunders, and lost the rod of its lightning, it is better for the artist not to live with Popes. It was a Pope who said of Cellini to a conclave of Cardinals that common laws and common authority were not made for men such as he; but it was a Pope who thrust Cellini into prison, and kept him there till he sickened with rage, and created unreal visions for himself, and saw the gilded sun enter his room, and grew so enamoured of it that he sought to escape, and crept out from tower to tower, and falling through dizzy

41

air at dawn, maimed himself, and was by a vine-dresser covered with vine leaves, and carried in a cart to one who, loving beautiful things, had care of him. There is danger in Popes. And as for the People, what of them and their authority? Perhaps of them and their authority one has spoken enough. Their authority is a thing blind, deaf, hideous, grotesque, tragic, amusing, serious, and obscene. It is impossible for the artist to live with the People. All despots bribe. The people bribe and brutalise. Who told them to exercise authority? They were made to live, to listen, and to love. Someone has done them a great wrong. They have marred themselves by imitation of their inferiors. They have taken the sceptre of the Prince. How should they use it? They have taken the triple tiara of the Pope. How should they carry its burden? They are as a clown whose heart is broken. They are as a priest whose soul is not yet born. Let all who love Beauty pity them. Though they themselves love not Beauty, yet let them pity themselves. Who taught them the trick of tyranny?

There are many other things that one might point out. One might point out how the Renaissance was great, because it sought to solve no social problem, and busied itself not about such things, but suffered the individual to develop freely, beautifully, and naturally, and so had great and individual artists, and great and individual men. One might point out how Louis XIV., by creating the modern state, destroyed the individualism of the artist, and made things monstrous in their monotony of repetition, and contemptible in their conformity to rule, and destroyed throughout all France all those fine freedoms of expression that had made tradition new in beauty, and new modes one with antique form. But the past is of no importance. The present is of no importance. It is with the future that we have to deal. For the past is what man should not have been. The present is what man ought not to be. The future is what artists are.

It will, of course, be said that such a scheme as is set forth here is quite unpractical, and goes against human nature. This is perfectly true. It is unpractical, and it goes against human nature. This is why it is worth carrying out, and that is why one proposes it. For what is a practical scheme? A practical scheme is either a scheme that is already in existence, or a scheme that could be carried out under existing conditions. But it is exactly the existing conditions that one objects to; and any scheme that could accept these conditions is wrong and foolish. The conditions will be done away with, and human nature will change. The only thing that one really knows about human nature is that it changes. Change is the one quality we can predicate of it. The systems that fail are those that rely on the permanency of human nature, and not on its growth and development. The error of Louis XIV. was that he thought human nature would always be the same. The result of his error was the French Revolution. It was an admirable result. All the results of the mistakes of governments are quite admirable.

It is to be noted also that Individualism does not come to man with any sickly cant about duty, which merely means doing what other people want because they want it; or any hideous cant about self-sacrifice, which is merely a survival of savage mutilation. In fact, it does not come to man with any claims upon him at all. It comes naturally and inevitably out of man. It is the point to which all development tends. It is the differentiation to which all organisms grow. It is the perfection that is inherent in every mode of life, and towards which every mode of life quickens. And so Individualism exercises no compulsion over man. On the contrary, it says to man that he should suffer no compulsion to be exercised over him. It does not try to force people to be good. It knows that people are good when they are let alone. Man will develop Individualism out of himself. Man is now so developing Individualism. To ask whether Individualism is practical is like asking whether Evolution is practical. Evolution is the law of life, and there is no evolution except towards Individualism. Where this tendency is not expressed, it is a case of artificially-arrested growth, or of disease, or of death.

Individualism will also be unselfish and unaffected. It has been pointed out that one of the results of the extraordinary tyranny of authority is that words are absolutely distorted from their proper and simple meaning, and are used to express the obverse of their right signification. What is true about Art is true about Life. A man is called affected, nowadays, if he dresses as he likes to dress. But in doing that he is acting in a perfectly natural manner. Affectation, in such matters, consists in dressing according to the views of one's neighbour, whose views, as they are the views of the majority, will probably be extremely stupid. Or a man is called selfish if he lives in the manner that seems to him most suitable for the full realisation of his own personality; if, in fact, the primary aim of his life is self-development. But this is the way in which everyone should live. Selfishness is not living as one wishes to live, it is asking others to live as one wishes to live. And unselfishness is letting other people's lives alone, not interfering with them. Selfishness always aims at creating around it an absolute uniformity of type. Unselfishness recognises infinite variety of type as a delightful thing, accepts it, acquiesces in it, enjoys it. It is not selfish to think for oneself. A man who does not think for himself does not think at all. It is grossly selfish to require of ones neighbour that he should think in the same way, and hold the same opinions. Why should he? If he can think, he will probably think differently. If he cannot think, it is monstrous to require thought of any kind from him. A red rose is not selfish because it wants to be a red rose. It would be horribly selfish if it wanted all the other flowers in the garden to be both red and roses. Under Individualism people will be quite natural and absolutely unselfish,and will know the meanings of the words, and realise them in their free, beautiful lives. Nor will men be egotistic as they are now. For the egotist is he who makes claims upon others, and the Individualist will not desire to do that. It will not give him pleasure. When man has realised Individualism, he will also realise sympathy and exercise it freely and spontaneously. Up to the present man has hardly cultivated sympathy at all. He has merely sympathy with pain, and sympathy with pain is not the highest form of sympathy. All sympathy is fine, but sympathy with suffering is the least fine mode. It is tainted with egotism. It is apt to become morbid. There is in it a certain element of terror for our own safety. We become afraid that we ourselves might be as the leper or as the blind, and that no man would have care of us. It is curiously limiting, too. One should sympathise with the entirety of life, not with life's sores and maladies merely, but with life's joy and beauty and energy and health and freedom. The wider sympathy is, of course, the more difficult. It requires more unselfishness. Anybody can sympathise with the sufferings of a friend, but it requires a very fine nature—it requires, in fact, the nature of a true Individualist—to sympathise with a friend's success.

In the modern stress of competition and struggle for place, such sympathy is naturally rare, and is also very much stifled by the immoral ideal of uniformity of type and conformity to rule which is so prevalent everywhere, and is perhaps most obnoxious in England.

Sympathy with pain there will, of course, always be. It is one of the first instincts of man. The animals which are individual, the higher animals, that is to say, share it with us. But it must be remembered that while sympathy with joy intensifies the sum of joy in the world, sympathy with pain does not really diminish the amount of pain. It may make man better able to endure evil, but the evil remains. Sympathy with consumption does not cure consumption; that is what Science does. And when Socialism has solved the problem of poverty, and Science solved the problem of disease, the area of the sentimentalists will be lessened, and the sympathy of man will be large, healthy, and spontaneous. Man will have joy in the contemplation of the joyous life of others.

For it is through joy that the Individualism of the future will develop itself. Christ made no attempt to reconstruct society, and consequently the Individualism that he preached to man could be realised only through pain or in solitude. The ideals that we owe to Christ are the ideals of the man who abandons society entirely, or of the man who resists society absolutely. But man is naturally social. Even the Thebaid became peopled at last. And though the cenobite realises his personality, it is often an impoverished personality that he so realises.

Upon the other hand, the terrible truth that pain is a mode through which man may realise himself exercises a wonderful fascination over the world. Shallow speakers and shallow thinkers in pulpits and on platforms often talk about the world's worship of pleasure, and whine against it. But it is rarely in the world's history that its ideal has been one of joy and beauty. The worship of pain has far more often dominated the world. Mediævalism, with its saints and martyrs, its love of self-torture, its wild passion for wounding itself, its gashing with knives, and its whipping with rods—Mediævalism is real Christianity, and the mediæval Christ is the real Christ. When the Renaissance dawned upon the world, and brought with it the new ideals of the beauty of life and the joy of living, men could not understand Christ. Even Art shows us that. The painters of the Renaissance drew Christ as a little boy playing with another boy in a palace or a garden, or lying back in his mother's arms, smiling at her, or at a flower, or at a bright bird; or as a noble, stately figure moving nobly through the world; or as a wonderful figure rising in a sort of ecstasy from death to life. Even when they drew him crucified they drew him as a beautiful God on whom evil men had inflicted suffering. But he did not preoccupy them much. What delighted them was to paint the men and women whom they admired, and to show the loveliness of this lovely earth. They painted many religious pictures—in fact, they painted far too many, and the monotony of type and motive is wearisome, and was bad for art. It was the result of the authority of the public in art-matters, and is to be deplored. But their soul was not in the subject. Raphael was a great artist when he painted his portrait of the Pope. When he painted his Madonnas and infant Christs, he is not a great artist at all. Christ had no message for the Renaissance, which was wonderful because it brought an ideal at variance with his, and to find the presentation of the real Christ we must go to mediæval art. There he is one maimed and marred; one who is not comely to look on, because Beauty is a joy; one who is not in fair raiment, because that may be a joy also: he is a beggar who has a marvellous soul; he is a leper whose soul is divine; he needs neither property nor health; he is a God realising his perfection through pain.

The evolution of man is slow. The injustice of men is great. It was necessary that pain should be put forward as a mode of self-realisation. Even now, in some places in the world, the message of Christ is necessary. No one who lived in modern Russia could possibly realise his perfection except by pain. A few Russian artists have realised themselves in Art; in a fiction that is mediæval in character, because its dominant note is the realisation of men through suffering. But for those who are not artists, and to whom there is no mode of life but the actual life of fact, pain is the only door to perfection. A Russian who lives happily under the present system of government in Russia must either believe that man has no soul, or that, if he has, it is not worth developing. A Nihilist who rejects all authority, because he knows authority to be evil, and welcomes all pain, because through that he realises his personality, is a real Christian. To him the Christian ideal is a true thing.

And yet, Christ did not revolt against authority. He accepted the imperial authority of the Roman Empire and paid tribute. He endured the ecclesiastical authority of the Jewish Church, and would not repel its violence by any violence of his own. He had, as I said before, no scheme for the reconstruction of society. But the modern world has schemes. It proposes to do away with poverty and the suffering that it entails. It desires to get rid of pain, and the suffering that pain entails. It trusts to Socialism and to Science as its methods. What it aims at is an Individualism expressing itself through joy. This Individualism will be larger, fuller, lovelier than any Individualism has ever been. Pain is not the ultimate mode of perfection. It is merely provisional and a protest. It has reference to wrong, unhealthy, unjust surroundings. When the wrong, and the disease, and the injustice are removed, it will have no further place. It will have done its work. It was a great work, but it is almost over. Its sphere lessens every day.

Nor will man miss it. For what man has sought for is, indeed, neither pain nor pleasure, but simply Life. Man has sought to live intensely, fully, perfectly. When he can do so without exercising restraint on others, or suffering it ever, and his activities are all pleasurable to him, he will be saner, healthier, more civilised, more himself. Pleasure is Nature's test, her sign of approval. When man is happy, he is in harmony with himself and his environment. The new Individualism, for whose service Socialism, whether it wills it or not, is working, will be perfect harmony. It will be what the Greeks sought for, but could not, except in Thought, realise completely, because they had slaves, and fed them; it will be what the Renaissance sought for, but could not realise completely except in Art, because they had slaves, and starved them. It will be complete, and through it each man will attain to his perfection. The new Individualism is the new Hellenism.

A CRITIC IN PALL MALL

THE TOMB OF KEATS

(Irish Monthly, July 1877.)

As one enters Rome from the Via Ostiensis by the Porta San Paolo, the first object that meets the eye is a marble pyramid which stands close at hand on the left.

There are many Egyptian obelisks in Rome—tall, snakelike spires of red sandstone, mottled with strange writings, which remind us of the pillars of flame which led the children of Israel through the desert away from the land of the Pharaohs; but more wonderful than these to look upon is this gaunt, wedge-shaped pyramid standing here in this Italian city, unshattered amid the ruins and wrecks of time, looking older than the Eternal City itself, like terrible impassiveness turned to stone. And so in the Middle Ages men supposed this to be the sepulchre of Remus, who was slain by his own brother at the founding of the city, so ancient and mysterious it appears; but we have now, perhaps unfortunately, more accurate information about it, and know that it is the tomb of one Caius Cestius, a Roman gentleman of small note, who died about 30 b.c.

Yet though we cannot care much for the dead man who lies in lonely state beneath it, and who is only known to the world through his sepulchre, still this pyramid will be ever dear to the eyes of all English-speaking people, because at evening its shadows fall on the tomb of one who walks with Spenser, and Shakespeare, and Byron, and Shelley, and Elizabeth Barrett Browning in the great procession of the sweet singers of England.

For at its foot there is a green sunny slope, known as the Old Protestant Cemetery, and on this a common-looking grave, which bears the following inscription:

This grave contains all that was mortal of a young English poet, who on his deathbed, in the bitterness of his heart, desired these words to be engraven on his tombstone: HERE LIES ONE WHOSE NAME WAS WRIT IN WATER. February 24, 1821.

And the name of the young English poet is John Keats.

Lord Houghton calls this cemetery 'one of the most beautiful spots on which the eye and heart of man can rest,' and Shelley speaks of it as making one 'in love with death, to think that one should be buried in so sweet a place'; and indeed when I saw the violets and the daisies and the poppies that overgrow the tomb, I remembered how the dead poet had once told his friend that he thought the 'intensest pleasure he had received in life was in watching the growth of flowers,' and how another time, after lying a while quite still, he murmured in some strange prescience of early death, 'I feel the flowers growing over me.'

But this time-worn stone and these wildflowers are but poor memorials [2] of one so great as Keats; most of all, too, in this city of Rome, which pays such honour to her dead; where popes, and emperors, and saints, and cardinals lie hidden in 'porphyry wombs,' or couched in baths of jasper and chalcedony and malachite, ablaze with precious stones and metals, and tended with continual service. For very noble is the site, and worthy of a noble monument; behind looms the grey pyramid, symbol of the world's age, and filled with memories of the sphinx, and the lotus leaf, and the glories of old Nile; in front is the Monte Testaccio, built, it is said, with the broken fragments of the vessels in which all the nations of the East and the West brought their tribute to Rome; and a little distance off, along the slope of the hill under the Aurelian wall, some tall gaunt cypresses rise, like burnt-out funeral torches, to mark the spot where Shelley's heart (that 'heart of hearts'!) lies in the earth; and, above all, the soil on which we tread is very Rome!

As I stood beside the mean grave of this divine boy, I thought of him as of a Priest of Beauty slain before his time; and the vision of Guido's St. Sebastian came before my eyes as I saw him at Genoa, a lovely brown boy, with crisp, clustering hair and red lips, bound by his evil enemies to a tree, and though pierced by arrows, raising his eyes with divine, impassioned gaze towards the Eternal Beauty of the opening heavens. And thus my thoughts shaped themselves to rhyme:

HEU MISERANDE PUER

Rid of the world's injustice and its pain,

He rests at last beneath God's veil of blue;

Taken from life while life and love were new

The youngest of the martyrs here is lain,

Fair as Sebastian and as foully slain.

No cypress shades his grave, nor funeral yew,

But red-lipped daisies, violets drenched with dew,

And sleepy poppies, catch the evening rain.

O proudest heart that broke for misery!

O saddest poet that the world hath seen!

O sweetest singer of the English land!

Thy name was writ in water on the sand,

But our tears shall keep thy memory green,

And make it flourish like a Basil-tree.

Rome, 1877.

Note.—A later version of this sonnet, under the title of 'The Grave of Keats,' is given in the *Poems*, page 157.

KEATS'S SONNET ON BLUE

(Century Guild Hobby Horse, July 1886.)

During my tour in America I happened one evening to find myself in Louisville, Kentucky. The subject I had selected to speak on was the Mission of Art in the Nineteenth Century, and in the course of my lecture I had occasion to quote Keats's Sonnet on Blue as an example of the poet's delicate sense of colour-harmonies. When my lecture was concluded there came round to see me a lady of middle age, with a sweet gentle manner and a most musical voice. She introduced herself to me as Mrs. Speed, the daughter of George Keats, and invited me to come and examine the Keats manuscripts in her possession. I spent most of the next day with her, reading the letters of Keats to her father, some of which were at that time unpublished, poring over torn yellow leaves and faded scraps of paper, and wondering at the little Dante in which Keats had written those marvellous notes on Milton. Some months afterwards, when I was in California, I received a letter from Mrs. Speed asking my acceptance of the original manuscript of the sonnet which I had quoted in my lecture. This manuscript I have had reproduced here, as it seems to me to possess much psychological interest. It shows us the conditions that preceded the perfected form, the gradual growth, not of the conception but of the expression, and the workings of that spirit of selection which is the secret of style. In the case of poetry, as in the case of the other arts, what may appear to be simply technicalities of method are in their essence spiritual not mechanical, and although, in all lovely work, what concerns us is the ultimate form, not the conditions that necessitate that form, yet the preference that precedes perfection, the evolution of the beauty, and the mere making of the music, have, if not their artistic value, at least their value to the artist.

It will be remembered that this sonnet was first published in 1848 by Lord Houghton in his *Life, Letters, and Literary Remains of John Keats.* Lord Houghton does not definitely state where he found it, but it was probably among the Keats manuscripts belonging to Mr. Charles Brown. It is evidently taken from a version later than that in my possession, as it accepts all the corrections, and makes three variations. As in my manuscript the first line is torn away, I give the sonnet here as it appears in Lord Houghton's edition.

ANSWER TO A SONNET ENDING THUS:

Dark eyes are dearer far

Than those that make the hyacinthine bell. [5]

By J. H. Reynolds.

Blue! 'Tis the life of heaven,—the domain

Of Cynthia,—the wide palace of the sun,—

The tent of Hesperus and all his train,—

    The bosomer of clouds, gold, grey and dun.

Blue! 'Tis the life of waters—ocean

    And all its vassal streams: pools numberless

May rage, and foam, and fret, but never can

    Subside if not to dark-blue nativeness.

Blue! gentle cousin of the forest green,

    Married to green in all the sweetest flowers,

Forget-me-not,—the blue-bell,—and, that queen

    Of secrecy, the violet: what strange powers

Hast thou, as a mere shadow! But how great,

    When in an Eye thou art alive with fate!

Feb. 1818.

In the Athenæum of the 3rd of June 1876 appeared a letter from Mr. A. J. Horwood, stating that he had in his possession a copy of The Garden of Florence in which this sonnet was transcribed. Mr. Horwood, who was unaware that the sonnet had been already published by Lord Houghton, gives the transcript at length. His version reads hue for life in the first line, and bright for wide in the second, and gives the sixth line thus:

With all his tributary streams, pools numberless,

a foot too long: it also reads to for of in the ninth line. Mr. Buxton Forman is of opinion that these variations are decidedly genuine, but indicative of an earlier state of the poem than that adopted in Lord Houghton's edition. However, now that we have before us Keats's first draft of his sonnet, it is difficult to believe that the sixth line in Mr. Horwood's version is really a genuine variation. Keats may have written,

Ocean

> His tributary streams, pools numberless,

and the transcript may have been carelessly made, but having got his line right in his first draft, Keats probably did not spoil it in his second. The Athenæum version inserts a comma after art in the last line, which seems to me a decided improvement, and eminently characteristic of Keats's method. I am glad to see that Mr. Buxton Forman has adopted it.

As for the corrections that Lord Houghton's version shows Keats to have made in the eighth and ninth lines of this sonnet, it is evident that they sprang from Keats's reluctance to repeat the same word in consecutive lines, except in cases where a word's music or meaning was to be emphasized. The substitution of 'its' for 'his' in the sixth line is more difficult of explanation. It was due probably to a desire on Keats's part not to mar by any echo the fine personification of Hesperus.

It may be noticed that Keats's own eyes were brown, and not blue, as stated by Mrs. Proctor to Lord Houghton. Mrs. Speed showed me a note to that effect written by Mrs. George Keats on the margin of the page in Lord Houghton's Life (p. 100, vol. i.), where Mrs. Proctor's description is given. Cowden Clarke made a similar correction in his Recollections, and in some of the later editions of Lord Houghton's book the word 'blue' is struck out. In Severn's portraits of Keats also the eyes are given as brown.

The exquisite sense of colour expressed in the ninth and tenth lines may be paralleled by

> The Ocean with its vastness, its blue green,

of the sonnet to George Keats.

DINNERS AND DISHES

(Pall Mall Gazette, March 7, 1885.)

A man can live for three days without bread, but no man can live for one day without poetry, was an aphorism of Baudelaire. You can live without pictures and music but you cannot live without eating, says the author of

Dinners and Dishes; and this latter view is, no doubt, the more popular. Who, indeed, in these degenerate days would hesitate between an ode and an omelette, a sonnet and a salmis? Yet the position is not entirely Philistine; cookery is an art; are not its principles the subject of South Kensington lectures, and does not the Royal Academy give a banquet once a year? Besides, as the coming democracy will, no doubt, insist on feeding us all on penny dinners, it is well that the laws of cookery should be explained: for were the national meal burned, or badly seasoned, or served up with the wrong sauce a dreadful revolution might follow.

Under these circumstances we strongly recommend Dinners and Dishes to every one: it is brief and concise and makes no attempt at eloquence, which is extremely fortunate. For even on ortolans who could endure oratory? It also has the advantage of not being illustrated. The subject of a work of art has, of course, nothing to do with its beauty, but still there is always something depressing about the coloured lithograph of a leg of mutton.

As regards the author's particular views, we entirely agree with him on the important question of macaroni. 'Never,' he says, 'ask me to back a bill for a man who has given me a macaroni pudding.' Macaroni is essentially a savoury dish and may be served with cheese or tomatoes but never with sugar and milk. There is also a useful description of how to cook risotto—a delightful dish too rarely seen in England; an excellent chapter on the different kinds of salads, which should be carefully studied by those many hostesses whose imaginations never pass beyond lettuce and beetroot; and actually a recipe for making Brussels sprouts eatable. The last is, of course, a masterpiece.

The real difficulty that we all have to face in life is not so much the science of cookery as the stupidity of cooks. And in this little handbook to practical Epicureanism the tyrant of the English kitchen is shown in her proper light. Her entire ignorance of herbs, her passion for extracts and essences, her total inability to make a soup which is anything more than a combination of pepper and gravy, her inveterate habit of sending up bread poultices with pheasants,—all these sins and many others are ruthlessly unmasked by the author. Ruthlessly and rightly. For the British cook is a foolish woman who should be turned for her iniquities into a pillar of salt which she never knows how to use.

But our author is not local merely. He has been in many lands; he has eaten back-hendl at Vienna and kulibatsch at St. Petersburg; he has had the courage to face the buffalo veal of Roumania and to dine with a German family at one o'clock; he has serious views on the right method of cooking those famous white truffles of Turin of which Alexandre Dumas was so fond; and, in the face of the Oriental Club, declares that Bombay curry is better than the curry of Bengal. In fact he seems to have had experience of almost every kind of meal except the 'square meal' of the Americans. This he should study at once; there is a great field for the philosophic epicure in the United States. Boston beans may be dismissed at once as delusions, but soft-shell crabs, terrapin, canvas-back ducks, blue fish and the pompono of New Orleans are all wonderful delicacies, particularly when one gets them at Delmonico's. Indeed, the two most remarkable bits of scenery in the States are undoubtedly Delmonico's and the Yosemité Valley; and the former place has done more to promote a good feeling between England and America than anything else has in this century.

We hope the 'Wanderer' will go there soon and add a chapter to Dinners and Dishes, and that his book will have in England the influence it deserves. There are twenty ways of cooking a potato and three hundred and sixty-five ways of cooking an egg, yet the British cook, up to the present moment, knows only three methods of sending up either one or the other.

Dinners and Dishes. By 'Wanderer.' (Simpkin and Marshall.)

SHAKESPEARE ON SCENERY

(Dramatic Review, March 14, 1885.)

I have often heard people wonder what Shakespeare would say, could he see Mr. Irving's production of his Much Ado About Nothing, or Mr. Wilson Barrett's setting of his Hamlet. Would he take pleasure in the glory of the scenery and the marvel of the colour? Would he be interested in the Cathedral of Messina, and the battlements of Elsinore? Or would he be indifferent, and say the play, and the play only, is the thing?

Speculations like these are always pleasurable, and in the present case happen to be profitable also. For it is not difficult to see what Shakespeare's attitude would be; not difficult, that is to say, if one reads Shakespeare himself, instead of reading merely what is written about him.

Speaking, for instance, directly, as the manager of a London theatre, through the lips of the chorus in Henry V., he complains of the smallness of the stage on which he has to produce the pageant of a big historical play, and of the want of scenery which obliges him to cut out many of its most picturesque incidents, apologises for the scanty number of supers who had to play the soldiers, and for the shabbiness of the properties, and, finally, expresses his regret at being unable to bring on real horses.

In the Midsummer Night's Dream, again, he gives us a most amusing picture of the straits to which theatrical managers of his day were reduced by the want of proper scenery. In fact, it is impossible to read him without seeing that he is constantly protesting against the two special limitations of the Elizabethan stage—the lack of suitable scenery, and the fashion of men playing women's parts, just as he protests against other difficulties with which managers of theatres have still to contend, such as actors who do not understand their words; actors who miss their cues; actors who overact their parts; actors who mouth; actors who gag; actors who play to the gallery, and amateur actors.

And, indeed, a great dramatist, as he was, could not but have felt very much hampered at being obliged continually to interrupt the progress of a play in order to send on some one to explain to the audience that the scene was to be changed to a particular place on the entrance of a particular character, and after his exit to somewhere else; that the stage was to represent the deck of a ship in a storm, or the interior of a Greek temple, or the streets of a certain town, to all of which inartistic devices Shakespeare is reduced, and for which he always amply apologizes. Besides this clumsy method, Shakespeare had two other substitutes for scenery—the hanging out of a placard, and his descriptions. The first of these could hardly have satisfied his passion for picturesqueness and his feeling for beauty, and certainly did not satisfy the dramatic critic of his day. But as regards the description, to those of us who look on Shakespeare not merely as a playwright but as a poet, and who enjoy reading him at home just as much as we enjoy seeing him acted, it may be a matter of congratulation that he had not at his command such skilled machinists as are in use now at the Princess's and at the Lyceum. For had Cleopatra's barge, for instance, been a structure of canvas and Dutch metal, it would probably have been painted over or broken up after the withdrawal of the piece, and, even had it survived to our own day, would, I am afraid, have become extremely shabby by this time. Whereas now the beaten gold of its poop is still bright, and the purple of its sails still beautiful; its silver oars are not tired of keeping time to the music of the flutes they follow, nor the Nereid's flower-soft hands of touching its silken tackle; the mermaid still lies at its helm, and still on its deck stand the boys with their coloured fans. Yet lovely as all Shakespeare's descriptive passages are, a description is in its essence undramatic. Theatrical audiences are far more impressed by what they look at than by what they listen to; and the modern dramatist, in having the surroundings of his play visibly presented to the audience when the curtain rises, enjoys an advantage for which Shakespeare often expresses his desire. It is true that Shakespeare's descriptions are not what descriptions are in modern plays—accounts of what the audience can observe for themselves; they are the imaginative method by which he creates in the mind of the spectators the image of that which he desires them to see. Still, the quality of the drama is action. It is always dangerous to pause for picturesqueness. And the introduction of self-explanatory scenery enables the modern method to be far more direct, while the loveliness of form and colour which it gives us, seems to me often to create an artistic temperament in the audience, and to produce that joy in beauty for beauty's sake, without which the great masterpieces of art can never be understood, to which, and to which only, are they ever revealed.

To talk of the passion of a play being hidden by the paint, and of sentiment being killed by scenery, is mere emptiness and folly of words. A noble play, nobly mounted, gives us double artistic pleasure. The eye as well as the ear is gratified, and the whole nature is made exquisitely receptive of the influence of imaginative work. And as regards a bad play, have we not all seen large audiences lured by the loveliness of scenic effect into listening to rhetoric posing as poetry, and to vulgarity doing duty for realism? Whether this be good or evil for the public I will not here discuss, but it is evident that the playwright, at any rate, never suffers.

Indeed, the artist who really has suffered through the modern mounting of plays is not the dramatist at all, but the scene-painter proper. He is rapidly being displaced by the stage-carpenter. Now and then, at Drury Lane, I have seen beautiful old front cloths let down, as perfect as pictures some of them, and pure painter's work, and there are many which we all remember at other theatres, in front of which some dialogue was reduced to graceful dumb-show through the hammer and tin-tacks behind. But as a rule the stage is overcrowded with enormous properties, which are not merely far more expensive and cumbersome than scene-paintings, but far less beautiful, and far less true. Properties kill perspective. A painted door is more like a real door than a real door is itself, for the proper conditions of light and shade can be given to it; and the excessive use of built-up structures always makes the stage too glaring, for as they have to be lit from behind, as well as from the front, the gas-jets become the absolute light of the scene instead of the means merely by which we perceive the conditions of light and shadow which the painter has desired to show us.

So, instead of bemoaning the position of the playwright, it were better for the critics to exert whatever influence they may possess towards restoring the scene-painter to his proper position as an artist, and not allowing him to be built over by the property man, or hammered to death by the carpenter. I have never seen any reason myself why such artists as Mr. Beverley, Mr. Walter Hann, and Mr. Telbin should not be entitled to become Academicians. They have certainly as good a claim as have many of those R.A.'s whose total inability to paint we can see every May for a shilling.

And lastly, let those critics who hold up for our admiration the simplicity of the Elizabethan stage remember that they are lauding a condition of things against which Shakespeare himself, in the spirit of a true artist, always strongly protested.

HENRY THE FOURTH AT OXFORD

(Dramatic Review, May 23, 1885.)

I have been told that the ambition of every Dramatic Club is to act Henry IV. I am not surprised. The spirit of comedy is as fervent in this play as is the spirit of chivalry; it is an heroic pageant as well as an heroic poem, and like most of Shakespeare's historical dramas it contains an extraordinary number of thoroughly good acting parts, each of which is absolutely individual in character, and each of which contributes to the evolution of the plot.

To Oxford belongs the honour of having been the first to present on the stage this noble play, and the production which I saw last week was in every way worthy of that lovely town, that mother of sweetness and of light. For, in spite of the roaring of the young lions at the Union, and the screaming of the rabbits in the home of the vivisector, in spite of Keble College, and the tramways, and the sporting prints, Oxford still remains the most beautiful thing in England, and nowhere else are life and art so exquisitely blended, so perfectly made one. Indeed, in most other towns art has often to present herself in the form of a reaction against the sordid ugliness of ignoble lives, but at Oxford she comes to us as an exquisite flower born of the beauty of life and expressive of life's joy. She finds her home by the Isis as once she did by the Ilissus; the Magdalen walks and the Magdalen cloisters are as dear to her as were ever the silver olives of Colonus and the golden gateway of the house of Pallas: she covers with fanlike tracery the vaulted entrance to Christ Church Hall, and looks out from the windows of Merton; her feet have stirred the Cumnor cowslips, and she gathers fritillaries in the river-fields. To her the clamour of the schools and the dullness of the lecture-room are a weariness and a vexation of spirit; she seeks not to define virtue, and cares little for the categories; she smiles on the swift athlete whose plastic grace has pleased her, and rejoices in the young Barbarians at their games; she watches the rowers from the reedy bank and gives myrtle to her lovers, and laurels to her poets, and rue to those who talk wisely in the street; she makes the earth lovely to all who dream with Keats; she opens high heaven to all who soar with Shelley; and turning away her head from pedant, proctor and Philistine, she has welcomed to her shrine a band of youthful actors, knowing that they have sought with much ardour for the stern secret of Melpomene, and caught with much gladness the sweet laughter of Thalia. And to me this ardour and this gladness were the two most fascinating qualities of the Oxford performance, as indeed they are qualities which are necessary to any fine dramatic production. For without quick and imaginative observation of life the most beautiful play becomes dull in presentation, and what is not conceived in delight by the actor can give no delight at all to others.

I know that there are many who consider that Shakespeare is more for the study than for the stage. With this view I do not for a moment agree. Shakespeare wrote the plays to be acted, and we have no right to alter the form which he himself selected for the full expression of his work. Indeed, many of the beauties of that work can be adequately conveyed to us only through the actor's art. As I sat in the Town Hall of Oxford the other night, the majesty of the mighty lines of the play seemed to me to gain new music from the clear young voices that uttered them, and the ideal grandeur of the heroism to be made more real to the spectators by the chivalrous bearing, the noble gesture and the fine passion of its exponents. Even the dresses had their dramatic value. Their archæological accuracy gave us, immediately on the rise of the curtain, a perfect picture of the time. As the knights and nobles moved across the stage in the flowing robes of peace and in the burnished steel of battle, we needed no dreary chorus to tell us in what age or land the play's action was passing, for the fifteenth century in all the dignity and grace of its apparel was living actually before us, and the delicate harmonies of colour struck from the first a dominant note of beauty which added to the intellectual realism of archæology the sensuous charm of art.

I have rarely seen a production better stage-managed. Indeed, I hope that the University will take some official notice of this delightful work of art. Why should not degrees be granted for good acting? Are they not given to those who misunderstand Plato and who mistranslate Aristotle? And should the artist be passed over? No. To Prince Hal, Hotspur and Falstaff, D.C.L.'s should be gracefully offered. I feel sure they would be gracefully accepted. To the rest of the company the crimson or the sheepskin hood might be assigned honoris causâ to the eternal confusion of the Philistine, and the rage of the industrious and the dull. Thus would Oxford confer honour on herself, and the artist be placed in his proper position. However, whether or not Convocation recognizes the claims of culture, I hope that the Oxford Dramatic Society will produce every summer for us some noble play like Henry IV. For, in plays of this kind, plays which deal with bygone times, there is always this peculiar charm, that they combine in one exquisite presentation the passions that are living with the picturesqueness that is dead. And when we have the modern spirit given to us in an antique form, the very remoteness of that form can be made a method of increased realism. This was Shakespeare's own attitude towards the ancient world, this is the attitude we in this century should adopt towards his plays, and with a feeling akin to this it seemed to me that these brilliant young Oxonians were working. If it was so, their aim is the right one. For while we look to the dramatist to give romance to realism, we ask of the actor to give realism to romance.

A HANDBOOK TO MARRIAGE

(Pall Mall Gazette, November 18, 1885.)

In spite of its somewhat alarming title this book may be highly recommended to every one. As for the authorities the author quotes, they are almost numberless, and range from Socrates down to Artemus Ward. He tells us of the wicked bachelor who spoke of marriage as 'a very harmless amusement' and advised a young friend of his to 'marry early and marry often'; of Dr. Johnson who proposed that marriage should be arranged by the Lord Chancellor, without the parties concerned having any choice in the matter; of the Sussex labourer who asked, 'Why should I give a woman half my victuals for cooking the other half?' and of Lord Verulam who thought that unmarried men did the best public work. And, indeed, marriage is the one subject on which all women agree and all men disagree. Our author, however, is clearly of the same opinion as the Scotch lassie who, on her father warning her what a solemn thing it was to get married, answered, 'I ken that, father, but it's a great deal solemner to be single.' He may be regarded as the champion of the married life. Indeed, he has a most interesting chapter on marriage-made men, and though he dissents, and we think rightly, from the view recently put forward by a lady or two on the Women's Rights platform that Solomon owed all his wisdom to the number of his wives, still he appeals to Bismarck, John Stuart Mill, Mahommed, and Lord Beaconsfield, as instances of men whose success can be traced to the influence of the women they married. Archbishop Whately once defined woman as 'a creature that does not reason and pokes the fire from the top,' but since his day the higher education of women has considerably altered their position. Women have always had an emotional sympathy with those they love; Girton and Newnham have rendered intellectual sympathy also possible. In our day it is best for a man to be married, and men must give up the tyranny in married life which was once so dear to them, and which, we are afraid, lingers still, here and there.

'Do you wish to be my wife, Mabel?' said a little boy. 'Yes,' incautiously answered Mabel. 'Then pull off my boots.'

On marriage vows our author has, too, very sensible views and very amusing stories. He tells of a nervous bridegroom who, confusing the baptismal and marriage ceremonies, replied when asked if he consented to take the bride for his wife: 'I renounce them all'; of a Hampshire rustic who, when giving the ring, said solemnly to the bride: 'With my body I thee wash up, and with all my hurdle goods I thee and thou'; of another who when asked whether he would take his partner to be his wedded wife, replied with shameful indecision: 'Yes, I'm willin'; but I'd a sight rather have her sister'; and of a Scotch lady who, on the occasion of her daughter's wedding, was asked by an old friend whether she might congratulate her on the event, and answered: 'Yes, yes, upon the whole it is very satisfactory; it is true Jeannie hates her gudeman, but then there's always a something!' Indeed, the good stories contained in this book are quite endless and make it very pleasant reading, while the good advice is on all points admirable.

Most young married people nowadays start in life with a dreadful collection of ormolu inkstands covered with sham onyxes, or with a perfect museum of salt-cellars. We strongly recommend this book as one of the best of wedding presents. It is a complete handbook to an earthly Paradise, and its author may be regarded as the Murray of matrimony and the Baedeker of bliss.

How to be Happy though Married: Being a Handbook to Marriage.
By a Graduate in the University of Matrimony. (T. Fisher Unwin.)

TO READ OR NOT TO READ

(Pall Mall Gazette, February 8, 1886.)

Books, I fancy, may be conveniently divided into three classes:

1. Books to read, such as Cicero's Letters, Suetonius, Vasari's Lives of the Painters, the Autobiography of Benvenuto Cellini, Sir John Mandeville, Marco Polo, St. Simon's Memoirs, Mommsen, and (till we get a better one) Grote's History of Greece.

2. Books to re-read, such as Plato and Keats: in the sphere of poetry, the masters not the minstrels; in the sphere of philosophy, the seers not the savants.

3. Books not to read at all, such as Thomson's Seasons, Rogers's Italy, Paley's Evidences, all the Fathers except St. Augustine, all John Stuart Mill except the essay on Liberty, all Voltaire's plays without any exception, Butler's Analogy, Grant's Aristotle, Hume's England, Lewes's History of Philosophy, all argumentative books and all books that try to prove anything.

The third class is by far the most important. To tell people what to read is, as a rule, either useless or harmful; for, the appreciation of literature is a question of temperament not of teaching; to Parnassus there is no primer and nothing that one can learn is ever worth learning. But to tell people what not to read is a very different matter, and I venture to recommend it as a mission to the University Extension Scheme.

Indeed, it is one that is eminently needed in this age of ours, an age that reads so much, that it has no time to admire, and writes so much, that it has no time to think. Whoever will select out of the chaos of our modern curricula 'The Worst Hundred Books,' and publish a list of them, will confer on the rising generation a real and lasting benefit.

After expressing these views I suppose I should not offer any suggestions at all with regard to 'The Best Hundred Books,' but I hope you will allow me the pleasure of being inconsistent, as I am anxious to put in a claim for a book that has been strangely omitted by most of the excellent judges who have contributed to your columns. I mean the Greek Anthology. The beautiful poems contained in this collection seem to me to hold the same position with regard to Greek dramatic literature as do the delicate little figurines of Tanagra to the Phidian marbles, and to be quite as necessary for the complete understanding of the Greek spirit.

I am also amazed to find that Edgar Allan Poe has been passed over. Surely this marvellous lord of rhythmic expression deserves a place? If, in order to make room for him, it be necessary to elbow out some one else, I should elbow out Southey, and I think that Baudelaire might be most advantageously substituted for Keble.

No doubt, both in the Curse of Kehama and in the Christian Year there are poetic qualities of a certain kind, but absolute catholicity of taste is not without its dangers. It is only an auctioneer who should admire all schools of art.

THE LETTERS OF A GREAT WOMAN
(Pall Mall Gazette, March 6, 1886.)

Of the many collections of letters that have appeared in this century few, if any, can rival for fascination of style and variety of incident the letters of George Sand which have recently been translated into English by M. Ledos de Beaufort. They extend over a space of more than sixty years, from 1812 to 1876, in fact, and comprise the first letters of Aurore Dupin, a child of eight years old, as well as the last letters of George Sand, a woman of seventy-two.

The very early letters, those of the child and of the young married woman, possess, of course, merely a psychological interest; but from 1831, the date of Madame Dudevant's separation from her husband and her first entry into Paris life, the interest becomes universal, and the literary and political history of France is mirrored in every page.

For George Sand was an indefatigable correspondent; she longs in one of her letters, it is true, for 'a planet where reading and writing are absolutely unknown,' but still she had a real pleasure in letter-writing. Her greatest delight was the communication of ideas, and she is always in the heart of the battle. She discusses pauperism with Louis Napoleon in his prison at Ham, and liberty with Armand Barbes in his dungeon at Vincennes; she writes to Lamennais on philosophy, to Mazzini on socialism, to Lamartine on democracy, and to Ledru-Rollin on justice. Her letters reveal to us not merely the life of a great novelist but the soul of a great woman, of a woman who was one with all the noblest movements of her day and whose sympathy with humanity was boundless absolutely. For the aristocracy of intellect she had always the deepest veneration, but the democracy of suffering touched her more. She preached the regeneration of mankind, not with the noisy ardour of the paid advocate, but with the enthusiasm of the true evangelist. Of all the artists of this century she was the most altruistic; she felt every one's misfortunes except her own. Her faith never left her; to the end of her life, as she tells us, she was able to believe without illusions. But the people disappointed her a little. She saw that they followed persons not principles, and for 'the great man theory' George Sand had no respect. 'Proper names are the enemies of principles' is one of her aphorisms.

So from 1850 her letters are more distinctly literary. She discusses modern realism with Flaubert, and play-writing with Dumas fils; and protests with passionate vehemence against the doctrine of L'art pour l'art. 'Art for the sake of itself is an idle sentence,' she writes; 'art for the sake of truth, for the sake of what is beautiful and good, that is the creed I seek.' And in a delightful letter to M. Charles Poncy she repeats the same idea very charmingly. 'People say that birds sing for the sake of singing, but I doubt it. They sing their loves and happiness, and in that they are in keeping with nature. But man must do something more, and poets only sing in order to move people and to make them think.' She wanted M. Poncy to be the poet of the people and, if good advice were all that had been needed, he would certainly have been the Burns of the workshop. She drew out a delightful scheme for a volume to be called Songs of all Trades and saw the possibilities of making handicrafts poetic. Perhaps she valued good intentions in art a little too much, and she hardly understood that art for art's sake is not meant to express the final cause of art but is merely a formula of creation; but, as she herself had scaled Parnassus, we must not quarrel at her bringing Proletarianism with her. For George Sand must be ranked among our poetic geniuses. She regarded the novel as still within the domain of poetry. Her heroes are not dead photographs; they are great possibilities. Modern novels are dissections; hers are dreams. 'I make popular types,' she writes, 'such as I do no longer see, but such as they should and might be.' For realism, in M. Zola's acceptation of the word, she had no admiration. Art to her was a mirror that transfigured truths but did not represent realities. Hence she could not understand art without personality. 'I am aware,' she writes to Flaubert, 'that you are opposed to the exposition of personal doctrine in literature. Are you right? Does not your opposition proceed rather from a want of conviction than from a principle of æsthetics? If we have any philosophy in our brain it must needs break forth in our writings. But you, as soon as you handle literature, you seem anxious, I know not why, to be another man, the one who must disappear, who annihilates himself and is no more. What a singular mania! What a deficient taste! The worth of our productions depends entirely on our own. Besides, if we withhold our own opinions respecting the personages we create, we naturally leave the reader in uncertainty as to the opinion he should himself form of them. That amounts to wishing not to be understood, and the result of this is that the reader gets weary of us and leaves us.'

She herself, however, may be said to have suffered from too dominant a personality, and this was the reason of the failure of most of her plays.

Of the drama in the sense of disinterested presentation she had no idea, and what is the strength and life-blood of her novels is the weakness of her dramatic works. But in the main she was right. Art without personality is impossible. And yet the aim of art is not to reveal personality, but to please. This she hardly recognized in her æsthetics, though she realized it in her work. On literary style she has some excellent remarks. She dislikes the extravagances of the romantic school and sees the beauty of simplicity. 'Simplicity,' she writes, 'is the most difficult thing to secure in this world: it is the last limit of experience and the last effort of genius.' She hated the slang and argot of Paris life, and loved the words used by the peasants in the provinces. 'The provinces,' she remarks, 'preserve the tradition of the original tongue and create but few new words. I feel much respect for the language of the peasantry; in my estimation it is the more correct.'

She thought Flaubert too much preoccupied with the sense of form, and makes these excellent observations to him—perhaps her best piece of literary criticism. 'You consider the form as the aim, whereas it is but the effect. Happy expressions are only the outcome of emotion and emotion itself proceeds from a conviction. We are only moved by that which we ardently believe in.' Literary schools she distrusted. Individualism was to her the keystone of art as well as of life. 'Do not belong to any school: do not imitate any model,' is her advice. Yet she never encouraged eccentricity. 'Be correct,' she writes to Eugène Pelletan, 'that is rarer than being eccentric, as the time goes. It is much more common to please by bad taste than to receive the cross of honour.'

On the whole, her literary advice is sound and healthy. She never shrieks and she never sneers. She is the incarnation of good sense. And the whole collection of her letters is a perfect treasure-house of suggestions both on art and on politics.

Letters of George Sand. Translated and edited by Raphael Ledos de Beaufort. (Ward and Downey.)

BÉRANGER IN ENGLAND

(Pall Mall Gazette, April 21, 1886.)

A philosophic politician once remarked that the best possible form of government is an absolute monarchy tempered by street ballads.

Without at all agreeing with this aphorism we still cannot but regret that the new democracy does not use poetry as a means for the expression of political opinion. The Socialists, it is true, have been heard singing the later poems of Mr. William Morris, but the street ballad is really dead in England. The fact is that most modern poetry is so artificial in its form, so individual in its essence and so literary in its style, that the people as a body are little moved by it, and when they have grievances against the capitalist or the aristocrat they prefer strikes to sonnets and rioting to rondels.

Possibly, Mr. William Toynbee's pleasant little volume of translations from Béranger may be the herald of a new school. Béranger had all the qualifications for a popular poet. He wrote to be sung more than to be read; he preferred the Pont Neuf to Parnassus; he was patriotic as well as romantic, and humorous as well as humane. Translations of poetry as a rule are merely misrepresentations, but the muse of Béranger is so simple and naïve that she can wear our English dress with ease and grace, and Mr. Toynbee has kept much of the mirth and music of the original. Here and there, undoubtedly, the translation could be improved upon; 'rapiers' for instance is an abominable rhyme to 'forefathers'; 'the hated arms of Albion' in the same poem is a very feeble rendering of 'le léopard de l'Anglais,' and such a verse as

'Mid France's miracles of art,

Rare trophies won from art's own land,

I've lived to see with burning heart

The fog-bred poor triumphant stand,

reproduces very inadequately the charm of the original:

Dans nos palais, où, près de la victoire,

Brillaient les arts, doux fruits des beaux climats,

J'ai vu du Nord les peuplades sans gloire,

De leurs manteaux secouer les frimas.

On the whole, however, Mr. Toynbee's work is good; Les Champs, for example, is very well translated, and so are the two delightful poems Rosette and Ma République; and there is a good deal of spirit in Le Marquis de Carabas:

> Whom have we here in conqueror's rôle?
>
> Our grand old marquis, bless his soul!
>
> Whose grand old charger (mark his bone!)
>
> Has borne him back to claim his own.
>
> Note, if you please, the grand old style
>
> In which he nears his grand old pile;
>
> With what an air of grand old state
>
> He waves that blade immaculate!
>
> Hats off, hats off, for my lord to pass,
>
> The grand old Marquis of Carabas!—

though 'that blade immaculate' has hardly got the sting of 'un sabre innocent'; and in the fourth verse of the same poem, 'Marquise, you'll have the bed-chamber' does not very clearly convey the sense of the line 'La Marquise a le tabouret.' Béranger is not nearly well enough known in England, and though it is always better to read a poet in the original, still translations have their value as echoes have their music.

A Selection from the Songs of De Béranger in English Verse. By William Toynbee. (Kegan Paul.)

THE POETRY OF THE PEOPLE

(Pall Mall Gazette, May 13, 1886.)

The Countess Martinengo deserves well of all poets, peasants and publishers. Folk-lore is so often treated nowadays merely from the point of view of the comparative mythologist, that it is really delightful to come across a book that deals with the subject simply as literature. For the Folk-tale is the father of all fiction as the Folk-song is the mother of all poetry; and in the games, the tales and the ballads of primitive people it is easy to see the germs of such perfected forms of art as the drama, the novel and the epic. It is, of course, true that the highest expression of life is to be found not in the popular songs, however poetical, of any nation, but in the great masterpieces of self-conscious Art; yet it is pleasant sometimes to leave the summit of Parnassus to look at the wildflowers in the valley, and to turn from the lyre of Apollo to listen to the reed of Pan. We can still listen to it. To this day, the vineyard dressers of Calabria will mock the passer-by with satirical verses as they used to do in the old pagan days, and the peasants of the olive woods of Provence answer each other in amœbæan strains. The Sicilian shepherd has not yet thrown his pipe aside, and the children of modern Greece sing the swallow-song through the villages in spring-time, though Theognis is more than two thousand years dead. Nor is this popular poetry merely the rhythmic expression of joy and sorrow; it is in the highest degree imaginative; and taking its inspiration directly from nature it abounds in realistic metaphor and in picturesque and fantastic imagery. It must, of course, be admitted that there is a conventionality of nature as there is a conventionality of art, and that certain forms of utterance are apt to become stereotyped by too constant use; yet, on the whole, it is impossible not to recognize in the Folk-songs that the Countess Martinengo has brought together one strong dominant note of fervent and flawless sincerity. Indeed, it is only in the more terrible dramas of the Elizabethan age that we can find any parallel to the Corsican voceri with their shrill intensity of passion, their awful frenzies of grief and hate. And yet, ardent as the feeling is, the form is nearly always beautiful. Now and then, in the poems of the extreme South one meets with a curious crudity of realism, but, as a rule, the sense of beauty prevails.

Some of the Folk-poems in this book have all the lightness and loveliness of lyrics, all of them have that sweet simplicity of pure song by which mirth finds its own melody and mourning its own music, and even where there are conceits of thought and expression they are conceits born of fancy not of affectation. Herrick himself might have envied that wonderful love-song of

Provence:

> If thou wilt be the falling dew
>
> And fall on me alway,
>
> Then I will be the white, white rose
>
> On yonder thorny spray.
>
> If thou wilt be the white, white rose
>
> On yonder thorny spray,
>
> Then I will be the honey-bee
>
> And kiss thee all the day.
>
> If thou wilt be the honey-bee
>
> And kiss me all the day,
>
> Then I will be in yonder heaven
>
> The star of brightest ray.
>
> If thou wilt be in yonder heaven
>
> The star of brightest ray,
>
> Then I will be the dawn, and we
>
> Shall meet at break of day.

How charming also is this lullaby by which the Corsican mother sings her babe to sleep!

> Gold and pearls my vessel lade,
>
> Silk and cloth the cargo be,
>
> All the sails are of brocade
>
> Coming from beyond the sea;
>
> And the helm of finest gold,

Made a wonder to behold.

Fast awhile in slumber lie;

Sleep, my child, and hushaby.

After you were born full soon,

You were christened all aright;

Godmother she was the moon,

Godfather the sun so bright.

All the stars in heaven told

Wore their necklaces of gold.

Fast awhile in slumber lie;

Sleep, my child, and hushaby.

Or this from Roumania:

Sleep, my daughter, sleep an hour;

Mother's darling gilliflower.

Mother rocks thee, standing near,

She will wash thee in the clear

Waters that from fountains run,

To protect thee from the sun.

Sleep, my darling, sleep an hour,

Grow thou as the gilliflower.

As a tear-drop be thou white,

As a willow tall and slight;

Gentle as the ring-doves are,

And be lovely as a star!

We hardly know what poems are sung to English babies, but we hope they are as beautiful as these two. Blake might have written them.

The Countess Martinengo has certainly given us a most fascinating book. In a volume of moderate dimensions, not too long to be tiresome nor too brief to be disappointing, she has collected together the best examples of modern Folk-songs, and with her as a guide the lazy reader lounging in his armchair may wander from the melancholy pine-forests of the North to Sicily's orange-groves and the pomegranate gardens of Armenia, and listen to the singing of those to whom poetry is a passion, not a profession, and whose art, coming from inspiration and not from schools, if it has the limitations, at least has also the loveliness of its origin, and is one with blowing grasses and the flowers of the field.

Essays in the Study of Folk-Songs. By the Countess Evelyn Martinengo Césaresco. (Redway.)

THE CENCI

(Dramatic Review, May 15, 1886.)

The production of The Cenci last week at the Grand Theatre, Islington, may be said to have been an era in the literary history of this century, and the Shelley Society deserves the highest praise and warmest thanks of all for having given us an opportunity of seeing Shelley's play under the conditions he himself desired for it. For The Cenci was written absolutely with a view to theatric presentation, and had Shelley's own wishes been carried out it would have been produced during his lifetime at Covent Garden, with Edmund Kean and Miss O'Neill in the principal parts. In working out his conception, Shelley had studied very carefully the æsthetics of dramatic art. He saw that the essence of the drama is disinterested presentation, and that the characters must not be merely mouthpieces for splendid poetry but must be living subjects for terror and for pity. 'I have endeavoured,' he says, 'as nearly as possible to represent the characters as they probably were, and have sought to avoid the error of making them actuated by my own conception of right or wrong, false or true: thus under a thin veil converting names and actions of the sixteenth century into cold impersonations of my own mind. . . .

'I have avoided with great care the introduction of what is commonly called mere poetry, and I imagine there will scarcely be found a detached simile or a single isolated description, unless Beatrice's description of the chasm appointed for her father's murder should be judged to be of that nature.'

He recognized that a dramatist must be allowed far greater freedom of expression than what is conceded to a poet. 'In a dramatic composition,' to use his own words, 'the imagery and the passion should interpenetrate one another, the former being reserved simply for the full development and illustration of the latter. Imagination is as the immortal God which should assume flesh for the redemption of mortal passion. It is thus that the most remote and the most familiar imagery may alike be fit for dramatic purposes when employed in the illustration of strong feeling, which raises what is low, and levels to the apprehension that which is lofty, casting over all the shadow of its own greatness. In other respects I have written more carelessly, that is, without an over-fastidious and learned choice of words. In this respect I entirely agree with those modern critics who assert that in order to move men to true sympathy we must use the familiar language of men.'

He knew that if the dramatist is to teach at all it must be by example, not by precept.

'The highest moral purpose,' he remarks, 'aimed at in the highest species of the drama, is the teaching the human heart, through its sympathies and antipathies, the knowledge of itself; in proportion to the possession of which knowledge every human being is wise, just, sincere, tolerant and kind. If dogmas can do more it is well: but a drama is no fit place for the enforcement of them.' He fully realizes that it is by a conflict between our artistic sympathies and our moral judgment that the greatest dramatic effects are produced. 'It is in the restless and anatomizing casuistry with which men seek the justification of Beatrice, yet feel that she has done what needs justification; it is in the superstitious horror with which they contemplate alike her wrongs and their revenge, that the dramatic character of what she did and suffered consists.'

In fact no one has more clearly understood than Shelley the mission of the dramatist and the meaning of the drama.

BALZAC IN ENGLISH

(Pall Mall Gazette, September 13, 1886.)

Many years ago, in a number of All the Year Round, Charles Dickens complained that Balzac was very little read in England, and although since then the public has become more familiar with the great masterpieces of French fiction, still it may be doubted whether the Comédie Humaine is at all appreciated or understood by the general run of novel readers. It is really the greatest monument that literature has produced in our century, and M. Taine hardly exaggerates when he says that, after Shakespeare, Balzac is our most important magazine of documents on human nature. Balzac's aim, in fact, was to do for humanity what Buffon had done for the animal creation. As the naturalist studied lions and tigers, so the novelist studied men and women. Yet he was no mere reporter. Photography and procès-verbal were not the essentials of his method. Observation gave him the facts of life, but his genius converted facts into truths, and truths into truth. He was, in a word, a marvellous combination of the artistic temperament with the scientific spirit. The latter he bequeathed to his disciples; the former was entirely his own. The distinction between such a book as M. Zola's L'Assommoir and such a book as Balzac's Illusions Perdues is the distinction between unimaginative realism and imaginative reality. 'All Balzac's characters,' said Baudelaire, 'are gifted with the same ardour of life that animated himself. All his fictions are as deeply coloured as dreams. Every mind is a weapon loaded to the muzzle with will. The very scullions have genius.' He was, of course, accused of being immoral. Few writers who deal directly with life escape that charge. His answer to the accusation was characteristic and conclusive. 'Whoever contributes his stone to the edifice of ideas,' he wrote, 'whoever proclaims an abuse, whoever sets his mark upon an evil to be abolished, always passes for immoral. If you are true in your portraits, if, by dint of daily and nightly toil, you succeed in writing the most difficult language in the world, the word immoral is thrown in your face.' The morals of the personages of the Comédie Humaine are simply the morals of the world around us. They are part of the artist's subject-matter; they are not part of his method. If there be any need of censure it is to life, not to literature, that it should be given. Balzac, besides, is essentially universal. He sees life from every point of view. He has no preferences and no prejudices. He does not try to prove anything. He feels that the spectacle of life contains its own secret. 'Il crée un monde et se tait.'

And what a world it is! What a panorama of passions! What a pell-mell of men and women! It was said of Trollope that he increased the number of our acquaintances without adding to our visiting list; but after the Comédie Humaine one begins to believe that the only real people are the people who never existed. Lucien de Rubempré, le Père Goriot, Ursule Mirouët, Marguerite Claës, the Baron Hulot, Madame Marneffe, le Cousin Pons, De Marsay—all bring with them a kind of contagious illusion of life. They have a fierce vitality about them: their existence is fervent and fiery-coloured; we not merely feel for them but we see them—they dominate our fancy and defy scepticism. A steady course of Balzac reduces our living friends to shadows, and our acquaintances to the shadows of shades. Who would care to go out to an evening party to meet Tomkins, the friend of one's boyhood, when one can sit at home with Lucien de Rubempré? It is pleasanter to have the entrée to Balzac's society than to receive cards from all the duchesses in Mayfair.

In spite of this, there are many people who have declared the Comédie Humaine to be indigestible. Perhaps it is: but then what about truffles? Balzac's publisher refused to be disturbed by any such criticism as that. 'Indigestible, is it?' he exclaimed with what, for a publisher, was rare good sense. 'Well, I should hope so; who ever thinks of a dinner that isn't?'

Balzac's Novels in English. *The Duchesse de Langeais and Other Stories; César Birotteau.* (Routledge and Sons.)

BEN JONSON

(Pall Mall Gazette, September 20, 1886.)

As for Mr. Symonds' estimate of Jonson's genius, it is in many points quite excellent. He ranks him with the giants rather than with the gods, with those who compel our admiration by their untiring energy and huge strength of intellectual muscle, not with those 'who share the divine gifts of creative imagination and inevitable instinct.' Here he is right. Pelion more than Parnassus was Jonson's home. His art has too much effort about it, too much definite intention. His style lacks the charm of chance. Mr. Symonds is right also in the stress he lays on the extraordinary combination in Jonson's work of the most concentrated realism with encyclopædic erudition. In Jonson's comedies London slang and learned scholarship go hand in hand. Literature was as living a thing to him as life itself. He used his classical lore not merely to give form to his verse, but to give flesh and blood to the persons of his plays. He could build up a breathing creature out of quotations. He made the poets of Greece and Rome terribly modern, and introduced them to the oddest company. His very culture is an element in his coarseness. There are moments when one is tempted to liken him to a beast that has fed off books.

We cannot, however, agree with Mr. Symonds when he says that Jonson 'rarely touched more than the outside of character,' that his men and women are 'the incarnations of abstract properties rather than living human beings,' that they are in fact mere 'masqueraders and mechanical puppets.' Eloquence is a beautiful thing but rhetoric ruins many a critic, and Mr. Symonds is essentially rhetorical. When, for instance, he tells us that 'Jonson made masks,' while 'Dekker and Heywood created souls,' we feel that he is asking us to accept a crude judgment for the sake of a smart antithesis. It is, of course, true that we do not find in Jonson the same growth of character that we find in Shakespeare, and we may admit that most of the characters in Jonson's plays are, so to speak, ready-made. But a ready-made character is not necessarily either mechanical or wooden, two epithets Mr. Symonds uses constantly in his criticism.

We cannot tell, and Shakespeare himself does not tell us, why Iago is evil, why Regan and Goneril have hard hearts, or why Sir Andrew Aguecheek is a fool. It is sufficient that they are what they are, and that nature gives warrant for their existence. If a character in a play is lifelike, if we recognize it as true to nature, we have no right to insist on the author explaining its genesis to us. We must accept it as it is: and in the hands of a good dramatist mere presentation can take the place of analysis, and indeed is often a more dramatic method, because a more direct one. And Jonson's characters are true to nature. They are in no sense abstractions; they are types. Captain Bobadil and Captain Tucca, Sir John Daw and Sir Amorous La Foole, Volpone and Mosca, Subtle and Sir Epicure Mammon, Mrs. Purecraft and the Rabbi Busy are all creatures of flesh and blood, none the less lifelike because they are labelled. In this point Mr. Symonds seems to us unjust towards Jonson.

We think, also, that a special chapter might have been devoted to Jonson as a literary critic. The creative activity of the English Renaissance is so great that its achievements in the sphere of criticism are often overlooked by the student. Then, for the first time, was language treated as an art. The laws of expression and composition were investigated and formularized. The importance of words was recognized. Romanticism, Realism and Classicism fought their first battles. The dramatists are full of literary and art criticisms, and amused the public with slashing articles on one another in the form of plays.

'English Worthies.' Edited by Andrew Lang. *Ben Jonson.* By John Addington Symonds. (Longmans, Green and Co.)

MR. SYMONDS' HISTORY OF THE RENAISSANCE
(Pall Mall Gazette, November 10, 1886.)

Mr. Symonds has at last finished his history of the Italian Renaissance. The two volumes just published deal with the intellectual and moral conditions in Italy during the seventy years of the sixteenth century which followed the coronation of Charles the Fifth at Bologna, an era to which Mr. Symonds gives the name of the Catholic Reaction, and they contain a most interesting and valuable account of the position of Spain in the Italian peninsula, the conduct of the Tridentine Council, the specific organization of the Holy Office and the Company of Jesus, and the state of society upon which those forces were brought to bear. In his previous volumes Mr. Symonds had regarded the past rather as a picture to be painted than as a problem to be solved. In these two last volumes, however, he shows a clearer appreciation of the office of history. The art of the picturesque chronicler is completed by something like the science of the true historian, the critical spirit begins to manifest itself, and life is not treated as a mere spectacle, but the laws of its evolution and progress are investigated also. We admit that the desire to represent life at all costs under dramatic conditions still accompanies Mr. Symonds, and that he hardly realizes that what seems romance to us was harsh reality to those who were engaged in it. Like most dramatists, also, he is more interested in the psychological exceptions than in the general rule. He has something of Shakespeare's sovereign contempt of the masses. The people stir him very little, but he is fascinated by great personalities. Yet it is only fair to remember that the age itself was one of exaggerated individualism, and that literature had not yet become a mouthpiece for the utterances of humanity. Men appreciated the aristocracy of intellect, but with the democracy of suffering they had no sympathy. The cry from the brickfields had still to be heard. Mr. Symonds' style, too, has much improved. Here and there, it is true, we come across traces of the old manner, as in the apocalyptic vision of the seven devils that entered Italy with the Spaniard, and the description of the Inquisition as a Belial-Moloch, a 'hideous idol whose face was blackened with soot from burning human flesh.' Such a sentence, also, as 'over the Dead Sea of social putrefaction floated the sickening oil of Jesuitical hypocrisy,' reminds us that rhetoric has not yet lost its charms for Mr. Symonds. Still, on the whole, the style shows far more reserve, balance and sobriety, than can be found in the earlier volumes where violent antithesis forms the predominant characteristic, and accuracy is often sacrificed to an adjective.

Amongst the most interesting chapters of the book are those on the Inquisition, on Sarpi, the great champion of the severance of Church from State, and on Giordano Bruno. Indeed, the story of Bruno's life, from his visit to London and Oxford, his sojourn in Paris and wanderings through

Germany, down to his betrayal at Venice and martyrdom at Rome, is most powerfully told, and the estimate of the value of his philosophy and the relation he holds to modern science, is at once just and appreciative. The account also of Ignatius Loyola and the rise of the Society of Jesus is extremely interesting, though we cannot think that Mr. Symonds is very happy in his comparison of the Jesuits to 'fanatics laying stones upon a railway' or 'dynamiters blowing up an emperor or a corner of Westminster Hall.' Such a judgment is harsh and crude in expression and more suitable to the clamour of the Protestant Union than to the dignity of the true historian. Mr. Symonds, however, is rarely deliberately unfair, and there is no doubt but that his work on the Catholic Reaction is a most valuable contribution to modern history—so valuable, indeed, that in the account he gives of the Inquisition in Venice it would be well worth his while to bring the picturesque fiction of the text into some harmony with the plain facts of the footnote.

On the poetry of the sixteenth century Mr. Symonds has, of course, a great deal to say, and on such subjects he always writes with ease, grace, and delicacy of perception. We admit that we weary sometimes of the continual application to literature of epithets appropriate to plastic and pictorial art. The conception of the unity of the arts is certainly of great value, but in the present condition of criticism it seems to us that it would be more useful to emphasize the fact that each art has its separate method of expression. The essay on Tasso, however, is delightful reading, and the position the poet holds towards modern music and modern sentiment is analysed with much subtlety. The essay on Marino also is full of interest. We have often wondered whether those who talk so glibly of Euphuism and Marinism in literature have ever read either Euphues or the Adone. To the latter they can have no better guide than Mr. Symonds, whose description of the poem is most fascinating. Marino, like many greater men, has suffered much from his disciples, but he himself was a master of graceful fancy and of exquisite felicity of phrase; not, of course, a great poet but certainly an artist in poetry and one to whom language is indebted. Even those conceits that Mr. Symonds feels bound to censure have something charming about them. The continual use of periphrases is undoubtedly a grave fault in style, yet who but a pedant would really quarrel with such periphrases as sirena de' boschi for the nightingale, or

85

il novello Edimione for Galileo?

From the poets Mr. Symonds passes to the painters: not those great artists of Florence and Venice of whom he has already written, but the Eclectics of Bologna, the Naturalists of Naples and Rome. This chapter is too polemical to be pleasant. The one on music is much better, and Mr. Symonds gives us a most interesting description of the gradual steps by which the Italian genius passed from poetry and painting to melody and song, till the whole of Europe thrilled with the marvel and mystery of this new language of the soul. Some small details should perhaps be noticed. It is hardly accurate, for instance, to say that Monteverde's Orfeo was the first form of the recitative-Opera, as Peri's Dafne and Euridice and Cavaliere's Rappresentazione preceded it by some years, and it is somewhat exaggerated to say that 'under the regime of the Commonwealth the national growth of English music received a check from which it never afterwards recovered,' as it was with Cromwell's auspices that the first English Opera was produced, thirteen years before any Opera was regularly established in Paris. The fact that England did not make such development in music as Italy and Germany did, must be ascribed to other causes than 'the prevalence of Puritan opinion.'

These, however, are minor points. Mr. Symonds is to be warmly congratulated on the completion of his history of the Renaissance in Italy. It is a most wonderful monument of literary labour, and its value to the student of Humanism cannot be doubted. We have often had occasion to differ from Mr. Symonds on questions of detail, and we have more than once felt it our duty to protest against the rhetoric and over-emphasis of his style, but we fully recognize the importance of his work and the impetus he has given to the study of one of the vital periods of the world's history. Mr. Symonds' learning has not made him a pedant; his culture has widened not narrowed his sympathies, and though he can hardly be called a great historian, yet he will always occupy a place in English literature as one of the remarkable men of letters in the nineteenth century.

Renaissance in Italy: The Catholic Reaction. In Two Parts. By John
Addington Symonds. (Smith, Elder and Co.)

MR. MORRIS'S ODYSSEY

(Pall Mall Gazette, April 26, 1887.)

Of all our modern poets, Mr. William Morris is the one best qualified by nature and by art to translate for us the marvellous epic of the wanderings of Odysseus. For he is our only true story-singer since Chaucer; if he is a Socialist, he is also a Saga-man; and there was a time when he was never wearied of telling us strange legends of gods and men, wonderful tales of chivalry and romance. Master as he is of decorative and descriptive verse, he has all the Greek's joy in the visible aspect of things, all the Greek's sense of delicate and delightful detail, all the Greek's pleasure in beautiful textures and exquisite materials and imaginative designs; nor can any one have a keener sympathy with the Homeric admiration for the workers and the craftsmen in the various arts, from the stainers in white ivory and the embroiderers in purple and gold, to the weaver sitting by the loom and the dyer dipping in the vat, the chaser of shield and helmet, the carver of wood or stone. And to all this is added the true temper of high romance, the power to make the past as real to us as the present, the subtle instinct to discern passion, the swift impulse to portray life.

It is no wonder the lovers of Greek literature have so eagerly looked forward to Mr. Morris's version of the Odyssean epic, and now that the first volume has appeared, it is not extravagant to say that of all our English translations this is the most perfect and the most satisfying. In spite of Coleridge's well-known views on the subject, we have always held that Chapman's Odyssey is immeasurably inferior to his Iliad, the mere difference of metre alone being sufficient to set the former in a secondary place; Pope's Odyssey, with its glittering rhetoric and smart antithesis, has nothing of the grand manner of the original; Cowper is dull, and Bryant dreadful, and Worsley too full of Spenserian prettinesses; while excellent though Messrs. Butcher and Lang's version undoubtedly is in many respects, still, on the whole, it gives us merely the facts of the Odyssey without providing anything of its artistic effect. Avia's translation even, though better than almost all its predecessors in the same field, is not worthy of taking rank beside Mr. Morris's, for here we have a true work of art, a rendering not merely of language into language, but of poetry into poetry, and though the new spirit added in the transfusion may seem to many rather Norse than Greek, and, perhaps at times, more boisterous than beautiful, there is yet a vigour of life in every line, a splendid ardour through each canto, that stirs the blood while one reads like the sound of a trumpet, and that, producing a physical as well as a spiritual delight, exults the senses no less than it exalts the soul. It may be admitted at once that, here and there, Mr. Morris has missed something of the marvellous dignity of the Homeric verse, and that, in his desire for rushing and ringing metre, he has occasionally sacrificed majesty to movement, and made stateliness give place to speed; but it is really only in such blank verse as Milton's that this effect of calm and lofty music can be attained, and in all other respects blank verse is the most inadequate medium for reproducing the full flow and fervour of the Greek hexameter. One merit, at any rate, Mr. Morris's version entirely and absolutely possesses. It is, in no sense of the word, literary; it seems to deal immediately with life itself, and to take from the reality of things its own form and colour; it is always direct and simple, and at its best has something of the 'large utterance of the early gods.'

As for individual passages of beauty, nothing could be better than the wonderful description of the house of the Phœacian king, or the whole telling of the lovely legend of Circe, or the manner in which the pageant of the pale phantoms in Hades is brought before our eyes. Perhaps the huge epic humour of the escape from the Cyclops is hardly realized, but there is always a linguistic difficulty about rendering this fascinating story into English, and where we are given so much poetry we should not complain about losing a pun; and the exquisite idyll of the meeting and parting with the daughter of Alcinous is really delightfully told. How good, for instance, is this passage taken at random from the Sixth Book:

But therewith unto the handmaids goodly Odysseus spake:

'Stand off I bid you, damsels, while the work in hand I take,

And wash the brine from my shoulders, and sleek them all around.

Since verily now this long while sweet oil they have not found.

But before you nought will I wash me, for shame I have indeed,

Amidst of fair-tressed damsels to be all bare of weed.'

So he spake and aloof they gat them, and thereof they told the may,

But Odysseus with the river from his body washed away

The brine from his back and shoulders wrought broad and mightily,

And from his head was he wiping the foam of the untilled sea;

But when he had thoroughly washed him, and the oil about him had shed,

He did upon the raiment the gift of the maid unwed.

But Athene, Zeus-begotten, dealt with him in such wise

That bigger yet was his seeming, and mightier to all eyes,

With the hair on his head crisp curling as the bloom of the daffodil.

And as when the silver with gold is o'erlaid by a man of skill,

Yea, a craftsman whom Hephæstus and Pallas Athene have taught

To be master over masters, and lovely work he hath wrought;

So she round his head and his shoulders shed grace abundantly.

It may be objected by some that the line

With the hair on his head crisp curling as the bloom of the daffodil,

is a rather fanciful version of

ουλας ηκε κομας, ὑακινθίνῳ ανθει ομοιασ

and it certainly seems probable that the allusion is to the dark colour of the hero's hair; still, the point is not one of much importance, though it may be worth noting that a similar expression occurs in Ogilby's superbly illustrated translation of the Odyssey, published in 1665, where Charles ii.'s Master of the Revels in Ireland gives the passage thus:

Minerva renders him more tall and fair,

Curling in rings like daffodils his hair.

No anthology, however, can show the true merit of Mr. Morris's translation, whose real merit does not depend on stray beauties, nor is revealed by chance selections, but lies in the absolute rightness and coherence of the whole, in its purity and justice of touch, its freedom from affectation and commonplace, its harmony of form and matter. It is sufficient to say that this is a poet's version of a poet, and for such surely we should be thankful. In these latter days of coarse and vulgar literature, it is something to have made the great sea-epic of the South native and natural to our northern isle, something to have shown that our English speech may be a pipe through which Greek lips can blow, something to have taught Nausicaa to speak the same language as Perdita.

The Odyssey of Homer. Done into English Verse by William Morris, author of *The Earthly Paradise.* In two volumes. Volume I. (Reeves and Turner.)

For review of Volume II. see *Mr. Morris's Completion of the Odyssey,* page 65.

RUSSIAN NOVELISTS

(Pall Mall Gazette, May 2, 1887.)

Of the three great Russian novelists of our time Tourgenieff is by far the finest artist. He has that spirit of exquisite selection, that delicate choice of detail, which is the essence of style; his work is entirely free from any personal intention; and by taking existence at its most fiery-coloured moments he can distil into a few pages of perfect prose the moods and passions of many lives.

Count Tolstoi's method is much larger, and his field of vision more extended. He reminds us sometimes of Paul Veronese, and, like that great painter, can crowd, without over-crowding, the giant canvas on which he works. We may not at first gain from his works that artistic unity of impression which is Tourgenieff's chief charm, but once that we have mastered the details the whole seems to have the grandeur and the simplicity of an epic. Dostoieffski differs widely from both his rivals. He is not so fine an artist as Tourgenieff, for he deals more with the facts than with the effects of life; nor has he Tolstoi's largeness of vision and epic dignity; but he has qualities that are distinctively and absolutely his own, such as a fierce intensity of passion and concentration of impulse, a power of dealing with the deepest mysteries of psychology and the most hidden springs of life, and a realism that is pitiless in its fidelity, and terrible because it is true. Some time ago we had occasion to draw attention to his marvellous novel Crime and Punishment, where in the haunt of impurity and vice a harlot and an assassin meet together to read the story of Dives and Lazarus, and the outcast girl leads the sinner to make atonement for his sin; nor is the book entitled Injury and Insult at all inferior to that great masterpiece. Mean and ordinary though the surroundings of the story may seem, the heroine Natasha is like one of the noble victims of Greek tragedy; she is Antigone with the passion of Phædra, and it is impossible to approach her without a feeling of awe. Greek also is the gloom of Nemesis that hangs over each character, only it is a Nemesis that does not stand outside of life, but is part of our own nature and of the same material as life itself. Aleósha, the beautiful young lad whom Natasha follows to her doom, is a second Tito Melema, and has all Tito's charm and grace and fascination. Yet he is different. He would never have denied Baldassare in the Square at Florence, nor lied to Romola about Tessa. He has a magnificent, momentary sincerity, a boyish unconsciousness of all that life signifies, an ardent enthusiasm for all that life cannot give. There is nothing calculating about him. He never thinks evil, he only does it. From a psychological point of view he is one of the most interesting characters of modern fiction, as from an artistic he is one of the most attractive. As we grow to know him he stirs strange questions for us, and makes us feel that it is not the wicked only who do wrong, nor the bad alone who work evil.

And by what a subtle objective method does Dostoieffski show us his characters! He never tickets them with a list nor labels them with a description. We grow to know them very gradually, as we know people whom we meet in society, at first by little tricks of manner, personal appearance, fancies in dress, and the like; and afterwards by their deeds and words; and even then they constantly elude us, for though Dostoieffski may lay bare for us the secrets of their nature, yet he never explains his personages away; they are always surprising us by something that they say or do, and keep to the end the eternal mystery of life.

Irrespective of its value as a work of art, this novel possesses a deep autobiographical interest also, as the character of Vania, the poor student who loves Natasha through all her sin and shame, is Dostoieffski's study of himself. Goethe once had to delay the completion of one of his novels till experience had furnished him with new situations, but almost before he had arrived at manhood Dostoieffski knew life in its most real forms; poverty and suffering, pain and misery, prison, exile, and love, were soon familiar to him, and by the lips of Vania he has told his own story. This note of personal feeling, this harsh reality of actual experience, undoubtedly gives the book something of its strange fervour and terrible passion, yet it has not made it egotistic; we see things from every point of view, and we feel, not that fiction has been trammelled by fact, but that fact itself has become ideal and imaginative. Pitiless, too, though Dostoieffski is in his method as an artist, as a man he is full of human pity for all, for those who do evil as well as for those who suffer it, for the selfish no less than for those whose lives are wrecked for others and whose sacrifice is in vain. Since Adam Bede and Le Père Goriot no more powerful novel has been written than Insult and Injury.

Injury and Insult. By Fedor Dostoieffski. Translated from the
Russian by Frederick Whishaw. (Vizetelly and Co.)

MR. PATER'S IMAGINARY PORTRAITS

(Pall Mall Gazette, June 11, 1887.)

To convey ideas through the medium of images has always been the aim of those who are artists as well as thinkers in literature, and it is to a desire to give a sensuous environment to intellectual concepts that we owe Mr. Pater's last volume. For these Imaginary or, as we should prefer to call them, Imaginative Portraits of his, form a series of philosophic studies in which the philosophy is tempered by personality, and the thought shown under varying conditions of mood and manner, the very permanence of each principle gaining something through the change and colour of the life through which it finds expression. The most fascinating of all these pictures is undoubtedly that of Sebastian Van Storck. The account of Watteau is perhaps a little too fanciful, and the description of him as one who was 'always a seeker after something in the world, that is there in no satisfying measure, or not at all,' seems to us more applicable to him who saw Mona Lisa sitting among the rocks than the gay and debonair peintre des fêtes galantes. But Sebastian, the grave young Dutch philosopher, is charmingly drawn. From the first glimpse we get of him, skating over the water-meadows with his plume of squirrel's tail and his fur muff, in all the modest pleasantness of boyhood, down to his strange death in the desolate house amid the sands of the Helder, we seem to see him, to know him, almost to hear the low music of his voice. He is a dreamer, as the common phrase goes, and yet he is poetical in this sense, that his theorems shape life for him, directly. Early in youth he is stirred by a fine saying of Spinoza, and sets himself to realize the ideal of an intellectual disinterestedness, separating himself more and more from the transient world of sensation, accident and even affection, till what is finite and relative becomes of no interest to him, and he feels that as nature is but a thought of his, so he himself is but a passing thought of God. This conception, of the power of a mere metaphysical abstraction over the mind of one so fortunately endowed for the reception of the sensible world, is exceedingly delightful, and Mr. Pater has never written a more subtle psychological study, the fact that Sebastian dies in an attempt to save the life of a little child giving to the whole story a touch of poignant pathos and sad irony.

Denys l'Auxerrois is suggested by a figure found, or said to be found, on some old tapestries in Auxerre, the figure of a 'flaxen and flowery creature, sometimes well-nigh naked among the vine-leaves, sometimes muffled in skins against the cold, sometimes in the dress of a monk, but always with a strong impress of real character and incident from the veritable streets' of the town itself. From this strange design Mr. Pater has fashioned a curious mediæval myth of the return of Dionysus among men, a myth steeped in colour and passion and old romance, full of wonder and full of worship, Denys himself being half animal and half god, making the world mad with a new ecstasy of living, stirring the artists simply by his visible presence, drawing the marvel of music from reed and pipe, and slain at last in a stage-play by those who had loved him. In its rich affluence of imagery this story is like a picture by Mantegna, and indeed Mantegna might have suggested the description of the pageant in which Denys rides upon a gaily-painted chariot, in soft silken raiment and, for head-dress, a strange elephant scalp with gilded tusks.

If Denys l'Auxerrois symbolizes the passion of the senses and Sebastian Van Storck the philosophic passion, as they certainly seem to do, though no mere formula or definition can adequately express the freedom and variety of the life that they portray, the passion for the imaginative world of art is the basis of the story of Duke Carl of Rosenmold. Duke Carl is not unlike the late King of Bavaria, in his love of France, his admiration for the Grand Monarque and his fantastic desire to amaze and to bewilder, but the resemblance is possibly only a chance one. In fact Mr. Pater's young hero is the precursor of the Aufklärung of the last century, the German precursor of Herder and Lessing and Goethe himself, and finds the forms of art ready to his hand without any national spirit to fill them or make them vital and responsive. He too dies, trampled to death by the soldiers of the country he so much admired, on the night of his marriage with a peasant girl, the very failure of his life lending him a certain melancholy grace and dramatic interest.

On the whole, then, this is a singularly attractive book. Mr. Pater is an intellectual impressionist. He does not weary us with any definite doctrine or seek to suit life to any formal creed. He is always looking for exquisite moments and, when he has found them, he analyses them with delicate and delightful art and then passes on, often to the opposite pole of thought or feeling, knowing that every mood has its own quality and charm and is justified by its mere existence. He has taken the sensationalism of Greek philosophy and made it a new method of art criticism. As for his style, it is curiously ascetic. Now and then, we come across phrases with a strange sensuousness of expression, as when he tells us how Denys l'Auxerrois, on his return from a long journey, 'ate flesh for the first time, tearing the hot, red morsels with his delicate fingers in a kind of wild greed,' but such passages are rare. Asceticism is the keynote of Mr. Pater's prose; at times it is almost too severe in its self-control and makes us long for a little more freedom. For indeed, the danger of such prose as his is that it is apt to become somewhat laborious. Here and there, one is tempted to say of Mr. Pater that he is 'a seeker after something in language, that is there in no satisfying measure, or not at all.' The continual preoccupation with phrase and epithet has its drawbacks as well as its virtues. And yet, when all is said, what wonderful prose it is, with its subtle preferences, its fastidious purity, its rejection of what is common or ordinary! Mr. Pater has the true spirit of selection, the true art of omission. If he be not among the greatest prose writers of our literature he is, at least, our greatest artist in prose; and though it may be admitted that the best style is that which seems an unconscious result rather than a conscious aim, still in these latter days when violent rhetoric does duty for eloquence and vulgarity usurps the name of nature, we should be grateful for a style that deliberately aims at perfection of form, that seeks to produce its effect by artistic means and sets before itself an ideal of grave and chastened beauty.

Imaginary Portraits. By Walter Pater, M.A., Fellow of Brasenose College, Oxford. (Macmillan and Co.)

A GERMAN PRINCESS

(Woman's World, November 1887.)

The Princess Christian's translation of the Memoirs of Wilhelmine, Margravine of Baireuth, is a most fascinating and delightful book. The Margravine and her brother, Frederick the Great, were, as the Princess herself points out in an admirably written introduction, 'among the first of those questioning minds that strove after spiritual freedom' in the last century. 'They had studied,' says the Princess, 'the English philosophers, Newton, Locke, and Shaftesbury, and were roused to enthusiasm by the writings of Voltaire and Rousseau. Their whole lives bore the impress of the influence of French thought on the burning questions of the day. In the eighteenth century began that great struggle of philosophy against tyranny and worn-out abuses which culminated in the French Revolution. The noblest minds were engaged in the struggle, and, like most reformers, they pushed their conclusions to extremes, and too often lost sight of the need of a due proportion in things. The Margravine's influence on the intellectual development of her country is untold. She formed at Baireuth a centre of culture and learning which had before been undreamt of in Germany.'

The historical value of these Memoirs is, of course, well known. Carlyle speaks of them as being 'by far the best authority' on the early life of Frederick the Great. But considered merely as the autobiography of a clever and charming woman, they are no less interesting, and even those who care nothing for eighteenth-century politics, and look upon history itself as an unattractive form of fiction, cannot fail to be fascinated by the Margravine's wit, vivacity and humour, by her keen powers of observation, and by her brilliant and assertive egotism. Not that her life was by any means a happy one. Her father, to quote the Princess Christian, 'ruled his family with the same harsh despotism with which he ruled his country, taking pleasure in making his power felt by all in the most galling manner,' and the Margravine and her brother 'had much to suffer, not only from his ungovernable temper, but also from the real privations to which they were subjected.' Indeed, the picture the Margravine gives of the King is quite extraordinary. 'He despised all learning,' she writes, 'and wished me to occupy myself with nothing but needlework and household duties or details. Had he found me writing or reading, he would probably have whipped me.' He 'considered music a capital offence, and maintained that every one should devote himself to one object: men to the military service, and women to their household duties. Science and the arts he counted among the "seven deadly sins."' Sometimes he took to religion, 'and then,' says the Margravine, 'we lived like trappists, to the great grief of my brother and myself. Every afternoon the King preached a sermon, to which we had to listen as attentively as if it proceeded from an Apostle. My brother and I were often seized with such an intense sense of the ridiculous that we burst out laughing, upon which an apostolic curse was poured out on our heads, which we had to accept with a show of humility and penitence.' Economy and soldiers were his only topics of conversation; his chief social amusement was to make his guests intoxicated; and as for his temper, the accounts the Margravine gives of it would be almost incredible if they were not amply corroborated from other sources. Suetonius has written of the strange madness that comes on kings, but even in his melodramatic chronicles there is hardly anything that rivals what the Margravine has to tell us. Here is one of her pictures of family life at a Royal Court in the last century, and it is not by any means the worst scene she describes:

> On one occasion, when his temper was more than usually bad, he told the Queen that he had received letters from Anspach, in which the Margrave announced his arrival at Berlin for the beginning of May. He was coming there for the purpose of marrying my sister, and one of his ministers would arrive previously with the betrothal ring. My father asked my sister whether she were pleased at this prospect, and how she would arrange her household. Now my sister had always made a point of telling him whatever came into her head, even the greatest home-truths, and he had never taken her outspokenness amiss. On this occasion, therefore, relying on former experience, she answered him as follows: 'When I have a house of my own, I shall take care to have a well-appointed dinner-table, better than yours is, and if I have children of my own, I shall not plague them as you do yours, and force them to eat things they thoroughly dislike!'
>
> 'What is amiss with my dinner-table?' the King enquired, getting very red in the face.
>
> 'You ask what is the matter with it,' my sister replied; 'there is not enough on it for us to eat, and what there is cabbage and carrots, which we detest.' Her first answer had already angered my father, but now he gave vent to his fury. But instead of punishing my sister he poured it all on my mother, my brother, and myself. To begin with he threw his plate at my brother's head, who would have been struck had he not got out of the way; a second one he threw at me, which I also happily escaped; then torrents of abuse followed these first signs of hostility. He reproached the Queen with having brought up her children so badly. 'You will curse your mother,' he said to my brother, 'for having made you such a good-for-nothing creature.' . . . As my brother and I passed near him to leave the room, he hit out at us with his crutch. Happily we escaped the blow, for it would certainly have struck us down, and

we at last escaped without harm.

Yet, as the Princess Christian remarks, 'despite the almost cruel treatment Wilhelmine received from her father, it is noticeable that throughout her memoirs she speaks of him with the greatest affection. She makes constant reference to his "good heart"'; and says that his faults 'were more those of temper than of nature.' Nor could all the misery and wretchedness of her home life dull the brightness of her intellect. What would have made others morbid, made her satirical. Instead of weeping over her own personal tragedies, she laughs at the general comedy of life. Here, for instance, is her description of Peter the Great and his wife, who arrived at Berlin in 1718:

> The Czarina was small, broad, and brown-looking, without the slightest dignity or appearance. You had only to look at her to detect her low origin. She might have passed for a German actress, she had decked herself out in such a manner. Her dress had been bought second-hand, and was trimmed with some dirty looking silver embroidery; the bodice was trimmed with precious stones, arranged in such a manner as to represent the double eagle. She wore a dozen orders; and round the bottom of her dress hung quantities of relics and pictures of saints, which rattled when she walked, and reminded one of a smartly harnessed mule. The orders too made a great noise, knocking against each other.

> The Czar, on the other hand, was tall and well grown, with a handsome face, but his expression was coarse, and impressed one with fear. He wore a simple sailor's dress. His wife, who spoke German very badly, called her court jester to her aid, and spoke Russian with her. This poor creature was a Princess Gallizin, who had been obliged to undertake this sorry office to save her life, as she had been mixed up in a conspiracy against the Czar, and had twice been flogged with the knout!

* * * * *

The following day [the Czar] visited all the sights of Berlin, amongst others the very curious collection of coins and antiques. Amongst these last named was a statue, representing a heathen god. It was anything but attractive, but was the most valuable in the collection. The Czar admired it very much, and insisted on the Czarina kissing it. On her refusing, he said to her in bad German that she should lose her head if she did not at once obey him. Being terrified at the Czar's anger she immediately complied with his orders without the least hesitation. The Czar asked the King to give him this and other statues, a request which he could not refuse. The same thing happened about a cupboard, inlaid with amber. It was the only one of its kind, and had cost King Frederick I. an enormous sum, and the consternation was general on its having to be sent to Petersburg.

This barbarous Court happily left after two days. The Queen rushed at once to Monbijou, which she found in a state resembling that of the fall of Jerusalem. I never saw such a sight. Everything was destroyed, so that the Queen was obliged to rebuild the whole house.

Nor are the Margravine's descriptions of her reception as a bride in the principality of Baireuth less amusing. Hof was the first town she came to, and a deputation of nobles was waiting there to welcome her. This is her account of them:

Their faces would have frightened little children, and, to add to their beauty, they had arranged their hair to resemble the wigs that were then in fashion. Their dresses clearly denoted the antiquity of their families, as they were composed of heirlooms, and were cut accordingly, so that most of them did not fit. In spite of their costumes being the 'Court Dresses,' the gold and silver trimmings were so black that you had a difficulty in making out of what they were made. The manners of these nobles suited their faces and their clothes. They might have passed for peasants. I could scarcely restrain my laughter when I first beheld these strange figures. I spoke to each in turn, but none of them understood what I said, and their replies sounded to me like Hebrew, because the dialect of the Empire is quite different from that spoken in Brandenburg.

The clergy also presented themselves. These were totally different creatures. Round their necks they wore great ruffs, which resembled washing baskets. They spoke very slowly, so that I might be able to understand them better. They said the most foolish things, and it was only with much difficulty that I was able to prevent myself from laughing. At last I got rid of all these people, and we sat down to dinner. I tried my best to converse with those at table, but it was useless. At last I touched on agricultural topics, and then they began to thaw. I was at once informed of all their different farmsteads and herds of cattle. An almost interesting discussion took place as to whether the oxen in the upper part of the country were fatter than those in the lowlands.

* * * * *

I was told that as the next day was Sunday, I must spend it at Hof, and listen to a sermon. Never before had I heard such a sermon! The clergyman began by giving us an account of all the marriages that had taken place from Adam's time to that of Noah. We were spared no detail, so that the gentlemen all laughed and the poor ladies blushed. The dinner went off as on the previous day. In the afternoon all the ladies came to pay me their respects. Gracious heavens! What ladies, too! They were all as ugly as the gentlemen, and their head-dresses were so curious that swallows might have built their nests in them.

As for Baireuth itself, and its petty Court, the picture she gives of it is exceedingly curious. Her father-in-law, the reigning Margrave, was a narrow-minded mediocrity, whose conversation 'resembled that of a sermon read aloud for the purpose of sending the listener to sleep,' and he had only two topics, Telemachus, and Amelot de la Houssaye's Roman History. The Ministers, from Baron von Stein, who always said 'yes' to everything, to Baron von Voit, who always said 'no,' were not by any means an intellectual set of men. 'Their chief amusement,' says the Margravine, 'was drinking from morning till night,' and horses and cattle were all they talked about. The palace itself was shabby, decayed and dirty. 'I was like a lamb among wolves,' cries the poor Margravine; 'I was settled in a strange country, at a Court which more resembled a peasant's farm, surrounded by coarse, bad, dangerous, and tiresome people.'

Yet her esprit never deserted her. She is always clever, witty, and entertaining. Her stories about the endless squabbles over precedence are extremely amusing. The society of her day cared very little for good manners, knew, indeed, very little about them, but all questions of etiquette were of vital importance, and the Margravine herself, though she saw the shallowness of the whole system, was far too proud not to assert her rights when circumstances demanded it, as the description she gives of her visit to the Empress of Germany shows very clearly. When this meeting was first proposed, the Margravine declined positively to entertain the idea. 'There was no precedent,' she writes, 'of a King's daughter and the Empress having met, and I did not know to what rights I ought to lay claim.' Finally, however, she is induced to consent, but she lays down three conditions for her reception:

I desired first of all that the Empress's Court should receive me at the foot of the stairs, secondly, that she should meet me at the door of her bedroom, and, thirdly, that she should offer me an armchair to sit on.

* * * * *

They disputed all day over the conditions I had made. The two first were granted me, but all that could be obtained with respect to the third was, that the Empress would use quite a small armchair, whilst she gave me a chair.

Next day I saw this Royal personage. I own that had I been in her place I would have made all the rules of etiquette and ceremony the excuse for not being obliged to appear. The Empress was small and stout, round as a ball, very ugly, and without dignity or manner. Her mind corresponded to her body. She was terribly bigoted, and spent her whole day praying. The old and ugly are generally the Almighty's portion. She received me trembling all over, and was so upset that she could not say a word.

After some silence I began the conversation in French. She answered me in her Austrian dialect that she could not speak in that language, and begged I would speak in German. The conversation did not last long, for the Austrian and low Saxon tongues are so different from each other that to those acquainted with only one the other is unintelligible. This is what happened to us. A third person would have laughed at our misunderstandings, for we caught only a word here and there, and had to guess the rest. The poor Empress was such a slave to etiquette that she would have thought it high treason had she spoken to me in a foreign language, though she understood French quite well.

Many other extracts might be given from this delightful book, but from the few that have been selected some idea can be formed of the vivacity and picturesqueness of the Margravine's style. As for her character, it is very well summed up by the Princess Christian, who, while admitting that she often appears almost heartless and inconsiderate, yet claims that, 'taken as a whole, she stands out in marked prominence among the most gifted women of the eighteenth century, not only by her mental powers, but by her goodness of heart, her self-sacrificing devotion, and true friendship.' An interesting sequel to her Memoirs would be her correspondence with Voltaire, and it is to be hoped that we may shortly see a translation of these letters from the same accomplished pen to which we owe the present volume. [63]

Memoirs of Wilhelmine Margravine of Baireuth. Translated and edited by Her Royal Highness Princess Christian of Schleswig-Holstein, Princess of Great Britain and Ireland. (David Stott.)

A VILLAGE TRAGEDY

One of the most powerful and pathetic novels that has recently appeared is A Village Tragedy by Margaret L. Woods. To find any parallel to this lurid little story, one must go to Dostoieffski or to Guy de Maupassant. Not that Mrs. Woods can be said to have taken either of these two great masters of fiction as her model, but there is something in her work that recalls their method; she has not a little of their fierce intensity, their terrible concentration, their passionless yet poignant objectivity; like them, she seems to allow life to suggest its own mode of presentation; and, like them, she recognizes that a frank acceptance of the facts of life is the true basis of all modern imitative art. The scene of Mrs. Woods's story lies in one of the villages near Oxford; the characters are very few in number, and the plot is extremely simple. It is a romance of modern Arcadia—a tale of the love of a farm-labourer for a girl who, though slightly above him in social station and education, is yet herself also a servant on a farm. True Arcadians they are, both of them, and their ignorance and isolation serve only to intensify the tragedy that gives the story its title. It is the fashion nowadays to label literature, so, no doubt, Mrs. Woods's novel will be spoken of as 'realistic.' Its realism, however, is the realism of the artist, not of the reporter; its tact of treatment, subtlety of perception, and fine distinction of style, make it rather a poem than a procès-verbal; and though it lays bare to us the mere misery of life, it suggests something of life's mystery also. Very delicate, too, is the handling of external Nature. There are no formal guide-book descriptions of scenery, nor anything of what Byron petulantly called 'twaddling about trees,' but we seem to breathe the atmosphere of the country, to catch the exquisite scent of the beanfields, so familiar to all who have ever wandered through the Oxfordshire lanes in June; to hear the birds singing in the thicket, and the sheep-bells tinkling from the hill.

Characterization, that enemy of literary form, is such an essential part of the method of the modern writer of fiction, that Nature has almost become to the novelist what light and shade are to the painter—the one permanent element of style; and if the power of A Village Tragedy be due to its portrayal of human life, no small portion of its charm comes from its Theocritean setting.

A Village Tragedy. By Margaret L. Woods. (Bentley and Son.)

MR. MORRIS'S COMPLETION OF THE ODYSSEY

(Pall Mall Gazette, November 24, 1887.)

Mr. Morris's second volume brings the great romantic epic of Greek literature to its perfect conclusion, and although there can never be an ultimate translation of either Iliad or Odyssey, as each successive age is sure to find pleasure in rendering the two poems in its own manner and according to its own canons of taste, still it is not too much to say that Mr. Morris's version will always be a true classic amongst our classical translations. It is not, of course, flawless. In our notice of the first volume we ventured to say that Mr. Morris was sometimes far more Norse than Greek, nor does the volume that now lies before us make us alter that opinion. The particular metre, also, selected by Mr. Morris, although admirably adapted to express 'the strong-winged music of Homer,' as far as its flow and freedom are concerned, misses something of its dignity and calm. Here, it must be admitted, we feel a distinct loss, for there is in Homer not a little of Milton's lofty manner, and if swiftness be an essential of the Greek hexameter, stateliness is one of its distinguishing qualities in Homer's hands. This defect, however, if we must call it a defect, seems almost unavoidable, as for certain metrical reasons a majestic movement in English verse is necessarily a slow movement; and, after all that can be said is said, how really admirable is this whole translation! If we set aside its noble qualities as a poem and look on it purely from the scholar's point of view, how straightforward it is, how honest and direct! Its fidelity to the original is far beyond that of any other verse-translation in our literature, and yet it is not the fidelity of a pedant to his text but rather the fine loyalty of poet to poet.

When Mr. Morris's first volume appeared many of the critics complained that his occasional use of archaic words and unusual expressions robbed his version of the true Homeric simplicity. This, however, is not a very felicitous criticism, for while Homer is undoubtedly simple in his clearness and largeness of vision, his wonderful power of direct narration, his wholesome sanity, and the purity and precision of his method, simple in language he undoubtedly is not. What he was to his contemporaries we have, of course, no means of judging, but we know that the Athenian of the fifth century b.c. found him in many places difficult to understand, and when the creative age was succeeded by the age of criticism and Alexandria began to take the place of Athens as the centre of culture for the Hellenistic world, Homeric dictionaries and glossaries seem to have been constantly published. Indeed, Athenæus tells us of a wonderful Byzantine blue-stocking, a précieuse from the Propontis, who wrote a long hexameter poem, called Mnemosyne, full of ingenious commentaries on difficulties in Homer, and in fact, it is evident that, as far as the language is concerned, such a phrase as 'Homeric simplicity' would have rather amazed an ancient Greek. As for Mr. Morris's tendency to emphasize the etymological meaning of words, a point commented on with somewhat flippant severity in a recent number of Macmillan's Magazine, here Mr. Morris seems to us to be in complete accord, not merely with the spirit of Homer, but with the spirit of all early poetry. It is quite true that language is apt to degenerate into a system of almost algebraic symbols, and the modern city-man who takes a ticket for Blackfriars Bridge, naturally never thinks of the Dominican monks who once had their monastery by Thames-side, and after whom the spot is named. But in earlier times it was not so. Men were then keenly conscious of the real meaning of words, and early poetry, especially, is full of this feeling, and, indeed, may be said to owe to it no small portion of its poetic power and charm. These old words, then, and this old use of words which we find in Mr. Morris's Odyssey can be amply justified upon historical grounds, and as for their artistic effect, it is quite excellent. Pope tried to put Homer into the ordinary language of his day, with what result we know only too well; but Mr. Morris, who uses his archaisms with the tact of a true artist, and to whom indeed they seem to come absolutely naturally, has succeeded in giving to his version by their aid that touch, not of 'quaintness,' for Homer is never quaint, but of old-world romance and old-world beauty, which we moderns find so pleasurable, and to which the Greeks themselves were so keenly sensitive.

As for individual passages of special merit, Mr. Morris's translation is no robe of rags sewn with purple patches for critics to sample. Its real value lies in the absolute rightness and coherence of the whole, in the grand architecture of the swift, strong verse, and in the fact that the standard is not merely high but everywhere sustained. It is impossible, however, to resist the temptation of quoting Mr. Morris's rendering of that famous passage in the twenty-third book of the epic, in which Odysseus eludes the trap laid for him by Penelope, whose very faith in the certainty of her husband's return makes her sceptical of his identity when he stands before her; an instance, by the way, of Homer's wonderful psychological knowledge of human nature, as it is always the dreamer himself who is most surprised when his dream comes true.

Thus she spake to prove her husband; but Odysseus, grieved at heart,

Spake thus unto his bed-mate well-skilled in gainful art:

'O woman, thou sayest a word exceeding grievous to me!

Who hath otherwhere shifted my bedstead? full hard for him should it be,

For as deft as he were, unless soothly a very God come here,

Who easily, if he willed it, might shift it otherwhere.

But no mortal man is living, how strong soe'er in his youth,

Who shall lightly hale it elsewhere, since a mighty wonder forsooth

Is wrought in that fashioned bedstead, and I wrought it, and I alone.

In the close grew a thicket of olive, a long-leaved tree full-grown,

That flourished and grew goodly as big as a pillar about,

So round it I built my bride-room, till I did the work right out

With ashlar stone close-fitting; and I roofed it overhead,

And thereto joined doors I made me, well-fitting in their stead.

Then I lopped away the boughs of the long-leafed olive-tree,

And, shearing the bole from the root up full well and cunningly,

I planed it about with the brass, and set the rule thereto,

And shaping thereof a bed-post, with the wimble I bored it through.

So beginning, I wrought out the bedstead, and finished it utterly,

And with gold enwrought it about, and with silver and ivory,

And stretched on it a thong of oxhide with the purple dye made bright.

Thus then the sign I have shown thee; nor, woman, know I aright

If my bed yet bideth steadfast, or if to another place

Some man hath moved it, and smitten the olive-bole from its base.'

These last twelve books of the Odyssey have not the same marvel of romance, adventure and colour that we find in the earlier part of the epic. There is nothing in them that we can compare to the exquisite idyll of Nausicaa or to the Titanic humour of the episode in the Cyclops' cave. Penelope has not the glamour of Circe, and the song of the Sirens may sound sweeter than the whizz of the arrows of Odysseus as he stands on the threshold of his hall. Yet, for sheer intensity of passionate power, for concentration of intellectual interest and for masterly dramatic construction, these latter books are quite unequalled. Indeed, they show very clearly how it was that, as Greek art developed, the epos passed into the drama. The whole scheme of the argument, the return of the hero in disguise, his disclosure of himself to his son, his terrible vengeance on his enemies and his final recognition by his wife, reminds us of the plot of more than one Greek play, and shows us what the great Athenian poet meant when he said that his own dramas were merely scraps from Homer's table. In rendering this splendid poem into English verse, Mr. Morris has done our literature a service that can hardly be over-estimated, and it is pleasant to think that, even should the classics be entirely excluded from our educational systems, the English boy will still be able to know something of Homer's delightful tales, to catch an echo of his grand music and to wander with the wise Odysseus round 'the shores of old romance.'

The Odyssey of Homer. Done into English Verse by William Morris, Author of *The Earthly Paradise.* Volume II. (Reeves and Turner.)

MRS. SOMERVILLE

(Pall Mall Gazette, November 30, 1887.)

Phyllis Browne's Life of Mrs. Somerville forms part of a very interesting little series, called 'The World's Workers'—a collection of short biographies catholic enough to include personalities so widely different as Turner and

Richard Cobden, Handel and Sir Titus Salt, Robert Stephenson and Florence Nightingale, and yet possessing a certain definite aim. As a mathematician and a scientist, the translator and popularizer of La Mécanique Céleste, and the author of an important book on physical geography, Mrs. Somerville is, of course, well known. The scientific bodies of Europe covered her with honours; her bust stands in the hall of the Royal Society, and one of the Women's Colleges at Oxford bears her name. Yet, considered simply in the light of a wife and a mother, she is no less admirable; and those who consider that stupidity is the proper basis for the domestic virtues, and that intellectual women must of necessity be helpless with their hands, cannot do better than read Phyllis Browne's pleasant little book, in which they will find that the greatest woman-mathematician of any age was a clever needlewoman, a good housekeeper, and a most skilful cook. Indeed, Mrs. Somerville seems to have been quite renowned for her cookery. The discoverers of the North-West Passage christened an island 'Somerville,' not as a tribute to the distinguished mathematician, but as a recognition of the excellence of some orange marmalade which the distinguished mathematician had prepared with her own hands and presented to the ships before they left England; and to the fact that she was able to make currant jelly at a very critical moment she owed the affection of some of her husband's relatives, who up to that time had been rather prejudiced against her on the ground that she was merely an unpractical Blue-stocking.

Nor did her scientific knowledge ever warp or dull the tenderness and humanity of her nature. For birds and animals she had always a great love. We hear of her as a little girl watching with eager eyes the swallows as they built their nests in summer or prepared for their flight in the autumn; and when snow was on the ground she used to open the windows to let the robins hop in and pick crumbs on the breakfast-table. On one occasion she went with her father on a tour in the Highlands, and found on her return that a pet goldfinch, which had been left in the charge of the servants, had been neglected by them and had died of starvation. She was almost heart-broken at the event, and in writing her Recollections, seventy years after, she mentioned it and said that, as she wrote, she felt deep pain. Her chief pet in her old age was a mountain sparrow, which used to perch on her arm and go to sleep there while she was writing. One day the sparrow fell into the water-jug and was drowned, to the great grief of its mistress who could hardly be consoled for its loss, though later on we hear of a beautiful paroquet taking the place of le moineau d'Uranie, and becoming Mrs. Somerville's constant companion. She was also very energetic, Phyllis Browne tells us, in trying to get a law passed in the Italian Parliament for the protection of animals, and said once, with reference to this subject, 'We English cannot boast of humanity so long as our sportsmen find pleasure in shooting down tame pigeons as they fly terrified out of a cage'—a remark with which I entirely agree. Mr. Herbert's Bill for the protection of land birds gave her immense pleasure, though, to quote her own words, she was 'grieved to find that "the lark, which at heaven's gate sings," is thought unworthy of man's protection'; and she took a great fancy to a gentleman who, on being told of the number of singing birds that is eaten in Italy—nightingales, goldfinches, and robins—exclaimed in horror, 'What! robins! our household birds! I would as soon eat a child!' Indeed, she believed to some extent in the immortality of animals on the ground that, if animals have no future, it would seem as if some were created for uncompensated misery—an idea which does not seem to me to be either extravagant or fantastic, though it must be admitted that the optimism on which it is based receives absolutely no support from science.

On the whole, Phyllis Browne's book is very pleasant reading. Its only fault is that it is far too short, and this is a fault so rare in modern literature that it almost amounts to a distinction. However, Phyllis Browne has managed to crowd into the narrow limits at her disposal a great many interesting anecdotes. The picture she gives of Mrs. Somerville working away at her translation of Laplace in the same room with her children is very charming, and reminds one of what is told of George Sand; there is an amusing account of Mrs. Somerville's visit to the widow of the young Pretender, the Countess of Albany, who, after talking with her for some time, exclaimed, 'So you don't speak Italian. You must have had a very bad education'! And this story about the Waverley Novels may possibly be new to some of my readers:

A very amusing circumstance in connection with Mrs. Somerville's acquaintance with Sir Walter arose out of the childish inquisitiveness of Woronzow Greig, Mrs. Somerville's little boy.

During the time Mrs. Somerville was visiting Abbotsford the Waverley Novels were appearing, and were creating a great sensation; yet even Scott's intimate friends did not know that he was the author; he enjoyed keeping the affair a mystery. But little Woronzow discovered what he was about. One day when Mrs. Somerville was talking about a novel that had just been published, Woronzow said, 'I knew all these stories long ago, for Mr. Scott writes on the dinner-table; when he has finished he puts the green cloth with the papers in a corner of the dining-room, and when he goes out Charlie Scott and I read the stories.'

Phyllis Browne remarks that this incident shows 'that persons who want to keep a secret ought to be very careful when children are about'; but the story seems to me to be far too charming to require any moral of the kind.

Bound up in the same volume is a Life of Miss Mary Carpenter, also written by Phyllis Browne. Miss Carpenter does not seem to me to have the charm and fascination of Mrs. Somerville. There is always something about her that is formal, limited, and precise. When she was about two years old she insisted on being called 'Doctor Carpenter' in the nursery; at the age of twelve she is described by a friend as a sedate little girl, who always spoke like a book; and before she entered on her educational schemes she wrote down a solemn dedication of herself to the service of humanity. However, she was one of the practical, hardworking saints of the nineteenth century, and it is no doubt quite right that the saints should take themselves very seriously. It is only fair also to remember that her work of rescue and reformation was carried on under great difficulties. Here, for instance, is the picture Miss Cobbe gives us of one of the Bristol night-schools:

It was a wonderful spectacle to see Mary Carpenter sitting patiently before the large school gallery in St. James's Back, teaching, singing, and praying with the wild street-boys, in spite of endless interruptions caused by such proceedings as shooting marbles at any object behind her, whistling, stamping, fighting, shrieking out 'Amen' in the middle of a prayer, and sometimes rising en masse and tearing like a troop of bisons in hob-nailed shoes down from the gallery, round the great schoolroom, and down the stairs, and into the street. These irrepressible outbreaks she bore with infinite good humour.

Her own account is somewhat pleasanter, and shows that 'the troop of bisons in hob-nailed shoes' was not always so barbarous.

I had taken to my class on the preceding week some specimens of ferns neatly gummed on white paper. . . . This time I took a piece of coal-shale, with impressions of ferns, to show them. . . . I told each to examine the specimen, and tell me what he thought it was. W. gave so bright a smile that I saw he knew; none of the others could tell; he said they were ferns, like what I showed them last week, but he thought they were chiselled on the stone. Their surprise and pleasure were great when I explained the matter to them.

The history of Joseph: they all found a difficulty in realizing that this had actually occurred. One asked if Egypt existed now, and if people lived in it. When I told them that buildings now stood which had been erected about the time of Joseph, one said that it was impossible, as they must have fallen down ere this. I showed them the form of a pyramid, and they were satisfied. One asked if all books were true.

The story of Macbeth impressed them very much. They knew the name of Shakespeare, having seen his name over a public-house.

A boy defined conscience as 'a thing a gentleman hasn't got, who, when a boy finds his purse and gives it back to him, doesn't give the boy sixpence.'

Another boy was asked, after a Sunday evening lecture on 'Thankfulness,' what pleasure he enjoyed most in the course of a year. He replied candidly, 'Cock-fightin', ma'am; there's a pit up by the "Black Boy" as is worth anythink in Brissel.'

There is something a little pathetic in the attempt to civilize the rough street-boy by means of the refining influence of ferns and fossils, and it is difficult to help feeling that Miss Carpenter rather over-estimated the value of elementary education. The poor are not to be fed upon facts. Even Shakespeare and the Pyramids are not sufficient; nor is there much use in giving them the results of culture, unless we also give them those conditions under which culture can be realized. In these cold, crowded cities of the North, the proper basis for morals, using the word in its wide Hellenic signification, is to be found in architecture, not in books.

Still, it would be ungenerous not to recognize that Mary Carpenter gave to the children of the poor not merely her learning, but her love. In early life, her biographer tells us, she had longed for the happiness of being a wife and a mother; but later she became content that her affection could be freely given to all who needed it, and the verse in the prophecies, 'I have given thee children whom thou hast not borne,' seemed to her to indicate what was to be her true mission. Indeed, she rather inclined to Bacon's opinion, that unmarried people do the best public work. 'It is quite striking,' she says in one of her letters, 'to observe how much the useful power and influence of woman has developed of late years. Unattached ladies, such as widows and unmarried women, have quite ample work to do in the world for the good of others to absorb all their powers. Wives and mothers have a very noble work given them by God, and want no more.' The whole passage is extremely interesting, and the phrase 'unattached ladies' is quite delightful, and reminds one of Charles Lamb.

Mrs. Somerville and Mary Carpenter. By Phyllis Browne, Author
of *What Girls Can Do, etc.* (Cassell and Co.)

ARISTOTLE AT AFTERNOON TEA

(Pall Mall Gazette, December 16, 1887.)

In society, says Mr. Mahaffy, every civilized man and woman ought to feel it their duty to say something, even when there is hardly anything to be said, and, in order to encourage this delightful art of brilliant chatter, he has published a social guide without which no débutante or dandy should ever dream of going out to dine. Not that Mr. Mahaffy's book can be said to be, in any sense of the word, popular. In discussing this important subject of conversation, he has not merely followed the scientific method of Aristotle which is, perhaps, excusable, but he has adopted the literary style of Aristotle for which no excuse is possible. There is, also, hardly a single anecdote, hardly a single illustration, and the reader is left to put the Professor's abstract rules into practice, without either the examples or the warnings of history to encourage or to dissuade him in his reckless career. Still, the book can be warmly recommended to all who propose to substitute the vice of verbosity for the stupidity of silence. It fascinates in spite of its form and pleases in spite of its pedantry, and is the nearest approach, that we know of, in modern literature to meeting Aristotle at an afternoon tea.

As regards physical conditions, the only one that is considered by Mr. Mahaffy as being absolutely essential to a good conversationalist, is the possession of a musical voice. Some learned writers have been of opinion that a slight stammer often gives peculiar zest to conversation, but Mr. Mahaffy rejects this view and is extremely severe on every eccentricity from a native brogue to an artificial catchword. With his remarks on the latter point, the meaningless repetition of phrases, we entirely agree. Nothing can be more irritating than the scientific person who is always saying 'Exactly so,' or the commonplace person who ends every sentence with 'Don't you know?' or the pseudo-artistic person who murmurs 'Charming, charming,' on the smallest-provocation. It is, however, with the mental and moral qualifications for conversation that Mr. Mahaffy specially deals. Knowledge he, naturally, regards as an absolute essential, for, as he most justly observes, 'an ignorant man is seldom agreeable, except as a butt.' Upon the other hand, strict accuracy should be avoided. 'Even a consummate liar,' says Mr. Mahaffy, is a better ingredient in a company than 'the scrupulously truthful man, who weighs every statement, questions every fact, and corrects every inaccuracy.' The liar at any rate recognizes that recreation, not instruction, is the aim of conversation, and is a far more civilized being than the blockhead who loudly expresses his disbelief in a story which is told simply for the amusement of the company. Mr. Mahaffy, however, makes an exception in favour of the eminent specialist and tells us that intelligent questions addressed to an astronomer, or a pure mathematician, will elicit many curious facts which will pleasantly beguile the time. Here, in the interest of Society, we feel bound to enter a formal protest. Nobody, even in the provinces, should ever be allowed to ask an intelligent question about pure mathematics across a dinner-table. A question of this kind is quite as bad as inquiring suddenly about the state of a man's soul, a sort of coup which, as Mr. Mahaffy remarks elsewhere, 'many pious people have actually thought a decent introduction to a conversation.'

As for the moral qualifications of a good talker, Mr. Mahaffy, following the example of his great master, warns us against any disproportionate excess of virtue. Modesty, for instance, may easily become a social vice, and to be continually apologizing for one's ignorance or stupidity is a grave injury to conversation, for, 'what we want to learn from each member is his free opinion on the subject in hand, not his own estimate of the value of that opinion.' Simplicity, too, is not without its dangers. The enfant terrible, with his shameless love of truth, the raw country-bred girl who always says what she means, and the plain, blunt man who makes a point of speaking his mind on every possible occasion, without ever considering whether he has a mind at all, are the fatal examples of what simplicity leads to. Shyness may be a form of vanity, and reserve a development of pride, and as for sympathy, what can be more detestable than the man, or woman, who insists on agreeing with everybody, and so makes 'a discussion, which implies differences in opinion,' absolutely impossible? Even the unselfish listener is apt to become a bore. 'These silent people,' says Mr. Mahaffy, 'not only take all they can get in Society for nothing, but they take it without the smallest gratitude, and have the audacity afterwards to censure those who have laboured for their amusement.' Tact, which is an exquisite sense of the symmetry of things, is, according to Mr. Mahaffy, the highest and best of all the moral conditions for conversation. The man of tact, he most wisely remarks, 'will instinctively avoid jokes about Blue Beard' in the company of a woman who is a man's third wife; he will never be guilty of talking like a book, but will rather avoid too careful an attention to grammar and the rounding of periods; he will cultivate the art of graceful interruption, so as to prevent a subject being worn threadbare by the aged or the inexperienced; and should he be desirous of telling a story, he will look round and consider each member of the party, and if there be a single stranger present will forgo the pleasure of anecdotage rather than make the social mistake of hurting even one of the guests. As for prepared or premeditated art, Mr. Mahaffy has a great contempt for it and tells us of a certain college don (let us hope not at Oxford or Cambridge) who always carried a jest-book in his pocket and had to refer to it when he wished to make a repartee. Great wits, too, are often very cruel, and great humorists often very vulgar, so it will be better to try and 'make good conversation without any large help from these brilliant but dangerous gifts.'

In a tête-à-tête one should talk about persons, and in general Society about things. The state of the weather is always an excusable exordium, but it is convenient to have a paradox or heresy on the subject always ready so as to direct the conversation into other channels. Really domestic people are almost invariably bad talkers as their very virtues in home life have dulled their interest in outer things. The very best mothers will insist on chattering of their babies and prattling about infant education. In fact, most women do not take sufficient interest in politics, just as most men are deficient in general reading. Still, anybody can be made to talk, except the very obstinate, and even a commercial traveller may be drawn out and become quite interesting. As for Society small talk, it is impossible, Mr. Mahaffy tells us, for any sound theory of conversation to depreciate gossip, 'which is perhaps the main factor in agreeable talk throughout Society.' The retailing of small personal points about great people always gives pleasure, and if one is not fortunate enough to be an Arctic traveller or an escaped Nihilist, the best thing one can do is to relate some anecdote of 'Prince Bismarck, or King Victor Emmanuel, or Mr. Gladstone.' In the case of meeting a genius and a Duke at dinner, the good talker will try to raise himself to the level of the former and to bring the latter down to his own level. To succeed among one's social superiors one must have no hesitation in contradicting them. Indeed, one should make bold criticisms and introduce a bright and free tone into a Society whose grandeur and extreme respectability make it, Mr. Mahaffy remarks, as pathetically as inaccurately, 'perhaps somewhat dull.' The best conversationalists are those whose ancestors have been bilingual, like the French and Irish, but the art of conversation is really within the reach of almost every one, except those who are morbidly truthful, or whose high moral worth requires to be sustained by a permanent gravity of demeanour and a general dullness of mind.

These are the broad principles contained in Mr. Mahaffy's clever little book, and many of them will, no doubt, commend themselves to our readers. The maxim, 'If you find the company dull, blame yourself,' seems to us somewhat optimistic, and we have no sympathy at all with the professional storyteller who is really a great bore at a dinner-table; but Mr. Mahaffy is quite right in insisting that no bright social intercourse is possible without equality, and it is no objection to his book to say that it will not teach people how to talk cleverly. It is not logic that makes men reasonable, nor the science of ethics that makes men good, but it is always useful to analyse, to formularize and to investigate. The only thing to be regretted in the volume is the arid and jejune character of the style. If Mr. Mahaffy would only write as he talks, his book would be much pleasanter reading.

The Principles of the Art of Conversation: A Social Essay. By J. P. Mahaffy. (Macmillan and Co.)

EARLY CHRISTIAN ART IN IRELAND
(Pall Mall Gazette, December 17, 1887.)

The want of a good series of popular handbooks on Irish art has long been felt, the works of Sir William Wilde, Petrie and others being somewhat too elaborate for the ordinary student; so we are glad to notice the appearance, under the auspices of the Committee of Council on Education, of Miss Margaret Stokes's useful little volume on the early Christian art of her country. There is, of course, nothing particularly original in Miss Stokes's book, nor can she be said to be a very attractive or pleasing writer, but it is unfair to look for originality in primers, and the charm of the illustrations fully atones for the somewhat heavy and pedantic character of the style.

This early Christian art of Ireland is full of interest to the artist, the archæologist and the historian. In its rudest forms, such as the little iron hand-bell, the plain stone chalice and the rough wooden staff, it brings us back to the simplicity of the primitive Christian Church, while to the period of its highest development we owe the great masterpieces of Celtic metal-work. The stone chalice is now replaced by the chalice of silver and gold; the iron bell has its jewel-studded shrine, and the rough staff its gorgeous casing; rich caskets and splendid bindings preserve the holy books of the Saints and, instead of the rudely carved symbol of the early missionaries, we have such beautiful works of art as the processional cross of Cong Abbey. Beautiful this cross certainly is with its delicate intricacy of ornamentation, its grace of proportion and its marvel of mere workmanship, nor is there any doubt about its history. From the inscriptions on it, which are corroborated by the annals of Innisfallen and the book of Clonmacnoise, we learn that it was made for King Turlough O'Connor by a native artist under the superintendence of Bishop O'Duffy, its primary object being to enshrine a portion of the true cross that was sent to the king in 1123. Brought to Cong some years afterwards, probably by the archbishop, who died there in 1150, it was concealed at the time of the Reformation, but at the beginning of the present century was still in the possession of the last abbot, and at his death it was purchased by Professor MacCullagh and presented by him to the museum of the Royal Irish Academy. This wonderful work is alone well worth a visit to Dublin, but not less lovely is the chalice of Ardagh, a two-handled silver cup, absolutely classical in its perfect purity of form, and decorated with gold and amber and crystal and with varieties of cloisonné and champlevé enamel. There is no mention of this cup, or of the so-called Tara brooch, in ancient Irish history. All that we know of them is that they were found accidentally, the former by a boy who was digging potatoes near the old Rath of Ardagh, the latter by a poor child who picked it up near the seashore. They both, however, belong probably to the tenth century.

Of all these works, as well as of the bell shrines, book-covers, sculptured crosses and illuminated designs in manuscripts, excellent pictures are given in Miss Stokes's handbook. The extremely interesting Fiachal Phadrig, or shrine of St. Patrick's tooth, might have been figured and noted as an interesting example of the survival of ornament, and one of the old miniatures of the scribe or Evangelist writing would have given an additional interest to the chapter on Irish MSS. On the whole, however, the book is wonderfully well illustrated, and the ordinary art student will be able to get some useful suggestions from it. Indeed, Miss Stokes, echoing the aspirations of many of the great Irish archæologists, looks forward to the revival of a native Irish school in architecture, sculpture, metal-work and painting. Such an aspiration is, of course, very laudable, but there is always a danger of these revivals being merely artificial reproductions, and it may be questioned whether the peculiar forms of Irish ornamentation could be made at all expressive of the modern spirit. A recent writer on house decoration has gravely suggested that the British householder should take his meals in a Celtic dining-room adorned with a dado of Ogham inscriptions, and such wicked proposals may serve as a warning to all who fancy that the reproduction of a form necessarily implies a revival of the spirit that gave the form life and meaning, and who fail to recognize the difference between art and anachronisms. Miss Stokes's proposal for an ark-shaped church in which the mural painter is to repeat the arcades and 'follow the architectural compositions of the grand pages of the Eusebian canons in the Book of Kells,' has, of course, nothing grotesque about it, but it is not probable that the artistic genius of the Irish people will, even when 'the land has rest,' find in such interesting imitations its healthiest or best expression. Still, there are certain elements of beauty in ancient Irish art that the modern artist would do well to study. The value of the intricate illuminations in the Book of Kells, as far as their adaptability to modern designs and modern material goes, has been very much overrated, but in the ancient Irish torques, brooches, pins, clasps and the like, the modern goldsmith will find a rich and, comparatively speaking, an untouched field; and now that the Celtic spirit has become the leaven of our politics, there is no reason why it should not contribute something to our decorative art. This result, however, will not be obtained by a patriotic misuse of old designs, and even the most enthusiastic Home Ruler must not be allowed to decorate his dining-room with a dado of Oghams.

Early Christian Art in Ireland. By Margaret Stokes. (Published for the Committee of Council on Education by Chapman and Hall.)

MADAME RISTORI

(Woman's World, January 1888.)

Madame Ristori's Etudes et Souvenirs is one of the most delightful books on the stage that has appeared since Lady Martin's charming volume on the Shakespearian heroines. It is often said that actors leave nothing behind them but a barren name and a withered wreath; that they subsist simply upon the applause of the moment; that they are ultimately doomed to the oblivion of old play-bills; and that their art, in a word, dies with them, and shares their own mortality. 'Chippendale, the cabinet-maker,' says the clever author of Obiter Dicta, 'is more potent than Garrick the actor. The vivacity of the latter no longer charms (save in Boswell); the chairs of the former still render rest impossible in a hundred homes.' This view, however, seems to me to be exaggerated. It rests on the assumption that acting is simply a mimetic art, and takes no account of its imaginative and intellectual basis. It is quite true, of course, that the personality of the player passes away, and with it that pleasure-giving power by virtue of which the arts exist. Yet the artistic method of a great actor survives. It lives on in tradition, and becomes part of the science of a school. It has all the intellectual life of a principle. In England, at the present moment, the influence of Garrick on our actors is far stronger than that of Reynolds on our painters of portraits, and if we turn to France it is easy to discern the tradition of Talma, but where is the tradition of David?

Madame Ristori's memoirs, then, have not merely the charm that always attaches to the autobiography of a brilliant and beautiful woman, but have also a definite and distinct artistic value. Her analysis of the character of Lady Macbeth, for instance, is full of psychological interest, and shows us that the subtleties of Shakespearian criticism are not necessarily confined to those who have views on weak endings and rhyming tags, but may also be suggested by the art of acting itself. The author of Obiter Dicta seeks to deny to actors all critical insight and all literary appreciation. The actor, he tells us, is art's slave, not her child, and lives entirely outside literature, 'with its words for ever on his lips, and none of its truths engraven on his heart.' But this seems to me to be a harsh and reckless generalization. Indeed, so far from agreeing with it, I would be inclined to say that the mere artistic process of acting, the translation of literature back again into life, and the presentation of thought under the conditions of action, is in itself a critical method of a very high order; nor do I think that a study of the careers of our great English actors will really sustain the charge of want of literary appreciation. It may be true that actors pass too quickly away from the form, in order to get at the feeling that gives the form beauty and colour, and that, where the literary critic studies the language, the actor looks simply for the life; and yet, how well the great actors have appreciated that marvellous music of words, which in Shakespeare, at any rate, is so vital an element of poetic power, if, indeed, it be not equally so in the case of all who have any claim to be regarded as true poets. 'The sensual life of verse,' says Keats, in a dramatic criticism published in the Champion, 'springs warm from the lips of Kean, and to one learned in Shakespearian hieroglyphics, learned in the spiritual portion of those lines to which Kean adds a sensual grandeur, his tongue must seem to have robbed the Hybla bees and left them honeyless.' This particular feeling, of which Keats speaks, is familiar to all who have heard Salvini, Sarah Bernhardt, Ristori, or any of the great artists of our day, and it is a feeling that one cannot, I think, gain merely by reading the passage to oneself. For my own part, I must confess that it was not until I heard Sarah Bernhardt in Phèdre that I absolutely realized the sweetness of the music of Racine. As for Mr. Birrell's statement that actors have the words of literature for ever on their lips, but none of its truths engraved on their hearts, all that one can say is that, if it be true, it is a defect which actors share with the majority of literary critics.

The account Madame Ristori gives of her own struggles, voyages and adventures, is very pleasant reading indeed. The child of poor actors, she made her first appearance when she was three months old, being brought on in a hamper as a New Year's gift to a selfish old gentleman who would not forgive his daughter for having married for love. As, however, she began to cry long before the hamper was opened, the comedy became a farce, to the immense amusement of the public. She next appeared in a mediæval melodrama, being then three years of age, and was so terrified at the machinations of the villain that she ran away at the most critical moment. However, her stage-fright seems to have disappeared, and we find her playing Silvio Pellico's Francesca da Rimini at fifteen, and at eighteen making her début as Marie Stuart. At this time the naturalism of the French method was gradually displacing the artificial elocution and academic poses of the Italian school of acting. Madame Ristori seems to have tried to combine simplicity with style, and the passion of nature with the self-restraint of the artist. 'J'ai voulu fondre les deux manières,' she tells us, 'car je sentais que toutes choses étant susceptibles de progrès, l'art dramatique aussi était appelé à subir des transformations.' The natural development, however, of the Italian drama was almost arrested by the ridiculous censorship of plays then existing in each town under Austrian or Papal rule. The slightest allusion to the sentiment of nationality or the spirit of freedom was prohibited. Even the word patria was regarded as treasonable, and Madame Ristori tells us an amusing story of the indignation of a censor who was asked to license a play, in which a dumb man returns home after an absence of many years, and on his entrance upon the stage makes gestures expressive of his joy in seeing his native land once more. 'Gestures of this kind,' said the censor, 'are obviously of a very revolutionary tendency, and cannot possibly be allowed. The only gestures that I could think of permitting would be gestures expressive of a dumb man's delight in scenery generally.' The stage directions were accordingly altered, and the word 'landscape' substituted for 'native land'! Another censor was extremely severe on an unfortunate poet who had used the expression 'the beautiful Italian sky,' and explained to him that 'the beautiful Lombardo-Venetian sky' was the proper official expression to use. Poor Gregory in Romeo and Juliet had to be rechristened, because Gregory is a name dear to the Popes; and the

Here I have a pilot's thumb,

Wrecked as homeward he did come,

of the first witch in Macbeth was ruthlessly struck out as containing an obvious allusion to the steersman of St. Peter's bark. Finally, bored and bothered by the political and theological Dogberrys of the day, with their inane prejudices, their solemn stupidity, and their entire ignorance of the conditions necessary for the growth of sane and healthy art, Madame Ristori made up her mind to leave the stage. She, however, was extremely anxious to appear once before a Parisian audience, Paris being at that time the centre of dramatic activity, and after some consideration left Italy for France in the year 1855. There she seems to have been a great success, particularly in the part of Myrrha; classical without being cold, artistic without being academic, she brought to the interpretation of the character of Alfieri's great heroine the colour-element of passion, the form-element of style. Jules Janin was loud in his praises, the Emperor begged Ristori to join the troupe of the Comédie Française, and Rachel, with the strange narrow jealousy of her nature, trembled for her laurels. Myrrha was followed by Marie Stuart, and Marie Stuart by Medea. In the latter part Madame Ristori excited the greatest enthusiasm. Ary Scheffer designed her costumes for her; and the Niobe that stands in the Uffizi Gallery at Florence, suggested to Madame Ristori her famous pose in the scene with the children. She would not consent, however, to remain in France, and we find her subsequently playing in almost every country in the world from Egypt to Mexico, from Denmark to Honolulu. Her representations of classical plays seem to have been always immensely admired. When she played at Athens, the King offered to arrange for a performance in the beautiful old theatre of Dionysos, and during her tour in Portugal she produced Medea before the University of Coimbra. Her description of the latter engagement is extremely interesting. On her arrival at the University, she was received by the entire body of the undergraduates, who still wear a costume almost mediæval in character. Some of them came on the stage in the course of the play as the handmaidens of Creusa, hiding their black beards beneath heavy veils, and as soon as they had finished their parts they took their places gravely among the audience, to Madame Ristori's horror, still in their Greek dress, but with their veils thrown back and smoking long cigars. 'Ce n'est pas la première fois,' she says, 'que j'ai dû empêcher, par un effort de volonté, la tragédie de se terminer en farce.' Very interesting, also, is her account of the production of Montanelli's Camma, and she tells an amusing story of the arrest of the author by the French police on the charge of murder, in consequence of a telegram she sent to him in which the words 'body of the victim' occurred. Indeed, the whole book is full of cleverly written stories, and admirable criticisms on dramatic art. I have quoted from the French version, which happens to be the one that lies before me, but whether in French or Italian the book is one of the most fascinating autobiographies that has appeared for some time, even in an age like ours when literary egotism has been brought to such an exquisite pitch of perfection.

Etudes et Souvenirs. By Madame Ristori. (Paul Ollendorff.)

ENGLISH POETESSES

(Queen, December 8, 1888.)

England has given to the world one great poetess, Elizabeth Barrett Browning. By her side Mr. Swinburne would place Miss Christina Rossetti, whose New Year hymn he describes as so much the noblest of sacred poems in our language, that there is none which comes near it enough to stand second. 'It is a hymn,' he tells us, 'touched as with the fire, and bathed as in the light of sunbeams, tuned as to chords and cadences of refluent sea-music beyond reach of harp and organ, large echoes of the serene and sonorous tides of heaven.' Much as I admire Miss Rossetti's work, her subtle choice of words, her rich imagery, her artistic naïveté, wherein curious notes of strangeness and simplicity are fantastically blended together, I cannot but think that Mr. Swinburne has, with noble and natural loyalty, placed her on too lofty a pedestal. To me, she is simply a very delightful artist in poetry. This is indeed something so rare that when we meet it we cannot fail to love it, but it is not everything. Beyond it and above it are higher and more sunlit heights of song, a larger vision, and an ampler air, a music at once more passionate and more profound, a creative energy that is born of the spirit, a winged rapture that is born of the soul, a force and fervour of mere utterance that has all the wonder of the prophet, and not a little of the consecration of the priest.

Mrs. Browning is unapproachable by any woman who has ever touched lyre or blown through reed since the days of the great Æolian poetess. But Sappho, who to the antique world was a pillar of flame, is to us but a pillar of shadow. Of her poems, burnt with other most precious work by Byzantine Emperor and by Roman Pope, only a few fragments remain. Possibly they lie mouldering in the scented darkness of an Egyptian tomb, clasped in the withered hand of some long-dead lover. Some Greek monk at Athos may even now be poring over an ancient manuscript, whose crabbed characters conceal lyric or ode by her whom the Greeks spoke of as 'the Poetess' just as they termed Homer 'the Poet,' who was to them the tenth Muse, the flower of the Graces, the child of Erôs, and the pride of Hellas—Sappho, with the sweet voice, the bright, beautiful eyes, the dark hyacinth coloured hair. But, practically, the work of the marvellous singer of Lesbos is entirely lost to us.

We have a few rose-leaves out of her garden, that is all. Literature nowadays survives marble and bronze, but in the old days, in spite of the Roman poet's noble boast, it was not so. The fragile clay vases of the Greeks still keep for us pictures of Sappho, delicately painted in black and red and white; but of her song we have only the echo of an echo.

Of all the women of history, Mrs. Browning is the only one that we could name in any possible or remote conjunction with Sappho.

Sappho was undoubtedly a far more flawless and perfect artist. She stirred the whole antique world more than Mrs. Browning ever stirred our modern age. Never had Love such a singer. Even in the few lines that remain to us the passion seems to scorch and burn. But, as unjust Time, who has crowned her with the barren laurels of fame, has twined with them the dull poppies of oblivion, let us turn from the mere memory of a poetess to one whose song still remains to us as an imperishable glory to our literature; to her who heard the cry of the children from dark mine and crowded factory, and made England weep over its little ones; who, in the feigned sonnets from the Portuguese, sang of the spiritual mystery of Love, and of the intellectual gifts that Love brings to the soul; who had faith in all that is worthy, and enthusiasm for all that is great, and pity for all that suffers; who wrote the Vision of Poets and Casa Guidi Windows and Aurora Leigh.

As one, to whom I owe my love of poetry no less than my love of country, said of her:

Still on our ears

The clear 'Excelsior' from a woman's lip

Rings out across the Apennines, although

The woman's brow lies pale and cold in death

With all the mighty marble dead in Florence.

For while great songs can stir the hearts of men,

Spreading their full vibrations through the world

In ever-widening circles till they reach

The Throne of God, and song becomes a prayer,

And prayer brings down the liberating strength

That kindles nations to heroic deeds,

She lives—the great-souled poetess who saw

From Casa Guidi windows Freedom dawn

On Italy, and gave the glory back

In sunrise hymns to all Humanity!

She lives indeed, and not alone in the heart of Shakespeare's England, but in the heart of Dante's Italy also. To Greek literature she owed her scholarly culture, but modern Italy created her human passion for Liberty. When she crossed the Alps she became filled with a new ardour, and from that fine, eloquent mouth, that we can still see in her portraits, broke forth such a noble and majestic outburst of lyrical song as had not been heard from woman's lips for more than two thousand years. It is pleasant to think that an English poetess was to a certain extent a real factor in bringing about that unity of Italy that was Dante's dream, and if Florence drove her great singer into exile, she at least welcomed within her walls the later singer that England had sent to her.

If one were asked the chief qualities of Mrs. Browning's work, one would say, as Mr. Swinburne said of Byron's, its sincerity and its strength. Faults it, of course, possesses. 'She would rhyme moon to table,' used to be said of her in jest; and certainly no more monstrous rhymes are to be found in all literature than some of those we come across in Mrs. Browning's poems. But her ruggedness was never the result of carelessness. It was deliberate, as her letters to Mr. Horne show very clearly. She refused to sandpaper her muse. She disliked facile smoothness and artificial polish. In her very rejection of art she was an artist. She intended to produce a certain effect by certain means, and she succeeded; and her indifference to complete assonance in rhyme often gives a splendid richness to her verse, and brings into it a pleasurable element of surprise.

In philosophy she was a Platonist, in politics an Opportunist. She attached herself to no particular party. She loved the people when they were king-like, and kings when they showed themselves to be men. Of the real value and motive of poetry she had a most exalted idea. 'Poetry,' she says, in the preface of one of her volumes, 'has been as serious a thing to me as life itself; and life has been a very serious thing. There has been no playing at skittles for me in either. I never mistook pleasure for the final cause of poetry, nor leisure for the hour of the poet. I have done my work so far, not as mere hand and head work apart from the personal being, but as the completest expression of that being to which I could attain.'

It certainly is her completest expression, and through it she realizes her fullest perfection. 'The poet,' she says elsewhere, 'is at once richer and poorer than he used to be; he wears better broadcloth, but speaks no more oracles.' These words give us the keynote to her view of the poet's mission. He was to utter Divine oracles, to be at once inspired prophet and holy priest; and as such we may, I think, without exaggeration, conceive her. She was a Sibyl delivering a message to the world, sometimes through stammering lips, and once at least with blinded eyes, yet always with the true fire and fervour of lofty and unshaken faith, always with the great raptures of a spiritual nature, the high ardours of an impassioned soul. As we read her best poems we feel that, though Apollo's shrine be empty and the bronze tripod overthrown, and the vale of Delphi desolate, still the Pythia is not dead. In our own age she has sung for us, and this land gave her new birth. Indeed, Mrs. Browning is the wisest of the Sibyls, wiser even than that mighty figure whom Michael Angelo has painted on the roof of the Sistine Chapel at Rome, poring over the scroll of mystery, and trying to decipher the secrets of Fate; for she realized that, while knowledge is power, suffering is part of knowledge.

To her influence, almost as much as to the higher education of women, I would be inclined to attribute the really remarkable awakening of woman's song that characterizes the latter half of our century in England. No country has ever had so many poetesses at once. Indeed, when one remembers that the Greeks had only nine muses, one is sometimes apt to fancy that we have too many. And yet the work done by women in the sphere of poetry is really of a very high standard of excellence. In England we have always been prone to underrate the value of tradition in literature. In our eagerness to find a new voice and a fresh mode of music, we have forgotten how beautiful Echo may be. We look first for individuality and personality, and these are, indeed, the chief characteristics of the masterpieces of our literature, either in prose or verse; but deliberate culture and a study of the best models, if united to an artistic temperament and a nature susceptible of exquisite impressions, may produce much that is admirable, much that is worthy of praise. It would be quite impossible to give a complete catalogue of all the women who since Mrs. Browning's day have tried lute and lyre. Mrs. Pfeiffer, Mrs. Hamilton King, Mrs. Augusta Webster, Graham Tomson, Miss Mary Robinson, Jean Ingelow, Miss May Kendall, Miss Nesbit, Miss May Probyn, Mrs. Craik, Mrs. Meynell, Miss Chapman, and many others have done really good work in poetry, either in the grave Dorian mode of thoughtful and intellectual verse, or in the light and graceful forms of old French song, or in the romantic manner of antique ballad, or in that 'moment's monument,' as Rossetti called it, the intense and concentrated sonnet. Occasionally one is tempted to wish that the quick, artistic faculty that women undoubtedly possess developed itself somewhat more in prose and somewhat less in verse. Poetry is for our highest moods, when we wish to be with the gods, and in our poetry nothing but the very best should satisfy us; but prose is for our daily bread, and the lack of good prose is one of the chief blots on our culture. French prose, even in the hands of the most ordinary writers, is always readable, but English prose is detestable. We have a few, a very few, masters, such as they are. We have Carlyle, who should not be imitated; and Mr. Pater, who, through the subtle perfection of his form, is inimitable absolutely; and Mr. Froude, who is useful; and Matthew Arnold, who is a model; and Mr. George Meredith, who is a warning; and Mr. Lang, who is the divine amateur; and Mr. Stevenson, who is the humane artist; and Mr. Ruskin, whose rhythm and colour and fine rhetoric and marvellous music of words are entirely unattainable. But the general prose that one reads in magazines and in newspapers is terribly dull and cumbrous, heavy in movement and uncouth or exaggerated in expression. Possibly some day our women of letters will apply themselves more definitely to prose.

Their light touch, and exquisite ear, and delicate sense of balance and proportion would be of no small service to us. I can fancy women bringing a new manner into our literature.

However, we have to deal here with women as poetesses, and it is interesting to note that, though Mrs. Browning's influence undoubtedly contributed very largely to the development of this new song-movement, if I may so term it, still there seems to have been never a time during the last three hundred years when the women of this kingdom did not cultivate, if not the art, at least the habit, of writing poetry.

Who the first English poetess was I cannot say. I believe it was the Abbess Juliana Berners, who lived in the fifteenth century; but I have no doubt that Mr. Freeman would be able at a moment's notice to produce some wonderful Saxon or Norman poetess, whose works cannot be read without a glossary, and even with its aid are completely unintelligible. For my own part, I am content with the Abbess Juliana, who wrote enthusiastically about hawking; and after her I would mention Anne Askew, who in prison and on the eve of her fiery martyrdom wrote a ballad that has, at any rate, a pathetic and historical interest. Queen Elizabeth's 'most sweet and sententious ditty' on Mary Stuart is highly praised by Puttenham, a contemporary critic, as an example of 'Exargasia, or the Gorgeous in Literature,' which somehow seems a very suitable epithet for such a great Queen's poems. The term she applies to the unfortunate Queen of Scots, 'the daughter of debate,' has, of course, long since passed into literature. The Countess of Pembroke, Sir Philip Sidney's sister, was much admired as a poetess in her day.

In 1613 the 'learned, virtuous, and truly noble ladie,' Elizabeth Carew, published a Tragedie of Marian, the Faire Queene of Jewry, and a few years later the 'noble ladie Diana Primrose' wrote A Chain of Pearl, which is a panegyric on the 'peerless graces' of Gloriana. Mary Morpeth, the friend and admirer of Drummond of Hawthornden; Lady Mary Wroth, to whom

Ben Jonson dedicated The Alchemist; and the Princess Elizabeth, the sister of Charles I., should also be mentioned.

After the Restoration women applied themselves with still greater ardour to the study of literature and the practice of poetry. Margaret, Duchess of Newcastle, was a true woman of letters, and some of her verses are extremely pretty and graceful. Mrs. Aphra Behn was the first Englishwoman who adopted literature as a regular profession. Mrs. Katharine Philips, according to Mr. Gosse, invented sentimentality. As she was praised by Dryden, and mourned by Cowley, let us hope she may be forgiven. Keats came across her poems at Oxford when he was writing Endymion, and found in one of them 'a most delicate fancy of the Fletcher kind'; but I fear nobody reads the Matchless Orinda now. Of Lady Winchelsea's Nocturnal Reverie Wordsworth said that, with the exception of Pope's Windsor Forest, it was the only poem of the period intervening between Paradise Lost and Thomson's Seasons that contained a single new image of external nature. Lady Rachel Russell, who may be said to have inaugurated the letter-writing literature of England; Eliza Haywood, who is immortalized by the badness of her work, and has a niche in The Dunciad; and the Marchioness of Wharton, whose poems Waller said he admired, are very remarkable types, the finest of them being, of course, the first named, who was a woman of heroic mould and of a most noble dignity of nature.

Indeed, though the English poetesses up to the time of Mrs. Browning cannot be said to have produced any work of absolute genius, they are certainly interesting figures, fascinating subjects for study. Amongst them we find Lady Mary Wortley Montague, who had all the caprice of Cleopatra, and whose letters are delightful reading; Mrs. Centlivre, who wrote one brilliant comedy; Lady Anne Barnard, whose Auld Robin Gray was described by Sir Walter Scott as 'worth all the dialogues Corydon and Phillis have together spoken from the days of Theocritus downwards,' and is certainly a very beautiful and touching poem; Esther Vanhomrigh and Hester Johnson, the Vanessa and the Stella of Dean Swift's life; Mrs. Thrale, the friend of the great lexicographer; the worthy Mrs. Barbauld; the excellent Miss Hannah More; the industrious Joanna Baillie; the admirable Mrs. Chapone, whose

Ode to Solitude always fills me with the wildest passion for society, and who will at least be remembered as the patroness of the establishment at which Becky Sharp was educated; Miss Anna Seward, who was called 'The Swan of Lichfield'; poor L. E. L. whom Disraeli described in one of his clever letters to his sister as 'the personification of Brompton—pink satin dress, white satin shoes, red cheeks, snub nose, and her hair à la Sappho'; Mrs. Ratcliffe, who introduced the romantic novel, and has consequently much to answer for; the beautiful Duchess of Devonshire, of whom Gibbon said that she was 'made for something better than a Duchess'; the two wonderful sisters, Lady Dufferin and Mrs. Norton; Mrs. Tighe, whose Psyche Keats read with pleasure; Constantia Grierson, a marvellous blue-stocking in her time; Mrs. Hemans; pretty, charming 'Perdita,' who flirted alternately with poetry and the Prince Regent, played divinely in the Winter's Tale, was brutally attacked by Gifford, and has left us a pathetic little poem on a Snowdrop; and Emily Brontë, whose poems are instinct with tragic power, and seem often on the verge of being great.

Old fashions in literature are not so pleasant as old fashions in dress. I like the costume of the age of powder better than the poetry of the age of Pope. But if one adopts the historical standpoint—and this is, indeed, the only standpoint from which we can ever form a fair estimate of work that is not absolutely of the highest order—we cannot fail to see that many of the English poetesses who preceded Mrs. Browning were women of no ordinary talent, and that if the majority of them looked upon poetry simply as a department of belles lettres, so in most cases did their contemporaries. Since Mrs. Browning's day our woods have become full of singing birds, and if I venture to ask them to apply themselves more to prose and less to song, it is not that I like poetical prose, but that I love the prose of poets.

VENUS OR VICTORY

(Pall Mall Gazette, February 24, 1888.)

There are certain problems in archæology that seem to possess a real romantic interest, and foremost among these is the question of the so-called

Venus of Melos. Who is she, this marble mutilated goddess whom Gautier loved, to whom Heine bent his knee? What sculptor wrought her, and for what shrine? Whose hands walled her up in that rude niche where the Melian peasant found her? What symbol of her divinity did she carry? Was it apple of gold or shield of bronze? Where is her city and what was her name among gods and men? The last writer on this fascinating subject is Mr. Stillman, who in a most interesting book recently published in America, claims that the work of art in question is no sea-born and foam-born Aphrodite, but the very Victory Without Wings that once stood in the little chapel outside the gates of the Acropolis at Athens. So long ago as 1826, that is to say six years after the discovery of the statue, the Venus hypothesis was violently attacked by Millingen, and from that time to this the battle of the archæologists has never ceased. Mr. Stillman, who fights, of course, under Millingen's banner, points out that the statue is not of the Venus type at all, being far too heroic in character to correspond to the Greek conception of Aphrodite at any period of their artistic development, but that it agrees distinctly with certain well-known statues of Victory, such as the celebrated 'Victory of Brescia.' The latter is in bronze, is later, and has the wings, but the type is unmistakable, and though not a reproduction it is certainly a recollection of the Melian statue. The representation of Victory on the coin of Agathocles is also obviously of the Melian type, and in the museum of Naples is a terra-cotta Victory in almost the identical action and drapery. As for Dumont d'Urville's statement that, when the statue was discovered, one hand held an apple and the other a fold of the drapery, the latter is obviously a mistake, and the whole evidence on the subject is so contradictory that no reliance can be placed on the statement made by the French Consul and the French naval officers, none of whom seems to have taken the trouble to ascertain whether the arm and hand now in the Louvre were really found in the same niche as the statue at all. At any rate, these fragments seem to be of extremely inferior workmanship, and they are so imperfect that they are quite worthless as data for measure or opinion. So far, Mr. Stillman is on old ground. His real artistic discovery is this. In working about the Acropolis of Athens, some years ago, he photographed among other sculptures the mutilated Victories in the Temple of Nikè Apteros, the 'Wingless Victory,' the little Ionic temple in which stood that statue of Victory of which it was said that 'the Athenians made her without wings that she might never leave Athens.' Looking over the photographs afterwards, when the impression of the comparatively diminutive size had passed, he was struck with the close resemblance of the type to that of the Melian statue. Now, this resemblance is so striking that it cannot be questioned by any one who has an eye for form. There are the same large heroic proportions, the same ampleness of physical development, and the same treatment of drapery, and there is also that perfect spiritual kinship which, to any true antiquarian, is one of the most valuable modes of evidence. Now it is generally admitted on both sides that the Melian statue is probably Attic in its origin, and belongs certainly to the period between Phidias and Praxiteles, that is to say, to the age of Scopas, if it be not actually the work of Scopas himself; and as it is to Scopas that these bas-reliefs have been always attributed, the similarity of style can, on Mr. Stillman's hypothesis, be easily accounted for.

As regards the appearance of the statue in Melos, Mr. Stillman points out that Melos belonged to Athens as late as she had any Greek allegiance, and that it is probable that the statue was sent there for concealment on the occasion of some siege or invasion. When this took place, Mr. Stillman does not pretend to decide with any degree of certainty, but it is evident that it must have been subsequent to the establishment of the Roman hegemony, as the brickwork of the niche in which the statue was found is clearly Roman in character, and before the time of Pausanias and Pliny, as neither of these antiquaries mentions the statue. Accepting, then, the statue as that of the Victory Without Wings, Mr. Stillman agrees with Millingen in supposing that in her left hand she held a bronze shield, the lower rim of which rested on the left knee where some marks of the kind are easily recognizable, while with her right hand she traced, or had just finished tracing, the names of the great heroes of Athens. Valentin's objection, that if this were so the left thigh would incline outwards so as to secure a balance, Mr. Stillman meets partly by the analogy of the Victory of Brescia and partly by the evidence of Nature herself; for he has had a model photographed in the same position as the statue and holding a shield in the manner he proposes in his restoration. The result is precisely the contrary to that which Valentin assumes. Of course, Mr.

Stillman's solution of the whole matter must not be regarded as an absolutely scientific demonstration. It is simply an induction in which a kind of artistic instinct, not communicable or equally valuable to all people, has had the greatest part, but to this mode of interpretation archæologists as a class have been far too indifferent; and it is certain that in the present case it has given us a theory which is most fruitful and suggestive.

The little temple of Nikè Apteros has had, as Mr. Stillman reminds us, a destiny unique of its kind. Like the Parthenon, it was standing little more than two hundred years ago, but during the Turkish occupation it was razed, and its stones all built into the great bastion which covered the front of the Acropolis and blocked up the staircase to the Propylæa. It was dug out and restored, nearly every stone in its place, by two German architects during the reign of Otho, and it stands again just as Pausanias described it on the spot where old Ægeus watched for the return of Theseus from Crete. In the distance are Salamis and Ægina, and beyond the purple hills lies Marathon. If the Melian statue be indeed the Victory Without Wings, she had no unworthy shrine.

There are some other interesting essays in Mr. Stillman's book on the wonderful topographical knowledge of Ithaca displayed in the Odyssey, and discussions of this kind are always interesting as long as there is no attempt to represent Homer as the ordinary literary man; but the article on the Melian statue is by far the most important and the most delightful. Some people will, no doubt, regret the possibility of the disappearance of the old name, and as Venus not as Victory will still worship the stately goddess, but there are others who will be glad to see in her the image and ideal of that spiritual enthusiasm to which Athens owed her liberty, and by which alone can liberty be won.

On the Track of Ulysses; together with an Excursion in Quest of the So-called Venus of Melos. By W. J. Stillman. (Houghton, Mifflin and Co., Boston.)

M. CARO ON GEORGE SAND

(Pall Mall Gazette, April 14, 1888.)

The biography of a very great man from the pen of a very ladylike writer—this is the best description we can give of M. Caro's Life of George Sand. The late Professor of the Sorbonne could chatter charmingly about culture, and had all the fascinating insincerity of an accomplished phrase-maker; being an extremely superior person he had a great contempt for Democracy and its doings, but he was always popular with the Duchesses of the Faubourg, as there was nothing in history or in literature that he could not explain away for their edification; having never done anything remarkable he was naturally elected a member of the Academy, and he always remained loyal to the traditions of that thoroughly respectable and thoroughly pretentious institution. In fact, he was just the sort of man who should never have attempted to write a Life of George Sand or to interpret George Sand's genius. He was too feminine to appreciate the grandeur of that large womanly nature, too much of a dilettante to realize the masculine force of that strong and ardent mind. He never gets at the secret of George Sand, and never brings us near to her wonderful personality. He looks on her simply as a littérateur, as a writer of pretty stories of country life and of charming, if somewhat exaggerated, romances. But George Sand was much more than this. Beautiful as are such books as Consuelo and Mauprat, François le Champi and La Mare au Diable, yet in none of them is she adequately expressed, by none of them is she adequately revealed. As Mr. Matthew Arnold said, many years ago, 'We do not know George Sand unless we feel the spirit which goes through her work as a whole.' With this spirit, however, M. Caro has no sympathy. Madame Sand's doctrines are antediluvian, he tells us, her philosophy is quite dead and her ideas of social regeneration are Utopian, incoherent and absurd. The best thing for us to do is to forget these silly dreams and to read Teverino and Le Secrétaire Intime. Poor M. Caro! This spirit, which he treats with such airy flippancy, is the very leaven of modern life. It is remoulding the world for us and fashioning our age anew. If it is antediluvian, it is so because the deluge is yet to come; if it is Utopian, then Utopia must be added to our geographies. To what curious straits M. Caro is driven by his violent prejudices may be estimated by the fact that he tries to class George Sand's novels with the old Chansons de geste, the stories of adventure characteristic of primitive literatures; whereas in using fiction as a vehicle of thought, and romance as a means of influencing the social ideals of her age, George Sand was merely carrying out the traditions of Voltaire and Rousseau, of Diderot and of Chateaubriand. The novel, says M. Caro, must be allied either to poetry or to science. That it has found in philosophy one of its strongest allies seems not to have occurred to him. In an English critic such a view might possibly be excusable. Our greatest novelists, such as Fielding, Scott and Thackeray, cared little for the philosophy of their age. But coming, as it does, from a French critic, the statement seems to show a strange want of recognition of one of the most important elements of French fiction. Nor, even in the narrow limits that he has imposed upon himself, can M. Caro be said to be a very fortunate or felicitous critic. To take merely one instance out of many, he says nothing of George Sand's delightful treatment of art and the artist's life. And yet how exquisitely does she analyse each separate art and present it to us in its relation to life! In Consuelo she tells us of music; in Horace of authorship; in Le Château des Désertes of acting; in Les Maîtres Mosaïstes of mosaic work; in Le Château de Pictordu of portrait painting; and in La Daniella of the painting of landscape. What Mr. Ruskin and Mr. Browning have done for England she did for France. She invented an art literature. It is unnecessary, however, to discuss any of M. Caro's minor failings, for the whole effect of the book, so far as it attempts to portray for us the scope and character of George Sand's genius, is entirely spoiled by the false attitude assumed from the beginning, and though the dictum may seem to many harsh and exclusive, we cannot help feeling that an absolute incapacity for appreciating the spirit of a great writer is no qualification for writing a treatise on the subject.

As for Madame Sand's private life, which is so intimately connected with her art (for, like Goethe, she had to live her romances before she could write them), M. Caro says hardly anything about it. He passes it over with a modesty that almost makes one blush, and for fear of wounding the susceptibilities of those grandes dames whose passions M. Paul Bourget analyses with such subtlety, he transforms her mother, who was a typical French grisette, into 'a very amiable and spirituelle milliner'! It must be admitted that Joseph Surface himself could hardly show greater tact and delicacy, though we ourselves must plead guilty to preferring Madame Sand's own description of her as an 'enfant du vieux pavé de Paris.'

George Sand. By the late Elmé Marie Caro. Translated by Gustave Masson, B.A., Assistant Master, Harrow School. 'Great French Writers' Series. (Routledge and Sons.)

A FASCINATING BOOK

(Woman's World, November 1888.)

Mr. Alan Cole's carefully-edited translation of M. Lefébure's history of Embroidery and Lace is one of the most fascinating books that has appeared on this delightful subject. M. Lefébure is one of the administrators of the Musée des Arts Décoratifs at Paris, besides being a lace manufacturer; and his work has not merely an important historical value, but as a handbook of technical instruction it will be found of the greatest service by all needle-women. Indeed, as the translator himself points out, M. Lefébure's book suggests the question whether it is not rather by the needle and the bobbin, than by the brush, the graver or the chisel, that the influence of woman should assert itself in the arts. In Europe, at any rate, woman is sovereign in the domain of art-needlework, and few men would care to dispute with her the right of using those delicate implements so intimately associated with the dexterity of her nimble and slender fingers; nor is there any reason why the productions of embroidery should not, as Mr. Alan Cole suggests, be placed on the same level with those of painting, engraving and sculpture, though there must always be a great difference between those purely decorative arts that glorify their own material and the more imaginative arts in which the material is, as it were, annihilated, and absorbed into the creation of a new form. In the beautifying of modern houses it certainly must be admitted—indeed, it should be more generally recognized than it is—that rich embroidery on hangings and curtains, portières, couches and the like, produces a far more decorative and far more artistic effect than can be gained from our somewhat wearisome English practice of covering the walls with pictures and engravings; and the almost complete disappearance of embroidery from dress has robbed modern costume of one of the chief elements of grace and fancy.

That, however, a great improvement has taken place in English embroidery during the last ten or fifteen years cannot, I think, be denied. It is shown, not merely in the work of individual artists, such as Mrs. Holiday, Miss May Morris and others, but also in the admirable productions of the South Kensington School of Embroidery (the best—indeed, the only real good—school that South Kensington has produced). It is pleasant to note on turning over the leaves of M. Lefébure's book, that in this we are merely carrying out certain old traditions of Early English art. In the seventh century, St. Ethelreda, first abbess of the monastery of Ely, made an offering to St. Cuthbert of a sacred ornament she had worked with gold and precious stones, and the cope and maniple of St. Cuthbert, which are preserved at Durham, are considered to be specimens of opus Anglicanum. In the year 800, the Bishop of Durham allotted the income of a farm of two hundred acres for life to an embroideress named Eanswitha, in consideration of her keeping in repair the vestments of the clergy in his diocese. The battle standard of King Alfred was embroidered by Danish Princesses; and the Anglo-Saxon Gudric gave Alcuid a piece of land, on condition that she instructed his daughter in needle-work. Queen Mathilda bequeathed to the Abbey of the Holy Trinity at Caen a tunic embroidered at Winchester by the wife of one Alderet; and when William presented himself to the English nobles, after the Battle of Hastings, he wore a mantle covered with Anglo-Saxon embroideries, which is probably, M. Lefébure suggests, the same as that mentioned in the inventory of the Bayeux Cathedral, where, after the entry relating to the broderie à telle (representing the conquest of England), two mantles are described—one of King William, 'all of gold, powdered with crosses and blossoms of gold, and edged along the lower border with an orphrey of figures.' The most splendid example of the opus Anglicanum now in existence is, of course, the Syon cope at the South Kensington Museum; but English work seems to have been celebrated all over the Continent. Pope Innocent iv. so admired the splendid vestments worn by the English clergy in 1246, that he ordered similar articles from Cistercian monasteries in England. St. Dunstan, the artistic English monk, was known as a designer for embroideries; and the stole of St. Thomas à Becket is still preserved in the cathedral at Sens, and shows us the interlaced scroll-forms used by Anglo-Saxon MS. illuminators.

How far this modern artistic revival of rich and delicate embroidery will bear fruit depends, of course, almost entirely on the energy and study that women are ready to devote to it; but I think that it must be admitted that all our decorative arts in Europe at present have, at least, this element of strength—that they are in immediate relationship with the decorative arts of Asia. Wherever we find in European history a revival of decorative art, it has, I fancy, nearly always been due to Oriental influence and contact with Oriental nations. Our own keenly intellectual art has more than once been ready to sacrifice real decorative beauty either to imitative presentation or to ideal motive. It has taken upon itself the burden of expression, and has sought to interpret the secrets of thought and passion. In its marvellous truth of presentation it has found its strength, and yet its weakness is there also. It is never with impunity that an art seeks to mirror life. If Truth has her revenge upon those who do not follow her, she is often pitiless to her worshippers. In Byzantium the two arts met—Greek art, with its intellectual sense of form, and its quick sympathy with humanity; Oriental art, with its gorgeous materialism, its frank rejection of imitation, its wonderful secrets of craft and colour, its splendid textures, its rare metals and jewels, its marvellous and priceless traditions. They had, indeed, met before, but in Byzantium they were married; and the sacred tree of the Persians, the palm of Zoroaster, was embroidered on the hem of the garments of the Western world. Even the Iconoclasts, the Philistines of theological history, who, in one of those strange outbursts of rage against Beauty that seem to occur only amongst European nations, rose up against the wonder and magnificence of the new art, served merely to distribute its secrets more widely; and in the Liber Pontificalis, written in 687 by Athanasius, the librarian, we read of an influx into Rome of gorgeous embroideries, the work of men who had arrived from Constantinople and from Greece. The triumph of the Mussulman gave the decorative art of Europe a new departure—that very principle of their religion that forbade the actual representation of any object in nature being of the greatest artistic service to them, though it was not, of course, strictly carried out. The Saracens introduced into Sicily the art of weaving silken and golden fabrics; and from Sicily the manufacture of fine stuffs spread to the North of Italy, and became localized in Genoa, Florence, Venice, and other towns. A still greater art-movement took place in Spain under the Moors and Saracens, who brought over workmen from Persia to make beautiful things for them. M. Lefébure tells us of Persian embroidery penetrating as far as Andalusia; and Almeria, like Palermo, had its Hôtel des Tiraz, which rivalled the Hôtel des Tiraz at Bagdad, tiraz being the generic name for ornamental tissues and costumes made with them. Spangles (those pretty little discs of gold, silver, or polished steel, used in certain embroidery for dainty glinting effects) were a Saracenic invention; and Arabic letters often took the place of letters in the Roman characters for use in inscriptions upon embroidered robes and Middle Age tapestries, their decorative value being so much greater. The book of crafts by Etienne Boileau, provost of the merchants in 1258–1268, contains a curious enumeration of the different craft-guilds of Paris, among which we find 'the tapiciers, or makers of the tapis sarrasinois (or Saracen cloths), who say that their craft is for the service only of churches, or great men like kings and counts'; and, indeed, even in our own day, nearly all our words descriptive of decorative textures and decorative methods point to an Oriental origin. What the inroads of the Mohammedans did for Sicily and Spain, the return of the Crusaders did for the other countries of Europe. The nobles who left for Palestine clad in armour, came back in the rich stuffs of the East; and their costumes, pouches (aumônières sarrasinoises), and caparisons excited the admiration of the needle-workers of the West. Matthew Paris says that at the sacking of Antioch, in 1098, gold, silver and priceless costumes were so equally distributed among the Crusaders, that many who the night before were famishing and imploring relief, suddenly found themselves overwhelmed with wealth; and Robert de Clair tells us of the wonderful fêtes that followed the capture of Constantinople. The thirteenth century, as M. Lefébure points out, was conspicuous for an increased demand in the West for embroidery. Many Crusaders made offerings to churches of plunder from Palestine; and St. Louis, on his return from the first Crusade, offered thanks at St. Denis to God for mercies bestowed on him during his six years' absence and travel, and presented some richly embroidered stuffs to be used on great occasions as coverings to the reliquaries containing the relics of holy martyrs. European embroidery, having thus become possessed of new materials and wonderful methods, developed on its own intellectual and imitative lines, inclining, as it went on, to the purely pictorial, and seeking to rival painting, and to produce landscapes and figure-subjects with elaborate perspective and subtle aerial effects. A fresh Oriental influence, however, came through the Dutch and the Portuguese, and the famous Compagnie des Grandes Indes; and M. Lefébure gives an illustration of a door-hanging now in the Cluny Museum, where we find the French fleurs-de-lys intermixed with Indian ornament. The hangings of Madame de Maintenon's room at Fontainebleau, which were embroidered at St. Cyr, represent Chinese scenery upon a jonquil-yellow ground.

Clothes were sent out ready cut to the East to be embroidered, and many of the delightful coats of the period of Louis xv. and Louis xvi. owe their dainty decoration to the needles of Chinese artists. In our own day the influence of the East is strongly marked. Persia has sent us her carpets for patterns, and Cashmere her lovely shawls, and India her dainty muslins finely worked with gold thread palmates, and stitched over with iridescent beetles' wings. We are beginning now to dye by Oriental methods, and the silk robes of China and Japan have taught us new wonders of colour-combination, and new subtleties of delicate design. Whether we have yet learned to make a wise use of what we have acquired is less certain. If books produce an effect, this book of M. Lefébure should certainly make us study with still deeper interest the whole question of embroidery, and by those who already work with their needles it will be found full of most fertile suggestion and most admirable advice.

Even to read of the marvellous works of embroidery that were fashioned in bygone ages is pleasant. Time has kept a few fragments of Greek embroidery of the fourth century b.c. for us. One is figured in M. Lefébure's book—a chain-stitch embroidery of yellow flax upon a mulberry-coloured worsted material, with graceful spirals and palmetto-patterns: and another, a tapestried cloth powdered with ducks, was reproduced in the Woman's World some months ago for an article by Mr. Alan Cole. [115] Now and then we find in the tomb of some dead Egyptian a piece of delicate work. In the treasury at Ratisbon is preserved a specimen of Byzantine embroidery on which the Emperor Constantine is depicted riding on a white palfrey, and receiving homage from the East and West. Metz has a red silk cope wrought with great eagles, the gift of Charlemagne, and Bayeux the needle-wrought epic of Queen Matilda. But where is the great crocus-coloured robe, wrought for Athena, on which the gods fought against the giants? Where is the huge velarium that Nero stretched across the Colosseum at Rome, on which was represented the starry sky, and Apollo driving a chariot drawn by steeds? How one would like to see the curious table-napkins wrought for Heliogabalus, on which were displayed all the dainties and viands that could be wanted for a feast; or the mortuary-cloth of King Chilperic, with its three hundred golden bees; or the fantastic robes that excited the indignation of the Bishop of Pontus, and were embroidered with 'lions, panthers, bears, dogs, forests, rocks, hunters—all, in fact, that painters can copy from nature.' Charles of Orleans had a coat, on the sleeves of which were embroidered the verses of a song beginning 'Madame, je suis tout joyeux,' the musical accompaniment of the words being wrought in gold thread, and each note, of square shape in those days, formed with four pearls. [116] The room prepared in the palace at Rheims for the use of Queen Joan of Burgundy was decorated with 'thirteen hundred and twenty-one papegauts (parrots) made in broidery and blazoned with the King's arms, and five hundred and sixty-one butterflies, whose wings were similarly ornamented with the Queen's arms—the whole worked in fine gold.' Catherine de Medicis had a mourning-bed made for her 'of black velvet embroidered with pearls and powdered with crescents and suns.' Its curtains were of damask, 'with leafy wreaths and garlands figured upon a gold and silver ground, and fringed along the edges with broideries of pearls,' and it stood in a room hung with rows of the Queen's devices in cut black velvet on cloth of silver. Louis xiv. had gold-embroidered caryatides fifteen feet high in his apartment. The state bed of Sobieski, King of Poland, was made of Smyrna gold brocade embroidered in turquoises and pearls, with verses from the Koran; its supports were of silver-gilt, beautifully chased and profusely set with enamelled and jewelled medallions. He had taken it from the Turkish camp before Vienna, and the standard of Mahomet had stood under it. The Duchess de la Ferté wore a dress of reddish-brown velvet, the skirt of which, adjusted in graceful folds, was held up by big butterflies made of Dresden china; the front was a tablier of cloth of silver, upon which was embroidered an orchestra of musicians arranged in a pyramidal group, consisting of a series of six ranks of performers, with beautiful instruments wrought in raised needle-work. 'Into the night go one and all,' as Mr. Henley sings in his charming Ballade of Dead Actors.

Many of the facts related by M. Lefébure about the embroiderers' guilds are also extremely interesting. Etienne Boileau, in his book of crafts, to which I have already alluded, tells us that a member of the guild was prohibited from using gold of less value than 'eight sous (about 6s.) the skein; he was bound to use the best silk, and never to mix thread with silk, because that made the work false and bad.' The test or trial piece prescribed for a worker who was the son of a master-embroiderer was 'a single figure, a sixth of the natural size, to be shaded in gold'; whilst one not the son of a master was required to produce 'a complete incident with many figures.' The book of crafts also mentions 'cutters-out and stencillers and illuminators' amongst those employed in the industry of embroidery. In 1551 the Parisian Corporation of Embroiderers issued a notice that 'for the future, the colouring in representations of nude figures and faces should be done in three or four gradations of carnation-dyed silk, and not, as formerly, in white silks.' During the fifteenth century every household of any position retained the services of an embroiderer by the year. The preparation of colours also, whether for painting or for dyeing threads and textile fabrics, was a matter which, M. Lefébure points out, received close attention from the artists of the Middle Ages. Many undertook long journeys to obtain the more famous recipes, which they filed, subsequently adding to and correcting them as experience dictated. Nor were great artists above making and supplying designs for embroidery. Raphael made designs for Francis i., and Boucher for Louis xv.; and in the Ambras collection at Vienna is a superb set of sacerdotal robes from designs by the brothers Van Eyck and their pupils. Early in the sixteenth century books of embroidery designs were produced, and their success was so great that in a few years French, German, Italian, Flemish, and English publishers spread broadcast books of design made by their best engravers. In the same century, in order to give the designers opportunity of studying directly from nature, Jean Robin opened a garden with conservatories, in which he cultivated strange varieties of plants then but little known in our latitudes. The rich brocades and brocadelles of the time are characterized by the introduction of large flowery patterns, with pomegranates and other fruits with fine foliage.

The second part of M. Lefébure's book is devoted to the history of lace, and though some may not find it quite as interesting as the earlier portion it will more than repay perusal; and those who still work in this delicate and fanciful art will find many valuable suggestions in it, as well as a large number of exceedingly beautiful designs. Compared to embroidery, lace seems comparatively modern. M. Lefébure and Mr. Alan Cole tell us that there is no reliable or documentary evidence to prove the existence of lace before the fifteenth century. Of course in the East, light tissues, such as gauzes, muslins, and nets, were made at very early times, and were used as veils and scarfs after the manner of subsequent laces, and women enriched them with some sort of embroidery, or varied the openness of them by here and there drawing out threads. The threads of fringes seem also to have been plaited and knotted together, and the borders of one of the many fashions of Roman toga were of open reticulated weaving. The Egyptian Museum at the Louvre has a curious network embellished with glass beads; and the monk Reginald, who took part in opening the tomb of St. Cuthbert at Durham in the twelfth century, writes that the Saint's shroud had a fringe of linen threads an inch long, surmounted by a border, 'worked upon the threads,' with representations of birds and pairs of beasts, there being between each such pair a branching tree, a survival of the palm of Zoroaster, to which I have before alluded. Our authors, however, do not in these examples recognize lace, the production of which involves more refined and artistic methods, and postulates a combination of skill and varied execution carried to a higher degree of perfection. Lace, as we know it, seems to have had its origin in the habit of embroidering linen. White embroidery on linen has, M. Lefébure remarks, a cold and monotonous aspect; that with coloured threads is brighter and gayer in effect, but is apt to fade in frequent washing; but white embroidery relieved by open spaces in, or shapes cut from, the linen ground, is possessed of an entirely new charm; and from a sense of this the birth may be traced of an art in the result of which happy contrasts are effected between ornamental details of close texture and others of open-work.

Soon, also, was suggested the idea that, instead of laboriously withdrawing threads from stout linen, it would be more convenient to introduce a needle-made pattern into an open network ground, which was called a lacis. Of this kind of embroidery many specimens are extant. The Cluny Museum possesses a linen cap said to have belonged to Charles v.; and an alb of linen drawn-thread work, supposed to have been made by Anne of Bohemia (1527), is preserved in the cathedral at Prague. Catherine de Medicis had a bed draped with squares of réseuil, or lacis, and it is recorded that 'the girls and servants of her household consumed much time in making squares of réseuil.' The interesting pattern-books for open-ground embroidery, of which the first was published in 1527 by Pierre Quinty, of Cologne, supply us with the means of tracing the stages in the transition from white thread embroidery to needle-point lace. We meet in them with a style of needle-work which differs from embroidery in not being wrought upon a stuff foundation. It is, in fact, true lace, done, as it were, 'in the air,' both ground and pattern being entirely produced by the lace-maker.

The elaborate use of lace in costume was, of course, largely stimulated by the fashion of wearing ruffs, and their companion cuffs or sleeves. Catherine de Medicis induced one Frederic Vinciolo to come from Italy and make ruffs and gadrooned collars, the fashion of which she started in France; and Henry iii. was so punctilious over his ruffs that he would iron and goffer his cuffs and collars himself rather than see their pleats limp and out of shape. The pattern-books also gave a great impulse to the art. M. Lefébure mentions German books with patterns of eagles, heraldic emblems, hunting scenes, and plants and leaves belonging to Northern vegetation; and Italian books, in which the motifs consist of oleander blossoms, and elegant wreaths and scrolls, landscapes with mythological scenes, and hunting episodes, less realistic than the Northern ones, in which appear fauns, and nymphs or amorini shooting arrows. With regard to these patterns, M. Lefébure notices a curious fact. The oldest painting in which lace is depicted is that of a lady, by Carpaccio, who died about 1523. The cuffs of the lady are edged with a narrow lace, the pattern of which reappears in Vecellio's Corona, a book not published until 1591. This particular pattern was, therefore, in use at least eighty years before it got into circulation with other published patterns.

It was not, however, till the seventeenth century that lace acquired a really independent character and individuality, and M. Duplessis states that the production of the more noteworthy of early laces owes more to the influence of men than to that of women. The reign of Louis xiv. witnessed the production of the most stately needle-point laces, the transformation of Venetian point, and the growth of Points d'Alençon, d'Argentan, de Bruxelles and d'Angleterre.

The king, aided by Colbert, determined to make France the centre, if possible, for lace manufacture, sending for this purpose both to Venice and to Flanders for workers. The studio of the Gobelins supplied designs. The dandies had their huge rabatos or bands falling from beneath the chin over the breast, and great prelates, like Bossuet and Fénelon, wore their wonderful albs and rochets. It is related of a collar made at Venice for Louis xiv. that the lace-workers, being unable to find sufficiently fine horse-hair, employed some of their own hairs instead, in order to secure that marvellous delicacy of work which they aimed at producing.

In the eighteenth century, Venice, finding that laces of lighter texture were sought after, set herself to make rose-point; and at the Court of Louis xv. the choice of lace was regulated by still more elaborate etiquette. The Revolution, however, ruined many of the manufactures. Alençon survived, and Napoleon encouraged it, and endeavoured to renew the old rules about the necessity of wearing point-lace at Court receptions. A wonderful piece of lace, powdered over with devices of bees, and costing 40,000 francs, was ordered. It was begun for the Empress Josephine, but in the course of its making her escutcheons were replaced by those of Marie Louise.

M. Lefébure concludes his interesting history by stating very clearly his attitude towards machine-made lace. 'It would be an obvious loss to art,' he says, 'should the making of lace by hand become extinct, for machinery, as skilfully devised as possible, cannot do what the hand does.' It can give us 'the results of processes, not the creations of artistic handicraft.' Art is absent 'where formal calculation pretends to supersede emotion'; it is absent 'where no trace can be detected of intelligence guiding handicraft, whose hesitancies even possess peculiar charm . . . cheapness is never commendable in respect of things which are not absolute necessities; it lowers artistic standard.' These are admirable remarks, and with them we take leave of this fascinating book, with its delightful illustrations, its charming anecdotes, its excellent advice. Mr. Alan Cole deserves the thanks of all who are interested in art for bringing this book before the public in so attractive and so inexpensive a form.

Embroidery and Lace: Their Manufacture and History from the Remotest Antiquity to the Present Day. Translated and enlarged by Alan S. Cole from the French of Ernest Lefébure. (Grevel and Co.)

HENLEY'S POEMS

(Woman's World, December 1888.)

'If I were king,' says Mr. Henley, in one of his most modest rondeaus,

'Art should aspire, yet ugliness be dear;

Beauty, the shaft, should speed with wit for feather;

And love, sweet love, should never fall to sere,

If I were king.'

And these lines contain, if not the best criticism of his own work, certainly a very complete statement of his aim and motive as a poet. His little Book of Verses reveals to us an artist who is seeking to find new methods of expression and has not merely a delicate sense of beauty and a brilliant, fantastic wit, but a real passion also for what is horrible, ugly, or grotesque. No doubt, everything that is worthy of existence is worthy also of art—at least, one would like to think so—but while echo or mirror can repeat for us a beautiful thing, to render artistically a thing that is ugly requires the most exquisite alchemy of form, the most subtle magic of transformation. To me there is more of the cry of Marsyas than of the singing of Apollo in the earlier poems of Mr. Henley's volume, In Hospital: Rhymes and Rhythms, as he calls them. But it is impossible to deny their power. Some of them are like bright, vivid pastels; others like charcoal drawings, with dull blacks and murky whites; others like etchings with deeply-bitten lines, and abrupt contrasts, and clever colour-suggestions. In fact, they are like anything and everything, except perfected poems—that they certainly are not. They are still in the twilight. They are preludes, experiments, inspired jottings in a note-book, and should be heralded by a design of 'Genius Making Sketches.' Rhyme gives architecture as well as melody to verse; it gives that delightful sense of limitation which in all the arts is so pleasurable, and is, indeed, one of the secrets of perfection; it will whisper, as a French critic has said, 'things unexpected and charming, things with strange and remote relations to each other,' and bind them together in indissoluble bonds of beauty; and in his constant rejection of rhyme, Mr. Henley seems to me to have abdicated half his power. He is a roi en exil who has thrown away some of the strings of his lute; a poet who has forgotten the fairest part of his kingdom.

However, all work criticizes itself. Here is one of Mr. Henley's inspired jottings. According to the temperament of the reader, it will serve either as a model or as the reverse:

As with varnish red and glistening

Dripped his hair; his feet were rigid;

Raised, he settled stiffly sideways:

You could see the hurts were spinal.

He had fallen from an engine,

And been dragged along the metals.

It was hopeless, and they knew it;

So they covered him, and left him.

As he lay, by fits half sentient,

Inarticulately moaning,

With his stockinged feet protruded

Sharp and awkward from the blankets,

To his bed there came a woman,

Stood and looked and sighed a little,

And departed without speaking,

As himself a few hours after.

I was told she was his sweetheart.

They were on the eve of marriage.

She was quiet as a statue,

But her lip was gray and writhen.

In this poem, the rhythm and the music, such as it is, are obvious—perhaps a little too obvious. In the following I see nothing but ingeniously printed prose. It is a description—and a very accurate one—of a scene in a hospital ward. The medical students are supposed to be crowding round the doctor. What I quote is only a fragment, but the poem itself is a fragment:

So shows the ring

Seen, from behind, round a conjuror

Doing his pitch in the street.

High shoulders, low shoulders, broad shoulders, narrow ones,

Round, square, and angular, serry and shove;

While from within a voice,

Gravely and weightily fluent,

Sounds; and then ceases; and suddenly

(Look at the stress of the shoulders!)

Out of a quiver of silence,

Over the hiss of the spray,

Comes a low cry, and the sound

Of breath quick intaken through teeth

Clenched in resolve. And the master

Breaks from the crowd, and goes,

Wiping his hands,

To the next bed, with his pupils

Flocking and whispering behind him.

Now one can see.

Case Number One

Sits (rather pale) with his bedclothes

Stripped up, and showing his foot

(Alas, for God's image!)

Swaddled in wet white lint

Brilliantly hideous with red.

Théophile Gautier once said that Flaubert's style was meant to be read, and his own style to be looked at. Mr. Henley's unrhymed rhythms form very dainty designs, from a typographical point of view. From the point of view of literature, they are a series of vivid, concentrated impressions, with a keen grip of fact, a terrible actuality, and an almost masterly power of picturesque presentation. But the poetic form—what of that?

Well, let us pass to the later poems, to the rondels and rondeaus, the sonnets and quatorzains, the echoes and the ballades. How brilliant and fanciful this is! The Toyokuni colour-print that suggested it could not be more delightful. It seems to have kept all the wilful fantastic charm of the original:

Was I a Samurai renowned,

Two-sworded, fierce, immense of bow?

A histrion angular and profound?

A priest? a porter?—Child, although

I have forgotten clean, I know

That in the shade of Fujisan,

What time the cherry-orchards blow,

I loved you once in old Japan.

As here you loiter, flowing-gowned

And hugely sashed, with pins a-row

Your quaint head as with flamelets crowned,

Demure, inviting—even so,

When merry maids in Miyako

To feel the sweet o' the year began,

And green gardens to overflow,

I loved you once in old Japan.

Clear shine the hills; the rice-fields round

Two cranes are circling; sleepy and slow,

A blue canal the lake's blue bound

Breaks at the bamboo bridge; and lo!

Touched with the sundown's spirit and glow,

I see you turn, with flirted fan,

Against the plum-tree's bloomy snow . . .

I loved you once in old Japan!

ENVOY.

Dear, 'twas a dozen lives ago

But that I was a lucky man

The Toyokuni here will show:

I loved you—once—in old Japan!

This rondel, too—how light it is, and graceful!—

We'll to the woods and gather may

Fresh from the footprints of the rain.

We'll to the woods, at every vein

To drink the spirit of the day.

The winds of spring are out at play,

The needs of spring in heart and brain.

We'll to the woods and gather may

Fresh from the footprints of the rain.

The world's too near her end, you say?

Hark to the blackbird's mad refrain!

It waits for her, the vast Inane?

Then, girls, to help her on the way

We'll to the woods and gather may.

There are fine verses, also, scattered through this little book; some of them very strong, as—

Out of the night that covers me,

Black as the pit from pole to pole,

I thank whatever gods may be

For my unconquerable soul.

It matters not how strait the gate,

How charged with punishments the scroll,

I am the master of my fate:

I am the captain of my soul.

Others with a true touch of romance, as—

Or ever the knightly years were gone

With the old world to the grave,

I was a king in Babylon,

And you were a Christian slave.

And here and there we come across such felicitous phrases as—

In the sand

The gold prow-griffin claws a hold,

or—

The spires

Shine and are changed,

and many other graceful or fanciful lines, even 'the green sky's minor thirds' being perfectly right in its place, and a very refreshing bit of affectation in a volume where there is so much that is natural.

However, Mr. Henley is not to be judged by samples. Indeed, the

Oscar Wilde

most attractive thing in the book is no single poem that is in it, but the strong humane personality that stands behind both flawless and faulty work alike, and looks out through many masks, some of them beautiful, and some grotesque, and not a few misshapen. In the case with most of our modern poets, when we have analysed them down to an adjective, we can go no further, or we care to go no further; but with this book it is different. Through these reeds and pipes blows the very breath of life. It seems as if one could put one's hand upon the singer's heart and count its pulsations. There is something wholesome, virile and sane about the man's soul. Anybody can be reasonable, but to be sane is not common; and sane poets are as rare as blue lilies, though they may not be quite so delightful.

Let the great winds their worst and wildest blow,

Or the gold weather round us mellow slow;

We have fulfilled ourselves, and we can dare,

And we can conquer, though we may not share

In the rich quiet of the afterglow,

What is to come,

is the concluding stanza of the last rondeau—indeed, of the last poem in the collection, and the high, serene temper displayed in these lines serves at once as keynote and keystone to the book. The very lightness and slightness of so much of the work, its careless moods and casual fancies, seem to suggest a nature that is not primarily interested in art—a nature, like Sordello's, passionately enamoured of life, one to which lyre and lute are things of less importance. From this mere joy of living, this frank delight in experience for its own sake, this lofty indifference, and momentary unregretted ardours, come all the faults and all the beauties of the volume. But there is this difference between them—the faults are deliberate, and the result of much study; the beauties have the air of fascinating impromptus. Mr. Henley's healthy, if sometimes misapplied, confidence in the myriad suggestions of life gives him his charm. He is made to sing along the highways, not to sit down and write. If he took himself more seriously, his work would become trivial.

A Book of Verses. By William Ernest Henley. (David Nutt.)

SOME LITERARY LADIES

(Woman's World, January 1889.)

In a recent article on English Poetesses, I ventured to suggest that our women of letters should turn their attention somewhat more to prose and somewhat less to poetry. Women seem to me to possess just what our literature wants—a light touch, a delicate hand, a graceful mode of treatment, and an unstudied felicity of phrase. We want some one who will do for our prose what Madame de Sévigné did for the prose of France. George Eliot's style was far too cumbrous, and Charlotte Brontë's too exaggerated. However, one must not forget that amongst the women of England there have been some charming letter-writers, and certainly no book can be more delightful reading than Mrs. Ross's Three Generations of English Women, which has recently appeared. The three Englishwomen whose memoirs and correspondence Mrs. Ross has so admirably edited are Mrs. John Taylor, Mrs. Sarah Austin, and Lady Duff Gordon, all of them remarkable personalities, and two of them women of brilliant wit and European reputation. Mrs. Taylor belonged to that great Norwich family about whom the Duke of Sussex remarked that they reversed the ordinary saying that it takes nine tailors to make a man, and was for many years one of the most distinguished figures in the famous society of her native town. Her only daughter married John Austin, the great authority on jurisprudence, and her salon in Paris was the centre of the intellect and culture of her day. Lucie Duff Gordon, the only child of John and Sarah Austin, inherited the talents of her parents. A beauty, a femme d'esprit, a traveller, and clever writer, she charmed and fascinated her age, and her premature death in Egypt was really a loss to our literature. It is to her daughter that we owe this delightful volume of memoirs.

First we are introduced to Mrs. Ross's great-grandmother, Mrs. Taylor, who 'was called, by her intimate friends, "Madame Roland of Norwich," from her likeness to the portraits of the handsome and unfortunate Frenchwoman.' We hear of her darning her boy's grey worsted stockings while holding her own with Southey and Brougham, and dancing round the Tree of Liberty with Dr. Parr when the news of the fall of the Bastille was first known. Amongst her friends were Sir James Mackintosh, the most popular man of the day, 'to whom Madame de Staël wrote, "Il n'y a pas de société sans vous." "C'est très ennuyeux de dîner sans vous; la société ne va pas quand vous n'êtes pas là";' Sir James Smith, the botanist; Crabb Robinson; the Gurneys; Mrs. Barbauld; Dr. Alderson and his charming daughter, Amelia Opie; and many other well-known people. Her letters are extremely sensible and thoughtful. 'Nothing at present,' she says in one of them, 'suits my taste so well as Susan's Latin lessons, and her philosophical old master. . . . When we get to Cicero's discussions on the nature of the soul, or Virgil's fine descriptions, my mind is filled up. Life is either a dull round of eating, drinking, and sleeping, or a spark of ethereal fire just kindled. . . . The character of girls must depend upon their reading as much as upon the company they keep. Besides the intrinsic pleasure to be derived from solid knowledge, a woman ought to consider it as her best resource against poverty.' This is a somewhat caustic aphorism: 'A romantic woman is a troublesome friend, as she expects you to be as impudent as herself, and is mortified at what she calls coldness and insensibility.' And this is admirable: 'The art of life is not to estrange oneself from society, and yet not to pay too dear for it.' This, too, is good: 'Vanity, like curiosity, is wanted as a stimulus to exertion; indolence would certainly get the better of us if it were not for these two powerful principles'; and there is a keen touch of humour in the following: 'Nothing is so gratifying as the idea that virtue and philanthropy are becoming fashionable.' Dr. James Martineau, in a letter to Mrs. Ross, gives us a pleasant picture of the old lady returning from market 'weighted by her huge basket, with the shank of a leg of mutton thrust out to betray its contents,' and talking divinely about philosophy, poets, politics, and every intellectual topic of the day. She was a woman of admirable good sense, a type of Roman matron, and quite as careful as were the Roman matrons to keep up the purity of her native tongue.

Mrs. Taylor, however, was more or less limited to Norwich. Mrs. Austin was for the world. In London, Paris, and Germany, she ruled and dominated society, loved by every one who knew her. 'She is "My best and brightest" to Lord Jeffrey; "Dear, fair and wise" to Sydney Smith; "My great ally" to Sir James Stephen; "Sunlight through waste weltering chaos" to Thomas Carlyle (while he needed her aid); "La petite mère du genre humain" to Michael Chevalier; "Liebes Mütterlein" to John Stuart Mill; and "My own Professorin" to Charles Buller, to whom she taught German, as well as to the sons of Mr. James Mill.' Jeremy Bentham, when on his deathbed, gave her a ring with his portrait and some of his hair let in behind. 'There, my dear,' he said, 'it is the only ring I ever gave a woman.' She corresponded with Guizot, Barthelemy de St. Hilaire, the Grotes, Dr. Whewell, the Master of Trinity, Nassau Senior, the Duchesse d'Orléans, Victor Cousin, and many other distinguished people. Her translation of Ranke's History of the Popes is admirable; indeed, all her literary work was thoroughly well done, and her edition of her husband's Province of Jurisprudence deserves the very highest praise. Two people more unlike than herself and her husband it would have been difficult to find. He was habitually grave and despondent; she was brilliantly handsome, fond of society, in which she shone, and 'with an almost superabundance of energy and animal spirits,' Mrs. Ross tells us. She married him because she thought him perfect, but he never produced the work of which he was worthy, and of which she knew him to be worthy. Her estimate of him in the preface to the Jurisprudence is wonderfully striking and simple. 'He was never sanguine. He was intolerant of any imperfection. He was always under the control of severe love of truth. He lived and died a poor man.' She was terribly disappointed in him, but she loved him. Some years after his death, she wrote to M. Guizot:

> In the intervals of my study of his works I read his letters to me—forty-five years of love-letters, the last as tender and passionate as the first. And how full of noble sentiments! The midday of our lives was clouded and stormy, full of cares and disappointments; but the sunset was bright and serene—as bright as the morning, and more serene. Now it is night with me, and must remain so till the dawn of another day. I am always alone—that is, I live with him.

The most interesting letters in the book are certainly those to M. Guizot, with whom she maintained the closest intellectual friendship; but there is hardly one of them that does not contain something clever, or thoughtful, or witty, while those addressed to her, in turn, are very interesting. Carlyle writes her letters full of lamentations, the wail of a Titan in pain, superbly exaggerated for literary effect.

Literature, one's sole craft and staff of life, lies broken in abeyance; what room for music amid the braying of innumerable jackasses, the howling of innumerable hyænas whetting the tooth to eat them up? Alas for it! it is a sick disjointed time; neither shall we ever mend it; at best let us hope to mend ourselves. I declare I sometimes think of throwing down the Pen altogether as a worthless weapon; and leading out a colony of these poor starving Drudges to the waste places of their old Mother Earth, when for sweat of their brow bread will rise for them; it were perhaps the worthiest service that at this moment could be rendered our old world to throw open for it the doors of the New. Thither must they come at last, 'bursts of eloquence' will do nothing; men are starving and will try many things before they die. But poor I, ach Gott! I am no Hengist or Alaric; only a writer of Articles in bad prose; stick to thy last, O Tutor; the Pen is not worthless, it is omnipotent to those who have Faith.

Henri Beyle (Stendhal), the great, I am often tempted to think the greatest of French novelists, writes her a charming letter about nuances. 'It seems to me,' he says, 'that except when they read Shakespeare, Byron, or Sterne, no Englishman understands "nuances"; we adore them. A fool says to a woman "I love you"; the words mean nothing, he might as well say "Olli Batachor"; it is the nuance which gives force to the meaning.' In 1839 Mrs. Austin writes to Victor Cousin: 'I have seen young Gladstone, a distinguished Tory who wants to re-establish education based on the Church in quite a Catholic form'; and we find her corresponding with Mr. Gladstone on the subject of education. 'If you are strong enough to provide motives and checks,' she says to him, 'you may do two blessed acts—reform your clergy and teach your people. As it is, how few of them conceive what it is to teach a people'! Mr. Gladstone replies at great length, and in many letters, from which we may quote this passage:

You are for pressing and urging the people to their profit against their inclination: so am I. You set little value upon all merely technical instruction, upon all that fails to touch the inner nature of man: so do

I. And here I find ground of union broad and deep-laid. . . .

I more than doubt whether your idea, namely that of raising man to social sufficiency and morality, can be accomplished, except through the ancient religion of Christ; . . . or whether, the principles of eclecticism are legitimately applicable to the Gospel; or whether, if we find ourselves in a state of incapacity to work through the Church, we can remedy the defect by the adoption of principles contrary to hers.
. . .

But indeed I am most unfit to pursue the subject; private circumstances of no common interest are upon me, as I have become very recently engaged to Miss Glynne, and I hope your recollections will enable you in some degree to excuse me.

Lord Jeffrey has a very curious and suggestive letter on popular education, in which he denies, or at least doubts, the effect of this education on morals. He, however, supports it on the ground 'that it will increase the enjoyment of individuals,' which is certainly a very sensible claim. Humboldt writes to her about an old Indian language which was preserved by a parrot, the tribe who spoke it having been exterminated, and about 'young Darwin,' who had just published his first book. Here are some extracts from her own letters:

I heard from Lord Lansdowne two or three days ago. . . . I think he is ce que nous avons de mieux. He wants only the energy that great ambition gives. He says, 'We shall have a parliament of railway kings' . . . what can be worse than that?—The deification of money by a whole people. As Lord Brougham says, we have no right to give ourselves pharisaical airs. I must give you a story sent to me. Mrs. Hudson, the railway queen, was shown a bust of Marcus Aurelius at Lord Westminster's, on which she said, 'I suppose that is not the present Marquis.' To goûter this, you must know that the extreme vulgar (hackney coachmen, etc.) in England pronounce 'marquis' very like 'Marcus.'

Dec. 17th.—Went to Savigny's. Nobody was there but W. Grimm and his wife and a few men. Grimm told me he had received two volumes of Norwegian fairy-tales, and that they were delightful. Talking of them, I said, 'Your children appear to be the happiest in the world; they live in the midst of fairy-tales.' 'Ah,' said he, 'I must tell you about that. When we were at Göttingen, somebody spoke to my little son about his father's Mährchen. He had read them but never thought of their being mine. He came running to me, and said with an offended air, "Father, they say you wrote those fairy-tales; surely you never invented such silly rubbish?" He thought it below my dignity.'

Savigny told a Volksmährchen too:

'St. Anselm was grown old and infirm, and lay on the ground among thorns and thistles. Der liebe Gott said to him, "You are very badly lodged there; why don't you build yourself a house?" "Before I take the trouble," said Anselm, "I should like to know how long I have to live." "About thirty years," said Der liebe Gott. "Oh, for so short a time," replied he, "it's not worth while," and turned himself round among the thistles.'

Dr. Franck told me a story of which I had never heard before. Voltaire had for some reason or other taken a grudge against the prophet Habakkuk, and affected to find in him things he never wrote. Somebody took the Bible and began to demonstrate to him that he was mistaken. 'C'est égal,' he said impatiently, 'Habakkuk était capable de tout!'

Oct. 30, 1853.

I am not in love with the Richtung (tendency) of our modern novelists. There is abundance of talent; but writing a pretty, graceful, touching, yet pleasing story is the last thing our writers nowadays think of. Their novels are party pamphlets on political or social questions, like Sybil, or Alton Locke, or Mary Barton, or Uncle Tom; or they are the most minute and painful dissections of the least agreeable and beautiful parts of our nature, like those of Miss Brontë—Jane Eyre and Villette; or they are a kind of martyrology, like Mrs. Marsh's Emilia Wyndham, which makes you almost doubt whether any torments the heroine would have earned by being naughty could exceed those she incurred by her virtue.

Where, oh! where is the charming, humane, gentle spirit that dictated the Vicar of Wakefield—the spirit which Goethe so justly calls versöhnend (reconciling), with all the weaknesses and woes of humanity? . . . Have you read Thackeray's Esmond? It is a curious and very successful attempt to imitate the style of our old novelists. . . . Which of Mrs. Gore's novels are translated? They are very clever, lively, worldly, bitter, disagreeable, and entertaining. . . . Miss Austen's—are they translated? They are not new, and are Dutch paintings of every-day people—very clever, very true, very unæsthetic, but amusing. I have not seen Ruth, by Mrs. Gaskell. I hear it much admired—and blamed. It is one of the many proofs of the desire women now have to friser questionable topics, and to poser insoluble moral problems. George Sand has turned their heads in that direction. I think a few broad scenes or hearty jokes à la Fielding were very harmless in comparison. They confounded nothing. . . .

The Heir of Redcliffe I have not read. . . . I am not worthy of superhuman flights of virtue—in a novel. I want to see how people act and suffer who are as good-for-nothing as I am myself. Then I have the sinful pretension to be amused, whereas all our novelists want to reform us, and to show us what a hideous place this world is: Ma foi, je ne le sais que trop, without their help.

The Head of the Family has some merits. . . . But there is too much affliction and misery and frenzy. The heroine is one of those creatures now so common (in novels), who remind me of a poor bird tied to a stake (as was once the cruel sport of boys) to be 'shyed' at (i.e. pelted) till it died; only our gentle lady-writers at the end of all untie the poor battered bird, and assure us that it is never the worse for all the blows it has had—nay, the better—and that now, with its broken wings and torn feathers and bruised body, it is going to be quite happy. No, fair ladies, you know that it is not so—resigned, if you please, but make me no shams of happiness out of such wrecks.

In politics Mrs. Austin was a philosophical Tory. Radicalism she detested, and she and most of her friends seem to have regarded it as moribund. The

Radical party is evidently effete,' she writes to M. Victor Cousin; the probable 'leader of the Tory party' is Mr. Gladstone. 'The people must be instructed, must be guided, must be, in short, governed,' she writes elsewhere; and in a letter to Dr. Whewell, she says that the state of things in France fills 'me with the deepest anxiety on one point,—the point on which the permanency of our institutions and our salvation as a nation turn. Are our higher classes able to keep the lead of the rest? If they are, we are safe; if not, I agree with my poor dear Charles Buller—our turn must come. Now Cambridge and Oxford must really look to this.' The belief in the power of the Universities to stem the current of democracy is charming. She grew to regard Carlyle as 'one of the dissolvents of the age—as mischievous as his extravagances will let him be'; speaks of Kingsley and Maurice as 'pernicious'; and talks of John Stuart Mill as a 'demagogue.' She was no doctrinaire. 'One ounce of education demanded is worth a pound imposed. It is no use to give the meat before you give the hunger.' She was delighted at a letter of St. Hilaire's, in which he said, 'We have a system and no results; you have results and no system.' Yet she had a deep sympathy with the wants of the people. She was horrified at something Babbage told her of the population of some of the manufacturing towns who are worked out before they attain to thirty years of age. 'But I am persuaded that the remedy will not, cannot come from the people,' she adds. Many of her letters are concerned with the question of the higher education of women. She discusses Buckle's lecture on 'The Influence of Women upon the Progress of Knowledge,' admits to M. Guizot that women's intellectual life is largely coloured by the emotions, but adds: 'One is not precisely a fool because one's opinions are greatly influenced by one's affections. The opinions of men are often influenced by worse things.' Dr. Whewell consults her about lecturing women on Plato, being slightly afraid lest people should think it ridiculous; Comte writes her elaborate letters on the relation of women to progress; and Mr. Gladstone promises that Mrs. Gladstone will carry out at Hawarden the suggestions contained in one of her pamphlets. She was always very practical, and never lost her admiration for plain sewing.

All through the book we come across interesting and amusing things. She gets St. Hilaire to order a large, sensible bonnet for her in Paris, which was at once christened the 'Aristotelian,' and was supposed to be the only useful bonnet in England. Grote has to leave Paris after the coup d'état, he tells her, because he cannot bear to see the establishment of a Greek tyrant. Alfred de Vigny, Macaulay, John Stirling, Southey, Alexis de Tocqueville, Hallam, and Jean Jacques Ampère all contribute to these pleasant pages. She seems to have inspired the warmest feelings of friendship in those who knew her. Guizot writes to her: 'Madame de Staël used to say that the best thing in the world was a serious Frenchman. I turn the compliment, and say that the best thing in the world is an affectionate Englishman. How much more an Englishwoman! Given equal qualities, a woman is always more charming than a man.'

Lucie Austin, afterwards Lady Duff Gordon, was born in 1821. Her chief playfellow was John Stuart Mill, and Jeremy Bentham's garden was her playground. She was a lovely, romantic child, who was always wanting the flowers to talk to her, and used to invent the most wonderful stories about animals, of whom she was passionately fond. In 1834 Mrs. Austin decided on leaving England, and Sydney Smith wrote his immortal letter to the little girl:

> Lucie, Lucie, my dear child, don't tear your frock: tearing frocks is not of itself a proof of genius. But write as your mother writes, act as your mother acts: be frank, loyal, affectionate, simple, honest, and then integrity or laceration of frock is of little import. And Lucie, dear child, mind your arithmetic. You know in the first sum of yours I ever saw there was a mistake. You had carried two (as a cab is licensed to do), and you ought, dear Lucie, to have carried but one. Is this a trifle? What would life be without arithmetic but a scene of horrors? You are going to Boulogne, the city of debts, peopled by men who have never understood arithmetic. By the time you return, I shall probably have received my first paralytic stroke, and shall have lost all recollection of you. Therefore I now give you my parting advice—don't marry anybody who has not a tolerable understanding and a thousand a year. And God bless you, dear child.

At Boulogne she sat next Heine at table d'hôte. 'He heard me speak

162

German to my mother, and soon began to talk to me, and then said, "When you go back to England, you can tell your friends that you have seen Heinrich Heine." I replied, "And who is Heinrich Heine?" He laughed heartily and took no offence at my ignorance; and we used to lounge on the end of the pier together, where he told me stories in which fish, mermaids, water-sprites and a very funny old French fiddler with a poodle were mixed up in the most fanciful manner, sometimes humorous, and very often pathetic, especially when the water-sprites brought him greetings from the "Nord See." He was . . . so kind to me and so sarcastic to every one else.' Twenty years afterwards the little girl whose 'braune Augen' Heine had celebrated in his charming poem Wenn ick an deinem Hause, used to go and see the dying poet in Paris. 'It does one good,' he said to her, 'to see a woman who does not carry about a broken heart, to be mended by all sorts of men, like the women here, who do not see that a total want of heart is their real failing.' On another occasion he said to her: 'I have now made peace with the whole world, and at last also with God, who sends thee to me as a beautiful angel of death: I shall certainly soon die.' Lady Duff Gordon said to him: 'Poor Poet, do you still retain such splendid illusions, that you transform a travelling Englishwoman into Azrael? That used not to be the case, for you always disliked us.' He answered: 'Yes, I do not know what possessed me to dislike the English, . . . it really was only petulance; I never hated them, indeed, I never knew them. I was only once in England, but knew no one, and found London very dreary, and the people and the streets odious. But England has revenged herself well; she has sent me most excellent friends—thyself and Milnes, that good Milnes.'

There are delightful letters from Dicky Doyle here, with the most amusing drawings, one of the present Sir Robert Peel as he made his maiden speech in the House being excellent; and the various descriptions of Hassan's performances are extremely amusing. Hassan was a black boy, who had been turned away by his master because he was going blind, and was found by Lady Duff Gordon one night sitting on her doorstep. She took care of him, and had him cured, and he seems to have been a constant source of delight to every one. On one occasion, 'when Prince Louis Napoleon (the late Emperor of the French) came in unexpectedly, he gravely said: "Please, my lady, I ran out and bought twopennyworth of sprats for the Prince, and for the honour

163

of the house."' Here is an amusing letter from Mrs. Norton:

> MY DEAR LUCIE,—We have never thanked you for the red Pots, which no early Christian should be without, and which add that finishing stroke to the splendour of our demesne, which was supposed to depend on a roc's egg, in less intelligent times. We have now a warm Pompeian appearance, and the constant contemplation of these classical objects favours the beauty of the facial line; for what can be deducted from the great fact, apparent in all the states of antiquity, that straight noses were the ancient custom, but the logical assumption that the constant habit of turning up the nose at unsightly objects—such as the National Gallery and other offensive and obtrusive things—has produced the modern divergence from the true and proper line of profile? I rejoice to think that we ourselves are exempt. I attribute this to our love of Pompeian Pots (on account of the beauty and distinction of this Pot's shape I spell it with a big P), which has kept us straight in a world of crookedness. The pursuit of profiles under difficulties—how much more rare than a pursuit of knowledge! Talk of setting good examples before our children! Bah! let us set good Pompeian Pots before our children, and when they grow up they will not depart from them.

Lady Duff Gordon's Letters from the Cape, and her brilliant translation of The Amber Witch, are, of course, well known. The latter book was, with Lady Wilde's translation of Sidonia the Sorceress, my favourite romantic reading when a boy. Her letters from Egypt are wonderfully vivid and picturesque. Here is an interesting bit of art criticism:

> Sheykh Yoosuf laughed so heartily over a print in an illustrated paper from a picture of Hilton's of Rebekah at the well, with the old 'wekeel' of 'Sidi Ibraheem' (Abraham's chief servant) kneeling before the girl he was sent to fetch, like an old fool without his turban, and Rebekah and the other girls in queer fancy dresses, and the camels with snouts like pigs. 'If the painter could not go into "Es Sham" to see how the Arab really look,' said Sheykh Yoosuf, 'why did he not paint a well in England, with girls like English peasants—at least it would have looked natural to English people? and the wekeel would not seem so

like a madman if he had taken off a hat!' I cordially agree with Yoosuf's art criticism. Fancy pictures of Eastern things are hopelessly absurd.

Mrs. Ross has certainly produced a most fascinating volume, and her book is one of the books of the season. It is edited with tact and judgment.

Three Generations of English Women. Memoirs and Correspondence of Susannah Taylor, Sarah Austin, and Lady Duff Gordon. By Janet Ross, author of Italian Sketches, Land of Manfred, etc. (Fisher Unwin.)

POETRY AND PRISON

(Pall Mall Gazette, January 3, 1889.)

Prison has had an admirable effect on Mr. Wilfrid Blunt as a poet. The Love Sonnets of Proteus, in spite of their clever Musset-like modernities and their swift brilliant wit, were but affected or fantastic at best. They were simply the records of passing moods and moments, of which some were sad and others sweet, and not a few shameful. Their subject was not of high or serious import. They contained much that was wilful and weak. In Vinculis, upon the other hand, is a book that stirs one by its fine sincerity of purpose, its lofty and impassioned thought, its depth and ardour of intense feeling. 'Imprisonment,' says Mr. Blunt in his preface, 'is a reality of discipline most useful to the modern soul, lapped as it is in physical sloth and self-indulgence. Like a sickness or a spiritual retreat it purifies and ennobles; and the soul emerges from it stronger and more self-contained.' To him, certainly, it has been a mode of purification. The opening sonnets, composed in the bleak cell of Galway Gaol, and written down on the flyleaves of the prisoner's prayer-book, are full of things nobly conceived and nobly uttered, and show that though Mr. Balfour may enforce 'plain living' by his prison regulations, he cannot prevent 'high thinking' or in any way limit or constrain the freedom of a man's soul. They are, of course, intensely personal in expression. They could not fail to be so. But the personality that they reveal has nothing petty or ignoble about it. The petulant cry of the shallow egoist which was the chief

165

characteristic of the Love Sonnets of Proteus is not to be found here. In its place we have wild grief and terrible scorn, fierce rage and flame-like passion. Such a sonnet as the following comes out of the very fire of heart and brain:

God knows, 'twas not with a fore-reasoned plan

I left the easeful dwellings of my peace,

And sought this combat with ungodly Man,

And ceaseless still through years that do not cease

Have warred with Powers and Principalities.

My natural soul, ere yet these strifes began,

Was as a sister diligent to please

And loving all, and most the human clan.

God knows it. And He knows how the world's tears

Touched me. And He is witness of my wrath,

How it was kindled against murderers

Who slew for gold, and how upon their path

I met them. Since which day the World in arms

Strikes at my life with angers and alarms.

And this sonnet has all the strange strength of that despair which is but the prelude to a larger hope:

I thought to do a deed of chivalry,

An act of worth, which haply in her sight

Who was my mistress should recorded be

And of the nations. And, when thus the fight

Faltered and men once bold with faces white

Turned this and that way in excuse to flee,

I only stood, and by the foeman's might

Was overborne and mangled cruelly.

Then crawled I to her feet, in whose dear cause

I made this venture, and 'Behold,' I said,

'How I am wounded for thee in these wars.'

But she, 'Poor cripple, would'st thou I should wed

A limbless trunk?' and laughing turned from me.

Yet she was fair, and her name 'Liberty.'

The sonnet beginning

A prison is a convent without God—

Poverty, Chastity, Obedience

Its precepts are:

is very fine; and this, written just after entering the gaol, is powerful:

Naked I came into the world of pleasure,

And naked come I to this house of pain.

Here at the gate I lay down my life's treasure,

My pride, my garments and my name with men.

The world and I henceforth shall be as twain,

No sound of me shall pierce for good or ill

These walls of grief. Nor shall I hear the vain

Laughter and tears of those who love me still.

Within, what new life waits me! Little ease,

Cold lying, hunger, nights of wakefulness,

Harsh orders given, no voice to soothe or please,

Poor thieves for friends, for books rules meaningless;

This is the grave—nay, hell. Yet, Lord of Might,

Still in Thy light my spirit shall see light.

But, indeed, all the sonnets are worth reading, and The Canon of Aughrim, the longest poem in the book, is a most masterly and dramatic description of the tragic life of the Irish peasant. Literature is not much indebted to Mr. Balfour for his sophistical Defence of Philosophic Doubt, which is one of the dullest books we know, but it must be admitted that by sending Mr. Blunt to gaol he has converted a clever rhymer into an earnest and deep-thinking poet. The narrow confines of a prison cell seem to suit the 'sonnet's scanty plot of ground,' and an unjust imprisonment for a noble cause strengthens as well as deepens the nature.

In Vinculis. By Wilfrid Scawen Blunt, Author of *The Wind and the Whirlwind, The Love Sonnets of Proteus, etc. etc.* (Kegan Paul.)

THE GOSPEL ACCORDING TO WALT WHITMAN
(Pall Mall Gazette, January 25, 1889.)

'No one will get to my verses who insists upon viewing them as a literary performance . . . or as aiming mainly towards art and æstheticism.' 'Leaves of Grass . . . has mainly been the outcropping of my own emotional and other personal nature—an attempt, from first to last, to put a Person, a human being (myself, in the latter half of the Nineteenth Century in America,) freely, fully and truly on record. I could not find any similar personal record in current literature that satisfied me.' In these words Walt Whitman gives us the true attitude we should adopt towards his work, having, indeed, a much saner view of the value and meaning of that work than either his eloquent admirers or noisy detractors can boast of possessing. His last book, November Boughs, as he calls it, published in the winter of the old man's life, reveals to us, not

168

indeed a soul's tragedy, for its last note is one of joy and hope, and noble and unshaken faith in all that is fine and worthy of such faith, but certainly the drama of a human soul, and puts on record with a simplicity that has in it both sweetness and strength the record of his spiritual development, and of the aim and motive both of the manner and the matter of his work. His strange mode of expression is shown in these pages to have been the result of deliberate and self-conscious choice. The 'barbaric yawp' which he sent over 'the roofs of the world' so many years ago, and which wrung from Mr. Swinburne's lip such lofty panegyric in song and such loud clamorous censure in prose, appears here in what will be to many an entirely new light. For in his very rejection of art Walt Whitman is an artist. He tried to produce a certain effect by certain means and he succeeded. There is much method in what many have termed his madness, too much method, indeed, some may be tempted to fancy.

In the story of his life, as he tells it to us, we find him at the age of sixteen beginning a definite and philosophical study of literature:

> Summers and falls, I used to go off, sometimes for a week at a stretch, down in the country, or to Long Island's seashores—there, in the presence of outdoor influences, I went over thoroughly the Old and New Testaments, and absorb'd (probably to better advantage for me than in any library or indoor room—it makes such difference where you read) Shakspere, Ossian, the best translated versions I could get of Homer, Eschylus, Sophocles, the old German Nibelungen, the ancient Hindoo poems, and one or two other masterpieces, Dante's among them. As it happen'd, I read the latter mostly in an old wood. The Iliad . . . I read first thoroughly on the peninsula of Orient, northeast end of Long Island, in a shelter'd hollow of rock and sand, with the sea on each side. (I have wonder'd since why I was not overwhelm'd by those mighty masters. Likely because I read them, as described, in the full presence of Nature, under the sun, with the far-spreading landscapes and vistas, or the sea rolling in.)

Edgar Allan Poe's amusing bit of dogmatism that, for our occasions and our day, 'there can be no such thing as a long poem,' fascinated him. 'The same thought had been haunting my mind before,' he said, 'but Poe's argument . . . work'd the sum out, and proved it to me,' and the English translation of the Bible seems to have suggested to him the possibility of a poetic form which, while retaining the spirit of poetry, would still be free from the trammels of rhyme and of a definite metrical system. Having thus, to a certain degree, settled upon what one might call the 'technique' of Whitmanism, he began to brood upon the nature of that spirit which was to give life to the strange form. The central point of the poetry of the future seemed to him to be necessarily 'an identical body and soul, a personality,' in fact, which personality, he tells us frankly, 'after many considerations and ponderings I deliberately settled should be myself.' However, for the true creation and revealing of this personality, at first only dimly felt, a new stimulus was needed. This came from the Civil War. After describing the many dreams and passions of his boyhood and early manhood, he goes on to say:

> These, however, and much more might have gone on and come to naught (almost positively would have come to naught,) if a sudden, vast, terrible, direct and indirect stimulus for new and national declamatory expression had not been given to me. It is certain, I say, that although I had made a start before, only from the occurrence of the Secession War, and what it show'd me as by flashes of lightning, with the emotional depths it sounded and arous'd (of course, I don't mean in my own heart only, I saw it just as plainly in others, in millions)—that only from the strong flare and provocation of that war's sights and scenes the final reasons-for-being of an autochthonic and passionate song definitely came forth.

> I went down to the war fields of Virginia . . . lived thenceforward in camp—saw great battles and the days and nights afterward—partook of all the fluctuations, gloom, despair, hopes again arous'd, courage evoked—death readily risk'd—the cause, too—along and filling those agonistic and lurid following years . . . the real parturition years . . . of this henceforth homogeneous Union. Without those three or four years and the experiences they gave, Leaves of Grass would not now be existing.

Having thus obtained the necessary stimulus for the quickening and awakening of the personal self, some day to be endowed with universality, he sought to find new notes of song, and, passing beyond the mere passion for expression, he aimed at 'Suggestiveness' first.

> I round and finish little, if anything; and could not, consistently with my scheme. The reader will have his or her part to do, just as much as I have had mine. I seek less to state or display any theme or thought, and more to bring you, reader, into the atmosphere of the theme or thought—there to pursue your own flight.

Another 'impetus-word' is Comradeship, and other 'word-signs' are Good Cheer, Content and Hope. Individuality, especially, he sought for:

> I have allow'd the stress of my poems from beginning to end to bear upon American individuality and assist it—not only because that is a great lesson in Nature, amid all her generalizing laws, but as counterpoise to the leveling tendencies of Democracy—and for other reasons. Defiant of ostensible literary and other conventions, I avowedly chant 'the great pride of man in himself,' and permit it to be more or less a motif of nearly all my verse. I think this pride is indispensable to an American. I think it not inconsistent with obedience, humility, deference, and self-questioning.

A new theme also was to be found in the relation of the sexes, conceived in a natural, simple and healthy form, and he protests against poor Mr. William Rossetti's attempt to Bowdlerise and expurgate his song.

> From another point of view Leaves of Grass is avowedly the song of Sex and Amativeness, and even Animality—though meanings that do not usually go along with these words are behind all, and will duly emerge; and all are sought to be lifted into a different light and atmosphere. Of this feature, intentionally palpable in a few lines, I shall only say the espousing principle of those lines so gives breath to my whole scheme that the bulk of the pieces might as well have been left unwritten were those lines omitted. . . .

Universal as are certain facts and symptoms of communities . . . there

171

is nothing so rare in modern conventions and poetry as their normal recognizance. Literature is always calling in the doctor for consultation and confession, and always giving evasions and swathing suppressions in place of that 'heroic nudity' on which only a genuine diagnosis . . . can be built. And in respect to editions of Leaves of Grass in time to come (if there should be such) I take occasion now to confirm those lines with the settled convictions and deliberate renewals of thirty years, and to hereby prohibit, as far as word of mine can do so, any elision of them.

But beyond all these notes and moods and motives is the lofty spirit of a grand and free acceptance of all things that are worthy of existence. He desired, he says, 'to formulate a poem whose every thought or fact should directly or indirectly be or connive at an implicit belief in the wisdom, health, mystery, beauty of every process, every concrete object, every human or other existence, not only consider'd from the point of view of all, but of each.' His two final utterances are that 'really great poetry is always . . . the result of a national spirit, and not the privilege of a polish'd and select few'; and that 'the strongest and sweetest songs yet remain to be sung.'

Such are the views contained in the opening essay A Backward Glance O'er Travel'd Roads, as he calls it; but there are many other essays in this fascinating volume, some on poets such as Burns and Lord Tennyson, for whom Walt Whitman has a profound admiration; some on old actors and singers, the elder Booth, Forrest, Alboni and Mario being his special favourites; others on the native Indians, on the Spanish element in American nationality, on Western slang, on the poetry of the Bible, and on Abraham Lincoln. But Walt Whitman is at his best when he is analysing his own work and making schemes for the poetry of the future. Literature, to him, has a distinctly social aim. He seeks to build up the masses by 'building up grand individuals.' And yet literature itself must be preceded by noble forms of life. 'The best literature is always the result of something far greater than itself— not the hero but the portrait of the hero. Before there can be recorded history or poem there must be the transaction.' Certainly, in Walt Whitman's views there is a largeness of vision, a healthy sanity and a fine ethical purpose. He is not to be placed with the professional littérateurs of his country, Boston novelists, New York poets and the like. He stands apart, and the chief value of his work is in its prophecy, not in its performance. He has begun a prelude to larger themes. He is the herald to a new era. As a man he is the precursor of a fresh type. He is a factor in the heroic and spiritual evolution of the human being. If Poetry has passed him by, Philosophy will take note of him.

November Boughs. By Walt Whitman. (Alexander Gardner.)

IRISH FAIRY TALES

(Woman's World, February 1889.)

'The various collectors of Irish folk-lore,' says Mr. W. B. Yeats in his charming little book *Fairy and Folk Tales of the Irish Peasantry*, 'have, from our point of view, one great merit, and from the point of view of others, one great fault.'

They have made their work literature rather than science, and told us of the Irish peasantry rather than of the primitive religion of mankind, or whatever else the folk-lorists are on the gad after. To be considered scientists they should have tabulated all their tales in forms like grocers' bills—item the fairy king, item the queen. Instead of this they have caught the very voice of the people, the very pulse of life, each giving what was most noticed in his day. Croker and Lover, full of the ideas of harum-scarum Irish gentility, saw everything humorized. The impulse of the Irish literature of their time came from a class that did not—mainly for political reasons—take the populace seriously, and imagined the country as a humorist's Arcadia; its passion, its gloom, its tragedy, they knew nothing of. What they did was not wholly false; they merely magnified an irresponsible type, found oftenest among boatmen, carmen, and gentlemen's servants, into the type of a whole nation, and created the stage Irishman. The writers of 'Forty-eight, and the famine combined, burst their bubble. Their work had the dash as well as the shallowness of an ascendant and idle class, and in

Croker is touched everywhere with beauty—a gentle Arcadian beauty. Carleton, a peasant born, has in many of his stories, . . . more especially in his ghost stories, a much more serious way with him, for all his humour. Kennedy, an old bookseller in Dublin, who seems to have had a something of genuine belief in the fairies, comes next in time. He has far less literary faculty, but is wonderfully accurate, giving often the very words the stories were told in. But the best book since Croker is Lady Wilde's Ancient Legends. The humour has all given way to pathos and tenderness. We have here the innermost heart of the Celt in the moments he has grown to love through years of persecution, when, cushioning himself about with dreams, and hearing fairy-songs in the twilight, he ponders on the soul and on the dead. Here is the Celt, only it is the Celt dreaming.

Into a volume of very moderate dimensions, and of extremely moderate price, Mr. Yeats has collected together the most characteristic of our Irish folklore stories, grouping them together according to subject. First come The Trooping Fairies. The peasants say that these are 'fallen angels who were not good enough to be saved, nor bad enough to be lost'; but the Irish antiquarians see in them 'the gods of pagan Ireland,' who, 'when no longer worshipped and fed with offerings, dwindled away in the popular imagination, and now are only a few spans high.' Their chief occupations are feasting, fighting, making love, and playing the most beautiful music. 'They have only one industrious person amongst them, the lepra-caun—the shoemaker.' It is his duty to repair their shoes when they wear them out with dancing. Mr. Yeats tells us that 'near the village of Ballisodare is a little woman who lived amongst them seven years. When she came home she had no toes—she had danced them off.' On May Eve, every seventh year, they fight for the harvest, for the best ears of grain belong to them. An old man informed Mr. Yeats that he saw them fight once, and that they tore the thatch off a house. 'Had any one else been near they would merely have seen a great wind whirling everything into the air as it passed.' When the wind drives the leaves and straws before it, 'that is the fairies, and the peasants take off their hats and say "God bless them."' When they are gay, they sing. Many of the most beautiful tunes of Ireland 'are only their music, caught up by eavesdroppers.' No prudent peasant would hum The Pretty Girl Milking the Cow near a fairy rath, 'for they are jealous, and do not like to hear their songs on clumsy mortal lips.' Blake once saw a fairy's funeral. But this, as Mr. Yeats points out, must have been an English fairy, for the Irish fairies never die; they are immortal.

Then come The Solitary Fairies, amongst whom we find the little Lepracaun mentioned above. He has grown very rich, as he possesses all the treasure-crocks buried in war-time. In the early part of this century, according to Croker, they used to show in Tipperary a little shoe forgotten by the fairy shoemaker. Then there are two rather disreputable little fairies—the Cluricaun, who gets intoxicated in gentlemen's cellars, and the Red Man, who plays unkind practical jokes. 'The Fear-Gorta (Man of Hunger) is an emaciated phantom that goes through the land in famine time, begging an alms and bringing good luck to the giver.' The Water-sheerie is 'own brother to the English Jack-o'-Lantern.' 'The Leanhaun Shee (fairy mistress) seeks the love of mortals. If they refuse, she must be their slave; if they consent, they are hers, and can only escape by finding another to take their place. The fairy lives on their life, and they waste away. Death is no escape from her. She is the Gaelic muse, for she gives inspiration to those she persecutes. The Gaelic poets die young, for she is restless, and will not let them remain long on earth.' The Pooka is essentially an animal spirit, and some have considered him the forefather of Shakespeare's 'Puck.' He lives on solitary mountains, and among old ruins 'grown monstrous with much solitude,' and 'is of the race of the nightmare.' 'He has many shapes—is now a horse, . . . now a goat, now an eagle. Like all spirits, he is only half in the world of form.' The banshee does not care much for our democratic levelling tendencies; she loves only old families, and despises the parvenu or the nouveau riche. When more than one banshee is present, and they wail and sing in chorus, it is for the death of some holy or great one. An omen that sometimes accompanies the banshee is '. . . an immense black coach, mounted by a coffin, and drawn by headless horses driven by a Dullahan.' A Dullahan is the most terrible thing in the world. In 1807 two of the sentries stationed outside St. James's Park saw one climbing the railings, and died of fright. Mr. Yeats suggests that they are possibly 'descended from that Irish giant who swam across the Channel with his head in his teeth.'

Then come the stories of ghosts, of saints and priests, and of giants. The ghosts live in a state intermediary between this world and the next. They are held there by some earthly longing or affection, or some duty unfulfilled, or anger against the living; they are those who are too good for hell, and too bad for heaven. Sometimes they 'take the forms of insects, especially of butterflies.' The author of the Parochial Survey of Ireland 'heard a woman say to a child who was chasing a butterfly, "How do you know it is not the soul of your grandfather?" On November eve they are abroad, and dance with the fairies.' As for the saints and priests, 'there are no martyrs in the stories.' That ancient chronicler Giraldus Cambrensis 'taunted the Archbishop of Cashel, because no one in Ireland had received the crown of martyrdom. "Our people may be barbarous," the prelate answered, "but they have never lifted their hands against God's saints; but now that a people have come amongst us who know how to make them (it was just after the English invasion), we shall have martyrs plentifully."' The giants were the old pagan heroes of Ireland, who grew bigger and bigger, just as the gods grew smaller and smaller. The fact is they did not wait for offerings; they took them vi et armis.

Some of the prettiest stories are those that cluster round Tír-na-n-Og. This is the Country of the Young, 'for age and death have not found it; neither tears nor loud laughter have gone near it.' 'One man has gone there and returned. The bard, Oisen, who wandered away on a white horse, moving on the surface of the foam with his fairy Niamh, lived there three hundred years, and then returned looking for his comrades. The moment his foot touched the earth his three hundred years fell on him, and he was bowed double, and his beard swept the ground. He described his sojourn in the Land of Youth to Patrick before he died.' Since then, according to Mr. Yeats, 'many have seen it in many places; some in the depths of lakes, and have heard rising therefrom a vague sound of bells; more have seen it far off on the horizon, as they peered out from the western cliffs. Not three years ago a fisherman imagined that he saw it.'

Mr. Yeats has certainly done his work very well. He has shown great critical capacity in his selection of the stories, and his little introductions are charmingly written. It is delightful to come across a collection of purely imaginative work, and Mr. Yeats has a very quick instinct in finding out the best and the most beautiful things in Irish folklore.

I am also glad to see that he has not confined himself entirely to prose, but has included Allingham's lovely poem on The Fairies:

> Up the airy mountain,
>
> Down the rushy glen,
>
> We daren't go a-hunting
>
> For fear of little men;
>
> Wee folk, good folk,
>
> Trooping all together;
>
> Green jacket, red cap,
>
> And white owl's feather!
>
> Down along the rocky shore
>
> Some make their home,
>
> They live on crispy pancakes
>
> Of yellow tide-foam;
>
> Some in the reeds
>
> Of the black mountain lake,
>
> With frogs for their watch-dogs
>
> All night awake.
>
> High on the hill-top
>
> The old King sits;
>
> He is now so old and gray

He's nigh lost his wits.

With a bridge of white mist

Columbkill he crosses,

On his stately journeys

From Slieveleague to Rosses;

Or going up with music,

On cold starry nights,

To sup with the Queen

Of the gay Northern Lights.

All lovers of fairy tales and folklore should get this little book. The Horned Women, The Priest's Soul, [157] and Teig O'Kane, are really marvellous in their way; and, indeed, there is hardly a single story that is not worth reading and thinking over.

Fairy and Folk Tales of the Irish Peasantry. Edited and Selected by
W. B. Yeats. (Walter Scott.)

MR. W. B. YEATS

(Woman's World, March 1889.)

'*The Wanderings of Oisin and Other Poems is*, I believe, the first volume of poems that Mr. Yeats has published, and it is certainly full of promise. It must be admitted that many of the poems are too fragmentary, too incomplete. They read like stray scenes out of unfinished plays, like things only half remembered, or, at best, but dimly seen. But the architectonic power of construction, the power to build up and make perfect a harmonious whole, is nearly always the latest, as it certainly is the highest, development of the artistic temperament. It is somewhat unfair to expect it in early work. One quality Mr. Yeats has in a marked degree, a quality that is not common in the work of our minor poets, and is therefore all the more welcome to

178

us—I mean the romantic temper. He is essentially Celtic, and his verse, at its best, is Celtic also. Strongly influenced by Keats, he seems to study how to 'load every rift with ore,' yet is more fascinated by the beauty of words than by the beauty of metrical music. The spirit that dominates the whole book is perhaps more valuable than any individual poem or particular passage, but this from The Wanderings of Oisin is worth quoting. It describes the ride to the Island of Forgetfulness:

And the ears of the horse went sinking away in the hollow light,

For, as drift from a sailor slow drowning the gleams of the world and the sun,

Ceased on our hands and faces, on hazel and oak leaf, the light,

And the stars were blotted above us, and the whole of the world was one;

Till the horse gave a whinny; for cumbrous with stems of the hazel and oak,

Of hollies, and hazels, and oak-trees, a valley was sloping away

From his hoofs in the heavy grasses, with monstrous slumbering folk,

Their mighty and naked and gleaming bodies heaped loose where they lay.

More comely than man may make them, inlaid with silver and gold,

Were arrow and shield and war-axe, arrow and spear and blade,

And dew-blanched horns, in whose hollows a child of three years old

Could sleep on a couch of rushes, round and about them laid.

And this, which deals with the old legend of the city lying under the waters of a lake, is strange and interesting:

The maker of the stars and worlds

Sat underneath the market cross,

And the old men were walking, walking,

And little boys played pitch-and-toss.

'The props,' said He, 'of stars and worlds

Are prayers of patient men and good.

The boys, the women, and old men,

Listening, upon their shadows stood.

A grey professor passing cried,

'How few the mind's intemperance rule!

What shallow thoughts about deep things!

The world grows old and plays the fool.'

The mayor came, leaning his left ear—

There were some talking of the poor—

And to himself cried, 'Communist!'

And hurried to the guardhouse door.

The bishop came with open book,

Whispering along the sunny path;

There was some talking of man's God,

His God of stupor and of wrath.

The bishop murmured, 'Atheist!

How sinfully the wicked scoff!'

And sent the old men on their way,

And drove the boys and women off.

The place was empty now of people;

A cock came by upon his toes;

An old horse looked across the fence,

And rubbed along the rail his nose.

The maker of the stars and worlds

To His own house did Him betake,

And on that city dropped a tear,

And now that city is a lake.

Mr. Yeats has a great deal of invention, and some of the poems in his book, such as Mosada, Jealousy, and The Island of Statues, are very finely conceived. It is impossible to doubt, after reading his present volume, that he will some day give us work of high import. Up to this he has been merely trying the strings of his instrument, running over the keys.

The Wanderings of Oisin and Other Poems. By W. B. Yeats.
(Kegan Paul.)

MR. YEATS'S WANDERINGS OF OISIN

(Pall Mall Gazette, July 12, 1889.)

Books of poetry by young writers are usually promissory notes that are never met. Now and then, however, one comes across a volume that is so far above the average that one can hardly resist the fascinating temptation of recklessly prophesying a fine future for its author. Such a book Mr. Yeats's Wanderings of Oisin certainly is. Here we find nobility of treatment and nobility of subject-matter, delicacy of poetic instinct and richness of imaginative resource. Unequal and uneven much of the work must be admitted to be. Mr. Yeats does not try to 'out-baby' Wordsworth, we are glad to say; but he occasionally succeeds in 'out-glittering' Keats, and, here and there, in his book we come across strange crudities and irritating conceits. But when he is at his best he is very good. If he has not the grand simplicity of epic treatment, he has at least something of the largeness of vision that belongs to the epical temper. He does not rob of their stature the great heroes of Celtic mythology. He is very naïve and very primitive and speaks of his giants with the air of a child. Here is a characteristic passage from the account of Oisin's return from the Island of Forgetfulness:

And I rode by the plains of the sea's edge, where all is barren and grey,

   Grey sands on the green of the grasses and over the dripping trees,

Dripping and doubling landward, as though they would hasten away

   Like an army of old men longing for rest from the moan of the seas.

Long fled the foam-flakes around me, the winds fled out of the vast,

   Snatching the bird in secret, nor knew I, embosomed apart,

When they froze the cloth on my body like armour riveted fast,

   For Remembrance, lifting her leanness, keened in the gates of my heart.

Till fattening the winds of the morning, an odour of new-mown hay

   Came, and my forehead fell low, and my tears like berries fell down;

Later a sound came, half lost in the sound of a shore far away,

   From the great grass-barnacle calling, and later the shore-winds brown.

If I were as I once was, the gold hooves crushing the sand and the shells,

   Coming forth from the sea like the morning with red lips murmuring a
song,

   Not coughing, my head on my knees, and praying, and wroth with the bells,

   I would leave no Saint's head on his body, though spacious his lands were
and strong.

Making way from the kindling surges, I rode on a bridle-path,

   Much wondering to see upon all hands, of wattle and woodwork made,

Thy bell-mounted churches, and guardless the sacred cairn and the earth,

And a small and feeble populace stooping with mattock and spade.

In one or two places the music is faulty, the construction is sometimes too involved, and the word 'populace' in the last line is rather infelicitous; but, when all is said, it is impossible not to feel in these stanzas the presence of the true poetic spirit.

The Wanderings of Oisin and other Poems. By W. B. Yeats. (Kegan Paul.)

MR. WILLIAM MORRIS'S LAST BOOK

(Pall Mall Gazette, March 2, 1889.)

Mr. Morris's last book is a piece of pure art workmanship from beginning to end, and the very remoteness of its style from the common language and ordinary interests of our day gives to the whole story a strange beauty and an unfamiliar charm. It is written in blended prose and verse, like the mediæval 'cante-fable,' and tells the tale of the House of the Wolfings in its struggles against the legionaries of Rome then advancing into Northern Germany. It is a kind of Saga, and the language in which the folk-epic, as we may call it, is set forth recalls the antique dignity and directness of our English tongue four centuries ago. From an artistic point of view it may be described as an attempt to return by a self-conscious effort to the conditions of an earlier and a fresher age. Attempts of this kind are not uncommon in the history of art. From some such feeling came the Pre-Raphaelite movement of our own day and the archaistic movement of later Greek sculpture. When the result is beautiful the method is justified, and no shrill insistence upon a supposed necessity for absolute modernity of form can prevail against the value of work that has the incomparable excellence of style. Certainly, Mr. Morris's work possesses this excellence. His fine harmonies and rich cadences create in the reader that spirit by which alone can its own spirit be interpreted, awake in him something of the temper of romance and, by taking him out of his own age, place him in a truer and more vital relation to the great masterpieces of

183

all time. It is a bad thing for an age to be always looking in art for its own reflection. It is well that, now and then, we are given work that is nobly imaginative in its method and purely artistic in its aim. As we read Mr. Morris's story with its fine alternations of verse and prose, its decorative and descriptive beauties, its wonderful handling of romantic and adventurous themes, we cannot but feel that we are as far removed from the ignoble fiction as we are from the ignoble facts of our own day. We breathe a purer air, and have dreams of a time when life had a kind of poetical quality of its own, and was simple and stately and complete.

The tragic interest of The House of the Wolfings centres round the figure of Thiodolf, the great hero of the tribe. The goddess who loves him gives him, as he goes to battle against the Romans, a magical hauberk on which rests this strange fate: that he who wears it shall save his own life and destroy the life of his land. Thiodolf, finding out this secret, brings the hauberk back to the Wood-Sun, as she is called, and chooses death for himself rather than the ruin of his cause, and so the story ends.

But Mr. Morris has always preferred romance to tragedy, and set the development of action above the concentration of passion. His story is like some splendid old tapestry crowded with stately images and enriched with delicate and delightful detail. The impression it leaves on us is not of a single central figure dominating the whole, but rather of a magnificent design to which everything is subordinated, and by which everything becomes of enduring import. It is the whole presentation of the primitive life that really fascinates. What in other hands would have been mere archæology is here transformed by quick artistic instinct and made wonderful for us, and human and full of high interest. The ancient world seems to have come to life again for our pleasure.

Of a work so large and so coherent, completed with no less perfection than it is conceived, it is difficult by mere quotation to give any adequate idea. This, however, may serve as an example of its narrative power. The passage describes the visit of Thiodolf to the Wood-Sun:

The moonlight lay in a great flood on the grass without, and the dew was falling in the coldest hour of the night, and the earth smelled sweetly: the whole habitation was asleep now, and there was no sound to be known as the sound of any creature, save that from the distant meadow came the lowing of a cow that had lost her calf, and that a white owl was flitting about near the eaves of the Roof with her wild cry that sounded like the mocking of merriment now silent. Thiodolf turned toward the wood, and walked steadily through the scattered hazel-trees, and thereby into the thick of the beech-trees, whose boles grew smooth and silver-grey, high and close-set: and so on and on he went as one going by a well-known path, though there was no path, till all the moonlight was quenched under the close roof of the beech-leaves, though yet for all the darkness, no man could go there and not feel that the roof was green above him. Still he went on in despite of the darkness, till at last there was a glimmer before him, that grew greater till he came unto a small wood-lawn whereon the turf grew again, though the grass was but thin, because little sunlight got to it, so close and thick were the tall trees round about it. . . . Nought looked Thiodolf either at the heavens above, or the trees, as he strode from off the husk-strewn floor of the beech wood on to the scanty grass of the lawn, but his eyes looked straight before him at that which was amidmost of the lawn: and little wonder was that; for there on a stone chair sat a woman exceeding fair, clad in glittering raiment, her hair lying as pale in the moonlight on the grey stone as the barley acres in the August night before the reaping-hook goes in amongst them. She sat there as though she were awaiting some one, and he made no stop nor stay, but went straight up to her, and took her in his arms, and kissed her mouth and her eyes, and she him again; and then he sat himself down beside her.

As an example of the beauty of the verse we would take this from the song of the Wood-Sun. It at least shows how perfectly the poetry harmonizes with the prose, and how natural the transition is from the one to the other:

In many a stead Doom dwelleth, nor sleepeth day nor night:

The rim of the bowl she kisseth, and beareth the chambering light

When the kings of men wend happy to the bride-bed from the board.

It is little to say that she wendeth the edge of the grinded sword,

When about the house half builded she hangeth many a day;

The ship from the strand she shoveth, and on his wonted way

By the mountain hunter fareth where his foot ne'er failed before:

She is where the high bank crumbles at last on the river's shore:

The mower's scythe she whetteth; and lulleth the shepherd to sleep

Where the deadly ling-worm wakeneth in the desert of the sheep.

Now we that come of the God-kin of her redes for ourselves we wot,

But her will with the lives of men-folk and their ending know we not.

So therefore I bid thee not fear for thyself of Doom and her deed.

But for me: and I bid thee hearken to the helping of my need.

Or else—Art thou happy in life, or lusteth thou to die

In the flower of thy days, when thy glory and thy longing bloom on high?

The last chapter of the book in which we are told of the great feast made for the dead is so finely written that we cannot refrain from quoting this passage:

> Now was the glooming falling upon the earth; but the Hall was bright within even as the Hall-Sun had promised. Therein was set forth the Treasure of the Wolfings; fair cloths were hung on the walls, goodly broidered garments on the pillars: goodly brazen cauldrons and fair-carven chests were set down in nooks where men could see them well, and vessels of gold and silver were set all up and down the tables of the feast. The pillars also were wreathed with flowers, and flowers hung garlanded from the walls over the precious hangings; sweet gums and spices were burning in fair-wrought censers of brass, and so many candles were alight under the Roof, that scarce had it looked more

ablaze when the Romans had litten the faggots therein for its burning amidst the hurry of the Morning Battle.

There then they fell to feasting, hallowing in the high-tide of their return with victory in their hands: and the dead corpses of Thiodolf and Otter, clad in precious glittering raiment, looked down on them from the High-seat, and the kindreds worshipped them and were glad; and they drank the Cup to them before any others, were they Gods or men.

In days of uncouth realism and unimaginative imitation, it is a high pleasure to welcome work of this kind. It is a work in which all lovers of literature cannot fail to delight.

A Tale of the House of the Wolfings and all the Kindreds of the Mark.
Written in Prose and in Verse by William Morris. (Reeves and Turner.)

SOME LITERARY NOTES

(Woman's World, April 1889.)

'In modern life,' said Matthew Arnold once, 'you cannot well enter a monastery; but you can enter the Wordsworth Society.' I fear that this will sound to many a somewhat uninviting description of this admirable and useful body, whose papers and productions have been recently published by Professor Knight, under the title of Wordsworthiana. 'Plain living and high thinking' are not popular ideals. Most people prefer to live in luxury, and to think with the majority. However, there is really nothing in the essays and addresses of the Wordsworth Society that need cause the public any unnecessary alarm; and it is gratifying to note that, although the society is still in the first blush of enthusiasm, it has not yet insisted upon our admiring Wordsworth's inferior work. It praises what is worthy of praise, reverences what should be reverenced, and explains what does not require explanation. One paper is quite delightful; it is from the pen of Mr. Rawnsley, and deals with such reminiscences of Wordsworth as still linger among the peasantry of Westmoreland. Mr. Rawnsley grew up, he tells us, in the immediate vicinity of the present Poet-Laureate's old home in Lincolnshire, and had been struck with the swiftness with which,

As year by year the labourer tills

His wonted glebe, or lops the glades,

the memories of the poet of the Somersby Wold had 'faded from off the circle of the hills'—had, indeed, been astonished to note how little real interest was taken in him or his fame, and how seldom his works were met with in the houses of the rich or poor in the very neighbourhood. Accordingly, when he came to reside in the Lake Country, he endeavoured to find out what of Wordsworth's memory among the men of the Dales still lingered on—how far he was still a moving presence among them—how far his works had made their way into the cottages and farmhouses of the valleys. He also tried to discover how far the race of Westmoreland and Cumberland farm-folk—the 'Matthews' and the 'Michaels' of the poet, as described by him—were real or fancy pictures, or how far the characters of the Dalesmen had been altered in any remarkable manner by tourist influences during the thirty-two years that have passed since the Lake poet was laid to rest.

With regard to the latter point, it will be remembered that Mr. Ruskin, writing in 1876, said that 'the Border peasantry, painted with absolute fidelity by Scott and Wordsworth,' are, as hitherto, a scarcely injured race; that in his fields at Coniston he had men who might have fought with Henry v. at Agincourt without being distinguished from any of his knights; that he could take his tradesmen's word for a thousand pounds, and need never latch his garden gate; and that he did not fear molestation, in wood or on moor, for his girl guests. Mr. Rawnsley, however, found that a certain beauty had vanished which the simple retirement of old valley days fifty years ago gave to the men among whom Wordsworth lived. 'The strangers,' he says, 'with their gifts of gold, their vulgarity, and their requirements, have much to answer for.' As for their impressions of Wordsworth, to understand them one must understand the vernacular of the Lake District. 'What was Mr. Wordsworth like in personal appearance?' said Mr. Rawnsley once to an old retainer, who still lives not far from Rydal Mount. 'He was a ugly-faäced man, and a meän-liver,' was the answer; but all that was really meant was that he was a man of marked features, and led a very simple life in matters of food and raiment. Another old man, who believed that Wordsworth 'got most of his poetry out of Hartley,' spoke of the poet's wife as 'a very onpleasant woman, very onpleasant indeed. A close-fisted woman, that's what she was.' This, however, seems to have been merely a tribute to Mrs. Wordsworth's admirable housekeeping qualities.

The first person interviewed by Mr. Rawnsley was an old lady who had been once in service at Rydal Mount, and was, in 1870, a lodging-house keeper at Grasmere. She was not a very imaginative person, as may be gathered from the following anecdote:—Mr. Rawnsley's sister came in from a late evening walk, and said, 'O Mrs. D---, have you seen the wonderful sunset?' The good lady turned sharply round and, drawing herself to her full height, as if mortally offended, answered: 'No, miss; I'm a tidy cook, I know, and "they say" a decentish body for a landlady, but I don't knaw nothing about sunsets or them sort of things, they've never been in my line.' Her reminiscence of Wordsworth was as worthy of tradition as it was explanatory, from her point of view, of the method in which Wordsworth composed, and was helped in his labours by his enthusiastic sister. 'Well, you know,' she said, 'Mr. Wordsworth went humming and booing about, and she, Miss Dorothy, kept close behint him, and she picked up the bits as he let 'em fall, and tak' 'em down, and put 'em together on paper for him. And you may be very well sure as how she didn't understand nor make sense out of 'em, and I doubt that he didn't know much about them either himself, but, howivver, there's a great many folk as do, I dare say.' Of Wordsworth's habit of talking to himself, and composing aloud, we hear a great deal. 'Was Mr. Wordsworth a sociable man?' asked Mr. Rawnsley of a Rydal farmer. 'Wudsworth, for a' he had noa pride nor nowt,' was the answer, 'was a man who was quite one to hissel, ye kna. He was not a man as folks could crack wi', nor not a man as could crack wi' folks. But there was another thing as kep' folk off, he had a ter'ble girt deep voice, and ye might see his faace agaan for long enuff. I've knoan folks, village lads and lasses, coming over by old road above, which runs from Grasmere to Rydal, flayt a'most to death there by Wishing Gaate to hear the girt voice a groanin' and mutterin' and thunderin' of a still evening. And he had a way of standin' quite still by the rock there in t' path under Rydal, and folks could hear sounds like a wild beast coming from the rocks, and childer were scared fit to be dead a'most.'

Wordsworth's description of himself constantly recurs to one:

And who is he with modest looks,

And clad in sober russet gown?

He murmurs by the running brooks,

A music sweeter than their own;

He is retired as noontide dew,

Or fountain in a noonday grove.

But the corroboration comes in strange guise. Mr. Rawnsley asked one of the Dalesmen about Wordsworth's dress and habits. This was the reply: 'Wudsworth wore a Jem Crow, never seed him in a boxer in my life,—a Jem Crow and an old blue cloak was his rig, and as for his habits, he had noan; niver knew him with a pot i' his hand, or a pipe i' his mouth. But he was a greät skater, for a' that—noan better in these parts—why, he could cut his own naäme upo' the ice, could Mr. Wudsworth.' Skating seems to have been Wordsworth's one form of amusement. He was 'over feckless i' his hands'—could not drive or ride—'not a bit of fish in him,' and 'nowt of a mountaineer.' But he could skate. The rapture of the time when, as a boy, on Esthwaite's frozen lake, he had

wheeled about,

Proud and exulting like an untired horse

That cares not for his home, and, shod with steel,

Had hissed along the polished ice,

was continued, Mr. Rawnsley tells us, into manhood's later day; and Mr. Rawnsley found many proofs that the skill the poet had gained, when

Not seldom from the uproar he retired,

Into a silent bay, or sportively

> Glanced sideways, leaving the tumultuous throng
>
> To cut across the reflex of a star,

was of such a kind as to astonish the natives among whom he dwelt. The recollection of a fall he once had, when his skate caught on a stone, still lingers in the district. A boy had been sent to sweep the snow from the White Moss Tarn for him. 'Did Mr. Wudsworth gie ye owt?' he was asked, when he returned from his labour. 'Na, but I seed him tumlle, though!' was the answer. 'He was a ter'ble girt skater, was Wudsworth now,' says one of Mr. Rawnsley's informants; 'he would put one hand i' his breast (he wore a frill shirt i' them days), and t' other hand i' his waistband, same as shepherds does to keep their hands warm, and he would stand up straight and sway and swing away grandly.'

Of his poetry they did not think much, and whatever was good in it they ascribed to his wife, his sister, and Hartley Coleridge. He wrote poetry, they said, 'because he couldn't help it—because it was his hobby'—for sheer love, and not for money. They could not understand his doing work 'for nowt,' and held his occupation in somewhat light esteem because it did not bring in 'a deal o' brass to the pocket.' 'Did you ever read his poetry, or see any books about in the farmhouses?' asked Mr. Rawnsley. The answer was curious: 'Ay, ay, time or two. But ya're weel aware there's potry and potry. There's potry wi' a li'le bit pleasant in it, and potry sic as a man can laugh at or the childer understand, and some as takes a deal of mastery to make out what's said, and a deal of Wudsworth's was this sort, ye kna. You could tell fra the man's faace his potry would niver have no laugh in it. His potry was quite different work from li'le Hartley. Hartley 'ud goa running along beside o' the brooks and mak his, and goa in the first oppen door and write what he had got upo' paper. But Wudsworth's potry was real hard stuff, and bided a deal of makking, and he'd keep it in his head for long enough. Eh, but it's queer, mon, different ways folks hes of making potry now. . . . Not but what Mr. Wudsworth didn't stand very high, and was a well-spoken man enough.' The best criticism on Wordsworth that Mr. Rawnsley heard was this: 'He was an open-air man, and a great critic of trees.'

There are many useful and well-written essays in Professor Knight's volume, but Mr. Rawnsley's is far the most interesting of all. It gives us a graphic picture of the poet as he appeared in outward semblance and manner to those about whom he wrote.

Wordsworthiana: A Selection from Papers read to the Wordsworth Society. Edited by William Knight. (Macmillan and Co.)

MR. SWINBURNE'S POEMS AND BALLADS (third series)
(Pall Mall Gazette, June 27, 1889.)

Mr. Swinburne once set his age on fire by a volume of very perfect and very poisonous poetry. Then he became revolutionary and pantheistic, and cried out against those that sit in high places both in heaven and on earth. Then he invented Marie Stuart and laid upon us the heavy burden of Bothwell. Then he retired to the nursery and wrote poems about children of a somewhat over-subtle character. He is now extremely patriotic, and manages to combine with his patriotism a strong affection for the Tory party. He has always been a great poet. But he has his limitations, the chief of which is, curiously enough, the entire lack of any sense of limit. His song is nearly always too loud for his subject. His magnificent rhetoric, nowhere more magnificent than in the volume that now lies before us, conceals rather than reveals. It has been said of him, and with truth, that he is a master of language, but with still greater truth it may be said that Language is his master. Words seem to dominate him. Alliteration tyrannizes over him. Mere sound often becomes his lord. He is so eloquent that whatever he touches becomes unreal.

Let us turn to the poem on the Armada:

The wings of the south-west wind are widened; the breath of his fervent lips,

More keen than a sword's edge, fiercer than fire, falls full on the plunging ships.

The pilot is he of the northward flight, their stay and their steersman he;

A helmsman clothed with the tempest, and girdled with strength to constrain the sea.

And the host of them trembles and quails, caught fast in his hand as a bird in the toils:

For the wrath and the joy that fulfil him are mightier than man's, whom he slays and spoils.

And vainly, with heart divided in sunder, and labour of wavering will,

The lord of their host takes counsel with hope if haply their star shine still.

Somehow we seem to have heard all this before. Does it come from the fact that of all the poets who ever lived Mr. Swinburne is the one who is the most limited in imagery? It must be admitted that he is so. He has wearied us with his monotony. 'Fire' and the 'Sea' are the two words ever on his lips. We must confess also that this shrill singing—marvellous as it is—leaves us out of breath. Here is a passage from a poem called A Word with the Wind:

Be the sunshine bared or veiled, the sky superb or shrouded,

   Still the waters, lax and languid, chafed and foiled,

Keen and thwarted, pale and patient, clothed with fire or clouded,

   Vex their heart in vain, or sleep like serpents coiled.

Thee they look for, blind and baffled, wan with wrath and weary,

   Blown for ever back by winds that rock the bird:

Winds that seamews breast subdue the sea, and bid the dreary

   Waves be weak as hearts made sick with hope deferred.

Let the clarion sound from westward, let the south bear token

   How the glories of thy godhead sound and shine:

Bid the land rejoice to see the land-wind's broad wings broken,

   Bid the sea take comfort, bid the world be thine.

Verse of this kind may be justly praised for the sustained strength and vigour of its metrical scheme. Its purely technical excellence is extraordinary. But is it more than an oratorical tour de force? Does it really convey much? Does it charm? Could we return to it again and again with renewed pleasure? We think not. It seems to us empty.

Of course, we must not look to these poems for any revelation of human life. To be at one with the elements seems to be Mr. Swinburne's aim. He seeks to speak with the breath of wind and wave. The roar of the fire is ever in his ears. He puts his clarion to the lips of Spring and bids her blow, and the Earth wakes from her dreams and tells him her secret. He is the first lyric poet who has tried to make an absolute surrender of his own personality, and he has succeeded. We hear the song, but we never know the singer. We never even get near to him. Out of the thunder and splendour of words he himself says nothing. We have often had man's interpretation of Nature; now we have Nature's interpretation of man, and she has curiously little to say. Force and Freedom form her vague message. She deafens us with her clangours.

But Mr. Swinburne is not always riding the whirlwind and calling out of the depths of the sea. Romantic ballads in Border dialect have not lost their fascination for him, and this last volume contains some very splendid examples of this curious artificial kind of poetry. The amount of pleasure one gets out of dialect is a matter entirely of temperament. To say 'mither' instead of 'mother' seems to many the acme of romance. There are others who are not quite so ready to believe in the pathos of provincialism. There is, however, no doubt of Mr. Swinburne's mastery over the form, whether the form be quite legitimate or not. The Weary Wedding has the concentration and colour of a great drama, and the quaintness of its style lends it something of the power of a grotesque. The ballad of The Witch-Mother, a mediæval Medea who slays her children because her lord is faithless, is worth reading on account of its horrible simplicity. The Bride's Tragedy, with its strange refrain of

In, in, out and in,

Blaws the wind and whirls the whin:

The Jacobite's Exile—

O lordly flow the Loire and Seine,

And loud the dark Durance:

But bonnier shine the braes of Tyne

Than a' the fields of France;

And the waves of Till that speak sae still

Gleam goodlier where they glance:

The Tyneside Widow and A Reiver's Neck-verse are all poems of fine imaginative power, and some of them are terrible in their fierce intensity of passion. There is no danger of English poetry narrowing itself to a form so limited as the romantic ballad in dialect. It is of too vital a growth for that. So we may welcome Mr. Swinburne's masterly experiments with the hope that things which are inimitable will not be imitated. The collection is completed by a few poems on children, some sonnets, a threnody on John William Inchbold, and a lovely lyric entitled The Interpreters.

In human thought have all things habitation;

Our days

Laugh, lower, and lighten past, and find no station

That stays.

But thought and faith are mightier things than time

Can wrong,

Made splendid once by speech, or made sublime

By song.

Remembrance, though the tide of change that rolls

Wax hoary,

Gives earth and heaven, for song's sake and the soul's,

Their glory.

Certainly, 'for song's sake' we should love Mr. Swinburne's work, cannot, indeed, help loving it, so marvellous a music-maker is he. But what of the soul? For the soul we must go elsewhere.

Poems and Ballads. Third Series. By Algernon Charles
Swinburne. (Chatto and Windus.)

A CHINESE SAGE

(Speaker, February 8, 1890.)

An eminent Oxford theologian once remarked that his only objection to modern progress was that it progressed forward instead of backward—a view that so fascinated a certain artistic undergraduate that he promptly wrote an essay upon some unnoticed analogies between the development of ideas and the movements of the common sea-crab. I feel sure the Speaker will not be suspected even by its most enthusiastic friends of holding this dangerous heresy of retrogression. But I must candidly admit that I have come to the conclusion that the most caustic criticism of modern life I have met with for some time is that contained in the writings of the learned Chuang Tzŭ, recently translated into the vulgar tongue by Mr. Herbert Giles, Her Majesty's Consul at Tamsui.

The spread of popular education has no doubt made the name of this great thinker quite familiar to the general public, but, for the sake of the few and the over-cultured, I feel it my duty to state definitely who he was, and to give a brief outline of the character of his philosophy.

Chuang Tzŭ, whose name must carefully be pronounced as it is not written, was born in the fourth century before Christ, by the banks of the Yellow River, in the Flowery Land; and portraits of the wonderful sage seated on the flying dragon of contemplation may still be found on the simple tea-trays and pleasing screens of many of our most respectable suburban households. The honest ratepayer and his healthy family have no doubt often mocked at the dome-like forehead of the philosopher, and laughed over the strange perspective of the landscape that lies beneath him. If they really knew who he was, they would tremble. Chuang Tzŭ spent his life in preaching the great creed of Inaction, and in pointing out the uselessness of all useful things. 'Do nothing, and everything will be done,' was the doctrine which he inherited from his great master Lao Tzŭ. To resolve action into thought, and thought into abstraction, was his wicked transcendental aim. Like the obscure philosopher of early Greek speculation, he believed in the identity of contraries; like Plato, he was an idealist, and had all the idealist's contempt for utilitarian systems; he was a mystic like Dionysius, and Scotus Erigena, and Jacob Böhme, and held, with them and with Philo, that the object of life was to get rid of self-consciousness, and to become the unconscious vehicle of a higher illumination. In fact, Chuang Tzŭ may be said to have summed up in himself almost every mood of European metaphysical or mystical thought, from Heraclitus down to Hegel. There was something in him of the Quietist also; and in his worship of Nothing he may be said to have in some measure anticipated those strange dreamers of mediæval days who, like Tauler and Master Eckhart, adored the purum nihil and the Abyss. The great middle classes of this country, to whom, as we all know, our prosperity, if not our civilization, is entirely due, may shrug their shoulders over all this and ask, with a certain amount of reason, what is the identity of contraries to them, and why they should get rid of that self-consciousness which is their chief characteristic. But Chuang Tzŭ was something more than a metaphysician and an illuminist. He sought to destroy society, as we know it, as the middle classes know it; and the sad thing is that he combines with the passionate eloquence of a Rousseau the scientific reasoning of a Herbert Spencer. There is nothing of the sentimentalist in him. He pities the rich more than the poor, if he even pities at all, and prosperity seems to him as tragic a thing as suffering. He has nothing of the modern sympathy with failures, nor does he propose that the prizes should always be given on moral grounds to those who come in last in the race. It is the race itself that he objects to; and as for active sympathy, which has become the profession of so many worthy people in our own day, he thinks that trying to make others good is as silly an occupation as 'beating a drum in a forest in order to find a fugitive.' It is a mere waste of energy. That is all. While, as for a thoroughly sympathetic man, he is, in the eyes of Chuang Tzŭ, simply a man who is always trying to be somebody else, and so misses the only possible excuse for his own existence.

Yes; incredible as it may seem, this curious thinker looked back with a sigh of regret to a certain Golden Age when there were no competitive examinations, no wearisome educational systems, no missionaries, no penny dinners for the people, no Established Churches, no Humanitarian Societies, no dull lectures about one's duty to one's neighbour, and no tedious sermons about any subject at all. In those ideal days, he tells us, people loved each other without being conscious of charity, or writing to the newspapers about it. They were upright, and yet they never published books upon Altruism. As every man kept his knowledge to himself, the world escaped the curse of scepticism; and as every man kept his virtues to himself, nobody meddled in other people's business. They lived simple and peaceful lives, and were contented with such food and raiment as they could get. Neighbouring districts were in sight, and 'the cocks and dogs of one could be heard in the other,' yet the people grew old and died without ever interchanging visits. There was no chattering about clever men, and no laudation of good men. The intolerable sense of obligation was unknown. The deeds of humanity left no trace, and their affairs were not made a burden for prosperity by foolish historians.

In an evil moment the Philanthropist made his appearance, and brought with him the mischievous idea of Government. 'There is such a thing,' says Chuang Tzŭ, 'as leaving mankind alone: there has never been such a thing as governing mankind.' All modes of government are wrong. They are unscientific, because they seek to alter the natural environment of man; they are immoral because, by interfering with the individual, they produce the most aggressive forms of egotism; they are ignorant, because they try to spread education; they are self-destructive, because they engender anarchy. 'Of old,' he tells us, 'the Yellow Emperor first caused charity and duty to one's neighbour to interfere with the natural goodness of the heart of man. In consequence of this, Yao and Shun wore the hair off their legs in endeavouring to feed their people. They disturbed their internal economy in order to find room for artificial virtues. They exhausted their energies in framing laws, and they were failures.' Man's heart, our philosopher goes on to say, may be 'forced down or stirred up,' and in either case the issue is fatal. Yao made the people too happy, so they were not satisfied. Chieh made them too wretched, so they grew discontented. Then every one began to argue about the best way of tinkering up society. 'It is quite clear that something must be done,' they said to each other, and there was a general rush for knowledge. The results were so dreadful that the Government of the day had to bring in Coercion, and as a consequence of this 'virtuous men sought refuge in mountain caves, while rulers of state sat trembling in ancestral halls.' Then, when everything was in a state of perfect chaos, the Social Reformers got up on platforms, and preached salvation from the ills that they and their system had caused. The poor Social Reformers! 'They know not shame, nor what it is to blush,' is the verdict of Chuang Tzŭ upon them.

The economic question, also, is discussed by this almond-eyed sage at great length, and he writes about the curse of capital as eloquently as Mr. Hyndman. The accumulation of wealth is to him the origin of evil. It makes the strong violent, and the weak dishonest. It creates the petty thief, and puts him in a bamboo cage. It creates the big thief, and sets him on a throne of white jade. It is the father of competition, and competition is the waste, as well as the destruction, of energy. The order of nature is rest, repetition, and peace. Weariness and war are the results of an artificial society based upon capital; and the richer this society gets, the more thoroughly bankrupt it really is, for it has neither sufficient rewards for the good nor sufficient punishments for the wicked. There is also this to be remembered—that the prizes of the world degrade a man as much as the world's punishments. The age is rotten with its worship of success. As for education, true wisdom can neither be learnt nor taught. It is a spiritual state, to which he who lives in harmony with nature attains. Knowledge is shallow if we compare it with the extent of the unknown, and only the unknowable is of value. Society produces rogues, and education makes one rogue cleverer than another. That is the only result of School Boards. Besides, of what possible philosophic importance can education be, when it serves simply to make each man differ from his neighbour? We arrive ultimately at a chaos of opinions, doubt everything, and fall into the vulgar habit of arguing; and it is only the intellectually lost who ever argue. Look at Hui Tzu. 'He was a man of many ideas. His work would fill five carts. But his doctrines were paradoxical.' He said that there were feathers in an egg, because there were feathers on a chicken; that a dog could be a sheep, because all names were arbitrary; that there was a moment when a swift-flying arrow was neither moving nor at rest; that if you took a stick a foot long, and cut it in half every day, you would never come to the end of it; and that a bay horse and a dun cow were three, because taken separately they were two, and taken together they were one, and one and two made up three. 'He was like a man running a race with his own shadow, and making a noise in order to drown the echo. He was a clever gadfly, that was all. What was the use of him?'

Morality is, of course, a different thing. It went out of fashion, says Chuang Tzŭ, when people began to moralize. Men ceased then to be spontaneous and to act on intuition. They became priggish and artificial, and were so blind as to have a definite purpose in life. Then came Governments and Philanthropists, those two pests of the age. The former tried to coerce people into being good, and so destroyed the natural goodness of man. The latter were a set of aggressive busybodies who caused confusion wherever they went. They were stupid enough to have principles, and unfortunate enough to act up to them. They all came to bad ends, and showed that universal altruism is as bad in its results as universal egotism. 'They tripped people up over charity, and fettered them with duties to their neighbours.' They gushed over music, and fussed over ceremonies. As a consequence of all this, the world lost its equilibrium, and has been staggering ever since.

Who, then, according to Chuang Tzŭ, is the perfect man? And what is his manner of life? The perfect man does nothing beyond gazing at the universe. He adopts no absolute position. 'In motion, he is like water. At rest, he is like a mirror. And, like Echo, he answers only when he is called upon.' He lets externals take care of themselves. Nothing material injures him; nothing spiritual punishes him. His mental equilibrium gives him the empire of the world. He is never the slave of objective existences. He knows that, 'just as the best language is that which is never spoken, so the best action is that which is never done.' He is passive, and accepts the laws of life. He rests in inactivity, and sees the world become virtuous of itself. He does not try to 'bring about his own good deeds.' He never wastes himself on effort. He is not troubled about moral distinctions. He knows that things are what they are, and that their consequences will be what they will be. His mind is the 'speculum of creation,' and he is ever at peace.

All this is of course excessively dangerous, but we must remember that Chuang Tzŭ lived more than two thousand years ago, and never had the opportunity of seeing our unrivalled civilization. And yet it is possible that, were he to come back to earth and visit us, he might have something to say to Mr. Balfour about his coercion and active misgovernment in Ireland; he might smile at some of our philanthropic ardours, and shake his head over many of our organized charities; the School Board might not impress him, nor our race for wealth stir his admiration; he might wonder at our ideals, and grow sad over what we have realized. Perhaps it is well that Chuang Tzŭ cannot return.

Meanwhile, thanks to Mr. Giles and Mr. Quaritch, we have his book to console us, and certainly it is a most fascinating and delightful volume. Chuang Tzŭ is one of the Darwinians before Darwin. He traces man from the germ, and sees his unity with nature. As an anthropologist he is excessively interesting, and he describes our primitive arboreal ancestor living in trees through his terror of animals stronger than himself, and knowing only one parent, the mother, with all the accuracy of a lecturer at the Royal Society. Like Plato, he adopts the dialogue as his mode of expression, 'putting words into other people's mouths,' he tells us, 'in order to gain breadth of view.' As a story-teller he is charming. The account of the visit of the respectable Confucius to the great Robber Chê is most vivid and brilliant, and it is impossible not to laugh over the ultimate discomfiture of the sage, the barrenness of whose moral platitudes is ruthlessly exposed by the successful brigand. Even in his metaphysics, Chuang Tzŭ is intensely humorous. He personifies his abstractions, and makes them act plays before us. The Spirit of the Clouds, when passing eastward through the expanse of air, happened to fall in with the Vital Principle. The latter was slapping his ribs and hopping about: whereupon the Spirit of the Clouds said, 'Who are you, old man, and what are you doing?' 'Strolling!' replied the Vital Principle, without stopping, for all activities are ceaseless. 'I want to know something,' continued the Spirit of the Clouds. 'Ah!' cried the Vital Principle, in a tone of disapprobation, and a marvellous conversation follows, that is not unlike the dialogue between the Sphinx and the Chimera in Flaubert's curious drama. Talking animals, also, have their place in Chuang Tzŭ's parables and stories, and through myth and poetry and fancy his strange philosophy finds musical utterance.

Of course it is sad to be told that it is immoral to be consciously good, and that doing anything is the worst form of idleness. Thousands of excellent and really earnest philanthropists would be absolutely thrown upon the rates if we adopted the view that nobody should be allowed to meddle in what does not concern him. The doctrine of the uselessness of all useful things would not merely endanger our commercial supremacy as a nation, but might bring discredit upon many prosperous and serious-minded members of the shop-keeping classes. What would become of our popular preachers, our Exeter Hall orators, our drawing-room evangelists, if we said to them, in the words of Chuang Tzŭ, 'Mosquitoes will keep a man awake all night with their biting, and just in the same way this talk of charity and duty to one's neighbour drives us nearly crazy. Sirs, strive to keep the world to its own original simplicity, and, as the wind bloweth where it listeth, so let Virtue establish itself. Wherefore this undue energy?' And what would be the fate of governments and professional politicians if we came to the conclusion that there is no such thing as governing mankind at all? It is clear that Chuang Tzŭ is a very dangerous writer, and the publication of his book in English, two thousand years after his death, is obviously premature, and may cause a great deal of pain to many thoroughly respectable and industrious persons. It may be true that the ideal of self-culture and self-development, which is the aim of his scheme of life, and the basis of his scheme of philosophy, is an ideal somewhat needed by an age like ours, in which most people are so anxious to educate their neighbours that they have actually no time left in which to educate themselves. But would it be wise to say so? It seems to me that if we once admitted the force of any one of Chuang Tzŭ's destructive criticisms we should have to put some check on our national habit of self-glorification; and the only thing that ever consoles man for the stupid things he does is the praise he always gives himself for doing them. There may, however, be a few who have grown wearied of that strange modern tendency that sets enthusiasm to do the work of the intellect. To these, and such as these, Chuang Tzŭ will be welcome. But let them only read him. Let them not talk about him. He would be disturbing at dinner-parties, and impossible at afternoon teas, and his whole life was a protest against platform speaking. 'The perfect man ignores self; the divine man ignores action; the true sage ignores reputation.' These are the principles of Chuang Tzŭ.

Chuang Tzŭ: Mystic, Moralist, and Social Reformer. Translated from the Chinese by Herbert A. Giles, H.B.M.'s Consul at Tamsui.
(Bernard Quaritch.)

MR. PATER'S APPRECIATIONS
(Speaker, March 22, 1890.)

When I first had the privilege—and I count it a very high one—of meeting Mr. Walter Pater, he said to me, smiling, 'Why do you always write poetry? Why do you not write prose? Prose is so much more difficult.'

It was during my undergraduate days at Oxford; days of lyrical ardour and of studious sonnet-writing; days when one loved the exquisite intricacy and musical repetitions of the ballade, and the villanelle with its linked long-drawn echoes and its curious completeness; days when one solemnly sought to discover the proper temper in which a triolet should be written; delightful days, in which, I am glad to say, there was far more rhyme than reason.

I may frankly confess now that at the time I did not quite comprehend what Mr. Pater really meant; and it was not till I had carefully studied his beautiful and suggestive essays on the Renaissance that I fully realized what a wonderful self-conscious art the art of English prose-writing really is, or may be made to be. Carlyle's stormy rhetoric, Ruskin's winged and passionate eloquence, had seemed to me to spring from enthusiasm rather than from art. I do not think I knew then that even prophets correct their proofs. As for Jacobean prose, I thought it too exuberant; and Queen Anne prose appeared to me terribly bald, and irritatingly rational. But Mr. Pater's essays became to me 'the golden book of spirit and sense, the holy writ of beauty.' They are still this to me. It is possible, of course, that I may exaggerate about them. I certainly hope that I do; for where there is no exaggeration there is no love, and where there is no love there is no understanding. It is only about things that do not interest one, that one can give a really unbiassed opinion; and this is no doubt the reason why an unbiassed opinion is always valueless.

But I must not allow this brief notice of Mr. Pater's new volume to degenerate into an autobiography. I remember being told in America that whenever Margaret Fuller wrote an essay upon Emerson the printers had always to send out to borrow some additional capital 'I's,' and I feel it right to accept this transatlantic warning.

Appreciations, in the fine Latin sense of the word, is the title given by Mr. Pater to his book, which is an exquisite collection of exquisite essays, of delicately wrought works of art—some of them being almost Greek in their purity of outline and perfection of form, others mediæval in their strangeness of colour and passionate suggestion, and all of them absolutely modern, in the true meaning of the term modernity. For he to whom the present is the only thing that is present, knows nothing of the age in which he lives. To realize the nineteenth century one must realize every century that has preceded it, and that has contributed to its making. To know anything about oneself, one must know all about others. There must be no mood with which one cannot sympathize, no dead mode of life that one cannot make alive. The legacies of heredity may make us alter our views of moral responsibility, but they cannot but intensify our sense of the value of Criticism; for the true critic is he who bears within himself the dreams and ideas and feelings of myriad generations, and to whom no form of thought is alien, no emotional impulse obscure.

Perhaps the most interesting, and certainly the least successful, of the essays contained in the present volume is that on Style. It is the most interesting because it is the work of one who speaks with the high authority that comes from the noble realization of things nobly conceived. It is the least successful, because the subject is too abstract. A true artist like Mr. Pater is most felicitous when he deals with the concrete, whose very limitations give him finer freedom, while they necessitate more intense vision. And yet what a high ideal is contained in these few pages! How good it is for us, in these days of popular education and facile journalism, to be reminded of the real scholarship that is essential to the perfect writer, who, 'being a true lover of words for their own sake, a minute and constant observer of their physiognomy,' will avoid what is mere rhetoric, or ostentatious ornament, or negligent misuse of terms, or ineffective surplusage, and will be known by his tact of omission, by his skilful economy of means, by his selection and self-restraint, and perhaps above all by that conscious artistic structure which is the expression of mind in style. I think I have been wrong in saying that the subject is too abstract. In Mr. Pater's hands it becomes very real to us indeed, and he shows us how, behind the perfection of a man's style, must lie the passion of a man's soul.

As one passes to the rest of the volume, one finds essays on Wordsworth and on Coleridge, on Charles Lamb and on Sir Thomas Browne, on some of Shakespeare's plays and on the English kings that Shakespeare fashioned, on Dante Rossetti, and on William Morris. As that on Wordsworth seems to be Mr. Pater's last work, so that on the singer of the Defence of Guenevere is certainly his earliest, or almost his earliest, and it is interesting to mark the change that has taken place in his style. This change is, perhaps, at first sight not very apparent. In 1868 we find Mr. Pater writing with the same exquisite care for words, with the same studied music, with the same temper, and something of the same mode of treatment. But, as he goes on, the architecture of the style becomes richer and more complex, the epithet more precise and intellectual. Occasionally one may be inclined to think that there is, here and there, a sentence which is somewhat long, and possibly, if one may venture to say so, a little heavy and cumbersome in movement. But if this be so, it comes from those side-issues suddenly suggested by the idea in its progress, and really revealing the idea more perfectly; or from those felicitous after-thoughts that give a fuller completeness to the central scheme, and yet convey something of the charm of chance; or from a desire to suggest the secondary shades of meaning with all their accumulating effect, and to avoid, it may be, the violence and harshness of too definite and exclusive an opinion. For in matters of art, at any rate, thought is inevitably coloured by emotion, and so is fluid rather than fixed, and, recognizing its dependence upon the moods and upon the passion of fine moments, will not accept the rigidity of a scientific formula or a theological dogma. The critical pleasure, too, that we receive from tracing, through what may seem the intricacies of a sentence, the working of the constructive intelligence, must not be overlooked. As soon as we have realized the design, everything appears clear and simple. After a time, these long sentences of Mr. Pater's come to have the charm of an elaborate piece of music, and the unity of such music also.

I have suggested that the essay on Wordsworth is probably the most recent bit of work contained in this volume. If one might choose between so much that is good, I should be inclined to say it is the finest also. The essay on Lamb is curiously suggestive; suggestive, indeed, of a somewhat more tragic, more sombre figure, than men have been wont to think of in connection with the author of the Essays of Elia. It is an interesting aspect under which to regard Lamb, but perhaps he himself would have had some difficulty in recognizing the portrait given of him. He had, undoubtedly, great sorrows, or motives for sorrow, but he could console himself at a moment's notice for the real tragedies of life by reading any one of the Elizabethan tragedies, provided it was in a folio edition. The essay on Sir Thomas Browne is delightful, and has the strange, personal, fanciful charm of the author of the Religio Medici, Mr. Pater often catching the colour and accent and tone of whatever artist, or work of art, he deals with. That on Coleridge, with its insistence on the necessity of the cultivation of the relative, as opposed to the absolute spirit in philosophy and in ethics, and its high appreciation of the poet's true position in our literature, is in style and substance a very blameless work. Grace of expression and delicate subtlety of thought and phrase, characterize the essays on Shakespeare. But the essay on Wordsworth has a spiritual beauty of its own. It appeals, not to the ordinary Wordsworthian with his uncritical temper, and his gross confusion of ethical and æsthetical problems, but rather to those who desire to separate the gold from the dross, and to reach at the true Wordsworth through the mass of tedious and prosaic work that bears his name, and that serves often to conceal him from us. The presence of an alien element in Wordsworth's art is, of course, recognized by Mr. Pater, but he touches on it merely from the psychological point of view, pointing out how this quality of higher and lower moods gives the effect in his poetry 'of a power not altogether his own, or under his control'; a power which comes and goes when it wills, 'so that the old fancy which made the poet's art an enthusiasm, a form of divine possession, seems almost true of him.' Mr. Pater's earlier essays had their purpurei panni, so eminently suitable for quotation, such as the famous passage on Mona Lisa, and that other in which Botticelli's strange conception of the Virgin is so strangely set forth. From the present volume it is difficult to select any one passage in preference to another as specially characteristic of Mr. Pater's treatment. This, however, is worth quoting at length. It contains a truth eminently suitable for our age:

> That the end of life is not action but contemplation—being as distinct from doing—a certain disposition of the mind: is, in some shape or other, the principle of all the higher morality. In poetry, in art, if you enter into their true spirit at all, you touch this principle in a measure; these, by their sterility, are a type of beholding for the mere joy of beholding. To treat life in the spirit of art is to make life a thing in which means and ends are identified: to encourage such treatment, the true moral significance of art and poetry. Wordsworth, and other poets who have been like him in ancient or more recent times, are the masters, the experts, in this art of impassioned contemplation. Their work is not to teach lessons, or enforce rules, or even to stimulate us to noble ends, but to withdraw the thoughts for a while from the mere machinery of life, to fix them, with appropriate emotions, on the spectacle of those great facts in man's existence which no machinery affects, 'on the great and universal passions of men, the most general and interesting of their occupations, and the entire world of nature'—on 'the operations of the elements and the appearances of the visible universe, on storm and sunshine, on the revolutions of the seasons, on cold and heat, on loss of friends and kindred, on injuries and resentments, on gratitude and hope, on fear and sorrow.' To witness this spectacle with appropriate emotions is the aim of all culture; and of these emotions poetry like Wordsworth's is a great nourisher and stimulant. He sees nature full of sentiment and excitement; he sees men and women as parts of nature, passionate, excited, in strange grouping and connection with the grandeur and beauty of the natural world:—images, in his own words,

'of men suffering; amid awful forms and powers.'

Certainly the real secret of Wordsworth has never been better expressed. After having read and reread Mr. Pater's essay—for it requires re-reading—one returns to the poet's work with a new sense of joy and wonder, and with something of eager and impassioned expectation. And perhaps this might be roughly taken as the test or touchstone of the finest criticism.

Finally, one cannot help noticing the delicate instinct that has gone to fashion the brief epilogue that ends this delightful volume. The difference between the classical and romantic spirits in art has often, and with much over-emphasis, been discussed. But with what a light sure touch does Mr. Pater write of it! How subtle and certain are his distinctions! If imaginative prose be really the special art of this century, Mr. Pater must rank amongst our century's most characteristic artists. In certain things he stands almost alone. The age has produced wonderful prose styles, turbid with individualism, and violent with excess of rhetoric. But in Mr. Pater, as in Cardinal Newman, we find the union of personality with perfection. He has no rival in his own sphere, and he has escaped disciples. And this, not because he has not been imitated, but because in art so fine as his there is something that, in its essence, is inimitable.

Appreciations, with an Essay on Style. By Walter Pater, Fellow of Brasenose College. (Macmillan and Co.)

SENTENTIAE

(Extracted from Reviews)

Perhaps he will write poetry some day. If he does we would earnestly appeal to him to give up calling a cock 'proud chanticleer.' Few synonyms are so depressing.

A young writer can gain more from the study of a literary poet than from the study of a lyrist.

I have seen many audiences more interesting than the actors, and have often heard better dialogue in the foyer than I have on the stage.

The Dramatic College might take up the education of spectators as well as that of players, and teach people that there is a proper moment for the throwing of flowers as well as a proper method.

Life remains eternally unchanged; it is art which, by presenting it to us under various forms, enables us to realize its many-sided mysteries, and to catch the quality of its most fiery-coloured moments. The originality, I mean, which we ask from the artist, is originality of treatment, not of subject. It is only the unimaginative who ever invents. The true artist is known by the use he makes of what he annexes, and he annexes everything.

If I ventured on a bit of advice, which I feel most reluctant to do, it would be to the effect that while one should always study the method of a great artist, one should never imitate his manner. The manner of an artist is essentially individual, the method of an artist is absolutely universal. The first is personality, which no one should copy; the second is perfection, which all should aim at.

A critic who posed as an authority on field sports assured me that no one ever went out hunting when roses were in full bloom. Personally, that is exactly the season I would select for the chase, but then I know more about flowers than I do about foxes, and like them much better.

The nineteenth century may be a prosaic age, but we fear that, if we are to judge by the general run of novels, it is not an age of prose.

Perhaps in this century we are too altruistic to be really artistic.

I am led to hope that the University will some day have a theatre of its own, and that proficiency in scene-painting will be regarded as a necessary qualification for the Slade Professorship. On the stage, literature returns to life and archæology becomes art. A fine theatre is a temple where all the muses may meet, a second Parnassus.

It would be sad indeed if the many volumes of poems that are every year published in London found no readers but the authors themselves and the authors' relations; and the real philanthropist should recognize it as part of his duties to buy every new book of verse that appears.

A fifteen-line sonnet is as bad a monstrosity as a sonnet in dialogue.

Antiquarian books, as a rule, are extremely dull reading. They give us facts without form, science without style, and learning without life.

The Roman patron, in fact, kept the Roman poet alive, and we fancy that many of our modern bards rather regret the old system. Better, surely, the humiliation of the sportula than the indignity of a bill for printing! Better to accept a country-house as a gift than to be in debt to one's landlady! On the whole, the patron was an excellent institution, if not for poetry at least for the poets; . . . every poet longs for a Mæcenas.

The two things the Greeks valued most in actors were grace of gesture and music of voice. Indeed, to gain these virtues their actors used to subject themselves to a regular course of gymnastics and a particular regime of diet, health being to the Greeks not merely a quality of art, but a condition of its production.

One should not be too severe on English novels: they are the only relaxation of the intellectually unemployed.

Most modern novels are more remarkable for their crime than for their culture.

Not that a tramp's mode of life is at all unsuited to the development of the poetic faculty. Far from it! He, if any one, should possess that freedom of mood which is so essential to the artist, for he has no taxes to pay and no relations to worry him. The man who possesses a permanent address, and whose name is to be found in the Directory, is necessarily limited and localized. Only the tramp has absolute liberty of living. Was not Homer himself a vagrant, and did not Thespis go about in a caravan?

In art as in life the law of heredity holds good. On est toujours fils de quelqu'un.

He has succeeded in studying a fine poet without stealing from him—a very difficult thing to do.

Morocco is a sort of paradox among countries, for though it lies westward of Piccadilly, yet it is purely Oriental in character, and though it is but three hours' sail from Europe, yet it makes you feel (to use the forcible expression of an American writer) as if you had been taken up by the scruff of the neck and set down in the Old Testament.

As children themselves are the perfect flowers of life, so a collection of the best poems written on children should be the most perfect of all anthologies.

No English poet has written of children with more love and grace and delicacy [than Herrick]. His Ode on the Birth of Our Saviour, his poem To His Saviour, A Child: A Present by a Child, his Graces for Children, and his many lovely epitaphs on children are all of them exquisite works of art, simple, sweet and sincere.

As the cross-benches form a refuge for those who have no minds to make up, so those who cannot make up their minds always take to Homeric studies. Many of our leaders have sulked in their tents with Achilles after some violent political crisis and, enraged at the fickleness of fortune, more than one has given up to poetry what was obviously meant for party.

There are two ways of misunderstanding a poem. One is to misunderstand it and the other to praise it for qualities it does not possess.

Most modern calendars mar the sweet simplicity of our lives by reminding us that each day that passes is the anniversary of some perfectly uninteresting event. It is true that such aphorisms as

> Graves are a *mother's dimples*
>
> When we complain,

or

> The primrose wears a constant smile,
>
> And captive takes the heart,

can hardly be said to belong to the very highest order of poetry, still, they

211

are preferable, on the whole, to the date of Hannah More's birth, or of the burning down of Exeter Change, or of the opening of the Great Exhibition; and though it would be dangerous to make calendars the basis of Culture, we should all be much improved if we began each day with a fine passage of English poetry.

Even the most uninteresting poet cannot survive bad editing.

Prefixed to the Calendar is an introductory note . . . displaying that intimate acquaintance with Sappho's lost poems which is the privilege only of those who are not acquainted with Greek literature.

Mediocre critics are usually safe in their generalities; it is in their reasons and examples that they come so lamentably to grief.

All premature panegyrics bring their own punishment upon themselves.

No one survives being over-estimated.

Henry Wadsworth Longfellow was one of the first true men of letters America produced, and as such deserves a high place in any history of American civilization. To a land out of breath in its greed for gain he showed the example of a life devoted entirely to the study of literature; his lectures, though not by any means brilliant, were still productive of much good; he had a most charming and gracious personality, and he wrote some pretty poems. But his poems are not of the kind that call for intellectual analysis or for elaborate description or, indeed, for any serious discussion at all.

Though the Psalm of Life be shouted from Maine to California, that would not make it true poetry.

Longfellow has no imitators, for of echoes themselves there are no echoes and it is only style that makes a school.

Poe's marvellous lines To Helen, a poem as beautiful as a Greek gem and as musical as Apollo's lute.

Good novelists are much rarer than good sons, and none of us would part readily with Micawber and Mrs. Nickleby. Still, the fact remains that a man who was affectionate and loving to his children, generous and warm-hearted to his friends, and whose books are the very bacchanalia of benevolence, pilloried his parents to make the groundlings laugh, and this fact every biographer of Dickens should face and, if possible, explain.

No age ever borrows the slang of its predecessor.

What we do not know about Shakespeare is a most fascinating subject, and one that would fill a volume, but what we do know about him is so meagre and inadequate that when it is collected together the result is rather depressing.

They show a want of knowledge that must be the result of years of study.

Rossetti's was a great personality, and personalities such as his do not easily survive shilling primers.

We are sorry to find an English dramatic critic misquoting Shakespeare, as we had always been of opinion that this was a privilege reserved specially for our English actors.

Biographies of this kind rob life of much of its dignity and its wonder, add to death itself a new terror, and make one wish that all art were anonymous.

A pillar of fire to the few who knew him, and of cloud to the many who knew him not, Dante Gabriel Rossetti lived apart from the gossip and tittle-tattle of a shallow age. He never trafficked with the merchants for his soul, nor brought his wares into the market-place for the idle to gape at. Passionate and romantic though he was, yet there was in his nature something of high austerity. He loved seclusion, and hated notoriety, and would have shuddered at the idea that within a few years after his death he was to make his appearance in a series of popular biographies, sandwiched between the author of Pickwick and the Great Lexicographer.

We sincerely hope that a few more novels like these will be published, as the public will then find out that a bad book is very dear at a shilling.

The only form of fiction in which real characters do not seem out of place is history. In novels they are detestable.

Shilling literature is always making demands on our credulity without ever appealing to our imagination.

Pathology is rapidly becoming the basis of sensational literature, and in art, as in politics, there is a great future for monsters.

It is only mediocrities and old maids who consider it a grievance to be misunderstood.

As truly religious people are resigned to everything, even to mediocre poetry, there is no reason at all why Madame Guyon's verses should not be popular with a large section of the community.

A simile committing suicide is always a depressing spectacle.

Such novels as Scamp are possibly more easy to write than they are to read.

We have no doubt that when Bailey wrote to Lord Houghton that common-sense and gentleness were Keats's two special characteristics the worthy Archdeacon meant extremely well, but we prefer the real Keats, with his passionate wilfulness, his fantastic moods and his fine inconsistence. Part of Keats's charm as a man is his fascinating incompleteness.

The Apostolic dictum, that women should not be suffered to teach, is no longer applicable to a society such as ours, with its solidarity of interests, its recognition of natural rights, and its universal education, however suitable it may have been to the Greek cities under Roman rule. Nothing in the United States struck me more than the fact that the remarkable intellectual progress of that country is very largely due to the efforts of American women, who edit many of the most powerful magazines and newspapers, take part in the discussion of every question of public interest, and exercise an important influence upon the growth and tendencies of literature and art. Indeed, the women of America are the one class in the community that enjoys that leisure which is so necessary for culture. The men are, as a rule, so absorbed in business, that the task of bringing some element of form into the chaos of daily life is left almost entirely to the opposite sex, and an eminent Bostonian once assured me that in the twentieth century the whole culture of his country

214

would be in petticoats. By that time, however, it is probable that the dress of the two sexes will be assimilated, as similarity of costume always follows similarity of pursuits.

The aim of social comedy, in Menander no less than in Sheridan, is to mirror the manners, not to reform the morals, of its day, and the censure of the Puritan, whether real or affected, is always out of place in literary criticism, and shows a want of recognition of the essential distinction between art and life. After all, it is only the Philistine who thinks of blaming Jack Absolute for his deception, Bob Acres for his cowardice, and Charles Surface for his extravagance, and there is very little use in airing one's moral sense at the expense of one's artistic appreciation.

The Æneid bears almost the same relation to the Iliad that the Idylls of the King do to the old Celtic romances of Arthur. Like them it is full of felicitous modernisms, of exquisite literary echoes and of delicate and delightful pictures; as Lord Tennyson loves England so did Virgil love Rome; the pageants of history and the purple of empire are equally dear to both poets; but neither of them has the grand simplicity or the large humanity of the early singers, and, as a hero, Æneas is no less a failure than Arthur.

There is always a certain amount of danger in any attempt to cultivate impossible virtues.

As far as the serious presentation of life is concerned, what we require is more imaginative treatment, greater freedom from theatric language and theatric convention. It may be questioned, also, whether the consistent reward of virtue and punishment of wickedness be really the healthiest ideal for an art that claims to mirror nature.

True originality is to be found rather in the use made of a model than in the rejection of all models and masters. Dans l'art comme dans la nature on est toujours fils de quelqu'un, and we should not quarrel with the reed if it whispers to us the music of the lyre. A little child once asked me if it was the nightingale who taught the linnets how to sing.

In France they have had one great genius, Balzac, who invented the modern method of looking at life; and one great artist, Flaubert, who is the impeccable master of style; and to the influence of these two men we may trace almost all contemporary French fiction. But in England we have had no schools worth speaking of. The fiery torch lit by the Brontës has not been passed on to other hands; Dickens has influenced only journalism; Thackeray's delightful superficial philosophy, superb narrative power, and clever social satire have found no echoes; nor has Trollope left any direct successors behind him—a fact which is not much to be regretted, however, as, admirable though Trollope undoubtedly is for rainy afternoons and tedious railway journeys, from the point of view of literature he is merely the perpetual curate of Pudlington Parva.

George Meredith's style is chaos illumined by brilliant flashes of lightning. As a writer he has mastered everything, except language; as a novelist he can do everything, except tell a story; as an artist he is everything, except articulate. Too strange to be popular, too individual to have imitators, the author of Richard Feverel stands absolutely alone. It is easy to disarm criticism, but he has disarmed the disciple. He gives us his philosophy through the medium of wit, and is never so pathetic as when he is humorous. To turn truth into a paradox is not difficult, but George Meredith makes all his paradoxes truths, and no Theseus can thread his labyrinth, no Œdipus solve his secret.

The most perfect and the most poisonous of all modern French poets once remarked that a man can live for three days without bread, but that no one can live for three days without poetry. This, however, can hardly be said to be a popular view, or one that commends itself to that curiously uncommon quality which is called common-sense. I fancy that most people, if they do not actually prefer a salmis to a sonnet, certainly like their culture to repose on a basis of good cookery.

A cynical critic once remarked that no great poet is intelligible and no little poet worth understanding, but that otherwise poetry is an admirable thing. This, however, seems to us a somewhat harsh view of the subject. Little poets are an extremely interesting study. The best of them have often some new beauty to show us, and though the worst of them may bore yet they rarely brutalize.

It is a curious thing that when minor poets write choruses to a play they should always consider it necessary to adopt the style and language of a bad translator. We fear that Mr. Bohn has much to answer for.

In one sonnet he makes a distinct attempt to be original and the result is extremely depressing.

> Earth wears her grandest robe, by autumn spun,
>
> *Like some stout matron who of youth has run*
>
> *The course, . . .*

is the most dreadful simile we have ever come across even in poetry. Mr. Griffiths should beware of originality. Like beauty, it is a fatal gift.

There is a wide difference between the beautiful Tuscan city and the sea-city of the Adriatic. Florence is a city full of memories of the great figures of the past. The traveller cannot pass along her streets without treading in the very traces of Dante, without stepping on soil made memorable by footprints never to be effaced. The greatness of the surroundings, the palaces, churches, and frowning mediæval castles in the midst of the city, are all thrown into the background by the greatness, the individuality, the living power and vigour of the men who are their originators, and at the same time their inspiring soul. But when we turn to Venice the effect is very different. We do not think of the makers of that marvellous city, but rather of what they made. The idealized image of Venice herself meets us everywhere. The mother is not overshadowed by the too great glory of any of her sons. In her records the city is everything—the republic, the worshipped ideal of a community in which every man for the common glory seems to have been willing to sink his own. We know that Dante stood within the red walls of the arsenal, and saw the galleys making and mending, and the pitch flaming up to heaven; Petrarch came to visit the great Mistress of the Sea, taking refuge there, 'in this city, true home of the human race,' from trouble, war and pestilence outside; and Byron, with his facile enthusiasms and fervent eloquence, made his home for a time in one of the stately, decaying palaces; but with these exceptions no great poet has ever associated himself with the life of Venice. She had architects, sculptors and painters, but no singer of her own.

To realize the popularity of the great poets one should turn to the minor poets and see whom they follow, what master they select, whose music they echo.

Ordinary theology has long since converted its gold into lead, and words and phrases that once touched the heart of the world have become wearisome and meaningless through repetition. If Theology desires to move us, she must re-write her formulas.

It takes a great artist to be thoroughly modern. Nature is always a little behind the age.

Mr. Nash, who styles himself 'a humble soldier in the army of Faith,' expresses a hope that his book may 'invigorate devotional feeling, especially among the young, to whom verse is perhaps more attractive than to their elders,' but we should be sorry to think that people of any age could admire such a paraphrase as the following:

> Foxes have holes in which to slink for rest,
>
> The birds of air find shelter in the nest;
>
> But He, the Son of Man and Lord of all,
>
> Has no abiding place His own to call.

It is a curious fact that the worst work is always done with the best intentions, and that people are never so trivial as when they take themselves very seriously.

Mr. Foster is an American poet who has read Hawthorne, which is wise of him, and imitated Longfellow, which is not quite so commendable.

Andiatoroctè is the title of a volume of poems by the Rev. Clarence Walworth, of Albany, N.Y. It is a word borrowed from the Indians, and should, we think, be returned to them as soon as possible. The most curious poem of the book is called Scenes at the Holy Home:

> Jesus and Joseph at work! Hurra!
>
> Sight never to see again,

A prentice Deity plies the saw,

While the Master ploughs with the plane.

Poems of this kind were popular in the Middle Ages when the cathedrals of every Christian country served as its theatres. They are anachronisms now, and it is odd that they should come to us from the United States. In matters of this kind we should have some protection.

As for the triolets, and the rondels, and the careful study of metrical subtleties, these things are merely the signs of a desire for perfection in small things and of the recognition of poetry as an art. They have had certainly one good result—they have made our minor poets readable, and have not left us entirely at the mercy of geniuses.

Poetry has many modes of music; she does not blow through one pipe alone. Directness of utterance is good, but so is the subtle recasting of thought into a new and delightful form. Simplicity is good, but complexity, mystery, strangeness, symbolism, obscurity even, these have their value. Indeed, properly speaking, there is no such thing as Style; there are merely styles, that is all.

Writers of poetical prose are rarely good poets.

Poetry may be said to need far more self-restraint than prose. Its conditions are more exquisite. It produces its effects by more subtle means. It must not be allowed to degenerate into mere rhetoric or mere eloquence. It is, in one sense, the most self-conscious of all the arts, as it is never a means to an end but always an end in itself.

It may be difficult for a poet to find English synonyms for Asiatic expressions, but even if it were impossible it is none the less a poet's duty to find them. As it is, Sir Edwin Arnold has translated Sa'di and some one must translate Sir Edwin Arnold.

Lounging in the open air is not a bad school for poets, but it largely depends on the lounger.

People are so fond of giving away what they do not want themselves, that charity is largely on the increase. But with this kind of charity I have not much sympathy. If one gives away a book, it should be a charming book—so charming, that one regrets having given it.

Mr. Whistler, for some reason or other, always adopted the phraseology of the minor prophets. Possibly it was in order to emphasize his well-known claims to verbal inspiration, or perhaps he thought with Voltaire that Habakkuk était capable de tout, and wished to shelter himself under the shield of a definitely irresponsible writer none of whose prophecies, according to the French philosopher, has ever been fulfilled. The idea was clever enough at the beginning, but ultimately the manner became monotonous. The spirit of the Hebrews is excellent but their mode of writing is not to be imitated, and no amount of American jokes will give it that modernity which is essential to a good literary style. Admirable as are Mr. Whistler's fireworks on canvas, his fireworks in prose are abrupt, violent and exaggerated.

'The decisive events of the world,' as has been well said, 'take place in the intellect,' and as for Board-schools, academic ceremonies, hospital wards and the like, they may be well left to the artists of the illustrated papers, who do them admirably and quite as well as they need be done. Indeed, the pictures of contemporary events, Royal marriages, naval reviews and things of this kind that appear in the Academy every year, are always extremely bad; while the very same subjects treated in black and white in the Graphic or the London News are excellent. Besides, if we want to understand the history of a nation through the medium of art, it is to the imaginative and ideal arts that we have to go and not to the arts that are definitely imitative. The visible aspect of life no longer contains for us the secret of life's spirit.

The difficulty under which the novelists of our day labour seems to me to be this: if they do not go into society, their books are unreadable; and if they do go into society, they have no time left for writing.

I must confess that most modern mysticism seems to me to be simply a method of imparting useless knowledge in a form that no one can understand. Allegory, parable, and vision have their high artistic uses, but their philosophical and scientific uses are very small.

220

The object of most modern fiction is not to give pleasure to the artistic instinct, but rather to portray life vividly for us, to draw attention to social anomalies, and social forms of injustice. Many of our novelists are really pamphleteers, reformers masquerading as story-tellers, earnest sociologists seeking to mend as well as to mirror life.

The book is certainly characteristic of an age so practical and so literary as ours, an age in which all social reforms have been preceded and have been largely influenced by fiction.

Mr. Stopford Brooke said some time ago that Socialism and the socialistic spirit would give our poets nobler and loftier themes for song, would widen their sympathies and enlarge the horizon of their vision, and would touch, with the fire and fervour of a new faith, lips that had else been silent, hearts that but for this fresh gospel had been cold. What Art gains from contemporary events is always a fascinating problem and a problem that is not easy to solve. It is, however, certain that Socialism starts well equipped. She has her poets and her painters, her art lecturers and her cunning designers, her powerful orators and her clever writers. If she fails it will not be for lack of expression. If she succeeds her triumph will not be a triumph of mere brute force.

Socialism is not going to allow herself to be trammelled by any hard and fast creed or to be stereotyped into an iron formula. She welcomes many and multiform natures. She rejects none and has room for all. She has the attraction of a wonderful personality and touches the heart of one and the brain of another, and draws this man by his hatred and injustice, and his neighbour by his faith in the future, and a third, it may be, by his love of art or by his wild worship of a lost and buried past. And all of this is well. For, to make men Socialists is nothing, but to make Socialism human is a great thing.

The Reformation gained much from the use of popular hymn-tunes, and the Socialists seem determined to gain by similar means a similar hold upon the people. However, they must not be too sanguine about the result. The walls of Thebes rose up to the sound of music, and Thebes was a very dull city indeed.

We really must protest against Mr. Matthews' efforts to confuse the poetry of Piccadilly with the poetry of Parnassus. To tell us, for instance, that Mr. Austin Dobson's verse 'has not the condensed clearness nor the incisive vigor of Mr. Locker's' is really too bad even for Transatlantic criticism. Nobody who lays claim to the slightest knowledge of literature and the forms of literature should ever bring the two names into conjunction.

Mr. Dobson has produced work that is absolutely classical in its exquisite beauty of form. Nothing more artistically perfect in its way than the Lines to a Greek Girl has been written in our time. This little poem will be remembered in literature as long as Thyrsis is remembered, and Thyrsis will never be forgotten. Both have that note of distinction that is so rare in these days of violence, exaggeration and rhetoric. Of course, to suggest, as Mr. Matthews does, that Mr. Dobson's poems belong to 'the literature of power' is ridiculous. Power is not their aim, nor is it their effect. They have other qualities, and in their own delicately limited sphere they have no contemporary rivals; they have none even second to them.

The heroine is a sort of well-worn Becky Sharp, only much more beautiful than Becky, or at least than Thackeray's portraits of her, which, however, have always seemed to me rather ill-natured. I feel sure that Mrs. Rawdon Crawley was extremely pretty, and I have never understood how it was that Thackeray could caricature with his pencil so fascinating a creation of his pen.

A critic recently remarked of Adam Lindsay Gordon that through him Australia had found her first fine utterance in song. This, however, is an amiable error. There is very little of Australia in Gordon's poetry. His heart and mind and fancy were always preoccupied with memories and dreams of England and such culture as England gave him. He owed nothing to the land of his adoption. Had he stayed at home he would have done much better work.

That Australia, however, will some day make amends by producing a poet of her own we cannot doubt, and for him there will be new notes to sound and new wonders to tell of.

The best that we can say of him is that he wrote imperfectly in Australia those poems that in England he might have made perfect.

Judges, like the criminal classes, have their lighter moments.

There seems to be some curious connection between piety and poor rhymes.

The South African poets, as a class, are rather behind the age. They seem to think that 'Aurora' is a very novel and delightful epithet for the dawn. On the whole they depress us.

The only original thing in the volume is the description of Mr. Robert Buchanan's 'grandeur of mind.' This is decidedly new.

Dr. Cockle tells us that Müllner's Guilt and The Ancestress of Grillparzer are the masterpieces of German fate-tragedy. His translation of the first of these two masterpieces does not make us long for any further acquaintance with the school. Here is a specimen from the fourth act of the fate-tragedy.

SCENE VIII.

ELVIRA.   HUGO.

ELVIRA (*after long silence, leaving the harp, steps to Hugo, and seeks his gaze*).

HUGO (*softly*). Though I made sacrifice of thy sweet life, the Father has forgiven. Can the wife—forgive?

ELVIRA (*on his breast*). She can!

HUGO (*with all the warmth of love*). Dear wife!

ELVIRA (*after a pause, in deep sorrow*). Must it be so, beloved one?

HUGO (*sorry to have betrayed himself*). What?

The Renaissance had for its object the development of great personalities. The perfect freedom of the temperament in matters of art, the perfect freedom of the intellect in intellectual matters, the full development of the individual, were the things it aimed at. As we study its history we find it full of great anarchies. It solved no political or social problems; it did not seek to solve them. The ideal of the 'Grand Siècle,' and of Richelieu, in whom the forces of that great age were incarnate, was different. The ideas of citizenship, of the building up of a great nation, of the centralization of forces, of collective action, of ethnic unity of purpose, came before the world.

The creation of a formal tradition upon classical lines is never without its danger, and it is sad to find the provincial towns of France, once so varied and individual in artistic expression, writing to Paris for designs and advice. And yet, through Colbert's great centralizing scheme of State supervision and State aid, France was the one country in Europe, and has remained the one country in Europe, where the arts are not divorced from industry.

Hawthorne re-created for us the America of the past with the incomparable grace of a very perfect artist, but Mr. Bret Harte's emphasized modernity has, in its own sphere, won equal, or almost equal, triumphs.

It is pleasant to come across a heroine [Bret Harte's Cressy] who is not identified with any great cause, and represents no important principle, but is simply a wonderful nymph from American backwoods, who has in her something of Artemis, and not a little of Aphrodite.

It is always a pleasure to come across an American poet who is not national, and who tries to give expression to the literature that he loves rather than to the land in which he lives. The Muses care so little for geography!

Blue-books are generally dull reading, but Blue-books on Ireland have always been interesting. They form the record of one of the great tragedies of modern Europe. In them England has written down her indictment against herself and has given to the world the history of her shame. If in the last century she tried to govern Ireland with an insolence that was intensified by race hatred and religious prejudice, she has sought to rule her in this century with a stupidity that is aggravated by good intentions.

Like most penmen he [Froude] overrates the power of the sword. Where England has had to struggle she has been wise. Where physical strength has been on her side, as in Ireland, she has been made unwieldy by that strength. Her own strong hands have blinded her. She has had force but no direction.

There are some who will welcome with delight the idea of solving the Irish question by doing away with the Irish people. There are others who will remember that Ireland has extended her boundaries, and that we have now to reckon with her not merely in the Old World but in the New.

Plastic simplicity of outline may render for us the visible aspect of life; it is different when we come to deal with those secrets which self-consciousness alone contains, and which self-consciousness itself can but half reveal. Action takes place in the sunlight, but the soul works in the dark. There is something curiously interesting in the marked tendency of modern poetry to become obscure. Many critics, writing with their eyes fixed on the masterpieces of past literature, have ascribed this tendency to wilfulness and to affectation. Its origin is rather to be found in the complexity of the new problems, and in the fact that self-consciousness is not yet adequate to explain the contents of the Ego. In Mr. Browning's poems, as in life itself, which has suggested, or rather necessitated, the new method, thought seems to proceed not on logical lines, but on lines of passion. The unity of the individual is being expressed through its inconsistencies and its contradictions. In a strange twilight man is seeking for himself, and when he has found his own image, he cannot understand it. Objective forms of art, such as sculpture and the drama, sufficed one for the perfect presentation of life; they can no longer so suffice.

As he is not a genius he, naturally, behaves admirably on every occasion.

Certainly dialect is dramatic. It is a vivid method of re-creating a past that never existed. It is something between 'A Return to Nature' and 'A Return to the Glossary.' It is so artificial that it is really naïve. From the point of view of mere music, much may be said for it. Wonderful diminutives lend new notes of tenderness to the song. There are possibilities of fresh rhymes, and in search for a fresh rhyme poets may be excused if they wander from the broad highroad of classical utterance into devious byways and less-trodden paths. Sometimes one is tempted to look on dialect as expressing simply the pathos of provincialisms, but there is more in it than mere mispronunciation. With that revival of an antique form, often comes the revival of an antique spirit. Through limitations that are sometimes uncouth, and always narrow, comes Tragedy herself; and though she may stammer in her utterance, and deck herself in cast-off weeds and trammelling raiment, still we must hold ourselves in readiness to accept her, so rare are her visits to us now, so rare her presence in an age that demands a happy ending from every play, and that sees in the theatre merely a source of amusement.

There is a great deal to be said in favour of reading a novel backwards. The last page is, as a rule, the most interesting, and when one begins with the catastrophe or the dénoûment one feels on pleasant terms of equality with the author. It is like going behind the scenes of a theatre. One is no longer taken in, and the hairbreadth escapes of the hero and the wild agonies of the heroine leave one absolutely unmoved.

He has every form of sincerity except the sincerity of the artist, a defect that he shares with most of our popular writers.

On the whole Primavera is a pleasant little book, and we are glad to welcome it. It is charmingly 'got up,' and undergraduates might read it with advantage during lecture hours.

Footnotes:

[2] Reverently some well-meaning persons have placed a marble slab on the wall of the cemetery with a medallion-profile of Keats on it and some mediocre lines of poetry. The face is ugly, and rather hatchet-shaped, with thick sensual lips, and is utterly unlike the poet himself, who was very beautiful to look upon. 'His countenance,' says a lady who saw him at one of Hazlitt's lectures, 'lives in my mind as one of singular beauty and brightness; it had the expression as if he had been looking on some glorious sight.' And this is the idea which Severn's picture of him gives. Even Haydon's rough pen-and-ink sketch of him is better than this 'marble libel,' which I hope will soon be taken down. I think the best representation of the poet would be a coloured bust, like that of the young Rajah of Koolapoor at Florence, which is a lovely and lifelike work of art.

[5] 'Make' is of course a mere printer's error for 'mock,' and was subsequently corrected by Lord Houghton. The sonnet as given in The Garden of Florence reads 'orbs for 'those.'

[63] The Margravine of Baireuth and Voltaire. (David Stott, 1888.)

[115] September 1888.

[116] See The Picture of Dorian Gray, chapter xi., page 222.

[157] From Lady Wilde' Ancient Legends of Ireland.

About Author

Oscar Fingal O'Flahertie Wills Wilde (16 October 1854 – 30 November 1900) was an Irish poet and playwright. After writing in different forms throughout the 1880s, the early 1890s saw him become one of the most popular playwrights in London. He is best remembered for his epigrams and plays, his novel The Picture of Dorian Gray, and the circumstances of his criminal conviction for "gross indecency", imprisonment, and early death at age 46.

Wilde's parents were successful Anglo-Irish intellectuals in Dublin. A young Wilde learned to speak fluent French and German. At university, Wilde read Greats; he demonstrated himself to be an exceptional classicist, first at Trinity College Dublin, then at Oxford. He became associated with the emerging philosophy of aestheticism, led by two of his tutors, Walter Pater and John Ruskin. After university, Wilde moved to London into fashionable cultural and social circles.

As a spokesman for aestheticism, he tried his hand at various literary activities: he published a book of poems, lectured in the United States and Canada on the new "English Renaissance in Art" and interior decoration, and then returned to London where he worked prolifically as a journalist. Known for his biting wit, flamboyant dress and glittering conversational skill, Wilde became one of the best-known personalities of his day. At the turn of the 1890s, he refined his ideas about the supremacy of art in a series of dialogues and essays, and incorporated themes of decadence, duplicity, and beauty into what would be his only novel, The Picture of Dorian Gray (1890). The opportunity to construct aesthetic details precisely, and combine them with larger social themes, drew Wilde to write drama. He wrote Salome (1891) in French while in Paris but it was refused a licence for England due to an absolute prohibition on the portrayal of Biblical subjects on the English stage. Unperturbed, Wilde produced four society comedies in the early 1890s, which made him one of the most successful playwrights of late-Victorian London.

At the height of his fame and success, while The Importance of Being Earnest (1895) was still being performed in London, Wilde had the Marquess of Queensberry prosecuted for criminal libel. The Marquess was the father of Wilde's lover, Lord Alfred Douglas. The libel trial unearthed evidence that caused Wilde to drop his charges and led to his own arrest and trial for gross indecency with men. After two more trials he was convicted and sentenced to two years' hard labour, the maximum penalty, and was jailed from 1895 to 1897. During his last year in prison, he wrote De Profundis (published posthumously in 1905), a long letter which discusses his spiritual journey through his trials, forming a dark counterpoint to his earlier philosophy of pleasure. On his release, he left immediately for France, never to return to Ireland or Britain. There he wrote his last work, The Ballad of Reading Gaol (1898), a long poem commemorating the harsh rhythms of prison life.

Early life

Oscar Wilde was born at 21 Westland Row, Dublin (now home of the Oscar Wilde Centre, Trinity College), the second of three children born to Anglo-Irish Sir William Wilde and Jane Wilde, two years behind his brother William ("Willie"). Wilde's mother had distant Italian ancestry,and under the pseudonym "Speranza" (the Italian word for 'hope'), wrote poetry for the revolutionary Young Irelanders in 1848; she was a lifelong Irish nationalist. She read the Young Irelanders' poetry to Oscar and Willie, inculcating a love of these poets in her sons. Lady Wilde's interest in the neo-classical revival showed in the paintings and busts of ancient Greece and Rome in her home.

William Wilde was Ireland's leading oto-ophthalmologic (ear and eye) surgeon and was knighted in 1864 for his services as medical adviser and assistant commissioner to the censuses of Ireland. He also wrote books about Irish archaeology and peasant folklore. A renowned philanthropist, his dispensary for the care of the city's poor at the rear of Trinity College, Dublin, was the forerunner of the Dublin Eye and Ear Hospital, now located at Adelaide Road. On his father's side Wilde was descended from a Dutchman, Colonel de Wilde, who went to Ireland with King William of Orange's invading army in 1690, and numerous Anglo-Irish ancestors. On his mother's side, Wilde's ancestors included a bricklayer from County Durham, who emigrated to Ireland sometime in the 1770s.

Wilde was baptised as an infant in St. Mark's Church, Dublin, the local Church of Ireland (Anglican) church. When the church was closed, the records were moved to the nearby St. Ann's Church, Dawson Street. Davis Coakley mentions a second baptism by a Catholic priest, Father Prideaux Fox, who befriended Oscar's mother circa 1859. According to Fox's testimony in Donahoe's Magazine in 1905, Jane Wilde would visit his chapel in Glencree, County Wicklow, for Mass and would take her sons with her. She asked Father Fox in this period to baptise her sons.

Fox described it in this way:

"I am not sure if she ever became a Catholic herself but it was not long before she asked me to instruct two of her children, one of them being the future erratic genius, Oscar Wilde. After a few weeks I baptized these two children, Lady Wilde herself being present on the occasion.

In addition to his children with his wife, Sir William Wilde was the father of three children born out of wedlock before his marriage: Henry Wilson, born in 1838 to one woman, and Emily and Mary Wilde, born in 1847 and 1849, respectively, to a second woman. Sir William acknowledged paternity of his illegitimate or "natural" children and provided for their education, arranging for them to be reared by his relatives rather than with his legitimate children in his family household with his wife.

In 1855, the family moved to No. 1 Merrion Square, where Wilde's sister, Isola, was born in 1857. The Wildes' new home was larger. With both his parents' success and delight in social life, the house soon became the site of a "unique medical and cultural milieu". Guests at their salon included Sheridan Le Fanu, Charles Lever, George Petrie, Isaac Butt, William Rowan Hamilton and Samuel Ferguson.

Until he was nine, Oscar Wilde was educated at home, where a French nursemaid and a German governess taught him their languages. He attended Portora Royal School in Enniskillen, County Fermanagh, from 1864 to 1871. Until his early twenties, Wilde summered at the villa, Moytura House, which his father had built in Cong, County Mayo. There the young Wilde and his brother Willie played with George Moore.

Isola died at age nine of meningitis. Wilde's poem "Requiescat" is written to her memory.

"Tread lightly, she is near

Under the snow

Speak gently, she can hear

the daisies grow"

University education: 1870s

Trinity College, Dublin

Wilde left Portora with a royal scholarship to read classics at Trinity College, Dublin, from 1871 to 1874, sharing rooms with his older brother Willie Wilde. Trinity, one of the leading classical schools, placed him with scholars such as R. Y. Tyrell, Arthur Palmer, Edward Dowden and his tutor, Professor J. P. Mahaffy, who inspired his interest in Greek literature. As a student Wilde worked with Mahaffy on the latter's book Social Life in Greece. Wilde, despite later reservations, called Mahaffy "my first and best teacher" and "the scholar who showed me how to love Greek things".For his part, Mahaffy boasted of having created Wilde; later, he said Wilde was "the only blot on my tutorship".

The University Philosophical Society also provided an education, as members discussed intellectual and artistic subjects such as Dante Gabriel Rossetti and Algernon Charles Swinburne weekly. Wilde quickly became an established member – the members' suggestion book for 1874 contains two pages of banter (sportingly) mocking Wilde's emergent aestheticism. He presented a paper titled "Aesthetic Morality". At Trinity, Wilde established himself as an outstanding student: he came first in his class in his first year, won a scholarship by competitive examination in his second and, in his finals, won the Berkeley Gold Medal in Greek, the University's highest academic award. He was encouraged to compete for a demyship to Magdalen College, Oxford – which he won easily, having already studied Greek for over nine years.

Magdalen College, Oxford

At Magdalen, he read Greats from 1874 to 1878, and from there he applied to join the Oxford Union, but failed to be elected.

Attracted by its dress, secrecy, and ritual, Wilde petitioned the Apollo Masonic Lodge at Oxford, and was soon raised to the "Sublime Degree of Master Mason".During a resurgent interest in Freemasonry in his third year, he commented he "would be awfully sorry to give it up if I secede from the Protestant Heresy". Wilde's active involvement in Freemasonry lasted only for the time he spent at Oxford; he allowed his membership of the Apollo University Lodge to lapse after failing to pay subscriptions.

Catholicism deeply appealed to him, especially its rich liturgy, and he discussed converting to it with clergy several times. In 1877, Wilde was left speechless after an audience with Pope Pius IX in Rome.He eagerly read the books of Cardinal Newman, a noted Anglican priest who had converted to Catholicism and risen in the church hierarchy. He became more serious in 1878, when he met the Reverend Sebastian Bowden, a priest in the Brompton Oratory who had received some high-profile converts. Neither his father, who threatened to cut off his funds, nor Mahaffy thought much of the plan; but mostly Wilde, the supreme individualist, balked at the last minute from pledging himself to any formal creed. On the appointed day of his baptism, Wilde sent Father Bowden a bunch of altar lilies instead. Wilde did retain a lifelong interest in Catholic theology and liturgy.

While at Magdalen College, Wilde became particularly well known for his role in the aesthetic and decadent movements. He wore his hair long, openly scorned "manly" sports though he occasionally boxed, and he decorated his rooms with peacock feathers, lilies, sunflowers, blue china and other objets d'art. He once remarked to friends, whom he entertained lavishly, "I find it harder and harder every day to live up to my blue china." The line quickly became famous, accepted as a slogan by aesthetes but used against them by critics who sensed in it a terrible vacuousness. Some elements disdained the aesthetes, but their languishing attitudes and showy costumes became a recognised pose. Wilde was once physically attacked by a group of four fellow students, and dealt with them single-handedly, surprising critics. By his third year Wilde had truly begun to develop himself and his myth, and considered his learning to be more expansive than what was within the prescribed texts. This attitude resulted in his being rusticated for one term, after he had returned late to a college term from a trip to Greece with Mahaffy.

Wilde did not meet Walter Pater until his third year, but had been enthralled by his Studies in the History of the Renaissance, published during Wilde's final year in Trinity. Pater argued that man's sensibility to beauty should be refined above all else, and that each moment should be felt to its fullest extent. Years later, in De Profundis, Wilde described Pater's Studies... as "that book that has had such a strange influence over my life".He learned tracts of the book by heart, and carried it with him on travels in later years. Pater gave Wilde his sense of almost flippant devotion to art, though he gained a purpose for it through the lectures and writings of critic John Ruskin. Ruskin despaired at the self-validating aestheticism of Pater, arguing that the importance of art lies in its potential for the betterment of society. Ruskin admired beauty, but believed it must be allied with, and applied to, moral good. When Wilde eagerly attended Ruskin's lecture series The Aesthetic and Mathematic Schools of Art in Florence, he learned about aesthetics as the non-mathematical elements of painting. Despite being given to neither early rising nor manual labour, Wilde volunteered for Ruskin's project to convert a swampy country lane into a smart road neatly edged with flowers.

Wilde won the 1878 Newdigate Prize for his poem "Ravenna", which reflected on his visit there the year before, and he duly read it at Encaenia. In November 1878, he graduated with a double first in his B.A. of Classical Moderations and Literae Humaniores (Greats). Wilde wrote to a friend, "The dons are 'astonied' beyond words – the Bad Boy doing so well in the end!"

Apprenticeship of an aesthete: 1880s

Debut in society

After graduation from Oxford, Wilde returned to Dublin, where he met again Florence Balcombe, a childhood sweetheart. She became engaged to Bram Stoker and they married in 1878. Wilde was disappointed but stoic:

he wrote to her, remembering "the two sweet years – the sweetest years of all my youth" during which they had been close. He also stated his intention to "return to England, probably for good." This he did in 1878, only briefly visiting Ireland twice after that.

Unsure of his next step, Wilde wrote to various acquaintances enquiring about Classics positions at Oxford or Cambridge. The Rise of Historical Criticism was his submission for the Chancellor's Essay prize of 1879, which, though no longer a student, he was still eligible to enter. Its subject, "Historical Criticism among the Ancients" seemed ready-made for Wilde – with both his skill in composition and ancient learning – but he struggled to find his voice with the long, flat, scholarly style. Unusually, no prize was awarded that year.

With the last of his inheritance from the sale of his father's houses, he set himself up as a bachelor in London. The 1881 British Census listed Wilde as a boarder at 1 (now 44) Tite Street, Chelsea, where Frank Miles, a society painter, was the head of the household. Wilde spent the next six years in London and Paris, and in the United States, where he travelled to deliver lectures.

He had been publishing lyrics and poems in magazines since entering Trinity College, especially in Kottabos and the Dublin University Magazine. In mid-1881, at 27 years old, he published Poems, which collected, revised and expanded his poems.

The book was generally well received, and sold out its first print run of 750 copies. Punch was less enthusiastic, saying "The poet is Wilde, but his poetry's tame". By a tight vote, the Oxford Union condemned the book for alleged plagiarism. The librarian, who had requested the book for the library, returned the presentation copy to Wilde with a note of apology. Biographer Richard Ellmann argues that Wilde's poem "Hélas!" was a sincere, though flamboyant, attempt to explain the dichotomies the poet saw in himself; one line reads: "To drift with every passion till my soul

Is a stringed lute on which all winds can play".

The book had further printings in 1882. It was bound in a rich, enamel parchment cover (embossed with gilt blossom) and printed on hand-made Dutch paper; over the next few years, Wilde presented many copies to the dignitaries and writers who received him during his lecture tours.

America: 1882

Aestheticism was sufficiently in vogue to be caricatured by Gilbert and Sullivan in Patience (1881). Richard D'Oyly Carte, an English impresario, invited Wilde to make a lecture tour of North America, simultaneously priming the pump for the US tour of Patience and selling this most charming aesthete to the American public. Wilde journeyed on the SS Arizona, arriving 2 January 1882, and disembarking the following day. Originally planned to last four months, it continued for almost a year due to the commercial success. Wilde sought to transpose the beauty he saw in art into daily life. This was a practical as well as philosophical project: in Oxford he had surrounded himself with blue china and lilies, and now one of his lectures was on interior design.

When asked to explain reports that he had paraded down Piccadilly in London carrying a lily, long hair flowing, Wilde replied, "It's not whether I did it or not that's important, but whether people believed I did it". Wilde believed that the artist should hold forth higher ideals, and that pleasure and beauty would replace utilitarian ethics.

Wilde and aestheticism were both mercilessly caricatured and criticised in the press; the Springfield Republican, for instance, commented on Wilde's behaviour during his visit to Boston to lecture on aestheticism, suggesting that Wilde's conduct was more a bid for notoriety rather than devotion to beauty and the aesthetic. T. W. Higginson, a cleric and abolitionist, wrote in "Unmanly Manhood" of his general concern that Wilde, "whose only distinction is that he has written a thin volume of very mediocre verse", would improperly influence the behaviour of men and women.

According to biographer Michèle Mendelssohn, Wilde was the subject of anti-Irish caricature and was portrayed as a monkey, a blackface performer and a Christy's Minstrel throughout his career. "Harper's Weekly put a sunflower-worshipping monkey dressed as Wilde on the front of the January 1882 issue. The magazine didn't let its reputation for quality impede its expression of what are now considered odious ethnic and racial ideologies. The drawing stimulated other American maligners and, in England, had a full-page reprint in the Lady's Pictorial. ... When the National Republican discussed Wilde, it was to explain 'a few items as to the animal's pedigree.' And on 22 January 1882 the Washington Post illustrated the Wild Man of Borneo alongside Oscar Wilde of England and asked 'How far is it from this to this?' "Though his press reception was hostile, Wilde was well received in diverse settings across America; he drank whiskey with miners in Leadville, Colorado, and was fêted at the most fashionable salons in many cities he visited.

London life and marriage

His earnings, plus expected income from The Duchess of Padua, allowed him to move to Paris between February and mid-May 1883. While there he met Robert Sherard, whom he entertained constantly. "We are dining on the Duchess tonight", Wilde would declare before taking him to an expensive restaurant. In August he briefly returned to New York for the production of Vera, his first play, after it was turned down in London. He reportedly entertained the other passengers with "Ave Imperatrix!, A Poem on England", about the rise and fall of empires. E. C. Stedman, in Victorian Poets, describes this "lyric to England" as "manly verse – a poetic and eloquent invocation". The play was initially well received by the audience, but when the critics wrote lukewarm reviews, attendance fell sharply and the play closed a week after it had opened.

Wilde had to return to England, where he continued to lecture on topics including Personal Impressions of America, The Value of Art in Modern Life, and Dress.

In London, he had been introduced in 1881 to Constance Lloyd, daughter of Horace Lloyd, a wealthy Queen's Counsel, and his wife. She happened to be visiting Dublin in 1884, when Wilde was lecturing at the Gaiety Theatre. He proposed to her, and they married on 29 May 1884 at the Anglican St James's Church, Paddington, in London. Although Constance had an annual allowance of £250, which was generous for a young woman (equivalent to about £25,600 in current value), the Wildes had relatively luxurious tastes. They had preached to others for so long on the subject of design that people expected their home to set new standards. No. 16, Tite Street was duly renovated in seven months at considerable expense. The couple had two sons together, Cyril (1885) and Vyvyan (1886). Wilde became the sole literary signatory of George Bernard Shaw's petition for a pardon of the anarchists arrested (and later executed) after the Haymarket massacre in Chicago in 1886.

Robert Ross had read Wilde's poems before they met at Oxford in 1886. He seemed unrestrained by the Victorian prohibition against homosexuality, and became estranged from his family. By Richard Ellmann's account, he was a precocious seventeen-year-old who "so young and yet so knowing, was determined to seduce Wilde". According to Daniel Mendelsohn, Wilde, who had long alluded to Greek love, was "initiated into homosexual sex" by Ross, while his "marriage had begun to unravel after his wife's second pregnancy, which left him physically repelled".

Prose writing: 1886–91

Journalism and editorship: 1886–89

Criticism over artistic matters in The Pall Mall Gazette provoked a letter in self-defence, and soon Wilde was a contributor to that and other journals during 1885–87. He enjoyed reviewing and journalism; the form suited his style. He could organise and share his views on art, literature and life, yet in a format less tedious than lecturing. Buoyed up, his reviews were largely chatty and positive. Wilde, like his parents before him, also supported the cause of Irish nationalism. When Charles Stewart Parnell was falsely accused of inciting murder, Wilde wrote a series of astute columns defending him in the Daily Chronicle.

His flair, having previously been put mainly into socialising, suited journalism and rapidly attracted notice. With his youth nearly over, and a family to support, in mid-1887 Wilde became the editor of The Lady's World magazine, his name prominently appearing on the cover. He promptly renamed it as The Woman's World and raised its tone, adding serious articles on parenting, culture, and politics, while keeping discussions of fashion and arts. Two pieces of fiction were usually included, one to be read to children, the other for the ladies themselves. Wilde worked hard to solicit good contributions from his wide artistic acquaintance, including those of Lady Wilde and his wife Constance, while his own "Literary and Other Notes" were themselves popular and amusing.

The initial vigour and excitement which he brought to the job began to fade as administration, commuting and office life became tedious. At the same time as Wilde's interest flagged, the publishers became concerned anew about circulation: sales, at the relatively high price of one shilling, remained low. Increasingly sending instructions to the magazine by letter, Wilde began a new period of creative work and his own column appeared less regularly.In October 1889, Wilde had finally found his voice in prose and, at the end of the second volume, Wilde left The Woman's World. The magazine outlasted him by one issue.

If Wilde's period at the helm of the magazine was a mixed success from an organizational point of view, it played a pivotal role in his development as a writer and facilitated his ascent to fame. Whilst Wilde the journalist supplied articles under the guidance of his editors, Wilde the editor was forced to learn to manipulate the literary marketplace on his own terms.

During the late 1880s, Wilde was a close friend of the artist James NcNeill Whistler and they dined together on many occasions. At one of these dinners, Whistler said a bon mot that Wilde found particularly witty, Wilde exclaimed that he wished that he had said it, and Whistler retorted "You will, Oscar, you will".Herbert Vivian—a mutual friend of Wilde and Whistler—attended the dinner and recorded it in his article The Reminiscences of a Short Life which appeared in The Sun in 1889. The article alleged that Wilde had a habit of passing off other people's witticisms as his own—especially Whistler's. Wilde considered Vivian's article to be a scurrilous betrayal, and it directly caused the broken friendship between Wilde and Whistler. The Reminiscences also caused great acrimony between Wilde and Vivian, Wilde accusing Vivian of "the inaccuracy of an eavesdropper with the method of a blackmailer" and banishing Vivian from his circle.

Shorter fiction

Wilde published The Happy Prince and Other Tales in 1888, and had been regularly writing fairy stories for magazines. In 1891 he published two more collections, Lord Arthur Savile's Crime and Other Stories, and in September A House of Pomegranates was dedicated "To Constance Mary Wilde". "The Portrait of Mr. W. H.", which Wilde had begun in 1887, was first published in Blackwood's Edinburgh Magazine in July 1889. It is a short story, which reports a conversation, in which the theory that Shakespeare's sonnets were written out of the poet's love of the boy actor "Willie Hughes", is advanced, retracted, and then propounded again. The only evidence for this is two supposed puns within the sonnets themselves.

The anonymous narrator is at first sceptical, then believing, finally flirtatious with the reader: he concludes that "there is really a great deal to be said of the Willie Hughes theory of Shakespeare's sonnets." By the end fact and fiction have melded together. Arthur Ransome wrote that Wilde "read something of himself into Shakespeare's sonnets" and became fascinated with the "Willie Hughes theory" despite the lack of biographical evidence for the historical William Hughes' existence. Instead of writing a short but serious essay on the question, Wilde tossed the theory amongst the three characters of the story, allowing it to unfold as background to the plot. The story thus is an early masterpiece of Wilde's combining many elements that interested him: conversation, literature and the idea that to shed oneself of an idea one must first convince another of its truth. Ransome concludes that Wilde succeeds precisely because the literary criticism is unveiled with such a deft touch.

Though containing nothing but "special pleading", it would not, he says "be possible to build an airier castle in Spain than this of the imaginary William Hughes" we continue listening nonetheless to be charmed by the telling. "You must believe in Willie Hughes," Wilde told an acquaintance, "I almost do, myself."

Essays and dialogues

Wilde, having tired of journalism, had been busy setting out his aesthetic ideas more fully in a series of longer prose pieces which were published in the major literary-intellectual journals of the day. In January 1889, The Decay of Lying: A Dialogue appeared in The Nineteenth Century, and Pen, Pencil and Poison, a satirical biography of Thomas Griffiths Wainewright, in The Fortnightly Review, edited by Wilde's friend Frank Harris. Two of Wilde's four writings on aesthetics are dialogues: though Wilde had evolved professionally from lecturer to writer, he retained an oral tradition of sorts. Having always excelled as a wit and raconteur, he often composed by assembling phrases, bons mots and witticisms into a longer, cohesive work.

Wilde was concerned about the effect of moralising on art; he believed in art's redemptive, developmental powers: "Art is individualism, and individualism is a disturbing and disintegrating force. There lies its immense value. For what it seeks is to disturb monotony of type, slavery of custom, tyranny of habit, and the reduction of man to the level of a machine." In his only political text, The Soul of Man Under Socialism, he argued political conditions should establish this primacy – private property should be abolished, and cooperation should be substituted for competition. At the same time, he stressed that the government most amenable to artists was no government at all. Wilde envisioned a society where mechanisation has freed human effort from the burden of necessity, effort which can instead be expended on artistic creation. George Orwell summarised, "In effect, the world will be populated by artists, each striving after perfection in the way that seems best to him."

This point of view did not align him with the Fabians, intellectual socialists who advocated using state apparatus to change social conditions, nor did it endear him to the monied classes whom he had previously entertained. Hesketh Pearson, introducing a collection of Wilde's essays in 1950, remarked how The Soul of Man Under Socialism had been an inspirational text for revolutionaries in Tsarist Russia but laments that in the Stalinist era "it is doubtful whether there are any uninspected places in which it could now be hidden".

Wilde considered including this pamphlet and The Portrait of Mr. W.H., his essay-story on Shakespeare's sonnets, in a new anthology in 1891, but eventually decided to limit it to purely aesthetic subjects. Intentions packaged revisions of four essays: The Decay of Lying, Pen, Pencil and Poison, The Truth of Masks (first published 1885), and The Critic as Artist in two parts. For Pearson the biographer, the essays and dialogues exhibit every aspect of Wilde's genius and character: wit, romancer, talker, lecturer, humanist and scholar and concludes that "no other productions of his have as varied an appeal". 1891 turned out to be Wilde's annus mirabilis; apart from his three collections he also produced his only novel.

The Picture of Dorian Gray

The first version of The Picture of Dorian Gray was published as the lead story in the July 1890 edition of Lippincott's Monthly Magazine, along with five others. The story begins with a man painting a picture of Gray. When Gray, who has a "face like ivory and rose leaves", sees his finished portrait, he breaks down. Distraught that his beauty will fade while the portrait stays beautiful, he inadvertently makes a Faustian bargain in which only the painted image grows old while he stays beautiful and young. For Wilde, the purpose of art would be to guide life as if beauty alone were its object. As Gray's portrait allows him to escape the corporeal ravages of his hedonism, Wilde sought to juxtapose the beauty he saw in art with daily life.

Reviewers immediately criticised the novel's decadence and homosexual allusions; The Daily Chronicle for example, called it "unclean", "poisonous", and "heavy with the mephitic odours of moral and spiritual putrefaction". Which he clarified his stance on ethics and aesthetics in art – "If a work of art is rich and vital and complete, those who have artistic instincts will see its beauty and those to whom ethics appeal more strongly will see its moral lesson." He nevertheless revised it extensively for book publication in 1891: six new chapters were added, some overtly decadent passages and homo-eroticism excised, and a preface was included consisting of twenty two epigrams, such as "Books are well written, or badly written. That is all."

Contemporary reviewers and modern critics have postulated numerous possible sources of the story, a search Jershua McCormack argues is futile because Wilde "has tapped a root of Western folklore so deep and ubiquitous that the story has escaped its origins and returned to the oral tradition." Wilde claimed the plot was "an idea that is as old as the history of literature but to which I have given a new form".Modern critic Robin McKie considered the novel to be technically mediocre, saying that the conceit of the plot had guaranteed its fame, but the device is never pushed to its full.On the other hand, Robert McCrum of The Guardian deemed it the 27th best novel ever written in English, calling it "an arresting, and slightly camp, exercise in late-Victorian gothic."

Theatrical career: 1892–95

Salomé

The 1891 census records the Wildes' residence at 16 Tite Street, where he lived with his wife Constance and two sons. Wilde though, not content with being better known than ever in London, returned to Paris in October 1891, this time as a respected writer. He was received at the salons littéraires, including the famous mardis of Stéphane Mallarmé, a renowned symbolist poet of the time. Wilde's two plays during the 1880s, Vera; or, The Nihilists and The Duchess of Padua, had not met with much success. He had continued his interest in the theatre and now, after finding his voice in prose, his thoughts turned again to the dramatic form as the biblical iconography of Salome filled his mind. One evening, after discussing depictions of Salome throughout history, he returned to his hotel and noticed a blank copybook lying on the desk, and it occurred to him to write in it what he had been saying. The result was a new play, Salomé, written rapidly and in French.

A tragedy, it tells the story of Salome, the stepdaughter of the tetrarch Herod Antipas, who, to her stepfather's dismay but mother's delight, requests the head of Jokanaan (John the Baptist) on a silver platter as a reward for dancing the Dance of the Seven Veils. When Wilde returned to London just before Christmas the Paris Echo referred to him as "le great event" of the season. Rehearsals of the play, starring Sarah Bernhardt, began but the play was refused a licence by the Lord Chamberlain, since it depicted biblical characters. Salome was published jointly in Paris and London in 1893, but was not performed until 1896 in Paris, during Wilde's later incarceration.

Comedies of society

Wilde, who had first set out to irritate Victorian society with his dress and talking points, then outrage it with Dorian Gray, his novel of vice hidden beneath art, finally found a way to critique society on its own terms. Lady Windermere's Fan was first performed on 20 February 1892 at St James's Theatre, packed with the cream of society. On the surface a witty comedy, there is subtle subversion underneath: "it concludes with collusive concealment rather than collective disclosure". The audience, like Lady Windermere, are forced to soften harsh social codes in favour of a more nuanced view. The play was enormously popular, touring the country for months, but largely trashed by conservative critics. It was followed by A Woman of No Importance in 1893, another Victorian comedy, revolving around the spectre of illegitimate births, mistaken identities and late revelations. Wilde was commissioned to write two more plays and An Ideal Husband, written in 1894, followed in January 1895.

Peter Raby said these essentially English plays were well-pitched, "Wilde, with one eye on the dramatic genius of Ibsen, and the other on the commercial competition in London's West End, targeted his audience with adroit precision".

Queensberry family

In mid-1891 Lionel Johnson introduced Wilde to Lord Alfred Douglas, Johnson's cousin and an undergraduate at Oxford at the time. Known to his family and friends as "Bosie", he was a handsome and spoilt young man. An intimate friendship sprang up between Wilde and Douglas and by 1893 Wilde was infatuated with Douglas and they consorted together regularly in a tempestuous affair. If Wilde was relatively indiscreet, even flamboyant, in the way he acted, Douglas was reckless in public. Wilde, who was earning up to £100 a week from his plays (his salary at The Woman's World had been £6), indulged Douglas's every whim: material, artistic or sexual.

Douglas soon initiated Wilde into the Victorian underground of gay prostitution and Wilde was introduced to a series of young working-class male prostitutes from 1892 onwards by Alfred Taylor. These infrequent rendezvous usually took the same form: Wilde would meet the boy, offer him

244

gifts, dine him privately and then take him to a hotel room. Unlike Wilde's idealised relations with Ross, John Gray, and Douglas, all of whom remained part of his aesthetic circle, these consorts were uneducated and knew nothing of literature. Soon his public and private lives had become sharply divided; in De Profundis he wrote to Douglas that "It was like feasting with panthers; the danger was half the excitement... I did not know that when they were to strike at me it was to be at another's piping and at another's pay."

Douglas and some Oxford friends founded a journal, The Chameleon, to which Wilde "sent a page of paradoxes originally destined for the Saturday Review". "Phrases and Philosophies for the Use of the Young" was to come under attack six months later at Wilde's trial, where he was forced to defend the magazine to which he had sent his work.In any case, it became unique: The Chameleon was not published again.

Lord Alfred's father, the Marquess of Queensberry, was known for his outspoken atheism, brutish manner and creation of the modern rules of boxing. Queensberry, who feuded regularly with his son, confronted Wilde and Lord Alfred about the nature of their relationship several times, but Wilde was able to mollify him. In June 1894, he called on Wilde at 16 Tite Street, without an appointment, and clarified his stance: "I do not say that you are it, but you look it, and pose at it, which is just as bad. And if I catch you and my son again in any public restaurant I will thrash you" to which Wilde responded: "I don't know what the Queensberry rules are, but the Oscar Wilde rule is to shoot on sight".His account in De Profundis was less triumphant: "It was when, in my library at Tite Street, waving his small hands in the air in epileptic fury, your father... stood uttering every foul word his foul mind could think of, and screaming the loathsome threats he afterwards with such cunning carried out". Queensberry only described the scene once, saying Wilde had "shown him the white feather", meaning he had acted in a cowardly way. Though trying to remain calm, Wilde saw that he was becoming ensnared in a brutal family quarrel. He did not wish to bear Queensberry's insults, but he knew to confront him could lead to disaster were his liaisons disclosed publicly.

The Importance of Being Earnest

Wilde's final play again returns to the theme of switched identities: the play's two protagonists engage in "bunburying" (the maintenance of alternative personas in the town and country) which allows them to escape Victorian social mores. Earnest is even lighter in tone than Wilde's earlier comedies. While their characters often rise to serious themes in moments of crisis, Earnest lacks the by-now stock Wildean characters: there is no "woman with a past", the principals are neither villainous nor cunning, simply idle cultivés, and the idealistic young women are not that innocent. Mostly set in drawing rooms and almost completely lacking in action or violence, Earnest lacks the self-conscious decadence found in The Picture of Dorian Gray and Salome.

The play, now considered Wilde's masterpiece, was rapidly written in Wilde's artistic maturity in late 1894. It was first performed on 14 February 1895, at St James's Theatre in London, Wilde's second collaboration with George Alexander, the actor-manager. Both author and producer assiduously revised, prepared and rehearsed every line, scene and setting in the months before the premiere, creating a carefully constructed representation of late-Victorian society, yet simultaneously mocking it. During rehearsal Alexander requested that Wilde shorten the play from four acts to three, which the author did. Premieres at St James's seemed like "brilliant parties", and the opening of The Importance of Being Earnest was no exception. Allan Aynesworth (who played Algernon) recalled to Hesketh Pearson, "In my fifty-three years of acting, I never remember a greater triumph than [that] first night." Earnest's immediate reception as Wilde's best work to date finally crystallised his fame into a solid artistic reputation. The Importance of Being Earnest remains his most popular play.

Wilde's professional success was mirrored by an escalation in his feud with Queensberry. Queensberry had planned to insult Wilde publicly by throwing a bouquet of rotting vegetables onto the stage; Wilde was tipped off and had Queensberry barred from entering the theatre. Fifteen weeks later Wilde was in prison.

Trials

246

Wilde v. Queensberry

On 18 February 1895, the Marquess left his calling card at Wilde's club, the Albemarle, inscribed: "For Oscar Wilde, posing somdomite" Wilde, encouraged by Douglas and against the advice of his friends, initiated a private prosecution against Queensberry for libel, since the note amounted to a public accusation that Wilde had committed the crime of sodomy.

Queensberry was arrested for criminal libel; a charge carrying a possible sentence of up to two years in prison. Under the 1843 Libel Act, Queensberry could avoid conviction for libel only by demonstrating that his accusation was in fact true, and furthermore that there was some "public benefit" to having made the accusation openly. Queensberry's lawyers thus hired private detectives to find evidence of Wilde's homosexual liaisons.

Wilde's friends had advised him against the prosecution at a Saturday Review meeting at the Café Royal on 24 March 1895; Frank Harris warned him that "they are going to prove sodomy against you" and advised him to flee to France. Wilde and Douglas walked out in a huff, Wilde saying "it is at such moments as these that one sees who are one's true friends". The scene was witnessed by George Bernard Shaw who recalled it to Arthur Ransome a day or so before Ransome's trial for libelling Douglas in 1913. To Ransome it confirmed what he had said in his 1912 book on Wilde; that Douglas's rivalry for Wilde with Robbie Ross and his arguments with his father had resulted in Wilde's public disaster; as Wilde wrote in De Profundis. Douglas lost his case. Shaw included an account of the argument between Harris, Douglas and Wilde in the preface to his play The Dark Lady of the Sonnets.

The libel trial became a cause célèbre as salacious details of Wilde's private life with Taylor and Douglas began to appear in the press. A team of private detectives had directed Queensberry's lawyers, led by Edward Carson QC, to the world of the Victorian underground. Wilde's association with blackmailers and male prostitutes, cross-dressers and homosexual brothels was recorded, and various persons involved were interviewed, some being coerced to appear as witnesses since they too were accomplices to the crimes of which Wilde was accused.

The trial opened on 3 April 1895 before Justice Richard Henn Collins amid scenes of near hysteria both in the press and the public galleries. The extent of the evidence massed against Wilde forced him to declare meekly, "I am the prosecutor in this case" Wilde's lawyer, Sir Edward George Clarke, opened the case by pre-emptively asking Wilde about two suggestive letters Wilde had written to Douglas, which the defence had in its possession. He characterised the first as a "prose sonnet" and admitted that the "poetical language" might seem strange to the court but claimed its intent was innocent. Wilde stated that the letters had been obtained by blackmailers who had attempted to extort money from him, but he had refused, suggesting they should take the £60 (equal to £6,800 today) offered, "unusual for a prose piece of that length". He claimed to regard the letters as works of art rather than something of which to be ashamed.

Carson, a fellow Dubliner who had attended Trinity College, Dublin at the same time as Wilde, cross-examined Wilde on how he perceived the moral content of his works. Wilde replied with characteristic wit and flippancy, claiming that works of art are not capable of being moral or immoral but only well or poorly made, and that only "brutes and illiterates", whose views on art "are incalculably stupid", would make such judgements about art. Carson, a leading barrister, diverged from the normal practice of asking closed questions. Carson pressed Wilde on each topic from every angle, squeezing out nuances of meaning from Wilde's answers, removing them from their aesthetic context and portraying Wilde as evasive and decadent. While Wilde won the most laughs from the court, Carson scored the most legal points. To undermine Wilde's credibility, and to justify Queensberry's description of Wilde as a "posing somdomite", Carson drew from the witness an admission of his capacity for "posing", by demonstrating that he had lied about his age on oath. Playing on this, he returned to the topic throughout his cross-examination. Carson also tried to justify Queensberry's characterisation by quoting from Wilde's novel, The Picture of Dorian Gray, referring in particular to a scene in the second chapter, in which Lord Henry Wotton explains his decadent philosophy to Dorian, an "innocent young man", in Carson's words.

Carson then moved to the factual evidence and questioned Wilde about his friendships with younger, lower-class men. Wilde admitted being on a first-name basis and lavishing gifts upon them, but insisted that nothing untoward had occurred and that the men were merely good friends of his. Carson repeatedly pointed out the unusual nature of these relationships and insinuated that the men were prostitutes. Wilde replied that he did not believe in social barriers, and simply enjoyed the society of young men. Then Carson asked Wilde directly whether he had ever kissed a certain servant boy, Wilde responded, "Oh, dear no. He was a particularly plain boy – unfortunately ugly – I pitied him for it." Carson pressed him on the answer, repeatedly asking why the boy's ugliness was relevant. Wilde hesitated, then for the first time became flustered: "You sting me and insult me and try to unnerve me; and at times one says things flippantly when one ought to speak more seriously."

In his opening speech for the defence, Carson announced that he had located several male prostitutes who were to testify that they had had sex with Wilde. On the advice of his lawyers, Wilde dropped the prosecution. Queensberry was found not guilty, as the court declared that his accusation that Wilde was "posing as a Somdomite " was justified, "true in substance and in fact".Under the Libel Act 1843, Queensberry's acquittal rendered Wilde legally liable for the considerable expenses Queensberry had incurred in his defence, which left Wilde bankrupt.

Regina v. Wilde

After Wilde left the court, a warrant for his arrest was applied for on charges of sodomy and gross indecency. Robbie Ross found Wilde at the Cadogan Hotel, Pont Street, Knightsbridge, with Reginald Turner; both men advised Wilde to go at once to Dover and try to get a boat to France; his mother advised him to stay and fight. Wilde, lapsing into inaction, could only say, "The train has gone. It's too late."On 6 April 1895, Wilde was arrested for "gross indecency" under Section 11 of the Criminal Law Amendment Act 1885, a term meaning homosexual acts not amounting to buggery (an offence under a separate statute). At Wilde's instruction, Ross and Wilde's butler forced their way into the bedroom and library of 16 Tite Street, packing some personal effects, manuscripts, and letters. Wilde was then imprisoned on remand at Holloway, where he received daily visits from Douglas.

Events moved quickly and his prosecution opened on 26 April 1895, before Mr Justice Charles. Wilde pleaded not guilty. He had already begged Douglas to leave London for Paris, but Douglas complained bitterly, even wanting to give evidence; he was pressed to go and soon fled to the Hotel du Monde. Fearing persecution, Ross and many others also left the United Kingdom during this time. Under cross examination Wilde was at first hesitant, then spoke eloquently:

Charles Gill (prosecuting): What is "the love that dare not speak its name"?

Wilde: "The love that dare not speak its name" in this century is such a great affection of an elder for a younger man as there was between David and Jonathan, such as Plato made the very basis of his philosophy, and such as you find in the sonnets of Michelangelo and Shakespeare. It is that deep spiritual affection that is as pure as it is perfect. It dictates and pervades great works of art, like those of Shakespeare and Michelangelo, and those two letters of mine, such as they are. It is in this century misunderstood, so much misunderstood that it may be described as "the love that dare not speak its name", and on that account of it I am placed where I am now. It is beautiful, it is fine, it is the noblest form of affection. There is nothing unnatural about it. It is intellectual, and it repeatedly exists between an older and a younger man, when the older man has intellect, and the younger man has all the joy, hope and glamour of life before him. That it should be so, the world does not understand. The world mocks at it, and sometimes puts one in the pillory for it.

This response was counter-productive in a legal sense as it only served to reinforce the charges of homosexual behaviour.

The trial ended with the jury unable to reach a verdict. Wilde's counsel, Sir Edward Clarke, was finally able to get a magistrate to allow Wilde and his friends to post bail. The Reverend Stewart Headlam put up most of the £5,000 surety required by the court, having disagreed with Wilde's treatment by the press and the courts. Wilde was freed from Holloway and, shunning attention, went into hiding at the house of Ernest and Ada Leverson, two of his firm friends. Edward Carson approached Frank Lockwood QC, the Solicitor General and asked "Can we not let up on the fellow now?" Lockwood answered that he would like to do so, but feared that the case had become too politicised to be dropped.

The final trial was presided over by Mr Justice Wills. On 25 May 1895 Wilde and Alfred Taylor were convicted of gross indecency and sentenced to two years' hard labour. The judge described the sentence, the maximum allowed, as "totally inadequate for a case such as this", and that the case was "the worst case I have ever tried". Wilde's response "And I? May I say nothing, my Lord?" was drowned out in cries of "Shame" in the courtroom.

Imprisonment

When first I was put into prison some people advised me to try and forget who I was. It was ruinous advice. It is only by realising what I am that I have found comfort of any kind. Now I am advised by others to try on my release to forget that I have ever been in a prison at all. I know that would be equally fatal. It would mean that I would always be haunted by an intolerable sense of disgrace, and that those things that are meant for me as much as for anybody else – the beauty of the sun and moon, the pageant of the seasons, the music of daybreak and the silence of great nights, the rain falling through the leaves, or the dew creeping over the grass and making it silver – would all be tainted for me, and lose their healing power, and their power of communicating joy. To regret one's own experiences is to arrest one's own development. To deny one's own experiences is to put a lie into the lips of one's own life. It is no less than a denial of the soul.

De Profundis

Wilde was incarcerated from 25 May 1895 to 18 May 1897.

He first entered Newgate Prison in London for processing, then was moved to Pentonville Prison, where the "hard labour" to which he had been sentenced consisted of many hours of walking a treadmill and picking oakum (separating the fibres in scraps of old navy ropes), and where prisoners were allowed to read only the Bible and The Pilgrim's Progress.

A few months later he was moved to Wandsworth Prison in London. Inmates there also followed the regimen of "hard labour, hard fare and a hard bed", which wore harshly on Wilde's delicate health. In November he collapsed during chapel from illness and hunger. His right ear drum was ruptured in the fall, an injury that later contributed to his death. He spent two months in the infirmary.

Richard B. Haldane, the Liberal MP and reformer, visited Wilde and had him transferred in November to Reading Gaol, 30 miles (48 km) west of London on 23 November 1895. The transfer itself was the lowest point of his incarceration, as a crowd jeered and spat at him on the railway platform. He spent the remainder of his sentence there, addressed and identified only as "C33" – the occupant of the third cell on the third floor of C ward.

About five months after Wilde arrived at Reading Gaol, Charles Thomas Wooldridge, a trooper in the Royal Horse Guards, was brought to Reading to await his trial for murdering his wife on 29 March 1896; on 17 June Wooldridge was sentenced to death and returned to Reading for his execution, which took place on Tuesday, 7 July 1896 – the first hanging at Reading in 18 years. From Wooldridge's hanging, Wilde later wrote The Ballad of Reading Gaol.

Wilde was not, at first, even allowed paper and pen but Haldane eventually succeeded in allowing access to books and writing materials. Wilde requested, among others: the Bible in French; Italian and German grammars; some Ancient Greek texts, Dante's Divine Comedy, Joris-Karl Huysmans's new French novel about Christian redemption En route, and essays by St Augustine, Cardinal Newman and Walter Pater.

Between January and March 1897 Wilde wrote a 50,000-word letter to Douglas. He was not allowed to send it, but was permitted to take it with him when released from prison. In reflective mode, Wilde coldly examines his career to date, how he had been a colourful agent provocateur in Victorian society, his art, like his paradoxes, seeking to subvert as well as sparkle. His own estimation of himself was: one who "stood in symbolic relations to the art and culture of my age". It was from these heights that his life with Douglas began, and Wilde examines that particularly closely, repudiating him for what Wilde finally sees as his arrogance and vanity: he had not forgotten Douglas' remark, when he was ill, "When you are not on your pedestal you are not interesting." Wilde blamed himself, though, for the ethical degradation of character that he allowed Douglas to bring about in him and took responsibility for his own fall, "I am here for having tried to put your father in prison." The first half concludes with Wilde forgiving Douglas, for his own sake as much as Douglas's. The second half of the letter traces Wilde's spiritual journey of redemption and fulfilment through his prison reading. He realised that his ordeal had filled his soul with the fruit of experience, however bitter it tasted at the time.

... I wanted to eat of the fruit of all the trees in the garden of the world ... And so, indeed, I went out, and so I lived. My only mistake was that I confined myself so exclusively to the trees of what seemed to me the sun-lit side of the garden, and shunned the other side for its shadow and its gloom.

Wilde was released from prison on 19 May 1897 and sailed that evening for Dieppe, France. He never returned to the UK.

On his release, he gave the manuscript to Ross, who may or may not have carried out Wilde's instructions to send a copy to Douglas (who later denied having received it). The letter was partially published in 1905 as De Profundis; its complete and correct publication first occurred in 1962 in The Letters of Oscar Wilde.

Decline: 1897–1900

Exile

Though Wilde's health had suffered greatly from the harshness and diet of prison, he had a feeling of spiritual renewal. He immediately wrote to the Society of Jesus requesting a six-month Catholic retreat; when the request was denied, Wilde wept. "I intend to be received into the Catholic Church before long", Wilde told a journalist who asked about his religious intentions.

He spent his last three years impoverished and in exile. He took the name "Sebastian Melmoth", after Saint Sebastian and the titular character of Melmoth the Wanderer (a Gothic novel by Charles Maturin, Wilde's great-uncle). Wilde wrote two long letters to the editor of the Daily Chronicle, describing the brutal conditions of English prisons and advocating penal reform. His discussion of the dismissal of Warder Martin for giving biscuits to an anaemic child prisoner repeated the themes of the corruption and degeneration of punishment that he had earlier outlined in The Soul of Man under Socialism.

Wilde spent mid-1897 with Robert Ross in the seaside village of Berneval-le-Grand in northern France, where he wrote The Ballad of Reading Gaol, narrating the execution of Charles Thomas Wooldridge, who murdered his wife in a rage at her infidelity. It moves from an objective story-telling to symbolic identification with the prisoners. No attempt is made to assess the justice of the laws which convicted them but rather the poem highlights the brutalisation of the punishment that all convicts share. Wilde juxtaposes the executed man and himself with the line "Yet each man kills the thing he loves". He adopted the proletarian ballad form and the author was credited as "C33", Wilde's cell number in Reading Gaol. He suggested that it be published in Reynolds' Magazine, "because it circulates widely among the criminal classes – to which I now belong – for once I will be read by my peers – a new experience for me". It was an immediate roaring commercial success, going through seven editions in less than two years, only after which "[Oscar" was added to the title page, though many in literary circles had known Wilde to be the author. It brought him a small amount of money.

Although Douglas had been the cause of his misfortunes, he and Wilde were reunited in August 1897 at Rouen. This meeting was disapproved of by the friends and families of both men. Constance Wilde was already refusing to meet Wilde or allow him to see their sons, though she sent him money – three pounds a week. During the latter part of 1897, Wilde and Douglas lived together near Naples for a few months until they were separated by their families under the threat of cutting off all funds.

Wilde's final address was at the dingy Hôtel d'Alsace (now known as L'Hôtel), on rue des Beaux-Arts in Saint-Germain-des-Prés, Paris. "This poverty really breaks one's heart: it is so sale , so utterly depressing, so hopeless. Pray do what you can" he wrote to his publisher.He corrected and published An Ideal Husband and The Importance of Being Earnest, the proofs of which, according to Ellmann, show a man "very much in command of himself and of the play" but he refused to write anything else: "I can write, but have lost the joy of writing".

He wandered the boulevards alone and spent what little money he had on alcohol. A series of embarrassing chance encounters with hostile English visitors, or Frenchmen he had known in better days, drowned his spirit. Soon Wilde was sufficiently confined to his hotel to joke, on one of his final trips outside, "My wallpaper and I are fighting a duel to the death. One of us has got to go". On 12 October 1900 he sent a telegram to Ross: "Terribly weak. Please come". His moods fluctuated; Max Beerbohm relates how their mutual friend Reginald 'Reggie' Turner had found Wilde very depressed after a nightmare. "I dreamt that I had died, and was supping with the dead!" "I am sure", Turner replied, "that you must have been the life and soul of the party."Turner was one of the few of the old circle who remained with Wilde to the end and was at his bedside when he died.

Death

By 25 November 1900 Wilde had developed meningitis, then called "cerebral meningitis". Robbie Ross arrived on 29 November, sent for a priest, and Wilde was conditionally baptised into the Catholic Church by Fr Cuthbert Dunne, a Passionist priest from Dublin,Wilde having been baptised in the Church of Ireland and having moreover a recollection of Catholic baptism as a child, a fact later attested to by the minister of the sacrament, Fr Lawrence Fox.Fr Dunne recorded the baptism,

> As the voiture rolled through the dark streets that wintry night, the sad story of Oscar Wilde was in part repeated to me... Robert Ross knelt by the bedside, assisting me as best he could while I administered conditional baptism, and afterwards answering the responses while I

gave Extreme Unction to the prostrate man and recited the prayers for the dying. As the man was in a semi-comatose condition, I did not venture to administer the Holy Viaticum; still I must add that he could be roused and was roused from this state in my presence. When roused, he gave signs of being inwardly conscious... Indeed I was fully satisfied that he understood me when told that I was about to receive him into the Catholic Church and gave him the Last Sacraments... And when I repeated close to his ear the Holy Names, the Acts of Contrition, Faith, Hope and Charity, with acts of humble resignation to the Will of God, he tried all through to say the words after me.

Wilde died of meningitis on 30 November 1900. Different opinions are given as to the cause of the disease: Richard Ellmann claimed it was syphilitic; Merlin Holland, Wilde's grandson, thought this to be a misconception, noting that Wilde's meningitis followed a surgical intervention, perhaps a mastoidectomy; Wilde's physicians, Dr Paul Cleiss and A'Court Tucker, reported that the condition stemmed from an old suppuration of the right ear (from the prison injury, see above) treated for several years (une ancienne suppuration de l'oreille droite d'ailleurs en traitement depuis plusieurs années) and made no allusion to syphilis.

Burial

Wilde was initially buried in the Cimetière de Bagneux outside Paris; in 1909 his remains were disinterred and transferred to Père Lachaise Cemetery, inside the city. His tomb there was designed by Sir Jacob Epstein. It was commissioned by Robert Ross, who asked for a small compartment to be made for his own ashes, which were duly transferred in 1950. The modernist angel depicted as a relief on the tomb was originally complete with male genitalia, which were initially censored by French Authorities with a golden leaf. The genitals have since been vandalised; their current whereabouts are unknown. In 2000, Leon Johnson, a multimedia artist, installed a silver prosthesis to replace them. In 2011, the tomb was cleaned of the many lipstick marks left there by admirers and a glass barrier was installed to prevent further marks or damage.

The epitaph is a verse from The Ballad of Reading Gaol,

And alien tears will fill for him

Pity's long-broken urn,

For his mourners will be outcast men,

And outcasts always mourn.

Posthumous pardon

In 2017, Wilde was among an estimated 50,000 men who were pardoned for homosexual acts that were no longer considered offences under the Policing and Crime Act 2017. The Act is known informally as the Alan Turing law.

Honours

In 2014 Wilde was one of the inaugural honorees in the Rainbow Honor Walk, a walk of fame in San Francisco's Castro neighbourhood noting LGBTQ people who have "made significant contributions in their fields."

Biographies

Wilde's life has been the subject of numerous biographies since his death. The earliest were memoirs by those who knew him: often they are personal or impressionistic accounts which can be good character sketches, but are sometimes factually unreliable. Frank Harris, his friend and editor, wrote a biography, Oscar Wilde: His Life and Confessions (1916); though prone to exaggeration and sometimes factually inaccurate, it offers a good literary portrait of Wilde. Lord Alfred Douglas wrote two books about his relationship with Wilde. Oscar Wilde and Myself (1914), largely ghost-written by T. W. H. Crosland, vindictively reacted to Douglas's discovery that De Profundis was addressed to him and defensively tried to distance him from Wilde's scandalous reputation. Both authors later regretted their work. Later, in Oscar Wilde: A Summing Up (1939) and his Autobiography he was more sympathetic to Wilde. Of Wilde's other close friends, Robert Sherard; Robert Ross, his literary executor; and Charles Ricketts variously published biographies, reminiscences or correspondence. The first more or less objective biography of Wilde came about when Hesketh Pearson wrote Oscar Wilde: His Life and Wit (1946). In 1954 Wilde's son Vyvyan Holland published his memoir Son of Oscar Wilde, which recounts the difficulties Wilde's wife and children faced after his imprisonment. It was revised and updated by Merlin Holland in 1989.

Oscar Wilde, a critical study by Arthur Ransome was published in 1912. The book only briefly mentioned Wilde's life, but subsequently Ransome (and The Times Book Club) were sued for libel by Lord Alfred Douglas. In April 1913 Douglas lost the libel action after a reading of De Profundis refuted his claims.

Richard Ellmann wrote his 1987 biography Oscar Wilde, for which he posthumously won a National (USA) Book Critics Circle Award in 1988and a Pulitzer Prize in 1989. The book was the basis for the 1997 film Wilde, directed by Brian Gilbert and starring Stephen Fry as the title character.

Neil McKenna's 2003 biography, The Secret Life of Oscar Wilde, offers an exploration of Wilde's sexuality. Often speculative in nature, it was widely criticised for its pure conjecture and lack of scholarly rigour. Thomas Wright's Oscar's Books (2008) explores Wilde's reading from his childhood in Dublin to his death in Paris. After tracking down many books that once belonged to Wilde's Tite Street library (dispersed at the time of his trials), Wright was the first to examine Wilde's marginalia.

Later on, I think everyone will recognise his achievements; his plays and essays will endure. Of course, you may think with others that his personality and conversation were far more wonderful than anything he wrote, so that his written works give only a pale reflection of his power. Perhaps that is so, and of course, it will be impossible to reproduce what is gone forever.

Robert Ross, 23 December 1900

In 2018, Matthew Sturgis' "Oscar: A Life," was published in London. The book incorporates rediscovered letters and other documents and is the most extensively researched biography of Wilde to appear since 1988.

Parisian literati, also produced several biographies and monographs on him. André Gide wrote In Memoriam, Oscar Wilde and Wilde also features in his journals. Thomas Louis, who had earlier translated books on Wilde into French, produced his own L'esprit d'Oscar Wilde in 1920. Modern books include Philippe Jullian's Oscar Wilde, and L'affaire Oscar Wilde, ou, Du danger de laisser la justice mettre le nez dans nos draps (The Oscar Wilde Affair, or, On the Danger of Allowing Justice to put its Nose in our Sheets) by Odon Vallet, a French religious historian. (Source: Wikipedia)

NOTABLE WORKS

ESSAYS

"The Decay of Lying" First published in Nineteenth Century (1889), republished in Intentions (1891).

"Pen, Pencil and Poison" First published in the Fortnightly Review (1889), republished in Intentions (1891).

"The Soul of Man under Socialism" First published in the Fortnightly Review (1891), republished in The Soul of Man (1895), privately printed.

Intentions (1891) Wilde revised his dialogues on aesthetic subjects for publication in this volume, which comprises:

- "The Critic as Artist"

- "The Decay of Lying"

- "Pen, Pencil and Poison"

- "The Truth of Masks"

"Phrases and Philosophies for the Use of the Young" first published in the Oxford student magazine The Chameleon, December 1894)

"A Few Maxims For The Instruction Of The Over-Educated" First published, anonymously, in the 1894 November 17 issue of Saturday Review.

FICTION

Novel

The Picture of Dorian Gray (1890/1891). The first version of "The Picture of Dorian Gray" was published, in a form highly edited by the magazine, as the lead story in the July 1890 edition of Lippincott's Monthly Magazine. Wilde published the longer and revised version in book form in 1891, with an added preface.

Stories

"The Portrait of Mr. W. H." (1889)

The Happy Prince and Other Tales (1888, a collection of fairy tales) consisting of:

- "The Happy Prince"
- "The Nightingale and the Rose"
- "The Selfish Giant"
- "The Devoted Friend"
- "The Remarkable Rocket"

A House of Pomegranates (1891, fairy tales)

Lord Arthur Savile's Crime and Other Stories (1891) Including "The Canterville Ghost" first published in periodical form in 1887.

Complete Short Fiction. Penguin Classics, 2003. Edited with an Introduction and Notes by Ian Small. Contains all works listed above plus Poems in Prose (1894) and one very short 'Elder-tree' (fragment).

POEMS

Ravenna (1878) Winner of the Newdigate Prize.

Poems (1881) Wilde's collection of poetry and first publication.

The Sphinx (1894)

Poems in Prose (1894)

The Ballad of Reading Gaol (1898)

PLAYS

Vera; or, The Nihilists (1880)

The Duchess of Padua (1883)

Lady Windermere's Fan (1892)

A Woman of No Importance (1893)

Salomé (French version) (1893, first performed in Paris 1896)

Salomé: A Tragedy in One Act: Translated from the French of Oscar Wilde by Lord Alfred Douglas, illustrated by Aubrey Beardsley (1894)

An Ideal Husband (1895) (text)

The Importance of Being Earnest (1895) (text)

La Sainte Courtisane and A Florentine Tragedy Fragmentary. First published 1908 in Methuen's Collected Works

(Dates are dates of first performance, which approximate better to the probable date of composition than dates of publication.)

The Importance of Being Earnest and Other Plays. Penguin Classics, 2000. Edited with an Introduction, Commentaries and Notes by Richard Allen Cave. Contains all from above save the first two. Salome is in English.

As an appendix there is one excised scene from The Importance of Being Earnest.

POSTHUMOUS (PREVIOUSLY UNPUBLISHED)

De Profundis (Written 1895-97, in Reading Gaol). Expurgated edition published 1905; suppressed portions 1913, expanded version in The Letters of Oscar Wilde (1962).

The Rise of Historical Criticism (Written while at college) First published in 1905 (Sherwood Press, Hartford, CT) privately printed. Reprinted in Miscellanies, the last volume of the First Collected Edition (1908).

The First Collected Edition (Methuen & Co., 14 volumes) appeared in 1908 and contained many previously unpublished works.

The Second Collected Edition (Methuen & Co., 12 volumes) appeared in installments between 1909–11 and contained several other unpublished works.

The Letters of Oscar Wilde (Written 1868-1900) Published in 1962. Republished as The Complete Letters of Oscar Wilde (2000), with letters discovered since 1962, and new annotations by Merlin Holland.

The Women of Homer (Written 1876, while at college). First published in Oscar Wilde: The Women of Homer (2008) by The Oscar Wilde Society.

The Philosophy of Dress First published in The New-York Tribune (1885), published for the first time in book form in Oscar Wilde On Dress (2013).

MISATTRIBUTED

Teleny, or The Reverse of the Medal (Paris, 1893) has been attributed to Wilde, but its authorship is unclear. One theory is that it was a combined effort by several of Wilde's friends, which he may have edited.

Constance On September 14, 2011, Wilde's grandson Merlin Holland contested Wilde's claimed authorship of this play entitled Constance, scheduled to open that week in the King's Head Theatre. It was not, in fact, "Oscar Wilde's final play," as its producers were claiming. Holland said Wilde did sketch out the play's scenario in 1894, but "never wrote a word" of it, and that "it is dishonest to foist this on the public." The Artistic Director Adam Spreadbury-Maher of the King's Head Theatre and producer of Constance pointed out that Wilde's son, Vyvyan Holland, wrote in 1954, "a significant amount of the dialogue (of Constance) bears the authentic stamp of my father's hand". There is further proof that the developed scenario that Constance was reconstituted from was written by Wilde between 1897 and his death in 1900, rather than the 1894 George Alexander scenario which Merlin Holland quotes.